Crime and Ravishment

Judith Summers

CORONET BOOKS
Hodder and Stoughton

Copyright © Judith Summers 1996

First published in Great Britain in 1996
by Hodder & Stoughton
First published in paperback in 1996
by Hodder and Stoughton
A division of Hodder Headline PLC
A Coronet Paperback

The right of Judith Summers to be identified as the Author of
the Work has been asserted by her in accordance with the
Copyright, Designs and Patents Act 1988.

10 9 8 7 6 5 4 3 2 1

British Library Cataloguing in Publication Data

Summers, Judith
Crime and Ravishment
1. English fiction – 20th century
I. Title
823.9′14 [F]

ISBN 0 340 63818 4

Printed and bound in Great Britain by
Cox & Wyman Ltd, Reading, Berkshire

Hodder and Stoughton
A division of Hodder Headline PLC
338 Euston Road
London NW1 3BH

For Udi

Acknowledgements

The author wishes to thank Joan Burstein and Lyndie Leventon of Browns of South Molton Street, and Denis Bellessort of Tiffany & Co, London.

Quotations from *The Dictionary of Psychotherapy* by Sue Walrond-Skinner on pages 177 and 179 reprinted by permission of Routledge (Routledge & Kegan Paul 1986).

Quotation from *Totem and Taboo* by Sigmund Freud reprinted by permission of Routledge.

Quotation from *The Psychology of Love* edited by Robert J. Sternberg and Michael L. Barnes reprinted by permission of Yale University Press (copyright © 1988 by Yale University Press).

One

―――――――――――

It was happening at last, and Miranda felt ecstatic.

Sixteen-year-old Justin was splayed out before her on a crisp white sheet.

'Oh Justin, you've no idea how long I've wanted you,' she whispered, slipping the shoe-string straps of her nightgown off her shoulders and letting the ivory satin column slither to the floor.

Then, without a moment's hesitation, she threw her slender body upon his and hungrily devoured his firm ebony flesh, tracing each hillock and valley of his muscle-bound torso with her lips. With a deep thrill she felt his penis burst into life against her, a majestic, exotic, potent bloom.

'Oh, Miranda,' he whispered, wrapping one powerful thigh around her hips while the other pushed between her legs, making way for him to enter her hot moist sex. She wanted him inside her so much, so much . . .

As he twisted her round, the bed springs squeaked loudly. Eaah! Eaah!

'Oh, Miranda!'

Eaah!

'Miranda, woman, you're so, so beautiful!'

Eaah! Eaah!

Miranda opened her eyes and blinked into the darkness. Justin let go of her. Arching with longing, she rolled over and looked guiltily at her husband, who lay fast asleep beside her like some pale, limp sea anemone washed up on a beach.

Why, why, oh why had she awoken?

Eaah!

She sat bolt upright, holding her breath. For a long while she heard nothing. Then . . .

Eaah!

Her heartbeat quickened. It was more of a rattle than a squeak, and it came from downstairs.

She glanced at the green glow of the alarm clock, balanced precariously on her copy of *Crime and Punishment*. At 2.26 in the morning, a rattle like that could only mean one thing.

A burglar.

Oh God, a burglar was trying to break into the house.

'Jack! Jack!' Miranda shook the sea anemone. When it didn't move, she slid out of bed and went out onto the landing, where she peered over the banisters into the deep, dark well. She waited for a few minutes, ears straining, but heard nothing more, only the frantic pounding of her heart and the ticking of the old Habitat wall clock echoing across the tiled hall.

Perhaps she had imagined the noise. Even if she hadn't, she ought to forget about it now and go back to bed. Because, if a burglar had been trying a window or a door, the battery of security locks would have defeated him by now, and he would have given up and gone away.

In which case there was nothing for her to be frightened of. And no reason for her not to go downstairs.

Clutching the wooden banister, she crept slowly down the creaking, carpeted treads into the sinister shadows. The front door was chained shut. The back door was bolted. Everything was as she had left it earlier on.

Except for one thing.

The kitchen door was gaping open. Miranda could have sworn she'd shut it on her way up to bed.

On tiptoes, she peered inside. A pencil-thin shaft of street

2

light had broken through a crack in the floor-to-ceiling curtains and drawn a sinister jagged yellow line across the floor, but the digital clock on the microwave blinked at her reassuringly. Her terror subsided and she let out her breath. Her hand groped the wall in search of the light switch.

Then, just as she was about to flick it on, she saw the intruder.

A bulky shape, he was crouched behind the door, his arms outstretched, ready to grasp her. Something – a small knife perhaps – glittered in his hand. With blood drumming in her ears, Miranda fled upstairs and shook Jack awake.

'Jack!' she whispered urgently. 'Jack!'

He rolled over on to his back, his right arm flopping across the pillows.

'Whah?'

'There's someone in the kitchen!'

The small 'o' of his mouth stretched into a yawn. 'For Chrissake! Whah time is it?'

'What does that matter? There's a burglar in the kitchen!'

His deep-set eyes opened a crack, and squinted at her disbelievingly. 'Don't be stupid.'

'I'm not being stupid.'

'Look, you must have been dreaming. No one could possibly break in here. There are so many locks that we can hardly get in. Come back to bed. You've imagined the whole thing.'

'I have not! I went downstairs, Jack! And I . . . I saw him!'

'Shit!'

In a flash Jack jumped out of bed, grabbed his spectacles, fell to the floor and began a frantic, but lengthy search under the bed.

'What on earth are you doing, Jack?'

'Looking for my slippers.'

'Oh, for God's sake! Hurry up! We've got to scare him off.'

Miranda dashed upstairs and pulled closed the children's

3

bedroom doors. The last thing she wanted was for them to wake up and get involved. As she came down, she said in a loud voice. *'I'll dial 999, Jack. You get your gun.'*

'My what?'

She grimaced at him. *'Hurry. It's in the wardrobe. Hello? Yes! Give me the police, and quickly, please!'*

While she conducted a loud, imaginary telephone conversation with the emergency services, Jack ran into the bedroom and threw open the wardrobe doors. After rummaging in the back of it, he returned empty-handed and perplexed.

'I don't have a gun!'

'Oh, for God's sake! *Great, you've got it, have you?'* she announced down the stairs. *'Come on, let's get him.'*

On the half-way landing, she picked up a vase of neglected stocks from the small pine chest, threw the withered, foul-smelling stems onto the carpet, and raised the painted china above her head. Jack grabbed it from her.

'That's my best Clarice Cliff!'

'But he's armed! He's got a knife!' Even in the dark, she could see him turn pale. *'The police will be here any minute now.'*

He cleared his throat. *'Yes. But don't worry,'* he said in a deep voice. *'I'll shoot him if I have to.'*

Jack gave the vase a wistful look, then clutched it under his arm and tiptoed on, pushing her ahead of him.

The front hall was silent but for their panting. No sound came from the kitchen. Either the intruder had fled or he was lying low and calling their bluff.

Miranda pointed to the kitchen. 'Behind the door!' she mouthed. 'Go on!'

With a weak smile, Jack dodged inside, shouting, 'OK, you bastard, the game's up! You. . . . Aaah!'

'Jack!'

Heedless of her own safety, she ran in after him and switched on the light, just in time to see him step on the

4

silver buckle of a school satchel and skid on the outstretched arm of a navy blue anorak, both of which were lying behind the door.

As his head thudded against the wall, the jug fell to the floor and smashed into a hundred shards, showering him with stagnant water.

There was a moment of silence, then Miranda burst into nervous giggles. Failing to see the funny side, Jack glared up at her from amidst the debris. His hands closed on the microfibre 'intruder', which he shook at her with barely-controlled fury.

'Miranda, you're so bloody neurotic! I can't believe you've done this to me again!'

At 7.30, she was summoned back to the kitchen.
'Mum?'
'*Mum*! Isn't there anything except cereal for breakfast?'
'Mu-um!'
With a small sigh, she kicked off her side of the duvet, pulled her old kimono over her crumpled cotton nightshirt and plodded down to the scene of her humiliation on long, slender legs.

By daylight, the kitchen looked as if it had indeed been burgled. Smelling strongly of last night's fish pie, a mountain of dirty crockery was stacked on the wooden draining board where she had left it after supper in the vain hope that someone other than herself would load the washing-up machine for a change. Garbage had spilt from the jammed-open top of the plastic swing-bin, and the dregs of a tin of tomatoes had dribbled down the front of it and congealed in a bloody pool on the lino. Two half-full bottles of milk were souring on the Aga, the battered, stripped-pine cupboard doors were hanging open, and plates, packets of cereal and pools of spilt juice were strewn across every horizontal surface.

'What a disgusting mess.' Miranda looked sternly at her sons, David and Thomas, who were both slumped over the round pine table in the window bay. 'Why are you both incapable of clearing up after yourselves?'

'Doesn't Mrs Weaving come today? Isn't that what she's paid to do?'

'David! How dare you talk like that! Mrs Weaving isn't a slave! Just because we have a cleaner once a week, that doesn't mean that you can drop things where you want to.' She took a deep breath in an attempt to calm herself down. 'Let's not start today with a silly quarrel. Good morning, darlings.' There was a long silence. 'I said good morning.'

Both boys grunted.

'David hit me before, Mum,' whined Thomas.

'I didn't, you little squirt!'

'Liar! You did!'

'Piss off, pervert!'

'David, don't speak to your brother like that.'

'Why not? It's true. He is a pervert.'

'I'm not!'

'Good morning, Diana, darling.'

'If it isn't Princess Di!'

'Shut up, David!' Wrapped in a huge, stained towelling dressing gown, a lank-haired waif shuffled into the room on pencil-thin ankles, her hollow eyes half-closed. 'Morning, Mum,' she said in a weak voice.

'Would you like some breakfast?' In vain, Miranda tried to keep the pleading note out of her voice. 'What can I make you? French toast, perhaps? Or pancakes? Scrambled eggs?'

'I'm a vegan. Remember?'

David snorted. 'Since when?'

Diana narrowed her eyes at him. 'Since last week, if you must know, pig-face. I don't eat eggs any more.'

'You don't eat anything any more.'

'Leave her alone, David. Well, how about some cereal, then, Diana? Weetabix? Corn Flakes? No? I know, I'll make you some porridge, with water! That's vegan, isn't it?'

'No, thanks, Mum.'

'How about some . . .'

6

'NO! Stop nagging, will you?'

'But I wasn't . . .'

'You're always trying to make me put on weight! I'm fourteen – old enough to make up my own mind about what I will or will not have for breakfast! OK?'

From larder shelves stacked with jars and boxes of nutritious, wholesome foods, Diana took out a packet of instant low-calorie soup, tore open the sachet, and tipped its powdered contents into a mug, to which she added a dash of warm tap-water. 'Less than 40 calories!' ran the claim on the front of the packet. Miranda bit her lip. The doctor had told her that making an issue of mealtimes would only make matters worse. But it was impossible not to nag. The alternative was standing by and watching her daughter slowly starve herself to death.

'What happened over there, Mum?'

A hot flush crept up her throat as Thomas's index finger pointed to the broken jug she had got as far last night as sweeping into a pile behind the door.

'Daddy fell over something. Over your satchel, actually, Thomas. Don't laugh, David, it's not funny. He could have hurt himself badly. He slipped on your anorak, too. Will you please both put your things away in future?'

'I did!' Thomas's voice rose to a dangerously high octave. 'You told me to keep my satchel behind the door. Can I have some pancakes, Mum?'

'Sorry, darling, I don't think I've got time.'

'But you just said you'd make some for Diana! That's not fair! Why can't you make some for me? What's so special about *her*?'

'She's bulimic, you poofter, that's what!' said David scornfully.

Diana pushed away her cup. 'I'm not!'

'OK, anorexic.'

'Piss off, David!'

'Diana, please! All of you, stop it! Can't we have a civilised breakfast for once?'

'I just want some pancakes! I'm starving! I'll die if you don't give me something to eat.'

'I wish you would die.'

'David!'

'Well, just look at him, Mum!' Miranda glanced at her youngest son with a sinking heart. 'Look, he's wearing Lily's necklace and earrings again!'

'So what?' said Diana, between slow, distasteful sips of soup. 'Why shouldn't he? Don't be so sexist, David.'

'Thomas, you don't need to wear so much jewellery for breakfast,' Miranda said feebly.

The elfin face beneath the shock of carrot-coloured hair puckered into a stubborn pout. 'I do.'

'Why, darling.'

'Because I'm a girl. I've got a regina. Ask Dad.'

Advised by Jack that both transexualism and transvesticism were normal, passing phases of male pre-adolescence, Miranda had tolerated ten-year-old Thomas's penchant for jewellery for the past two months. Today her tolerance suddenly snapped.

'For Heaven's sake, you're a boy. I know you're a boy, you know you're a boy, even your father knows you're a boy, whatever he might say. And you don't have a vagina – and that's vagina, with a V-A, regina means queen – don't snigger, David – you have a penis.'

'A prick,' agreed David. 'Like Dad and me.'

'Huh! You are a prick, David. A big prick.'

'Thomas! And Daddy and David don't wear earrings, do they? Certainly not for breakfast.'

'Well, I do.' Absent-mindedly, he flicked a large grey bogey onto the table, picked it up with his fingertip and put it in his mouth.

Diana shuddered. 'Christ! That's gross!'

'Please don't swear, Diana. Now, what are you going to eat, boys? How about some lovely home-made organic muesli . . .'

'There's nothing lovely about it. It tastes like gravel.'

8

'And it makes you fart! Pppffffhhh!'

'Toast, then.'

'Boring.'

'It's toast or nothing.' She got out the sugar-free peanut butter and cut some slices from the stoneground organic loaf she had bought the day before. The knife slipped on the lava-hard crust, cutting a deep flap in her little finger. A quiet 'Fuck!' slipped out before she could censor it.

Allies now, the children snorted gleefully, 'Fuck, fuck, fuck!'

Her hand swathed in a length of kitchen roll, Miranda slammed the slices down on to their plates.

David's face fell. 'Is that all we're getting? I want scrambled eggs.'

'I made you some yesterday and you left it all.'

'Yeah, well it wasn't cooked, was it? It was wet and slimey.'

'It was creamy, David. Scrambled eggs are meant to be creamy.'

'No, it was definitely slimey. It wasn't slimey when I had it at Justin's on Saturday.'

'Oh, I *am* sorry. Well, if you don't like my cooking, you'd better eat all your meals there, hadn't you? Alternatively, learn to cook yourself. I'm sure it's not beyond your skills.'

David muttered a string of obscenities under his breath.

'What was that?'

'Nothing.' His lips settled into the habitual sulky pout which so disfigured his handsome features. If Thomas took after Jack, with his red hair, densely freckled skin and concave chest, his sixteen-year-old brother was a male version of Miranda, with her over-large features: the eyes green and round; the mouth long and wide; the nose straight as a ruler and continuing a good half inch after it ought by rights to have ended. But whereas these features hinted at a hidden strength in Miranda, they made David look soft, even vulnerable. Not that he *was* soft or vulnerable. Miranda

9

had yet to find a chink in his emotional armour. The only time he'd ever expressed anything remotely resembling real feeling was when she'd unearthed, and confiscated, his carefully camouflaged stash of spliffs.

'This peanut butter tastes really bitter!' moaned Thomas. 'And look! My bread's got your blood on it! Eargh! I'm not eating it. I'll get AIDS if I do. Mum, why don't you ever buy proper bread, like Seamus has in his house? I've asked you to a billion times.'

Miranda gritted her teeth. Their next door neighbours, the Connors, were the last relics of the working classes who had inhabited all of Huddleston Avenue until seventies gentrification had brought in the venetian-blind-and-stripped-pine likes of Jack and herself. Eleven-year-old Seamus lived off bleached sliced bread, sweets, chocolate spread, jam, chips and sausages, washed down with an endless supply of fizzy drinks, ketchup and brown sauce. Fresh vegetables and fruit never passed his lips, which were permanently rainbow-stained with assorted E numbers, as were Thomas's whenever he came back from playing with him. Seamus Connor never seemed to wash or clean his teeth, which, annoyingly, remained perfect. Despite his fat-enriched, vitamin-depleted diet, so did his health.

'If you like it so much next door, darling, go and live there.'

'I wish I could.'

'Besides, brown bread is proper bread. It just happens to be better for you than white bread.'

'Bollocks.'

'And it tastes nicer.'

'It's mega-disgusting.'

'Look, just stop complaining and eat it, will you? Why don't you have some too, Diana?'

'But you know I've just eaten!'

'Goodness, you're all so spoiled! Really, most children in the world would be gratef . . .'

At this point, the door opened again, and Lily, David's

twin sister, came in, silky blonde hair skimming her buttocks, black over-the-knee socks revealing acres of slender, tanned thighs which disappeared into a pelmet of a navy school skirt. 'Oh, *pul-lease*, Mum! Not the starving millions *again*!' she said, flashing her huge, innocent-looking, blue eyes. 'I can't bear it! It's the same bloody argument about food, every bloody day. Really, why don't you just hire a cook and be bloody done with it?'

Miranda gasped. 'Pardon?'

'Hire a cook. If you got a job, you could afford to. God, this place stinks of fish! Why hasn't the washing up been done?'

'Because,' Miranda began, 'you haven't done . . .'

'Hold on, is that the phone? Don't worry, Mum, I'll get it!'

Lily dashed out into the hall. After a brief, bright 'Hello?' her voice dropped several octaves and purred sexily into the receiver. Her time-consuming telephonic life was only exceeded by her turbulent love life; frequently, as now, the two were inextricably intertwined.

'Come on, Mum!' moaned David. 'I've got to go in a minute! There must be something else we can have!'

Reluctantly, Miranda took down the marshmallow-sprinkled, chocolate-flavoured over-processed cereal she had secretly bought for herself and hidden on the top shelf of the larder.

'Awesome!'

'Wicked!'

How easy it was to be liked. Making herself a cup of instant coffee, Miranda went upstairs to get dressed. Her bedroom smelled like a second-hand clothes shop. She pulled open the faded Laura Ashley curtains and pushed up the sash. On the second floor balcony of the terraced house opposite, a half-naked man was pegging an assortment of garish underpants onto a string washing line. In the garden next door, a large and burly gnome – a new addition to the army of occupation – was squatting on Mary

Connor's pink-and-white crazy paving. On her own side of the trellis, a small, carefully-nurtured patch of green, the buds of the red rambling rose were entangling themselves with the white jasmine flowers which scrambled over the fence, and the feathery fronds of the astilbe, the proud blue delphiniums and the vivid orange poppies were swaying in the breeze. She sighed with pleasure. The garden was her pride and joy, a tiny slice of *rus* in the middle of the bleak, Tufnell Park *urbe*, at its best in the sunshine on this warm, late June morning.

Back in the room, a pale, freckled bottom peeked at her from beneath the colour co-ordinated duvet.

'Time to get up, darling.'

Jack gave a loud snort. Even asleep, he exuded an air of reproach for having been so unnecessarily awakened during the night. Miranda stifled an urge to smother him with the pillow. 'Time to get up!' She rocked him gently. 'Jack! Jack!' She gave him a sharp shove and he opened one bleary eye.

'Where's my tea?' he muttered.

'Oh. Sorry. It's in the bag.'

'What?'

'In the bag. The tea bag.'

'What?'

'It's a joke.'

'What?'

'A joke. Oh, forget it. Go back to sleep.'

Miranda rummaged in the jumble-sale depths of her wardrobe until she found a cleanish pair of black leggings. Since none of her t-shirts looked remotely wearable, she surreptitiously slipped an ironed shirt from the pile in Jack's orderly drawer.

'Put that back,' he mumbled without opening his eyes. 'I said, put it back.'

'OK.' Smiling to herself, she smuggled it into the corridor and slipped it on.

Hurtful as an insult, the front door slammed shut as David left for school without saying goodbye to her.

'Hurry up, Mum!' yelled Thomas. 'We'll be late!'

It was only when she passed the hall mirror on her way out of the house that she realised she had forgotten to wash her face or brush her long, tangled mane of auburn hair. There were shadows under her eyes, and her skin looked sallow. It was hard to believe she had once been voted the most kissable girl in her school class. She looked tired, drawn, every one of her forty years and a few more to boot.

With Diana, Thomas and Lily filing in front of her, she left the house. Next door, Seamus's mother leaned out of her bedroom window, the first floor watchtower from whence she guarded Huddleston Avenue every morning, a plump, beaming mass of black eye make-up, thick, peach foundation, and long, unruly blonde curls.

'Mornin', love!'

'Morning, Mary.'

Mary Connor twirled a lock of over-permed hair around a red-taloned finger. 'Late for school again, are ya?'

Miranda gave her a weak smile. She and Jack sometimes wondered if Mary's make-up was not tattooed onto her skin. In fifteen years of living in the street, they had never seen her without it. Jack despised make-up on women; soon after he had met Miranda, he had persuaded her to stop wearing it, saying that it made her look false and hard. After so long, she had now got used to her own pale face and invisible lashes. Yet whenever she saw Mary she felt dull without quite knowing why.

Biting her colourless lips, she unlocked Horace, the navy blue Morris Minor which was her pride and joy.

'I wish you'd get a new car,' said Diana. 'Or at least take us to school in Daddy's Golf. That may be dented and rusty, but at least it's vaguely twentieth century. It's really embarrassing being dropped at school in *this*.'

'Oh blast! I've forgotten my Vodaphone! Hold on, Mum, I won't be a minute!'

'Lily! You don't need to take that phone at school!' Miranda called after her as she ran back into the house. It was at times like these she wondered what kind of children she had brought up. 'There's nothing wrong with Horace,' she said fondly as she slipped into the driver's seat and unclamped the anti-theft device from the steering wheel. 'I've had him since I was a student. He's perfectly service-able. And he gets us from A to B. Besides, he's safer than a new car. I mean, no one's going to carjack us in him, are they, or reach in and grab my handbag?'

'Honestly, you're so neurotic!'

'I'm not, Diana. Really, these things do happen, you know. All the time.'

Lily reappeared, mobile phone in hand. It belonged to Derek, her current boyfriend, and a waiter in the Café Rouge. No sooner had she got into the car than she rang him on it. A curious conversation ensued – the second that morning, Miranda noted with silent dismay – marked, on Lily's side by giggles and thinly-veiled sexual innuendos.

Still under Mary's hawk-like gaze, Miranda pulled away. The traffic was murderous. When, she wondered, would she feel happy about letting Diana, Lily and Thomas go to school by public transport again? As Jack often reminded her, Thomas had only been mugged once at the bus stop. His attackers, three nine-year-olds armed with penknives, had divested him of a week's supply of bubble gum, nothing more.

What Jack failed to realise was that, along with Thomas's Bazookas, the little thugs had taken away his self-confidence, not to mention Miranda's peace of mind. What if they had been nineteen-year-olds? What if they had stabbed him? What if he had charged across a road to get away from them and been knocked down by a car? With his ridiculous red hair that would never lie down flat and his penchant for women's jewellery, he was so horribly vulnerable. And what if someone had mugged the girls? Driving the three of them to school didn't put her out that much. The strain of a little rush-hour traffic was nothing compared to the relief of knowing that her children were safe.

The girls insisted on being dropped around the corner from their school, and Thomas and Miranda drove on in silence. How would he cope in a year's time when he joined David at the comprehensive? If only he wasn't so eminently bulliable, she thought as she tore off his necklace and earrings and shoved him out of the car door. Samantha, his teacher, was standing by the school gate on security duty. Miranda waited for her to remark on the latest purple bruise on his forehead, and rehearsed saying to her, 'I'm thinking of getting him a crash helmet. He will keep falling upstairs!' It sounded such a lame excuse, completely unbelievable even to Miranda, who knew it was true. How long would it be before a social worker and three heavy policemen turned up at dawn to cart her children away?

Samantha flicked back her long black hair. 'Mrs Green?'

'Yes?'

'You have remembered that there's a NUT demo this afternoon, haven't you?'

'Oh. Actually . . .'

Samantha smiled brusquely. 'Against the revised National Curriculum. School ends at twelve.'

'Pick me up, Mum!' Thomas called over his shoulder as he ran off to join his friends.

Miranda felt oddly disappointed that the bruise had not been remarked upon. As she drove down to Camden Town, she could not help wondering whether she secretly wanted her children to be taken into care. It would certainly solve a lot of problems, like how to stop them taking drugs, what to do about Diana's diet, how to pay for their designer trainers and what, remotely healthy, to cook for them day after day after day. She would still see them, of course, because social services were very keen on children in care maintaining parental links nowadays, but she would not have to cope with the frustrating day-to-day element of their existence. While they were being taken care of by a warm-hearted foster mother, she and Jack could have that second honeymoon they so desperately needed. And she would be free at last to write that serious novel she had been meaning to start ever since leaving university nineteen years ago.

In a cold guilty sweat, Miranda slammed on the brakes at the traffic lights. Did she really want her precious children to be snatched away by Social Services just so that she could fulfill that stupid old ambition? Despite Thomas's transvesticism and tantrums, despite Diana's low-cal soups, despite Lily's endless boyfriend traumas and the exhausting battles with David over late nights and drugs, she adored all four of them. Of course she did. Why, then, was the thought of them being fostered so . . . so . . . yes, so horribly attractive? She must be unnatural. She didn't have the right to call herself a mother. She was sick, sick, sick.

She pulled down the driver's mirror. Her sick, sick, sick face stared back at her, reflecting the awfulness of her thoughts. 'You're a disgrace to womankind,' she said out loud, pulling her fingers through her hair.

Miranda looked away, disappointed in herself. Compared to 99.9 per cent of the world, she had Life as easy as it came. Middle-class and – once upon a time – good looking, she had been brought up during a period of unprecedented prosperity and peace. She had four healthy children who, despite her natural anxieties about them, never caused her any real grief. Her husband might not be the most exciting of men, but he was kind, faithful and fair minded, and, when nagged enough, he even did a fairish job of scouring the kitchen sink. Though not rich, he earned a good salary, enough to make Miranda feel guilty for being comfortably-off while thousands were homeless on the London streets. She had a five-up, two-down, re-roofed Victorian terraced house, complete with burglar alarm, window locks and automatic security lights. Her old stripped-pine Habitat kitchen was strewn with all the accessories deemed necessary for modern, urban, middle-class life: a steel egg stand in the shape of a chicken; an array of wicker whisks; bunches of dried herbs dangling picturesquely from hooks in the ceiling; a non-stick wok; an unused chicken brick. A washing machine, a tumble dryer, a Magimix, a microwave, a Dustbuster, a power shower, a blender, even an electric juice extractor which Jack had bought her for Christmas two years ago and she had not yet worked out how to use. Given these substantial blessings, only the most dissatisfied person in the world could fail to be ecstatically happy.

So, there it was: she was the most dissatisfied person in the world. She must be. Because she wasn't ecstatically happy. She wasn't even remotely happy.

'Oi! You!' Braking beside Horace, a lorry driver grinned down through his open window, and brandished a half-eaten banana at her. 'I'll cheer you up, darling!'

'Get lost, Tarzan!' she snapped back.

'Bitch!' With a grimace, he pulled out in front of her. Swerving to avoid him, she dashed Horace's wing against a lamp-post.

'Oh God!' she appealed to the deity she disbelieved in. 'What's wrong with me?'

Horace limped through the gates of Sainsbury's car park like an injured bird, his ripped bumper scraping along the ground. Sobbing like a child, Miranda steered him down the ramp into the dank depths of the basement.

And that was when her troubles began.

Two

Dressed in a purple shell suit, a man with shoulder-length grey hair was leaning against the concrete wall, his face half-hidden by his hand as he lit a cigarette. Miranda would not have given him a second glance as she passed him but for two curious things: he put the cigarette in his mouth back to front and lit the filter; and when he took out another, his hands shook so violently that he nearly dropped the packet onto the ground.

She glanced at him, registered him, then forgot him as she strode up the moving walkway into the light and, taking a trolley, entered the glare of the post-modern hangar. The piped fragrance of freshly-baked bread smacked her in the face like a reproach, smelling of everything she tried to be but was not – a fulfilled person, an Earth Mother, a happy and supportive wife.

She thought of the coming day with a rising sense of panic. What was she going to do with Thomas all afternoon? Time never dragged slower than when he was off school. Refusing to go out anywhere, he moped about the house, raiding her wardrobe and the girls' make-up, and demanding to be amused. She tried her best to keep him occupied with painting, cooking and crafts, but that was never enough for him. As Jack often pointedly remarked, a boy of his age ought to be able to amuse himself.

The implication was, of course, that *she* had spoiled him.

Had she? Miranda wondered as she selected a bag of apples from the shelves. Had she spoiled all of them? On mornings like today, she looked at them as if they were strangers and marvelled at how her sweet, innocent babes could have grown up into such insolent, petulant monsters. Lately she'd told herself that David and Lily were simply under enormous pressure to pass their GCSEs, but now their exams were over, and for the other two she could find no excuse. She'd tried her best to bring them all up with a sense of values, but it was obvious to anyone, even to herself, that she had failed. The ethics she had attempted to instil in them – thrift, selflessness and kindness to others – had run like water off a duck's back. If they had a moral code, it was 'I want to, therefore I will.'

But, as Jack often reminded her, it was no good blaming them. Since she was their mother, and, psychologically speaking, the biggest influence on them, it had to be her fault.

She sighed. There was no way round it: motherhood had opened up a whole new world for her to feel inadequate about. Something about it didn't suit her temperament. It might make some women glow like beacons, but she flickered dimly, a tired 25-watt light bulb which was about to blow.

Sainsbury's at 9.10 on a Monday morning was a model of order and efficiency – no queues at the checkouts, the fresh food piled mountain-high in dazzling varieties and amounts. Miranda took no notice of this conspicuous abundance. Choice didn't interest her. Like a riding school nag which has been around the same route so many times that it knows exactly when to trot and when to canter, she headed for the same counters and bought the same items week in, week out. When the cashier totted up the bill, she always experienced the same frisson of shock at the astronomical amount she had spent, and when she got the goods home and unpacked them, she invariably realised with dismay that there was still not enough food to last more than a couple of days. Still, shopping this way gave her the illusion of being efficient, though she knew in her heart she was anything but.

The truth was that she didn't want to be efficient, or so Jack had said on Saturday night, when she'd happened to remark that she'd been rushed off her feet all week. Efficiency would free her up, Jack had said, and deep down Miranda didn't want to be free. Because freedom, he'd added pointedly, represented a vacuum to her, a vacuum into which she was afraid of being sucked.

She slammed a large bag of King Edwards into the trolley. If only Jack had fulfilled his ambition to become a psychoanalyst, instead of settling for that social psychology lectureship at the local polytechnic, he'd have had plenty of other people to treat, and so mightn't have spent all his free time analysing her. As it was, he picked apart her every word and move, always to her disadvantage. Worst of all, his analysis was unerringly accurate, and invariably targeted well below the belt.

What he conveniently forgot, when he pointed out how little she had accomplished in her life, was that someone had to run a house and look after the children, and, in their marriage, that someone was her. She hadn't intended to give up being a freelance journalist when they got married. Far from it. After the twins were born there had seemed little alternative. It had just seemed so stupid struggling to forge a decent career when the daily help they then employed was earning so much more than she was. No sooner were Lily and David out of nappies than Diana arrived, the product of a forgotten Pill, and then, three-and-a-half years later, Thomas, after a similar accident – though there was no such thing as an accident, or so Jack said. With four under-sixes on her hands, she hadn't had a moment to herself. When she'd suggested getting an au pair, he'd put his foot down, insisting that it would do the children irreparable damage to grow up with a string of strangers living in the house.

By the age of thirty, Miranda had lost all of her self-confidence and most of her professional contacts, and her career, such as it had ever been, had slipped by the wayside.

Gradually, her domestic duties had expanded to fill all but the margins of her available time. In those margins, she had continued to write – not the serious features or fiction she had always been interested in, but short, non-topical, consumer-oriented fillers for women's magazines: 'What's New on the Yoghurt Counter', 'Dealing with Nappy Rash', 'Your Tampon and You'.

During the past few years, commissions for those had gradually dried up, too. Editor friends had moved on and up their respective career ladders, and inspiration had deserted her. Now, on the odd occasions when she had a clear hour to herself, she didn't know what to do with it. She might read the *Guardian*, looking for feature ideas she could steal, or leaf idly through one of her many recipe books, searching for wholesome dishes that the children might deign to eat. It hardly seemed worth starting anything remotely creative when she knew it would only be a matter of minutes till Jack phoned from his office, asking her to look something up in the Complete Works of Freud, or Thomas burst in in search of her jewellery box, or Diana needed taking to guitar lessons, or Lily wanted testing for an exam or dropping over in Hampstead, or David arrived with Justin and a gang of cronies, demanding a meal.

Her private time, it seemed, was expendable; theirs was sacrosanct. Their lectures, football matches, phone calls, cinema outings, parties, dates, meals, raves and homework could never be delayed, but her writing could always be put off for another hour, or day, or week. No one was breathing down her neck for delivery of anything, therefore there was no delivery. Conceived in rare moments of mental passion, any creative ideas she had survived for a week at most before self-aborting.

She halted beside the dried pasta counter, surprised at the strength of her anger towards Jack today. He might have the odd fault, but he wasn't a bad husband. Compared to others – wife beaters, alcoholics, serial killers, for instance – he was a paragon. A little pompous, perhaps, and, yes, smug as well, with perhaps a propensity for being over-critical. But if he did criticise her, it was only out of true concern for her. And, painful though it was, he was right in making her take responsibility for what she had or hadn't made of her life. When it came down to it, it was no one's fault but her own that her journalistic career had never taken off. Hadn't her contemporaries had brilliant careers, and didn't most of them have children too? Miranda's domestic prison was of her own making. She'd used motherhood as an excuse to opt out.

She had to learn to say *no* to things, as Jack had reminded her, at 2.00 a.m. on Sunday morning, when, in answer to a summoning phone call from the twins, she had driven off to Battersea to pick them both up from a house party. *No* to the tyranny of being a good wife and mother; *No* to her neurosis about urban crime. For only by learning to say *No* to these things would she learn to say *Yes* to herself.

With two crunchy cellophane bags of wholemeal rigatoni dangling from her hands, Miranda contemplated the truth of this. Jack *was* right. She *should* worry less about things over which she had no control. Things like the children's futures, drugs at school, muggers, car-jackers, axe-wielding murderers. And burglars breaking in during the middle of the night . . .

A flush of shame stole up her neck as she thought of Jack lying on the kitchen floor amidst the fragments of his broken Clarice Cliff jug.

He was certainly right in one thing – she did worry neurotically about crime, and to absolutely no purpose. Because however savage and endemic crime had become – and it was savage and endemic, you only had to flick through any local paper, or listen to the mugging stories at any dinner party to realise that – all the worrying in the world had absolutely no effect on one's fate. Worry didn't keep trouble at bay, it merely stopped you enjoying the times when there was nothing to worry about.

'*No, no, no!*' she rehearsed saying under her breath. She smiled to herself at the powerful simplicity of the word.

When she thought about it, a little bit of healthy neglect could only have a positive effect on her family. A few days of the kids having to go to school on public transport; of them having to wash and iron their own clothes; of there being nothing to eat in the house; of Jack finding his dirty socks were he'd left them – rolled up in little hard balls, like rabbit droppings, on the bedroom floor; of Thomas being fetched late from school.

She imagined him waiting in the playground that very day, his throat aching with suppressed wails of abandonment. But he would survive. After all, he was ten years old. Someone would step in to look after him. He might even toughen up and learn to look after himself.

She sighed. The truth was that she *would* turn up at the school gates on time. She'd drive him home, cook him lunch, and try to keep him happy while she prepared tonight's shepherd's pie. Later she'd collect the girls from school, drive Lily to her friend in Crouch End and then Diana to Brent Cross, where she'd promised to buy her a new baggy t-shirt if – only if – she first went to Lindy's and ate a sandwich or a cake. Back home, she'd lay the table and scrub the pesticide residue off the vegetables, and when Jack came home she'd ask him all about his day. She was just too conscientious to renege on all these responsibilities. Unlike the attractively selfish, she was cursed with a sense of duty which made it impossible for her to let anyone down. Anyone, that was, except herself.

'Miranda! Miranda?'

In a daze, she looked up into a pair of close-set, black-rimmed eyes.

'Miranda?'

The eyes crinkled up, and the gash of glossy burgundy beneath them lifted into a broad smile.

'Suzanne! Sorry! I was miles away. Gosh! How lovely to see you!'

24

She hoped she sounded convincing. Suzanne Jones was the last person she wanted to see in her present mood. A high-flyer even during their days at London's University College, since graduating Suzanne's media career had taken off into orbit so fast that, had it not been for Suzanne's genuine desire to keep up with her old friends, Miranda would have lost track of its meteoric rise.

The burgundy gash lunged towards her and planted noisy kisses somewhere past both her cheeks. 'Mmpuh! Mmpuh! How are you, darling?'

'Great!' As she took in Suzanne's beige Nicole Farhi trouser suit, her immaculate but subtle make-up, and her precision-cut bobbed black hair, Miranda became conscious of her own baggy M&S leggings, her unwashed face and her unbrushed, out-of-shape locks. 'How are you?'

'Great! Well, OK. Busy and exhausted, as per usual. You know how it is.' Miranda grunted in vague agreement. 'I just popped in here on my way to work because I didn't have a thing to eat in the house. I ate a tin of sardines for breakfast because there was literally nothing else! I probably stink of fish, don't I?' Her laughter rang out between the aisles. 'It's so nice to see you, Miranda. I've been meaning to ring you for ages, but . . . well, time goes so fast, doesn't it? It must be – what – a year since we last saw each other. To tell you the truth, darling, I'm dead on my feet. I desperately need a break, but what can one do? I've got two documentaries in pre-production, and we're in the middle of another series of *Nightfile*.'

'I've been watching it. It's really fantastic.' This was very hard for Miranda to admit. She had been riveted to every edition of Suzanne's twice-weekly, late-night arts programme, watching with one hand in a box of chocolates, and her shoulders hunched up with jealousy.

'Oh, you don't have to say that!'

'No, really, I mean it.'

'Thank you. You're very sweet. Actually, the Beeb are quite happy with it, too. They've even commissioned a new series for the spring. I should be pleased, but between you and me and Sainsbury's, it's a nightmare to produce. I simply hate doing live TV. I keep thinking that each show will be a disaster, and that everyone will discover at long last that I'm really not a capable producer, just a hopeless sham.'

This, perhaps, was the thing Miranda found hardest to take about Suzanne: that despite her fame, her success and her undoubted amassed fortune, she had remained so modest, so normal, so full of self-doubt. So bloody nice.

'How can you say that? Look, if it's all too much for you, can't Nick take over some of the work?' Nick Shaver, ex-TV-presenter, serious charmer and powerful and respected Left-wing intellect, was Suzanne's business partner and devoted husband of fifteen years' standing, and another source of the despicable jealousy which Miranda bore towards her old friend.

'Nick?'

'Yes. After all, he must see how overworked you are. Hey? What have I said? What's the matter?'

For Suzanne's up-turned nose was reddening at the tip. 'Don't you know?'

'Know what?'

'Nick and I. . . . We . . . split up.'

'*What?* You're joking! When?'

'In January. I'm surprised you didn't read about it. It was all over the *Daily Mail*.'

'I never see the *Mail*. Jack doesn't approve of it, and whenever I sneak it into the house, Lily whisks it up to her room.'

'I thought it was funny that you didn't ring me.'

'Oh, Suzanne! I'm so sorry! You must think me awful! You and Nick splitting up . . . God, it's so hard to believe!'

'I didn't believe it at first.' She wiped away a tear. 'Get this for a cliché – he ran off with our twenty-three-year-old secretary.'

'No! How *could* he?'

Sadly, but with resignation, Suzanne smiled. 'It's the way of the world, Miranda. Women of our age get left all the time for younger women. I keep asking myself what I did wrong, or what I should have done differently. Nick claims that I never had time for him. Well, I never had time for anything, neither of us had. Maybe I shouldn't have worked quite so hard . . . But then we both worked hard. We had to keep the business going. When you're running an independent television company, you either stay on the treadmill, or get the hell off.'

Miranda took her hand. 'Oh, Suzanne, how ghastly!'

'Isn't it just? You know, darling, sometimes I think you've been right all along.'

'Me?'

'Yes. Deciding to stay at home, and be your own person, and *enjoy* your life, instead of flogging your guts out at a career.'

'Well, I didn't exactly decide . . . I mean, I still try and do the odd article . . .' Miranda's sentence petered out as her voice lost conviction in her words. 'Most of the time I wish I had a job like yours,' she admitted.

Suzanne shook her head. 'Don't, darling. Believe me, it's stress, stress and more stress. True, I've made a name for myself, and quite a bit of money, but I haven't got a moment to spend it. And now I've no one to spend it on. At least you've got your four gorgeous children – and time to enjoy them. And you've got a wonderful, loyal husband like Jack. Don't ever knock it. That's got to be worth a lot.'

Mmpuah! Mmpuah! Before parting, they exchanged kisses and promises to have a girl's night out at the earliest opportunity. Then Miranda continued her supermarket round, shopping with dogged concentration. Piling the trolley high with food made her feel she was at least doing something useful with her life.

Butter: two sticks, one semi-salted and one unsalted. Polyunsaturated margarine for Jack. Two bags of brown rice which, David complained, was as gritty as sand. A dozen deep-frozen pizza bases. Six tins of plum tomatoes. Four packets of low-calorie soups for Diana – on reflection, forty calories were better than none.

She stopped by the yoghurt counter, bewildered by choice. There were plain yoghurts and fruit yoghurts. Full fat, diet and skimmed yoghurts. Sweetened and unsweetened yoghurts. Smooth yoghurts, and yoghurts with lumps of fruit. There were cartons with separate sections of fruit attached, and cartons with sugary sprinkles trapped inside their see-through lids. There were yoghurts for babies, and yoghurts for toddlers – Captain Scarlet yoghurts and Yogi Bear yoghurts and Power Ranger yoghurts and Mr Men yoghurts. Sheepsmilk, goatsmilk and cowsmilk yoghurts from Germany, France, England, Wales and Greece. She scoured the labels for additives which might make Thomas hyperactive or aggravate David's acne, then picked up a multi-pack sporting silly skeletons on the side and a long list of E-numbers which Thomas had once eaten, and loved, at Seamus's house.

Wonderful, loyal Jack, as Suzanne had referred to him, would not approve of these. He would probably raise his rusty eyebrows when he saw them in the fridge, and say that buying food with pictures of skeletons on it was in-dicative of something awful, like wishing your children dead. Implying that she wished their children dead. Which, naturally, she did not. The very thought of anything bad happening to them made her feel faint. She might sometimes wish her husband dead – what wife didn't every now and then? – but her children? Never!

It was just that, occasionally, she wished them, or herself, elsewhere.

Feeling defiant, she placed the skeleton yoghurts into the trolley and freewheeled into the next aisle in search of lentils. Suzanne's news had shocked her to the core. Nick Shaver running off with a younger woman? It was unbelievable! At least Jack was still there after nineteen years of marriage. That alone was something to be grateful for.

That being the case, why was she feeling so aggressive towards him this morning? Could it be because of his lack of humour when last night's intruder had turned out to be nothing more frightening than David's anorak?

Or was something else making her angry – that other thing, the thing which she had carefully avoided thinking about for the last few months?

Suddenly, in Technicolour detail, her erotic dream about Justin flooded back to her, and a hot stain of embarrassment stole up her neck. Justin had been David's best friend ever since they'd started at primary school, and over the past ten years she'd watched him metamorphose from a shy, skinny, suspicious-eyed child into a six-foot, burly, cocky Adonis. Given that her house had become almost a second home to him, and that she was almost a second mother – his own, a formidable, overworked Antiguan midwife, lived nearby – there was something extremely suspect in the fact that, of all the men in the world, her subconscious had time and again selected him as a partner in her dream sex life. To want to seduce your own son was forgivable, almost mythic, as Jack would probably say. But to fantasise about seducing your son's best friend was tacky in the extreme, and surely a sign of deep and abiding sexual frustration.

So what was new? It was now two long years since she and Jack had last done what was necessary to bring each other to simultaneous, if not exactly joyous, orgasm. Jack had always been a cerebral rather than a physical animal, and it was the cerebral which excited him. It hadn't been Miranda's endless legs and full, firm breasts which had first caught his attention nineteen years ago in that dreary student union bar, it had been her book: a copy (borrowed and unread, as it happened) of R. D. Laing's *Knots*.

Nineteen years! People got less than that for murder! Miranda dropped a bottle of blood-red ketchup into the trolley. For the first seventeen years of this extended sentence, Jack had performed his part in their sex life dutifully, rather than enthusiastically. There had been an initial burst of passion, naturally, a time when they hadn't been able to keep their hands out of each other's Levi's. But, when she looked back on it, even in the early days he had initiated their love-making with an ominous regularity. After their marriage, this regularity had slowed quite drastically: from daily to twice a week, then to once a week; and from that to once a fortnight, and, later, once a month.

Two years ago, the metronome of his passion had come to a complete halt.

Several months had passed before Miranda had even noticed. When she finally had, she'd discreetly attempted to take matters, i.e. Jack, into her own hands. Her caresses had aroused a wince of annoyance in him, and nothing more, so she'd soon given that up as a bad job. It had taken another full year for her to overcome her embarrassment enough to broach the subject, and when she had, late one night in bed, he just said he'd been rather tired lately, and that had been that. The next time she'd mentioned it – on the eve of their next wedding anniversary – he'd launched into a long, evasive lecture on the ageing process, in which he'd said how pleased he was that they'd both reached the time of life when sex, for its own sake, took a back seat.

At the time, she'd accepted this without disagreeing. She knew from experience that to disagree with Jack was useless, because he never, ever conceded a single point in an argument, let alone admitted defeat. Anyway, she hadn't minded that much. If he restrained from stirring up the dull ditchwater that their sex life had become over the years, so be it.

In the light of what Suzanne had just told her, however, she found herself wondering whether this breakdown in marital relations might lead to a breakdown of their marriage. Would Jack leave her for another, younger woman, as Nick Shaver had left Suzanne?

No, it was impossible. Sex had never been that important to Jack, who anyway regarded infidelity as a sign of psychological weakness, something he would never admit to.

Besides, he hated change. Even changing his underpants made him nervous.

Exactly when had their sex life started to go wrong? Miranda wondered as she deliberated between refills of biological and non-biological detergent. If she was honest, had it ever really been right for her? Jack had always been so cautious in bed, handling her as if she were a Meissen figurine, when what she secretly wanted was to be hurled across the room like a cheap plate in a Greek restaurant. Even after all these years of intimacy, her wild, uninhibited fantasies remained hidden from him. Sordid, almost pornographic scenes quite at odds with her daytime character took place inside her head when they'd made love, but she could never have told him about them. It would have been less embarrassing to have told a maiden aunt.

Sometimes she looked at Jack and wondered what on earth had drawn them together all those years ago. It hadn't been lust, and it definitely hadn't been a shared sense of humour. So had it been shared values? Perhaps, way back in the Seventies, when values still mattered. What about intellectual compatibility? Maybe. Jack *was* brainy. He had a point of view about everything, and she, too, had had an intellect, once upon a time. They still discussed things, of course – 'Can you take the car in to be serviced?' 'Would you rather watch Ben Elton tonight, or a Channel 4 documentary about suicide?' – but they seldom had what one might call a stimulating conversation. They stayed together because they were together. But – and this was a question she had never before dared ask herself – did she *want* to spend the rest of her life with him?

The answer came to her now: no, not particularly. And then again, not particularly not. Their marriage had become a bit like a pair of washed-out but serviceable knickers – one intended to throw them out, but somehow never got around to it.

Tears of self-pity pricked her eyes. Miranda had started out thinking that her marriage was going to be the greatest thing in the world. Now she pictured it as an unwanted undergarment, the kind one would disown if it accidentally dropped on a laundrette floor.

She stooped to reach for some fabric softener. The man in the purple shell suit must have been right behind her, because his empty shopping basket rammed into her back.

'Sorry,' she said automatically as he pushed brusquely past her.

I'm forty years old, and I feel as if I'm pushing sixty, she thought. It was too late for her to change now. After all, what could she possibly *do*? All she had to look forward to were more years of sexless and unexciting marriage, the menopause and HRT.

These were not the kind of negative thoughts which Miranda allowed herself for long, and as the trolley filled she methodically replaced them with comforting clichés. Life was what one made of it. Dangerous and crime-torn as London had become, it was still a safer place for the children to grow up than New York or Sarajevo. She really must be more positive about things. It was up to her, and her alone, what she made of the rest of her life.

Take today. If she got through the checkouts quickly, she'd have a clear hour between unpacking the shopping and picking up Thomas. An hour was actually quite a long time – certainly long enough to phone up a couple of magazine features editors and hassle them for work, or even to start the first chapter of a best-selling novel . . .

But when she reached the end of the aisle, her heart sank. Lines of shoppers were queueing at every checkout, their trollies piled siege-high. Like an Olympic runner who reaches the finishing line only to discover she has finished last, not first, she felt incredulous. How had the store filled up so quickly?

She dithered for a moment, then chose a queue at random. But within minutes Miranda realised that the queue next to her was moving twice as fast, and she trundled her trolley over and joined it. Suddenly ravenous, she gazed longingly at a bar of chocolate in the basket of the lady now in front of her. Overcome by a sudden craving for something sweet, she asked this woman to keep her place for her while she bolted off in search of a multi-pack of Maltesers.

By the time she returned, the woman had disappeared and the checkout was closed.

Bursting with frustration, she rejoined her original queue, which was now two trollies longer than it had been when she'd left it. At long last, the obese man in front of her began to unload his shopping onto the conveyor belt. She watched in a trance as vast quantities of custard creams, pork sausages, streaky bacon, white sliced bread, tinned meat pies and large tubs of lard skated towards the cashier. When he caught her staring, he glared back at her angrily. Feeling as embarrassed as if she had been caught reading his diary, Miranda turned around.

She started. The man in the purple shell suit was standing right behind her again, almost too close for comfort. His right hand was deep in his trouser pocket, and a near empty wire basket was looped around his other arm. His stooped shoulders and lowered head hinted at a lifetime of poverty and dejection. Dingy and grey as an old net curtain, his long shaggy hair and fringe hung over his face, making it almost impossible to see his features.

Between the matted strands, she caught a quick glimpse of a distinctly odd face: the cheeks were taut, immobile, and the tip of the nose had a kind of artificial sheen. Perhaps the man had had extensive skin grafts. Perhaps he'd been the victim of a bad road accident, or even a dreadful fire. She sighed. It must be so painful for the poor man, looking like that. People could be so cruel and insensitive.

Determined to act naturally with him, Miranda smiled and said, 'I'm afraid we're in for quite a wait! Who'd ever have thought Sainsbury's could get so busy this early in the day?'

Without a flicker of emotion to show he had heard her – perhaps his facial muscles had been destroyed in the accident, too – he lowered his head even more. Sensing that he was embarrassed, she went on, 'I do so hate doing the weekly shopping, don't you?'

It was a tactless remark. Judging from what he had in his basket – a tiny packet of frozen burgers and a single carton of own-brand strawberry yoghurt – he lived alone, without family, friends or money. She pictured him suddenly in a dreary bedsit devoid of personal possessions, frying the frozen burgers on a Baby Belling while his socks drip-dried on a nearby electric radiator and the TV blared loudly for company. The thinness of this existence hurt her so much that she was suddenly tempted to befriend him by asking him home for lunch.

He turned away from her, making odd, impatient clicking noises with his tongue, and shifted nervously from foot to foot. She changed her mind about inviting him home. He might think she was patronising him, which, in a way, she would be. He might – oh, God! – think she was inviting him home for sex instead of spaghetti. And when she pushed him away he'd presume she was rejecting him because of his scars.

Plink, plink, plink. Frozen chips and white sliced bread drifted across the laser till and were stuffed, unceremoniously, into the obese man's gingham shopping bags. As free space appeared on the conveyor belt, Miranda began to load her own stuff. Her relief at having decided not to ask the scarred man home was tempered with guilt. The conviction would not leave her that she ought, by rights, to do something for him. Because *he* had done something for *her*. Yes, his silent, proud suffering had put her own, petty problems into perspective.

Suddenly she knew just what to do. As she tapped him on the shoulder, he swung round as sharply as if she had pricked him with a pin.

'Look,' she said. 'Look, I've bought so much, and you've hardly got anything in that basket. Would you like to check out in front of me?'

Two red-rimmed eyes stared at her wildly. His lips parted in what looked like a sneer. Deep in his trouser pocket, his right hand jiggled up and down.

Oh Christ, he was playing with himself!

The next moment, his hand withdrew, clutching something hard, dark and shiny.

No, it wasn't his penis.

It was a gun.

Three

It was happening, the thing she'd lived in fear of for so long – needlessly lived in fear of, according to Jack. Never mind that the chances were statistically negligible, she was becoming a victim of violent crime.

She'd done everything she could to minimise the risk of it happening, but now Miranda saw that all her efforts had been useless. The two security locks on every window, the diligence with which she set the burglar alarm whenever she went out, the personal alarm which she usually carried everywhere but which, today, she'd left at home, in the pocket of her anorak – she'd relied on these to keep her safe, yet in the end none of them had made the slightest difference. Vigilance counted for nothing these days, when an innocent bystander could be shot dead in a supermarket queue.

She read about murders, muggings and robberies every day, but the victims were always unknown to her. A bank teller in Kilburn, a seventeen-year-old student in Preston, an eighty-six-year-old Nottingham grannie.

Tomorrow the newspaper headlines would read, 'A 40-year-old mother-of-four from North London'.

For once, Jack had been wrong in telling her she was being neurotic. But would she survive long enough to say, '*I told you so*'?

On one level, the situation seemed incredible, almost laughably so. Things like this happened to other people, they didn't touch her. Yet the man, and his gun, were real enough.

'Freeze!'

The word came out as a faint croak, so he cleared his throat and repeated it, this time in a blood-curdling bellow.

Now people nearby swung round to see what was happening. Miranda heard someone scream.

'FREEZE!' he yelled a third time – unnecessarily, as far as she was concerned, for her blood had already turned to ice and her legs were rigid under her.

Feeling completely helpless, she waited for someone to do something, but customers and staff alike merely stared at him, and at her, as if in cataleptic trances. The cashier behind the next till was trembling violently, her mouth agape, her hand resting on the open till tray.

Far off, the plink-plink of the lasers continued, a testament that not everyone had yet plunged, as Miranda had, over the precipice of normality.

Only one person seemed to be carrying on as before, and that was the fat man in front of her, who carried on loading his shopping into bags. He glanced up once, warily, but he was too ashamed to meet her eyes. When he'd finished packing, he picked the bags up and walked away, unchallenged. Seconds later, Miranda saw him pass by outside the plate glass window. A policewoman strode past him, but he said nothing to her about the gunman, he just walked on.

Was Miranda the only one to have noticed that he'd left the supermarket without paying? In a brief moment of near-hysterical levity she wondered if he and the gunman might be partners in some elaborate shoplifting plot.

But her captor didn't follow the fat man outside. He was behind her now, and his arm was under her chin, and he was pulling her against him so tightly that she could scarcely breathe. She could feel his hard body shaking against her, and smell his fast, hot sour breath. It was quite clear to her that he wasn't going anywhere. And neither was she.

Out of the corner of her eye, she saw a uniformed security guard at the customer services desk slip his arm under the counter.

'IF ANYONE CALLS THE POLICE OR SETS OFF THE ALARM, SHE'S DEAD. UNDERSTAND?'

Miranda understood. She'd patronised this stranger in the checkout queue, and now he was going to kill her for it. After forty years of struggling to live a more or less blameless life, this was to be her fate – to be shot dead for trying to do a kind deed.

The situation called for inner strength and heroism, but she felt neither brave nor angry. In the presence of that gun, she felt utterly powerless. Fear had paralysed every muscle in her body.

She was going to die, and she didn't want to. She wanted to see Thomas grow up and throw away his earrings. She wanted to persuade David to stay on at school to do his 'A' levels. She wanted Diana to put on half a stone, and Lily to spend an entire morning without talking to her boyfriend on the phone.

She wanted to live long enough to consummate her dream affair with Justin and, just once, to tell Jack how much she hated him.

'YOU! YES, YOU!'

The cashier's face tightened with terror as the gun was momentarily pointed in her direction.

'GET BAGS. PLASTIC BAGS. OPEN THE FUCKING TILLS. YOU – COLLECT THE MONEY. YES, YOU WITH THE BAGS! I SAID, COLLECT THE FUCK-ING MONEY AND PUT IT IN THE BAGS! WHAT'S WRONG WITH YOU? OPEN THE FUCKING BAGS!'

For the cashier was fumbling with the top of a plastic carrier.

'OPEN THAT FUCKING BAG!'

The woman screamed in terror as he carried on yell-ing at her. Miranda couldn't bear to see it. It was like watching a dog being beaten.

'Can't you see that she can't do it?' she heard her own voice say.

'*What*?' his voice rasped in her ear.

Miranda swallowed. 'She can't open the bag. It's hard. They're slippery. She can't get it to open.'

She could feel his whole body tense up as he brandished the gun again. 'DO IT OR I'LL KILL YOU!'

'No! Please!' Sobbing loudly, the cashier ran from till to till, collecting bank notes. Her skirt was rucked up behind, making her look pathetic and vulnerable. Miranda wanted to tell her to pull it down. She was amazed at herself. What was she thinking of? Here she was, a helpless child clamped in the jaws of a Rottweiller, and she was worried that a stranger's stocking tops were showing.

'HURRY UP!'

A small boy, sheltering behind his mother's skirt, started to cry.

'SHUT UP!'

There was a moment of absolute silence. Then a siren went off in the street outside. Startled, the gunman jerked backwards, pulling Miranda off her feet. As his arm tightened around her neck, her hands reached upwards, clutching at him, trying to drag it away. It was useless. He was not made of flesh, but of solid steel. Black spots danced before her eyes. For a moment she thought she was going to be strangled.

'TURN THAT OFF! TURN THE ALARM OFF OR I'LL BLOW HER BRAINS OUT!'

Someone – a security guard, perhaps – called out something inaudible.

'WHAT?'

'It's not us. It . . . it's outside. A car alarm.'

'YOU'RE LYING! TURN IT OFF!'

A police tow-away vehicle cruised past the plate glass window, bearing a maroon estate car, its sidelights flashing. As it disappeared from sight the alarm faded, then stopped.

'Shit!' the robber muttered, loosening his grip on her

40

neck. 'HURRY UP!' he yelled at the cashier, who was running towards him holding the two bulging carrier bags. 'PUT THEM THERE.' He pointed to the end of the counter, then sidled towards them, dragging Miranda with him. His elbow jerked into her back. 'Pick them up.'

She did as she was told. Maybe now he'd let go of her, grab the money and run. But no, he still held on to her tightly, pushed her in front of him like a human shield. The short, sharp bursts of his breath burned into her scalp.

'ANYONE TRIES TO STOP ME LEAVING HERE, AND SHE'S DONE FOR.'

His fingers dug into her upper arm as he dragged her backwards towards the exit. As her laden trolley receded into the distance, she wondered what would happen to it if she didn't return soon. Would Jack be called in to claim her shopping, or would a member of staff have to retrace her every footstep, painstakingly replacing every tin and packet on the shelves? The time she'd spent filling the trolley had been completely wasted. What would she give the children for dinner when he finally set her free?

In the covered trolley park, she waited for him to let go of her and make a run for it. But he didn't run. Instead, he slung his arm around her shoulder and dragged her down the moving ramp towards the car park. He was holding her close, as close as a lover. A family coming up on the other side did not give them a second glance.

The gun dug into her ribs. 'OK,' he muttered. 'Where's your car?'

Too terrified to rebel, she pointed towards Horace. With a grip like steel he steered her towards him, and pushed her against the driver's door. 'Open up.' She could feel the evil power of his body close behind her while she fumbled for her keys in the lucky dip of her handbag. The state of her handbag was disgusting, Jack had said so last week, its mess indicative of Miranda's disorganised state of mind. As she groped blindly in it now, she wished she'd cleared it out, as Jack had told her she ought. Her captor was getting impatient. Her handbag might well prove the death of her.

'Get a move on!'

'I'm sorry . . . The key . . . I'll find it in a min . . .'

He snatched the bag and tipped it upside down. A mulch of screwed-up tissues, copper coins and fluff-coated fruit pastilles rained down onto the bonnet, along with a grubby, unused tampon which had long ago escaped from its hygenic cellophane shell.

Out of the corner of her eye, Miranda noticed there was a grating under her feet. In a split-second of rebellion, she grabbed the keys and dropped them. By Sod's Law, they landed on the metal. Before she could kick them through the bars, he shoved her hard against the door.

'That was stupid.'

The gun dug into her back ribs again as he stooped down to pick the keys up. The door opened with a squeak and he shoved her inside. Pointing the gun at her through the windscreen he ran round to the other side and slid in beside her, violating the precious familiarity of the car.

Surely someone would come and rescue her soon? Surely the alarm must have been raised, the police called?

'Drive.'

She started the engine and reversed slowly out of the space, narrowly missing a concrete pillar. Fool! Why hadn't she slammed into it?

The robber jumped as Horace's broken bumper scraped against the ground. 'What the fuck's that?'

Miranda could scarcely talk. 'The car . . . a lorry . . . it was . . .'

'Shit! Drive!' Out of the corner of her eye she saw him rip off his purple jacket. Then he lowered his head and scratched at something at the back of his neck. As he lifted his arms over his head, his grey wig came off, revealing black, tousled hair. A moment later he dug his fingers into his scarred temples and his entire face peeled away.

She screamed. The car swerved.

'Shut up! Keep driving!'

Shaking violently, she drove up the ramp. Horace wouldn't be allowed out of the car park, of that she was sure. There would be police waiting at the top, armed marksmen, the SAS. After a short siege, her captor would surrender and she would be freed.

To her horror, the attendant in the glass booth grinned at her benignly. 'Ticket please, love.' She stared at him mutely. 'Got to have your ticket, love, or I can't let you out, now, can I?'

Just then, a loud alarm went off nearby, and a telephone rang inside the booth. The attendant was about to pick it up when the gunman leaned across Miranda.

'Sorry, mate,' he said, cool as ice. 'The sodding ticket blew out of her hands. Give us a break and let us out this time – we've got to pick the kids up in half an hour!'

Why the hell didn't the attendant pick up the phone? He hesitated, then suddenly put out his arm, pressed a button and raised the barrier. 'You'll get me shot!' he said with a conspiratorial grin. The gunman gave him a thumbs-up sign. Miranda noticed that his fingernails were bitten to the quick.

'Move it!'

The traffic lights at the car park entrance were red. Glancing in the mirror while she waited for them to change, she saw the attendant speaking on the phone. Mouth open, he stared at the back of Horace with a doubtful look. Sensing what was happening, the robber leaned over and kissed Miranda on the cheek. She winced. The attendant was fooled, though: he shook his head and mouthed a clear no. The barrier closed behind them. The lights changed to green.

'Go! Go, go, GO!'

As she drove off, he swung round and looked over his shoulder, his arm looped oppressively across the top of her seat. 'Keep your eyes on the road,' he said hoarsely. 'And whatever you do, don't look at me.'

She did as she was told. She had already glimpsed enough of him to give the police a basic description. About thirty-five to forty. East London accent, white skin, dark hair. Nose shortish, sort of squattish. Those bitten nails.

But, in all probability, she wouldn't live to pass this information on, because he'd now force her to drive to some deserted back street where he'd blast her brains out before making off with the loot. Yet another senseless, callous crime in the huge catalogue of senseless, violent crimes committed every day. Her scarcely-recognisable corpse would be discovered later this afternoon by a couple of kids on their way home from school, or by a traffic warden on her rounds. Tomorrow the tabloid headlines would read, 'Meter Rita in Faceless Mother-of-Four Horror.'

Feeling sick, she pulled up at some traffic lights. A shrieking squad car shot past in the opposite direction, headlights blazing, siren blasting. She felt like crying. The man beside her snorted contemptuously, and produced a pack of cigarettes. His hands were shaking so much that he could scarcely light up. Hadn't he seen the large No Smoking sign dangling from the mirror?

'What . . . what do you want me to do?'

'WHAT?'

'I mean, where do you want me to drive? Which way?'

'Anywhere.' He sucked hard on the cigarette. A cloud of acrid smoke billowed in Miranda's face. 'Straight on. No, left. Next left.'

'Here? I can't . . .'

'I SAID . . .'

'It's a one-way street.'

'Right. Right then. RIGHT. NOW!'

'Are you sure?'

'YES!'

'OK, as long as you're sure,' she said, as calmly as she could. 'Because, you know, there are roadworks round there. We'll probably get stuck and . . .' Without thinking, she began to turn her head.

'Don't look at me!' he yelled. 'And don't try to be clever. There aren't any fucking roadworks.'

'OK.' She swung the car around the corner into an obstacle course of orange cones, white bunting and steaming resurfacing machines. The robber stifled a howl of panic as vehicles closed in on them. Lowering the gun, he pressed it against her thigh.

'Don't try anything, or you'll never walk again.'

Her fingers tightened on the wheel. 'My name's Miranda.' She cleared her throat. 'Miranda Green. I have . . . I have four children. Thomas is . . .'

'Shut up!'

'Thomas is ten. David and Lily, the twins, are sixteen. Diana, my other daughter . . .'

'I said, shut up!'

'She's just fourteen . . . I want you to know that they'd all be devastated if anything happened to me. So, if you're thinking of killing me, well, you won't just have my death on your conscience, you'll have their ruined lives, too.'

His laugh was frosted with hysteria, and it terrified her in a way all his yelling had somehow failed to do. Suddenly she realised that he was mad, and heartless, and indeed planning to kill her.

On automatic pilot, Miranda inched the car forward. Death, and the back of a number 24 bus, stared her in the face.

With a dizzying lack of logic, he directed her north, then east, then north, then south and then west again in an interminable journey through the greyest stretches of North London. Now and then she recognised a kebab house or a row of shops they had passed earlier on. He must have recognised them, too, because his teeth tore ferociously at his fingernails and he cursed under his breath. Had he lost his way, or didn't he know where to take her?

From time to time he glanced down at the bank notes stuffed into the plastic carrier bags between his feet. How much money could there be in them? A couple of thousand pounds? Surely only an amateur crook would rob a super-market at ten in the morning when the tills were relatively empty. And an amateur was probably more dangerous than a professional. A professional would have taken the money and run. He had taken her, too.

Miranda's life had spun out of control. She was in the hands of a maniac. Where was he taking her, and what was he planning to do with her once he got her there? She clung to the hope that he would suddenly leap out of the car and make a run for it, but it was a hope so thin that she could see right through it to the deserted mews where he'd point the gun at her forehead and, with-out flinching, pull the trigger.

And then her chance came, as she braked at some traffic lights. Two policemen were standing on the pavement, deep in conversation with the proprietor of a newstand. She tried to scream at them, but her throat felt so tight that no sound came out.

Stubbornly, they refused to look her way. She seethed. They must have got reports of the robbery by now, so why weren't they watching out for Horace? There weren't that many navy blue Morris Minors on the streets.

And then she realised: no one was looking for a Morris Minor, because no one had seen the gunman drive off in one. No one in the supermarket knew the identity of the gunman's hostage, and no one at home would know that something had happened to her until she failed to pick Thomas up from school. Even then, the teachers would probably send him home on the bus like all the other kids, and her absence wouldn't really be felt until she failed to produce supper that evening, when Jack would probably attribute it to some subconscious desire of her ego's to escape from responsibility. How long would it take him to put two and two together and report her missing? Probably not until the police phoned and asked him to come down to the morgue to identify her corpse.

One of the constables turned towards her, laughing. But when he saw the car his laughter died. Leaning forward, he squinted through the windscreen. Without taking his eyes off Horace, he nudged his companion and said a few words. Her captor's legs began to jiggle up and down. Whistling softly, he reached down and with one hand pushed the bags of money under his seat. Then, without warning, he lunged at her. She just had time to glimpse the look of terror in his eyes before he drew her to him and crushed her mouth in a fierce, wet kiss.

Revolted, Miranda pulled away and wiped her mouth on her sleeve. When she looked up, the policeman's face was level with the passenger window. The man's right hand dropped behind her seat. 'The gun's aimed at your spine,' he muttered through clenched teeth.

Slowly, with his left hand, he wound the window down. 'Yes, guv?'

'Are you aware that your front bumper is hanging off?'

'Too bloody right, guv!' He sounded so normal, so cool. 'A Roller just crashed into us without looking. And, would you believe it, drove off without stopping. We're just off to get a quote for the repair.'

'Ah. And there's something else.' A pink finger tapped the windscreen. 'Tax. It's nearly the end of June. Your disc runs out in a week.'

'Thanks for the reminder.'

The constable grinned. 'All part of the service in the new-look Met. Customer satisfaction and all that. By the way . . .'

'Yes?'

'There's the question of seatbelts.'

'Ah.'

'Neither you nor your lady-friend here are wearing them. I should book you for that.'

'Help . . .' said Miranda.

'Yes, guv.'

The lights turned to amber.

'Please, this man . . .'

'Darling?'

'This man is . . .'

Now the lights were green. The PC stood back and motioned for Miranda to drive on.

'But . . .' she called.

'Thanks a million, guv. We'll do them up right away.'

The pistol jabbed into her seat as he rolled up the window. 'Do what he said.'

She'd always been a good girl and done what she was told, and, true to form, she was proving an obedient victim. *Yes, she was actually buckling herself in!* Clunk click. A condemned woman strapping herself into an electric chair.

With tears streaming down her face, Miranda drove on and on and on, into Hackney. Now he seemed to know where he was. He directed her into a maze of dull, deserted roads where small terraced houses ran like blanket stitches along either side of the street.

'Slow down.'

A finger pointed to a dilapidated corner house, the ugliest house in the ugly street. Two stories high, and covered in brown pebble-dash, it had a peeling front door, grey net curtains and a front patch – one could not call such a thing a garden – spilling over with weeds.

He gestured at a small garage tacked on to the side of the house. 'In there.'

'What?'

'Drive in there.'

There was no knowing what he might do to her when he got her inside. A strong wave of terror gave her the strength to rebel.

'No, I won't! I can't!' Near to hysteria, Miranda slammed her foot on the brake.

'Do what I say!'

'No, I'm not going to! If you want to kill me, you can bloody well do it here!'

'Kill you?' He began to laugh again, then stopped

48

abruptly. 'I'm not going to kill you! I'm not even going to hurt you. Not if you do what I say, that is. Drive inside.' After a long pause he added, uneasily, 'Please.'

She crushed the accelerator to the floor. The car shot forward, and the gun fell out of his hand. With a yell of protest, he yanked the wheel round, forcing the car up the concrete slope and into the garage.

Just before they hit the wall, he pulled the handbrake up, and Horace screeched to a halt. Miranda struggled out of the car, but he was much too fast for her. Before she'd got to the garage doorway, he'd pulled down a thick steel shutter, blocking out the light.

His hand over her face, he dragged her through a door and into a narrow hallway. Between his fingers she caught glimpses of a small wrought iron telephone table, a bare light bulb, some torn, stripey wallpaper stained green with mould.

Now, in a small, cramped kitchen with old fashioned cream-painted fitments and shiny blue walls, he shoved her down on a chair, ran behind her and bound a tea-towel tightly around her eyes.

'What are you going to do to me? Don't hurt me! Please!'

He said nothing. She heard him move about the kitchen, slamming cupboard doors, rattling in drawers, then something hard and scratchy cut into her arms. Oh God, he was tying her to the chair! First her wrists, then her legs. The chair scraped as he pushed it across the floor into a cold, dank place. Just before he slammed the door on her, he ripped off the blindfold.

When her sobs of terror had subsided, she looked around her prison, an old-fashioned larder with a stone floor and cobwebs festooning the ceiling. Ladders of shelves surrounded her, stacked neatly but sparsely with food: a bottle of corn oil; a packet of Basmati rice; tins of Italian plum tomatoes; a dusty pot of Gentlemen's Relish; Greek olives; an ancient tin of Spam.

High up in one wall was a mesh-covered ventilation hole.

She stared out of it for what must have been hours, watching the cloudless sky turn a vivid blue.

Time passed, but she soon lost track of it. After a long while she guessed it must be late afternoon. Thomas would have made his own way home from school by now. He might even have telephoned Jack to complain that she hadn't picked him up. Rescue me, Jack! she willed. She imagined this plea travelling across London to Jack's small, book-lined office in the Balls Pond Road University. Rescue me! She was hoping against hope he'd hear this message, but he wouldn't, because he wouldn't be open to receiving it. He didn't believe in ESP.

A key turned. The larder door swung open. A figure stood outside, wearing jeans and a crumpled red t-shirt and holding the *Daily Mirror* in front of his face.

'Want anything?'

She swallowed. Her throat was horribly dry. 'I want to go home.'

His eyes squinted at her through the holes he'd cut in the headline: MP IN STRIP CLUB STORM.

'Look, I won't tell anyone where you live. I honestly don't know where I am, or who you are, and I don't care. I promise I won't go to the police. I just want to go home and see my children. Please set me free! Please!'

Without answering, he slammed the door on her.

She looked up at the tiny window and watched the sky. Time passed. It might be hot outside, but she could not stop shivering. Her buttocks hurt from having sat too long in one place, and the string bonds had cut into her skin. Boredom and terror battled within her. If she ever got out, she swore she'd never, ever complain again.

At last her abductor threw open the door, and, like a magician at a children's party, produced a mug of steaming, fragrant tea from behind his newspaper mask. Thirsty as she was, she refused to drink it, turning her head away when he held it to her lips.

Cold and congealed, the drink was still on one of the

shelves hours later, as the patch of sky grew dark. Now she could hear him at work in the kitchen, chopping something with a knife. While he worked, he whistled a tune that her own father had once played repeatedly on his Decca gramophone. Exhausted, Miranda closed her eyes and listened.

Come Fly With Me.

She knew the lyrics by heart. Of course, being a teenager at the time, she'd despised the song, just as her own children despised songs from the sixties when she now sang them. Only after her father's death six years ago had she suddenly learned to appreciate it.

Like her father, he whistled with perfect pitch. Miranda closed her eyes, and a picture of her father came to her, his tall body swaying, his fingers snapping, click-click, click-click. Suddenly she was back in the Cricklewood house where she'd grown up, watching him twirl her mother round the living room in a lively jive. Respectable salesman that he was, he had always nursed a secret ambition to become a jazz singer. At work, he had looked staid, almost stiff, but the moment he walked through his front door he'd loosened his tightly-knotted tie and thrown off his pinstriped jacket and become a different man – Bohemian, relaxed, squatting on the floor on bent daddy-long-legs, reading the *Evening News* to the mellifluous tones of Sinatra, George Shearing or Nat King Cole.

How strange that the robber should have chosen this of all tunes! When he came to the soaring refrain, she heard her father's voice, clear if slightly out-of-tune, singing the words, and she had to crush an urge to join in too.

She opened her eyes and looked at her bound wrists, the scummy tea, the locked door in front of her. With a sudden burst of anger Miranda realised that the song was now ruined for her. Whenever she heard it – if she was to have a whenever – she would think not of her adored father, but of this terrifying imprisonment.

'Shut up!'

In the silence that followed, she heard his footsteps walk towards the larder door.

'What?'

'Stop whistling that song!'

'Why?'

'Just stop.'

He stopped. Water gushed, knives chopped, oil sizzled in a pan. The irresistible smell of frying bacon wafted under the door. When he next opened it he was wearing the shiny latex mask and the wig he had had on in Sainsbury's.

And, in his right hand, was a long, serrated knife.

'Stop yelling! For Christ's sake, don't panic! I'm not going to hurt you!' he shouted above her hysterical screams. Then, the moment she calmed down, he lunged across her.

'Help! Someone!'

'Shut up! I just want to get the fucking bread!' Reaching over her head, he grabbed a paper bag from behind her. A shower of crumbs cascaded over her. The lethal blade waved in her face as he attempted to brush them away.

'Get your hands off me!'

'I was only . . .'

'Get *off*!'

He jumped back and, clutching the loaf like a shield, hovered outside the larder, staring in. 'I'm making a meal,' he said in an aggrieved voice. 'I figured you must be hungry.'

'Well, you figured wrong. I'm not hungry and won't eat anything. I just want to go home.'

'Well, you can't. Not yet.'

'When, then?'

He turned away, put the bread on the counter and cut it into wafer-thin slices.

'When can I go home?'

Still he didn't answer. Deliberately, he laid the knife down on the kitchen counter before returning to the larder. 'Butter,' he explained in a cool voice before reaching across her again. Leaving the door ajar, he bustled about between the gas stove and a Formica table with splayed metal legs.

At length he came towards her, bearing a large Union Jack tray on which were arranged a plate of tiny, crustless bread and butter triangles, a bowl of green salad and a plate of spaghetti. He balanced it on her lap, untied her hands then drew up a chair and sat down facing her, the gun cradled in his lap.

Despite his threatening presence, she ate up everything, and with surprising relish.

It was the first time in more than nineteen years that a man had cooked her a proper meal.

When she'd finished, he put down his weapon and took away her empty plates. 'That OK?' he asked in an off-hand manner. She nodded, anxious not to make him angry, but damned if she was going to admit the truth – it had been one of the tastiest meals she had ever eaten. Perfectly *al dente*, the spaghetti had been coated with a creamy carbonara sauce and garnished with freshly-grated parmesan, crispy lardons of bacon and a light dusting of crushed peppercorns. Tossed together in pre-Raphaelite profusion, the lollo rosso and rocket had glistened with dark balsamic vinegar, grains of Meaux mustard and golden walnut oil.

Lollo rosso, rocket, walnut oil and balsamic vinegar? Meaux mustard, lardons, and fresh parmesan? Why did these delicacies surprise her so much? In which sociological text book was it written that an armed East London gangster could not be a terrific cook? The depth of her own class prejudice shocked her almost as much as the oranges in caramel he now said he just happened to have knocked up. Would she like some?

Curiosity got the better of her determination not to collude with him. Bright as marigolds in their pool of golden sauce, they were refreshingly tart, thinly pared and sliced wafer thin. He was obviously a dab hand with that Kitchen Devil.

When he finally took the tray away, she looked at him with new eyes. He was no ordinary gunman, he was a gourmet gunman.

His back towards her, the gourmet gunman stood at the sink, and washed up in an orderly, organised manner. Afterwards he went out, turning the light off as if she were not there.

'Hey! What about me?' Miranda called out as his footsteps thundered up the stairs. Either he didn't hear her or he deliberately ignored her. A television was turned on in the room overhead, and the theme tune of the late-night news blared out.

There must have been something about the robbery on it because, after a sudden thud, the sound went off. Pacing back and forth across the room like a caged wolf, the gourmet gunman howled softly into the night.

Now it was pitch dark, and her body had turned to ice, all of it except her bladder which burned inside her like a fiery wound. She had not been to the lavatory since leaving home that morning, and she was in dire danger of peeing where she sat. Miranda imagined the bliss of letting the hot urine flood out of her onto the chair, warming her thighs and trickling down her legs, but the thought of him coming back to find her sitting in a cold, stinking puddle was unbearable. Holding onto her bladder was holding onto normality. If she let go, she would lose self-respect, hope, everything.

'Hello? Are you there?' she called into the darkness. 'I need to go to the loo.'

There was no answer, only a loud snort from upstairs where he had been sleeping for hours, snoring sporadically.

'Hey! Wake up, will you? I need a lavatory!'

There was a strange rattling sound, which she realised was the chattering of her own teeth. Was the gourmet gunman trying to freeze her to death, or was he putting her on ice until such time as he decided to slaughter her? Was he keeping her chill-fresh, so he could carve her up, casserole her and feed her to his next victim? Was he perhaps a necrophiliac, with a penchant for cold meat?

She mustn't panic. Not yet. She forced herself to think of

the children. Sometimes when she couldn't sleep at night, or after she'd woken up in a panic thinking that she'd heard a burglar, she'd creep silently into their rooms, kneel down by their beds and just gaze at their sleeping faces, wondering at the metamorphosis that nightly took place. For gone were the sullen, pouting mouths, the reproachful eyes, the brows creased by exam pressure, and peer pressure, and the sheer everyday pressure of urban life; in sleep, their faces resumed the innocent look of angels with which they'd been born. It was at times like these that she glimpsed the answer to the question that so often troubled her nowadays: what had she done with her life? If nothing else, she'd brought up four beautiful children. Now, in her mind's eye, she revisited each of their rooms, and watched them sleep. Tears poured down her face. The thought of them had never seemed so poignant. She imagined Jack lying alone in bed, sleeplessly fretting about her, and she imagined the joyful smile on his face if – no, *when* – she eventually came home. All the petty anger she'd ever felt towards him was washed away by a sudden rush of love and affection she longed, in vain, to express.

'Oh, darling, please, please get me out of here!' she muttered.

She was wasting her breath. Jack, bless him, couldn't help her. If he was awake in bed, he'd be reading Freud on losing a partner. If by any remote chance he was out searching for her, he'd never, ever find her. Why, he couldn't even find his front door key in his jacket pocket!

'Help! Help! Please, SOMEONE, HELP ME!'

The snoring stopped. Something overhead fell to the ground. She held her breath as heavy footsteps stumbled downstairs. The hall light went on, cutting a sharp slice across the kitchen, and a dishevelled silhouette shuffled into view.

'Did you just shout?'

She took a deep breath. 'I . . . I need to use the lavatory. Hey, I said . . . Wait! Come back!'

The gourmet gunman walked out on her, but came back a moment later, pulling his mask over his face. Squatting down in front of her, he placed the gun at her feet and attempted, unsuccessfully, to untie the string with which he'd bound her to the chair. After a minute he went across to the sink, and picked up a small Sabatier knife. Miranda flinched.

'Relax, I'm not going to cut you.'

She stood up with difficulty. Her legs were so stiff that he had to help her into the hall. With his back against the opposite wall and the gun in his hand, he stood guard while she entered the airless shoebox of an under-the-stairs lavatory.

There was a bolt on the door, so she slid it shut. As soon as she sat down, burning urine gushed out of her, a near-orgasmic release. Afterwards, she pulled her leggings up and sat down again on the seat, dreading the moment when she had to face him again. Biting back tears, she stared bleakly at the small, grubby sink, the threadbare towel, the cracked yellow soap lit up by the bare bulb. It was all so horribly sordid. Was this the way her life was going to end?

'Finished?' the gourmet gunman said through the door.

'No.'

Her eyes searched for a potential weapon: a clotheshanger, a hammer, even a lavatory brush. There, on a narrow shelf above the door, was a familiar cobalt blue plastic bottle. Bleach. Careful not to make any noise, Miranda took it down and read the warning on the label. Then she flushed the lavatory and rinsed her hands and face. Two dark, terrified eyes stared back at her from the small mirror above the sink. She looked a hundred years old.

With the bottle clutched behind her, she slid back the bolt and gently kicked the door open. The hall was in darkness, and the gourmet gunman wasn't there. Why had he turned the lights off? Where was he hiding? What was he planning to do to her next?

Still as a statue, she waited, deafened by the pulsing of blood in her ears. Then, very slowly, she crept out.

Scarcely six feet away from her was the front door. Through its frosted glass panel filtered the glow of an orange streetlight. She could almost smell freedom.

Stealthy as a thief, she tiptoed over to the door and pulled the handle gently towards her. The catch clicked, but the door would not budge. She pulled again, and again, each time more violently, but still nothing happened. The door was double locked. She was trapped.

She swung round, desperate to find an escape route. And then she saw him, barely an arm's length away from her, slumped at the foot of the stairs. The gun was cradled in his hands, and his pupils glittered coldly at her through the eyeslits of the mask.

Her fingers tightened around the bottle of bleach.

'Put that down.' He spoke slowly in a calm but hoarse voice. Miranda did not move. 'Throwing it won't help either of us. Things are bad enough as it is. If you want the key, it's under the mat. Right there, under your feet.'

The gourmet gunman raised his hand, and Miranda lifted the bottle threateningly. 'Don't you touch me!' she shrieked.

He put the gun down on the bottom step. 'I won't hurt you. God's honour. I won't stop you. Go.'

'What?'

'Go. Go on. You can go now, see? You're free. Don't look at me like that. Look, move aside, I'll get you the key. But don't throw that stuff at me. OK?'

It was a trick. A sadistic trick. Of course it was a trick. Why should she believe him? Without taking his eyes off her, the gourmet gunman slid to his knees, crawled towards her and lifted the corner of the doormat. His masked face was at her feet. She could pour the bleach into his eyes and blind him if she wanted to. She could even kick him in the teeth.

'Here.' He stood up slowly, and held out the key. 'Take it. Go on. Here, for fuck's sake, before I change my mind.'

He pressed the cold metal into her hands, but her fingers

57

were shaking so much that she dropped it. The gourmet gunman stooped and picked it up for her.

As she tried in vain to fit it in the lock, Miranda began to cry.

He was torturing her, that's what he was doing. He was waiting for the moment when she believed him, for that split second when her face lit up, thinking she was free, and then he would snatch the key back and shoot her in the face or in the back of her head, or maybe, just for fun, just to prolong the torture, maybe in the knees. This game was worse than the robbery, worse than the drive here, worse than all the hours of imprisonment.

'It doesn't fit! You know it doesn't fit!' Tears streaming down her face, she hurled the key to the ground and crumpled against the door. He stared at her for a moment, then crouched down beside her, picked up the key, put it in the lock and turned it. The door opened.

'Get up. Come on. Get out of here.'

When she didn't move, he pulled her roughly to her feet. 'I don't understand,' she sobbed, hanging limply in his arms. 'Why are you doing this?'

There was a long pause, then he shrugged. 'I fucked up. Now I don't know what else to do with you.'

The gourmet gunman gave her a small push, and she staggered out into the night. He followed close behind her and, at the gate, grabbed her firmly by the shoulder.

'I'm sorry,' he murmured. 'About putting you through all this. I didn't plan to drag you into it, it just happened. This whole thing's been a fucking fiasco. I never meant to hurt you, honest. And I'm letting you go now, aren't I? Remember to tell them that when you go to the police.'

Four

Pulling away from him, she stumbled into the street. When she glanced back, the gourmet gunman was still at the gate. He raised his hand. To wave or to shoot? Without waiting to find out, Miranda forced her legs to walk on. Once around the corner, she broke into a run. Her footsteps echoed across the otherwise silent street, making her swing round sharply from time to time, convinced that he was following her.

Soon she was out of breath and panting hard, and had to slow down. Gradually, her frantic heartbeat began to subside, and with it the immediate terror. She shivered – not because she was cold but with sudden elation. She had danced with Death and tripped it up; and now, given a second chance to live, she luxuriated in the amniotic caress of the night.

Scarcely noticing where she was going, led on by some sixth sense, Miranda walked steadily and fearlessly on through the deserted streets. Soon the odd car and taxi began to pass by her. Above the orange glow of the streetlights, the night sky bleached slowly into day. From a rooftop, a blackbird let loose a sweet aria into the stillness. Tears of happiness coursed down her face.

Suddenly she turned a corner and found herself in the Holloway Road, almost back on home territory. She sobbed with relief at its familiarity. Its second-hand furniture shops, kebab houses and greasy-spoon caffs had never looked so beautiful. With a warm breeze blowing in her face, she floated on, unaware of the ugliness around her: the ubiquitous litter, the grey metal security shutters tagged in fluorescent yellow by the local gangs; the crushed carpet of broken bottles in the gutter; the rosettes of dog faeces which bordered the cracked pavement like tiny brown rosebuds iced upon a cake.

At long last, she reached Huddleston Avenue. Squashed orange peel, empty crisp bags and torn milk cartons littered the pavement, evidence that, though it was very early and the residents were still sleeping behind the closed curtains, the dustman had already been and gone.

Of all the houses in the street, only her own appeared to be awake. It was hardly surprising since Jack and the children would have been up all night, as sick with worry as she herself would have been had one of them disappeared. How thrilled they'd be when they saw her! How tearful! How relieved! Behind her closed eyelids, she lived through her probable reunion with each of them, and felt herself washed in a love as soft and comforting and blissful as a warm, foamy, fragrant bath.

Determined to prolong this unique and precious moment, she stopped just short of the squad car which was double-parked outside her house. From where she was, she could see the car's erstwhile occupants sitting at her kitchen table in the bay window: a man and a woman in white, short-sleeved shirts with dark epaulettes, drinking mugs of tea, both totally unaware of her presence. A mischievous smile twisted her lips: what fun it would be to spend a few minutes secretly watching everyone, and then surprise them!

As the police woman swung round in order to push up the bottom half of the sash window, Miranda dodged out of sight behind the squad car. The next moment, the kitchen door opened, and Jack emerged from the hall, tousle-haired and yawning in his red dressing-gown. He said something to the officers, but she couldn't catch what it was. The female officer shook her head. When she spoke, her voice boomed across the street.

'Never mind, sir. No news can be good news sometimes.'

Jack nodded glumly. 'Anyone fancy a cup of tea?' Picking up the kettle from the Aga, he took it over to the sink, turned on the tap and filled it. Then he replaced it on the hot plate. Simple actions, but Miranda could not remember the last time she'd seen him perform them, certainly not without a show of feigned inefficiency.

Now he went over to the kitchen door, and called to the children to come downstairs.

Miranda's heart lurched with the desire to see and embrace her brood. She was about to stand up when the female officer spoke again.

'Your young lad's gone out already. Couldn't sleep. Your neighbour Mary was in earlier, and she made him breakfast. Now she's taken him to her house. I've never seen a boy eat so much so fast. He must have been half-starved, mustn't he, Col?'

Her colleague nodded. 'Salt of the earth, that Mary, isn't she? Don't get friendly neighbours like that every day, do you? In here at the crack of dawn, she was. Made breakfast for us, too. And she left some in the oven for you and your other kiddies. Eggs, bacon, mush, beans, the whole works.'

Jack took a full plate out of the Aga, and joined the officers at the table. As she watched him tuck in, Miranda frowned incredulously. Why, Jack loathed cholesterol-rich food! He scarcely allowed bacon in the house, and, as long as they'd been married, he'd only ever eaten yoghurt, prunes or bran flakes for breakfast. Yet here he was, tucking into Mary's fry-up, even going so far as to mop the plate with some forbidden white, sliced bread.

As if on cue, the front door of Mary's house clicked open, and Seamus and Thomas tumbled out between the gaggle of garden gnomes that lined the path. Both boys were wearing flat police hats, and each one carried a half-eaten ice-lolly which dripped livid pink spots down their clothes.

'Betchoo can't run faster than me!'

'Betch' I can!'

Oblivious of Miranda hiding behind the police car, they clambered over the gate and raced off towards the corner, lollies waving, the soles of their bare feet slapping blackly against the pavement.

Swathed in a filmy pink negligée, Mary ambled slowly out of the door behind them, and clopped down the short, cluttered path in a pair of tiny, high-heeled, fur-trimmed silver mules.

'Keep your voices down!' she bellowed after them. 'Some lucky buggers round here are still sleeping.' Her hair cascading in a wild yellow torrent down the ample acres of her back, she opened her gate and shuffled next door. 'Yoohoo!' With the practised ease of royalty, she waved through the kitchen window. 'Morning, all. Slept well, Jack?'

He cleared his throat. 'Considering.'

'Naturally, love. Considering. Any news of Miranda? Tsst.' Clicking her tongue, she shook her head sadly. Her hair fell over her forehead. 'Poor love,' she said, pushing it back with her long red talons. 'Dreadful thing to happen to her, isn't it? What with her being so afraid of burglars and things. Kidnapped in the supermarket! And us not knowing whether she's alive or dead!'

'Terrible.' Jack wiped his mouth on a napkin. 'Thanks for the food, Mary.'

'Anyway I can help, you know me. Anything I can do in your hour of need – shopping, cleaning, cooking. You got to help, haven't you? What else are neighbours for at a time like this? Aw, don't clear up, love! I'll do it. I hate to see a fellow doing women's work. Unless he's my old man!' Her glossy lips let loose a short, hyena-like bark. 'Well, do I have to stand here all day or are you going to let me in? Tommy! Seamus! Come back now!'

Without a murmur of dissent, the two boys ran back from the corner and followed Mary inside the house. Reappearing a moment later in the kitchen, they began to clown around with the police officers. Seamus jumped onto a bench, then leapt onto Jack's shoulders. Jack toppled out of sight,

Mary howled with laughter, and the female constable picked Seamus up by his collar, and held him dangling.

Now Diana came shuffling in in her stained dressing-gown. 'Hi, Dad. Oh, hallo, Mary. Any news about Mum?'

'I'm afraid not.'

'Oh God! Look, are you really sure it was her that robber kidnapped?'

The policewoman patted her shoulder. 'Seems like it, love. The last car seen leaving the carpark was a Morris Minor just like hers, and your Dad swears it was her on the security video. Don't you, sir?'

Jack nodded. Diana's head fell forward onto his chest, and he slipped his arm around her. Miranda strained her ears to hear his words of comfort, but couldn't catch them. After a short moment, Diana moved away, walked over to the window and stared blankly out. Hesitantly, her lips parted, closed, then parted again. 'Look, I know this sounds horrid, Dad, but . . . well . . . how am I going to get to my tap-dancing class after school if Mum's not back in time to take me? Could you drop me there?'

'You'll have to take the tube or the bus.'

'But then I'd have to change trains at Camden Town! Mum never lets me, because of all the drug dealers.'

'I'm sure she wouldn't mind, just this once.'

Diana nodded, sniffed back tears. Then her nose crinkled. 'Can I smell bacon?'

'You certainly can, Di, love. It's my special fry-up.'

'Oh.' Diana fell silent for a moment. 'Is there . . . I don't suppose there's any left, Mary?'

Miranda's mouth dropped open.

'Might be some still in the cooker, love. Take a look.'

Crouching down, Diana peeped inside. 'Yes, there is. Can I have it?'

'Course. That's what it's there for.'

Incredulous, Miranda watched her anorexic daughter sit down and eat with real gusto. Now David and Lily came in too and, without making a fuss, made themselves breakfast.

Not only that: when they'd finished, they quietly cleared up.

Filled with a deep sense of unease, Miranda squatted down on her haunches. Where had the long faces, moans and complaints which habitually greeted her in the morning gone to? How had the emotional battlefield of her kitchen become, in her absence, a haven of harmony in which even Jack appeared to be having fun?

She had always thought of herself as being like a sun in their lives – an essential, life-giving presence. Suddenly she saw that she'd been more of a cloud casting a dark shadow over them. From what she could see, none of them really missed her. No, they didn't miss her at all.

'Come on, you young scoundrels,' Mary scolded loudly. 'Time to get ready for school.'

'Oh, no! Do we have to go today, Dad? What if they find Mum?'

'I'll call you immediately, Thomas, I promise.'

'Please, Dad! It's not fair!'

'Life must go on, even without your mother. *I'm* going into work. It's important for all of us to preserve a semblance of normality.'

David guffawed. 'How can Thomas preserve that when he isn't normal to start with?'

Thomas ignored the taunt. 'Please, Dad! Please! I will be normal, I promise I will!'

'I said no.'

Miranda waited for him to start whingeing. Instead, he simply heaved a sigh of defeat and allowed Mary to usher him, and the others, out of the kitchen.

A moment later, she reappeared. 'If you two coppers haven't got anything better to do, Thomas'd like to show you his crystal collection. Come on, loves! You'll make his day.'

Shrugging, the officers left the room.

Alone for the first time, Jack walked over to the window, and running his hands through his thin hair, stared out. Dark shadows of sleeplessness surrounded his eyes, and his face suddenly looked so drawn and miserable that Miranda's sense of unease immediately disappeared. Of course he and the children were worried sick about her – how could she have doubted it for a moment? Their cheerfulness in front of Mary and the police had been nothing but an act.

It was time to stop torturing them. Unable to suppress a small, victorious whoop, she stood up and, waving brightly, walked straight towards the house. But Jack didn't see her, because at the exact same moment Mary came back in, and he turned away.

'That's got rid of them for a while. Well, hello again, lover boy.'

Mouth agape, Miranda ducked behind the front hedge, pulled apart the spindly branches, and stared through the foliage at the unfolding scene.

With a wicked leer on her face, Mary towered over Jack and drew him towards her with arms as soft, round and plump as feather bolsters. Like a bee searching for honey in a foxglove, his nose delved into the deep crack of her cleavage.

'Mmmm!'

Jack pushed Mary roughly against the Aga, pressing one hand against the balloon of her breast while the other fumbled with her knotted sash.

'Ouch! This bloody thing's hot, Jack! Jack!'

'So am I.'

The slippery pink nylon having slid off her shoulders, Jack rained wet kisses on her marshmallow flesh.

'Oh, God! I want to fuck you so much.'

Miranda's legs gave way. Dropping to her knees, she crawled up the front path.

'. . . because you smell so nice,' she heard Jack murmur. 'What are you wearing under this?'

'Not a stitch. Only Poison.'

'What?'

'Poison. It's perfume. Don't you remember nothing, love? You gave it to me last Christma . . . aah!'

Kneeling up between two pots of scarlet geraniums, Miranda peered over the sill. Jack had pulled Mary's head down towards him, and stopped her words with hungry lips. His hand was groping between her legs.

'Mmm . . . Muffin's soaking wet.'

'She always is when the Mule's around. Stop, Jack! This is far too risky.'

'Mmm.'

'Anyone could see us. My Brian could walk past! The kids could come in. Oooh! Or the cops! Then we'd be well and truly nabbed, wouldn't we? Mmm!'

As she dug her nails into the shallows of his curly, rust-coloured hair, Jack reached behind her and grabbed a long slender courgette from the vegetable basket. Roughly pulling apart her negligee, he slid it slowly into the abundant growth of black hair between her legs.

'Ooh! Oh, stop it, Jack! We shouldn't be doing this. Mmmah! Not with Miranda missing.'

'Miranda?' he muttered vaguely.

'Jack! Jack, love, no! Uhh! A bit deeper, love, and a bit to the side. Oh, yes! Just there! Oh, stop!'

'I can't!'

'Uuuuh! Love, you'd better, this is far too risky. Uhh! Deeper, yes, deeper!'

He fell to his knees and licked the waterfall of her undulating belly. 'Oh, Muffin!' Pulling the glistening courgette out of her, he bit the end off savagely. 'I will stop,' he said with his mouth full. 'In one minute. The trouble is, you're so . . . mmm, delicious, Oh, Muffin, you've no idea how much the Mule wants to pay you another visit. Four hours is too long without you. Let him in for a little bit! He's begging you. Please, please, *please!*'

Nausea scalding the back of her throat, Miranda crawled out into the street, scrambled to her feet and, blinded by tears, ran back towards the main road.

It couldn't be true! Jack and Mary, having an affair? Having an affair when she'd been kidnapped by a ruthless gunman, when she was missing and, for all they knew, maybe even dead?

Jack making love to Mary? How could this be when he despised Mary, when he never missed an opportunity to criticise her? If it wasn't her lack of taste he was laying into – the plethora of plaster gnomes and leprechauns in her garden, the nodding daschund on the back shelf of her Nissan Sunny, her frothy, festooned net curtains – it was her loud-mouthed ignorance, or her predilection for salacious local gossip, or her unerring ability to drop round, uninvited, in the middle of every Channel 4 programme of any worth. And if her personality wasn't under the hammer, it was her looks he couldn't abide: that glossy red lipstick and those matching, pointed talons; the pneumatic spare tyre rolling over the straining waistband of her clinging lycra bicycle shorts; the black roots of her untameable, corkscrewed, peroxided hair. According to Jack, every aspect of Mary grated on him. This being so, how could he possibly be having an affair with her?

Besides, Jack was impotent. Why, he hadn't been interested in sex for two years!

She closed her eyes. An image of Jack and Mary fucking against the Aga was scorched inside her lids.

As for that courgette . . .

She'd bought it in Queen's Crescent market on Saturday, so she could make Jack ratatouille, one of his favourite dishes. Long, shiny and green, it had lit up the kitchen counter like a blob of bright paint.

Now it had been washed in Mary's juices.

How many vegetables before it had received a similar marinade? Had she – oh, God – unknowingly cooked and eaten them, or, even worse, eaten them raw without washing them?

Just when had she first been betrayed?

When she and Jack had moved to Huddleston Avenue, and he'd laughingly called the scarlet 'smalls' bedecking Mary's washing line a 'contradiction in terms', had he even then been secretly longing to bury his face in them?

When had he done so? More to the point, where?

Maybe it had been in Miranda's own bedroom. On the floor, or standing up against the Laura Ashley wallpaper, or on the pale blue polycotton of their marital bed.

But what did such details matter? The important thing was that Jack had deceived her in the most banal and hypocritical way. He wasn't impotent. Nor did sex now take a back seat in his life, as he'd once claimed. Far from it, he was having a rip-roaring affair with their next-door neighbour, a woman he professed to despise.

Stunned by this betrayal, she sank down on a broken bench at the corner of Huddleston Avenue, carefully siting herself between two snow-white pools of bird shit. Traffic thundered past her, belching brown, poisonous fumes into the air. The romantic version of her homecoming which she'd been nurturing imploded inside her, leaving a black hole. The truth was that, even if she hadn't discovered Jack and Mary *in flagrante*, the future wouldn't have been all roses, not after the first couple of days. Everyone would have been relieved to see her at first, of course, but what then? Once she'd been interviewed by the police and a journalist or two, life would have returned to normal. The children would have gone back to school, and Jack would have raced off to work, leaving her alone at home with her terror. Perhaps she might have received a concerned phone call from him during the day, but his voice would have had a brusqueness to it, a sharp, distracted edge. Within forty-eight hours he'd have started hinting that it had been her own fault that the gunman had picked on her in Sainsbury's. Something to do with her looking and thinking like a victim.

As for the children, once the initial glamour of having a mother who'd been abducted at gunpoint had worn off, her relationship with them would have quickly regressed: to a sulky stand-off with David, open warfare with Diana, non-communication with Lily and strained aggravation with Thomas, who, today, and for the rest of his life, would no doubt hold it against her that she'd failed to pick him up at the school gates.

And after today would come tomorrow, and after that another tomorrow, and so on and on and on for the rest of her days. The constricting corset of motherhood awaited her, as did that callus-forming, shabby pair of shoes that was her marriage.

Bewildered, Miranda looked up and down the street. Like a character in a play who suddenly discovers, mid-performance, that the author has changed the ending, she had no idea where to go or whom to turn to.

And then it came to her: Suzanne Jones.

Stumbling to the nearest telephone kiosk, she took the scrap of paper with Suzanne's hastily-scribbled telephone number from the pocket of her shirt. But when she lifted the receiver and attempted to dial, a sign flashed on before her: Enter Money. She stared at it with a sinking heart. She had no money on her.

Then she saw the ten pence coin on the ground. Miranda picked it up, and examined it incredulously. It was a miracle – enough to make her believe in God. She put it in the slot and dialled.

'Hello. Suzanne Jones here.'

'Oh, God! Suzanne!' She broke down in tears. 'Suzanne! I can't tell you . . .'

But Suzanne took no notice of her. 'I'm afraid I can't come to the phone at the moment, but if you'd like to leave your name, your telephone number, your fax number, and your mobile phone number, and the time and date of your call I will ring you back as soon as I can. If possible, please explain the nature of your call. If you wish to send a fax now, please do so after the tone which will be coming up after this message. During business hours I can be reached on . . .'

'Hurry, hurry!' Miranda begged the receiver.

'Oh one seven one seven six six six eight seven eight. I repeat . . .'

'Come on!'

'Fax number oh one seven one seven six eight five eight seven two. I repeat . . .'

Miranda stared at the digital display, willing it not to change.

'If your call is urgent I can be reached on my mobile number oh nine five six two three five two . . .'

While she did her best to memorise the number, the 10p sign changed to zero, and the Enter Money flashed back on.

'I repeat oh nine five . . .'

She tapped her feet. 'Come on! *Come on!*'

'Alternatively, you can leave a message with my message service on . . .'

Enter Money. ENTER MONEY.

In vain, Miranda scoured the floor for more dropped treasure.

'Please leave your message or send your fax after this short tone.'

The bleep started. Then the telephone went dead.

Slamming down the receiver, she stumbled out into the street. What should she do? Who could she turn to? The last thing she could face at the moment was being questioned by the police.

She needed time to think. She needed a refuge. Her nose was running, and she urgently needed some tissues, but her tissues were inside her handbag, and her handbag was inside Horace.

And Horace was in the gourmet gunman's garage.

By the time Miranda had walked all the way back to East London, painful blisters had formed on her toes, and her mouth tasted as poisonous as mercury.

The gourmet gunman's street was even uglier than she remembered. Rusty windows closed, dingy curtains drawn against the daylight, letterbox falling off, his house looked like something out of a murder film. What on earth had she been thinking of in coming back here?

It occurred to her with sudden relief that her abductor would have fled long ago, thinking she was going to return with the police. All she had to do was open the garage door, take Horace and drive away.

For a long while she stood on the pavement, watching the house, waiting for something to happen. When nothing did, she walked slowly up the concrete slope and tried the garage door, which was locked.

She was about to walk away when she noticed a narrow alley at the side of the house, guarded ineffectually by a broken-down gate. Pushing this open, she squeezed past an array of festering dustbins and rusty bike wheels.

Two yards down was a door, which, when pushed open, revealed a narrow slice of the dark garage and the tip of Horace's wing.

With a pounding heart, Miranda tiptoed inside.

There was Horace, glowing in the dark, his curves as dear and familiar to her as those of a cat. He had been hers so long that his imperfections formed a map of her marriage: the old dent on the broken front bumper where she had crashed at Hyde Park Corner the moment after Jack had asked her to marry him; the indelible baby-sick stains on the back-seat upholstery; the remnants of Diana's My Little Pony sticker collection, permanently glued to the back windows; the outline of Jack's torso, indelibly impressed into the front passenger seat.

The moment she slipped inside, she burst into tears. With his split screen, bare dashboard and familiar leathery smell, Horace belonged to a bygone age: an age of mystical Glastonbury Festival weekends in her student days, and Sunday drives down leafy country lanes, and picnics and outings with her parents when the children were young. An age when she and Jack were convinced they and their generation could change the world for the better.

What a joke! Stuck in a time-warp within a transformed world, she alone had clung onto these half-baked ideals – and Horace – while her contemporaries now bulldozed their way through the hostile urban jungle in bulky four-wheel drives. Only she, it seemed, had not changed her philosophy or her style. A whole decade, the acquisitive eighties, had passed her by while she was mixing her own muesli, changing nappies, ironing the children's clothes, and trying, with Jack, to create for them, in the growing chaos of late twentieth century London, a safe, meaningful and, so she'd thought, vaguely stable life.

Closing her eyes for a moment, Miranda let exhaustion sweep over her, blotting out the unpalatable reality.

The next thing she knew, a hand grabbed her shoulder. Someone was dragging her backwards, out of sleep, out of the car and pushing her down onto the cold hard concrete of the garage floor.

The moment she screamed, something clamped over her mouth. Something, someone, lifted her off her feet.

Without thinking, she bit into the soft flesh pressed hard against her lips. With a loud yelp, he let go of her, but as she ran for the door he grabbed her arm and pulled her off balance, shouting, 'What the fuck . . .'

'No!'

As Miranda fell backwards towards him, knocking down a pyramid of old paint cans, she took a deep breath and jerked her elbow into his ribs with a force that surprised both of them.

'Bitch!'

'Let go! *Let go of me!*'

She wrenched out of his grip, but before she could get away from him he grabbed her again and swung her round towards him, pressing her face into the hard wall of his chest. With her arms now pinioned behind her, she could do little except butt her head into him, and attempt to stamp on his feet.

'Ow!'

After she'd crushed his foot hard under hers, she thought she'd get free, but he held on and on and on to her until sheer exhaustion and his strength overwhelmed her.

Victorious, the gourmet gunman dragged her limp body towards the kitchen. Miranda cursed herself for her stupidity. Freedom had been handed to her, a gift-wrapped gem, but she had tossed it aside as if it was a worthless bauble. Now she'd done it! She was helpless, helpless . . .

And yet . . . Suddenly five short words broke through the thick, viscous meniscus of fear: *knee him in the balls*. If anything would save her, that would. All she had to do was jerk her knee up into that ridiculous patch of vulnerable manhood she had learned, over the years, to treat with such unwarranted reverence and respect.

But what if it didn't work? What if she didn't do it properly? What if she only succeeded in making him angrier, and more violent, than he already was?

What if she didn't try? They were by the kitchen door. In another minute, she would be back in that larder, trussed up and ready to be dismembered. She remembered his skill with the Kitchen Devil. If she had any chance to get away, this was it.

Arching her spine, she pushed her knee back as far as she could, then thrust it up with as much force as she could muster. With a small thud, it smashed into something soft and squelchy.

For a moment, nothing happened. Then, with a loud sucking in of air, the gourmet gunman crumpled to the floor, taking her with him.

As he writhed on the ground, legs drawn up, hands clutching his genitals, she scrambled to her feet and ran for the front door. She had just opened it when he let out a bellow so deep and pitiful that she stopped in her tracks.

His gun was lying on the wrought iron telephone table. Gingerly, she picked it up and walked slowly over to where

73

he lay. Pointing it at him, she bent down, and, for the first time, took a good look at him.

Her lips parted. She drew in a long, shocked breath.

Like a B-movie starlet, whose make-up remains immaculate after surviving a near-fatal car accident and bursting into tears, even when contorted in agony his face was the most handsome she had ever seen.

His long, unruly black hair, run through with thin slivers of silver, begged to be ruffled. Bordering his screwed-up eyes were thick, dark eyelashes which gave tantalising glimpses of irises which were a startling swimming-pool blue. His broken nose looked like a diploma from the Hard Knocks School of Life, and his full sensual lips could have sold a million French cigarettes. As she stared at them in awe, they drew back in a grimace of pain to reveal two rows of tightly-clenched, sharp, evenly-spaced white teeth.

Her eyes drifted slowly past them to his strong, thick jaw, pierced with dark stubble, and the thumb-print cleft on his chin, and his bullish throat, and thence to the hair-flecked, muscular V which disappeared into the open collar of a creased denim shirt.

And there, just visible, on his left shoulder, was the delicate tracery of an indigo tattoo . . .

Desire scratched like a sharp unwelcome fingernail down Miranda's spine.

Kneeling beside him, she pressed the gun barrel hard against his temple, unreasonably angry that someone so extraordinarily attractive could be so evil inside.

Five

'Waaah! Waa-ah!'

It took some time for her to realise that he was no longer moaning, but asking for something.

'Waa-er!'

'Water?' She prodded his ribs with the gun. 'Why should I give you anything?' His torso was solid, muscular, glistening with a fine film of sweat. She fought back the urge to rip off his shirt and fall hungrily upon his nipples. 'Say please.'

The long, spidery lashes parted for a split second, and, with a venomous glint in his eyes, the gourmet gunman squinted up at her. 'Please.'

Miranda hesitated for a moment, then went into the kitchen, where, suddenly famished, she rooted amongst the debris for something to eat. Gnawing on a stale end of bread, she plucked a glass from the counter and filled it under the tap.

By the time she returned, he was sitting up, clutching his knees. She put the glass on the floor beside him, and stood at a distance, brandishing the gun. There seemed little need of it, for it appeared she'd kicked the power out of him. His skin was ashen, and his hands were shaking so much that the water spilled down his sleeves.

Putting down the glass, he wiped his mouth on his wrist. 'Why are you still here? Why didn't you go home?'

'I . . . I did. The police were at my house, waiting for me. Hey, don't move! Look, I said, don't move!'

Ignoring her, he crawled down the hall, pulled himself up on the front door, flipped open the letter box and peered out. 'Where are they?'

'Who?'

'The Filth. The Old Bill. Look, I want you to go outside, and tell them I won't give them no trouble. OK? Do that now, OK? OK babe?'

She raised the gun. 'Don't you dare call me *babe*!'

'Sure. Sorry. Whatever you say.' The letterbox snapped shut. 'Go on, then, call them in. What are you waiting for? Look, don't play games with me.'

'I'm not playing games.' She paused, enjoying the moment of power. 'You see, there is no *them*.'

The gourmet gunman looked at her again, this time with open suspicion. 'Who *are* you?'

She tightened her grip on the gun. To her surprise, she didn't dislike the weight of it in her hand. 'Actually, I think you owe me that explanation.'

Exasperated, he shook his head. 'What are you *doing* here?'

'You brought me here. Or have you forgotten?'

'I let you go, didn't I?'

She shrugged. 'I came back.'

'What the hell for?'

'I . . .' The heavy gun was slipping down, so she raised it at him again. It occurred to her that, since she was holding it, she had no need to answer him. She was controlling him now. She could do, and say, what she liked. 'I wanted your recipe for carbonara sauce,' she quipped, flashing him a cold smile.

'Don't fuck with me, lady!'

She turned scarlet. 'I'm not *fucking with you*! I . . . I wanted my car.'

'That bit of scrap metal?'

'As a matter of fact, it has sentimental value. Not that someone like you would understand that! Besides, my handbag's in the back.'

'Your handbag? Jesus! Haven't you got another one?'

'I can't get into my wardrobe!'

'Why not? Bedroom door stuck?'

At the mention of her bedroom, a vision of Jack and Mary flashed back into her mind, and, to her horror, she burst into tears. 'If you must know, my husband's having an affair!'

There was a long pause, during which he stared at her as if she were the crazy one. 'What the fuck's that got to do with me?'

'Everything! If you hadn't taken me hostage, I'd never have found out!' Raising her arm, she wiped her damp face on her sleeve. 'Stay where you are! I said . . .'

He took no notice. Very slowly, and with obvious pain, he got to his feet and, bent almost double, staggered into the under-the-stairs lavatory. There was a rattling sound, then he came out clutching a wad of tissue paper which he held out towards her.

Sniffing back her tears, Miranda pointed the gun at him.

'Don't come any closer, or I'll shoot!'

He gave a half-laugh. 'You've been watching too many films.'

'I mean it. I will. Look, stay where . . .'

Straightening up, he walked up to her and pressed the wad of tissue into her free hand. They were eye to eye, barely six inches apart, and she could see every pore on his crumpled paper bag of a face. She could feel the sexuality emanating from him. He made no attempt to take the weapon from her. Instead, his blue eyes stared down at her, cold, unflickering, trying to control her with their steady gaze.

'Go on,' he said. 'Put me out of my misery.'

She hooked her index finger around the trigger. To her horror, the catch clicked back. 'I . . . I will, if you don't stand back. Stand back, OK?' Her voice rose. 'Did you hear me? STAND BACK!'

But the gourmet gunman didn't back off, he just licked his glorious lips with a moist pink tongue. 'Shoot me. Go on.

No one would blame you, it's a dog-eat-dog world. Either you kill me or . . .'

He raised an eloquent eyebrow. His hand moved. Terrified, Miranda screwed her eyes shut and released the trigger. A blast of hot air hit her in the face. There was a loud thud as his body hit the floor.

Hysterical now, she began to scream. 'Oh my God! Oh, God, what have I done? Oh God, no!'

An eternity later, she plucked up the courage to open her eyes. At the end of the gun barrel burned a small yellow flame.

The corpse on the floor grinned up at her, got to its feet, reached into the back pocket of its jeans and extracted a pack of cigarettes.

'Cheers, doll,' he said, lighting up.

Open-mouthed, Miranda watched him limp away. Then her sense of shock turned to outrage.

Catching up with him in the kitchen, she rained her fists hard on his back. 'You bastard! How could you do that? Holding up Sainsbury's . . . taking me hostage . . . putting me through all this, *all this* . . . And all the time, it wasn't even a real gun! It was a cigarette lighter, a bloody cigarette lighter! Oh, God, I could kill you for this!'

With the speed of an animal, the gourmet gunman swung round, grabbed her wrists and stared into her eyes. Then his gaze travelled to her lips. For a split second she thought he was going to kiss her, but instead he let go of her so abruptly that she felt the floor shift under her feet.

'Look, I said I was sorry, didn't I?' Turning away, he filled the electric kettle and plugged it back in with shaking hands. 'Want a cuppa?' When she did not reply, he opened a cupboard above the sink, and sorted through its contents. 'Earl Grey . . . Fortnum's breakfast blend . . . Orange Pekoe . . . or, hold on a tick, there's some Lapsang Souchong in here somewhere. Nothing you fancy? Suit yourself.'

He warmed a small brown pot under the hot tap, and spooned in some loose tea from a rusty tin. For some reason, his expert actions made Miranda angrier than ever.

'I don't believe this! You kidnap me at gunpoint, you scare me half to death, you . . . you *ruin* my life! And then you say you're sorry and offer to make me tea. And that's supposed to be enough?'

'You already kicked the shit out of me. What more do you want?' He poured the boiling water into the pot. 'Want me to beat myself up? I'm already doing enough of that, believe me. Milk or lemon?'

'What are you, some kind of silver service waiter?'

'You a journalist?'

This remark did not displease her. She had not been asked what she did for many a year. She sat down at the table, and kicked her shoes off. 'What makes you say that?'

He shrugged. 'You ask a lot of questions.'

'I'm curious. It's not every day I'm offered a pot of Lapsang Souchong by a real live gangster.'

With a short, humourless laugh, he sat down opposite her. 'I'm not what you think. I'm like the gun – a sham.'

'You could have fooled me.'

'Yeah, well . . .' He sighed. 'Doing hold-ups isn't my usual style.'

'So what exactly is your usual style? No, don't tell me, let's play *What's My Line?*! Are you – let me guess – a . . . a paid killer? Or a forger? No? Do you rob banks for a living?'

'Look, I'm just an ordinary common-or-garden villain. A conman. A hoister.'

'A what?'

'Shoplifter. I don't do armed robbery, not normally. Well, I haven't for some time. I'm not in that league any more.' A lock of hair had flopped over his face. He pushed it back with surprisingly elegant, though well-chewed fingers. 'You don't believe me, do you?'

'What difference does that make? I'm sure the police will. And if they don't, you can always explain it to the jury.' Shocked at her own cruelty, she watched with relish as the colour bled from his face. 'Cheer up! The prison system's so overcrowded that sentences tend to be very lenient, don't they? What do they hand out for armed robbery nowadays? Ten years? But you must know all about that.' She gulped down the strong, fragrant tea. 'Oh no, I forgot – you're not a real armed robber, are you? You're just a cook who just happened to find himself in Sainsbury's on a Monday morning without the money for some crucial ingredient for . . . for beefburgers *en croute*. And since you just happened to have a gun in your pocket – correction, a replica gun – oh yes, and a handy disguise – you thought you'd hold the place up in order to get it. And then – how absent-minded can a person get? – you left the crucial ingredient on the counter, and took me home instead.' As she slammed down the mug, hot tea slopped over her hand. 'Ouch!'

He reached across the table. 'Here, let me take a butcher's at that.'

'Don't touch me!' Snatching her hand away, she went over to the sink and plunged the burn under the cold tap.

The gourmet gunman took out another cigarette. 'I know you don't believe a word I say. But just let me tell you something. I . . .'

Her anger bubbling over, she swung round. 'No, let me tell *you* something – you're full of crap. Just like my husband. Maybe all men are the same. Maybe you can't help being cowards and liars. Maybe you're all genetically incapable of taking responsibility for what you do.'

'Look, I'm sorry if . . .'

'And what's more pathetic, men think that all they've got to do is to say they're sorry and Mummy will forgive them. Well, I'm not your mother and I won't forgive you. I'll never get over the shock of what you've done to me! It was bad enough before, worrying about burglars breaking into the house, and muggers getting me in the street, and ordinary everyday things like that. But now I'll never even be able to go to Sainsbury's without worrying that some maniac is going to grab me in the queue! You've destroyed my life, understand? And so has

Jack! I mean, how could he make love to Mary – *Mary*, for God's sake – in my house? In my kitchen! With the police and the children upstairs!' Her angry voice rose to an orgasmic crescendo: 'While I'm being held prisoner by a lunatic!'

The lunatic gave her a clear, knowing look, and sighed. 'Listen, babe, you're just jealous and . . .'

'I am not *jealous* – not that it's any of your business. If you must know, I'm bloody furious! And not just with Jack! I mean, how dare the kids be having such a good time when I've been kidnapped . . . while I'm being held hostage . . . when I'm missing, maybe even dead?' She blew her nose again. 'Well, as far as I'm concerned they can all manage without me from now on. I'm never going home again, and that's that. Let them think I've been murdered.'

For a long time they sat together in silence. 'You'll have to go home sometime,' he said eventually. 'I mean, you'll have to give yourself up to the police.'

'Why? *I* haven't done anything!'

He chewed his fingertips. 'Look, I'm sorry about your old man and all that, but I don't want to be charged with murder because you decide to disappear.'

'You probably won't get caught. The clear-up rate's appalling.'

'But you know where I live, don't you?'

'True. That *was* stupid of you, bringing me here. Well, you'll just have to move – if you can bring yourself to leave this. . .' She glanced at the peeling walls. 'This palace. Otherwise you will have to murder me, to stop me going to the police,' she added recklessly. 'Unless . . .' She had no idea where this word had come from. Nevertheless, it hung threateningly in the air.

'Yeah?'

Unsure of her ground, she hesitated. 'Unless . . .' She swallowed.

He looked at her coldly. 'Want to do business? What do you want? The Sainsbury's dosh?'

'How dare you! *I'm* not a thief!'

81

'What then?'

'I think . . . I think I might want to teach Jack a lesson.'

'Want me to give him a good going over?'

'No! Of course not! No-o.' Her outrage faded as she contemplated this rather attractive proposition. However, she crushed down her murderous thoughts. 'I might . . . I might want somewhere to stay for a couple of weeks.'

'*You* want to stay *here*? For a couple of *weeks*?' He threw his head back, and a deep, throaty laugh escaped from his parted lips. 'Jesus! Do you think I'm off my trolley? Half the Met is out looking for you.'

'That didn't seem to bother you yesterday.'

'That was different, wasn't it? I fucked up. There's no way you can stay here now.'

'Why not?'

'Well . . . I . . .' He glanced around for a reason. 'Well, for a start it's too small here, isn't it? I need my space.'

'Think how much you'll get in prison. A six-foot cell, shared with – what? three other men. You'll never be alone, not even in the lavatory. And then there's the rest of it – the slopping out, the disgusting food – I bet you won't like that – and the beatings, and the gang rapes.' With a pleasure that shocked her, she watched the pale cheeks underneath the gourmet gunman's dark stubble turn grey. 'But I guess you must know all about that. OK. It's your choice, remember. In that case, I'll be on my way.'

Just one night. That was how long he said she could stay there. Just one night, then she had to leave. The day before, he'd tied her up and held her captive, but now that she wanted to stay, he couldn't wait to get rid of her.

Such was Miranda's effect on men nowadays.

She tried not to think about it. Instead, she pushed a chair under the plastic doorhandle of his small and dingy spare room to make it secure, then crawled into the narrow confines of a creaking single bed, and sought oblivion in sleep.

There, between the childish comfort of creased flannelette sheets, she slept better than she had for years.

From time to time she surfaced, aware of the late evening sun dying away behind the thin curtains, or of him knocking at the door with offers of drinks or food, but she didn't answer.

Then, in the early hours of the morning, she suddenly awoke, convinced that the last day and a half had been a terrible dream. But the peeling unfamiliar walls crowded in on her and her nostrils filled with the stuffy, unfamiliar stench of damp. As the grey dawn light seeped into the room, Miranda stared up at the bare bulb which hung down from the ceiling, dreading the moment when she would have to get up and deal with the reality of Jack's betrayal. Burying her head under the pillow, she suffocated herself back to sleep.

A series of loud raps on the door awoke her. When she didn't answer, there was a deafening thud and the bedroom door crashed back, sending the chair flying across the room.

Miranda screamed. Dressed in short shorts and a skin-tight t-shirt, her reluctant host sauntered in, a laden breakfast tray in his hands, and a wad of newspapers under his arm.

'Morning, sunshine. I made you something to eat.'

'Get out of here. I don't want anything from you. Just leave me alone, will you?'

'Go on – take it,' he said, thrusting the tray at her.

'No!'

'Have it your own way.' Dropping the newspapers on the end of the bed, he balanced the tray across her chest.

'Hey! Take it off!'

But he had gone, closing the broken door behind him.

Raising her head, she glanced sullenly at the tray, then struggled into a sitting position, amazed. On one side of it stood a small pot of tea, covered by a carefully-folded white napkin-cosy. Next to it, between two fans of toast soldiers were a pair of large brown eggs, the tops cracked open to reveal a stuffing of perfectly scrambled eggs garnished with fresh chives and grey caviar. Suddenly ravenous, she plumped up the lumpy pillows and ate every irresistible morsel, wondering where on earth he had learned to cook that way.

Afterwards, she sifted through the newspapers. It was now a full two days since she had gone missing, and her story had made several of the front pages. An unrecognisable identikit picture of the gunman in his disguise stared out at her, next to a ghastly photograph of herself dressed only in a skimpy bikini. Taken two years ago by David while they were on a camping holiday in Suffolk, the picture made her look fat, greasy-skinned and bulbous-nosed. She would have torn it up when it came back from the processors had Jack not stopped her. His handing it over to the press now was a betrayal on a par with his adultery.

Folding the offensive snapshot out of sight, she read the story under the headline: ***PROFESSOR'S WIFE FEARED DEAD***

> *Scotland Yard last night expressed growing concern for the safety of 40-year-old mother-of-four Miranda Green, the London woman missing since Monday's armed raid on Sainsbury's supermarket in Camden Town.*
>
> *It is believed that the robber, who was armed with a pistol, took Mrs Green hostage, using her car, a 1972 Morris Minor, as a getaway vehicle.*
>
> *Last night, Professor Jack Green, the missing woman's husband, expressed fears for his wife's health from their home in Tufnell Park. 'My wife is an extremely nervous and easily-frightened person,' he said. 'This kind of ordeal could have a devastating and lasting effect on her. If anyone is holding her hostage, I beg them to let her go, for the sake of her sanity, if not of ours.'*

The tray crashed to the floor as she leapt out of bed, seething with humiliation. Frustrated as a prize-fighter with no opponent to attack, she pulled on her clothes and headed downstairs, where she found the gourmet gunman lounging on a goat-skin rug in the front room, his head propped on a sofa, his bare, muscular, hair-flecked legs apart. Desire stabbed through her, throwing her into confusion. Gathering her defences, she shot him an icy glare.

The front room was furnished in something resembling modern style. From the ceiling, a small crystal chandelier cast a dreary glow over the anonymous furniture: an uncomfortable-looking black leather sofa, a grey canvas sling-back chair, a glass-fronted drinks cabinet displaying a plethora of unopened bottles and cut-crystal glasses. A volcano of cigarette ash spilt from a chrome ashtray on to a battered black coffee table. Sunlight streamed through a crack in the heavy tweed curtains, making the dust motes and tobacco smoke dance in the air. In this austere setting, the black wall-fitment crowded with old-fashioned knick-knacks and small Capo di Monte figurines looked completely out of place.

'Are these yours?' Miranda snapped, picking up a small, ornate silver platter from the nearest shelf. On the back was etched an inscription: *Happy Anniversary Fred and Mabel love from Ronnie and Reggie.* 'Thanks for the food,' she said, putting it down before he had time to answer. 'Where did you learn to do scrambled eggs that way?'

The gourmet gunman shrugged. 'I watched Anton Mossiman on TV the last time I was in the Scrubs. I wrote to him after that, and he sent me a copy of his book. They put me in charge of the kitchen after that. Can't say my efforts went down a bundle with everyone. But don't get too used to it. It's time you went home now. Your kids must be getting anxious about you.' He picked up his cigarettes.

'Can I have one of those?'

'I didn't know you smoked.' He held out the packet, and she took one. Then, picking up the gun, he took aim at her. 'Pow!'

'That's not funny.' She snatched it from him with

trembling fingers, pulled the trigger and lit up. The acrid smoke poured into her lungs like a hot, comforting poultice. 'Actually, I don't smoke. I mean, Jack and I used to, when we first met. But when the twins were born, we decided to give up.'

'Ah, the famous Jack! You missed him on the box this morning. Making an appeal for your safe return. He was in tears, you know.'

'Bloody hypocrite!'

'Sure you're right about that other woman?'

'Perfectly sure, thank you.'

'Don't you think you should go home and have it out with him, just in case?'

She dragged deeply on the cigarette. 'You won't get rid of me as easily as that.'

'Uh-huh.' Slowly and lazily, he scratched his bare thigh. 'Mind if I ask you a question?' Shrugging indifferently, she blew out smoke in a defensive stream. 'What do you see in him?'

'In Jack? For God's sake! What a stupid question to ask! He's my husband!'

'And?'

'And . . . I love him, of course!'

'Mind me asking why?'

'Yes, I do mind, actually. I love him because . . .' Racking her brains, she failed to come up with a single convincing answer. 'It's none of your business!' she snapped angrily. 'I mean, why on earth should I have to justify my feelings to you?'

'You don't have to do anything.'

She tried to sit down elegantly in the low chair, but fell backwards, her legs apart. 'Look, if you must know, he's a very interesting and intelligent person and . . .' Miranda hesitated. 'He may have his faults, but he's extremely kind and caring and supportive and loyal . . . I mean, I always thought he was loyal before this . . . And, well, he's interesting to be with . . . I mean, interesting-ish . . . and knowledgable and . . . and . . .' She fell into an uncomfortable silence, unable to think of anything else to say.

'Bit of a nerd, isn't he?'

'*A nerd?* Jack? He's a psychology lecturer!'

'Ah! That explains it.'

'Explains what? He's definitely not a nerd! He's not! He's . . . he's . . . he's a . . . a . . .' She searched for the right word. Suddenly, it came to her in a blinding flash. In an attempt to hold it back, she bit hard on her bottom lip, but the word escaped anyway. '. . . a weed. A weed!' Unable to stop herself, she broke down in giggles. 'A deceitful, adulterous, dishonest weed! Oh, God! I shouldn't have said that!'

'Why not?' A grin smoothed out the creases of the gourmet gunman's craggy face. 'That's the first time I've heard you laugh.' His voice was like molasses, thick and sweet, and it threw her into confusion.

'I haven't had much to laugh about. Being kidnapped at gunpoint isn't my idea of fun. Even when the gun turns out to be a . . . to be a . . . a cigarette lighter.' She pursed her lips tightly together, but it did no good: they curled, parted, and let another giggle escape. She took a deep breath to calm herself. 'What are *you* grinning at? Armed robbery isn't funny.'

'True enough. But you look very pretty when you smile.'

A blush stole up her neck. Still looking at her, he reached a long, bare arm out to the coffee table, and stubbed out his cigarette.

'So, what're you going to do about her?'

'Who?'

'The old bird next door.'

She sighed. 'She's not old. She's five years younger than I am. What can I do if Jack's in love with her?'

He whistled softly, a long, sad downward note. 'The trouble with you middle-class women is you're too fucking controlled. Now, if any of the women I knew found out her husband was screwing the woman next door, she'd go round her house and turn her face into Chicken Vindaloo.

87

She wouldn't just shrug it off, like you have.'

'I haven't shrugged it off, thank you very much. But there are better ways of dealing with problems than beating people up. I happen to abhor physical violence. It's detestable.'

'So what isn't *detestable*? Standing back and letting them get on with it?'

Was it true? She tried to locate the place inside her where her anger should be, but all she could find were feelings of inadequacy – as if Jack having an affair with Mary was all her fault.

The gourmet gunman shook his head. 'I don't understand you. Isn't there nothing you want to do to her? No way you can get back at her?'

'No, there isn't! There really isn' . . .'

Then it came to her in another blinding flash, stopping her mid-sentence. As he watched her, a slow smile spread across his lips.

'Yeah?' he prompted. 'Go on! Spit it out!'

She shook her head. 'There's no point in discussing it,' she said primly. 'Because I could never, ever do it. Not in a million years.'

The stolen van rattled through the night, bouncing over sleeping policemen, crashing into potholes, flying along the empty roads. Seated on the bare floor at the back, Miranda clung onto a metal bar that ran across the low roof, her spine banging against the drum of the walls.

'Can't you slow down a bit?'

The gourmet gunman couldn't have heard her above the roar of the engine, for, as they careered round the next corner, his foot pressed down on the accelerator and the van tilted dangerously to one side. For a horrible moment, she thought it was going to turn over. But, at the last minute, it righted itself and she was thrown sideways across the floor.

'I *said*, slow down!'

He looked over his shoulder. 'What?'

'SLOW DOWN! Hey, turn around! TURN AROUND! Watch where you're going!'

There was the sound of angry hooting from outside, as he swerved to the left to avoid an oncoming bus. As soon as they'd passed it, he looked round and grinned at her.

'Won't be long.'

She clenched her teeth. After what seemed like an eternity of jolting, he swung the van into a side street and slowed to a crawl. At long last, he pulled up and got out. A moment later he opened the back doors and threw something soft at her.

'Here,' he said. 'Put this on.'

She pulled the knitted mask over her head, and he did the same with his. The scratchy wool pricked her cheeks, and pressed tight over her face. As she looked out through the slits, feeling like a bird-watcher camouflaged in a hide, her eyes met the two pinpricks of glitter in his otherwise invisible face.

'This is ridiculous!' she hissed. 'I really don't want to go through with it.'

The quick jerk of his chin was like a command. Reluctantly, she scrambled out of the van and dropped down into the dark road.

'Which one?' he muttered. She pointed to the house, and his eyes widened. 'You've got your work cut out!'

Reaching into the van, he unrolled a heavy blanket and handed her an axe. When she didn't move, he pushed her gently forward.

'Go on. What are you waiting for?'

She was trembling so much that her teeth were chattering. 'Please! Don't make me! I . . . I can't!'

'Course you can.'

Filled with foreboding, she looked up at the dark house. Then, pushing the garden gate gently open, she tiptoed nervously up to the steps.

Ten ugly faces stared eerily at her through the darkness. Ten pairs of pointed ears flapped towards her. Ten rigid mouths grinned inanely.

Her eyes settled on a small, plump fellow perched on top of a red-and-white toadstool, dangling his rod into the small, stone wishing-well beneath his wrinkled, slipper-shod feet. She'd always born a particular hatred towards him. He seemed to represent the triumph of hope over experience, for he'd been fishing in the same place for the past ten years, and had never caught anything.

Until now.

Taking a deep breath, she swung the axe back, then brought it forward. The blade glinted in the moonlight for a split second before catching the fisherman a glancing blow on his waist.

For a moment nothing happened. Then his torso tipped forward and plopped loudly into the water.

With a small gasp, Miranda turned to look at the gourmet gunman. 'Is that enough?'

'Go on!'

Swinging the axe back again, she took aim and smashed it into the neck of a jovial gnome pushing a wheelbarrow. *Thwack*! His head flew off like a golf ball, and landed with a soft thud in a pot of Busy Lizzies. Trembling, she stared at the face peeping up at her through the foliage. The eyes were Jack's, superior and full of reproach. With a sudden burst of fury, she brought the axe down on the flowerpot, splitting the gnome's forehead assunder, embedding the blade deep in his skull.

Suddenly a frenzy of destruction overtook her. Pulling the axe free, Miranda began to hack furiously at the rest of the gnomes and leprechauns and woodland animals. Limbs and torsos splintered under her savage punishment. Squirrels' tails and rabbits' ears flew into the street.

Now, overhead, a sash was thrown up and a man leaned out.

'What the bloody hell is going on?' There was a short

pause, pregnant with horror, while Brian registered what was happening. 'I don't believe it! Mary? Vandals!'

'Time for us to piss off,' said the gourmet gunman calmly, heading for the van.

She took no notice, but swung the axe again, sending the pre-cast concrete bird-table toppling into the bamboo tee-pee which protected Mary's prize sweet peas.

'Why, you . . .'

'*Come on!*'

'What's going on?' Mary's voice called from inside. Now she joined Brian at the window. When she saw the devastation, her eyes bulged. She looked like a huge, angry Pekinese dog. 'My lovely garden! Why, you bleeding bastards! I'll bleeding fucking kill you!'

She dodged inside. A moment later, the light went on in the inside hall.

'*Hurry up!*' Though the gourmet gunman yanked on her arm, Miranda refused to move. As heavy footsteps thundered down the stairs, she tore free, raised the axe again and brought it down on a porky, naked cherub, parting him for ever from the shrivelled stone penis with which, when the pump was switched on, he peed into a small, heart-shaped wishing-well.

The front door flew open, and Mary appeared, backlit in a thin nightdress, broomstick in hand.

Grabbing Miranda by the hand, the gourmet gunman pulled her out of the gate and threw her into the back of the van. The wheels screeched over the tarmac as he pulled away with the back doors still flapping open. Her heart racing, her breath short and fast, Miranda clung to the roof bar, and watched Mary shrink to nothing as they shot down the street.

In a small, unlit mews a mile away, the gourmet gunman slammed on the brakes, jumped out, and, tearing off Miranda's Balaclava, dragged her out onto the cobbles where he shook her furiously. His eyes flared at her like two blazing gas jets.

'Why didn't you stop when I told you? You could have got caught!'

Miranda scarcely heard him, for the drumming of blood in her ears. 'I did it! I really did it, didn't I?' she whispered. 'Did I do OK?'

'No, you bloody didn't!'

'Oh?'

He shook her again. 'You were brilliant, woman. Fucking brilliant.'

The next moment, he slid his arms around her, and crushed her mouth under his. Exquisite pleasure coursed through her, potent as a narcotic. Everything was blotted out except the warmth of his arms and his hands on her back and his wonderful, wonderful mouth on hers. It felt so right to kiss his mouth, that it could have been made to measure for her. Her lips drank in the tip of his sweet tongue, then, more, more. Given her way, she would have taken him all inside her, just for the sheer pleasure of feeling him fill her up.

But, after a while – how long, she had no idea, she only knew it was much too short – he suddenly drew back and stared at her, astonished. 'Jesus!' he breathed.

For a horrible moment, Miranda thought he wasn't going to kiss her again. Feeling like a starving woman suddenly offered an exquisite meal only to have it snatched away, she pulled him back and, raising the front of his t-shirt, pressed herself against his chest.

This time, when they kissed, he didn't let go of her. His hands travelled down over her body, tracing each one of her curves, then he pushed her shirt roughly up and tore off her bra. With firm, hard fingertips, he explored her breasts like a blind man reading Braille. 'Oh, you're beautiful!' he moaned hoarsely.

The skin under his T-shirt was hot, firm, silky-soft. As he lifted her up and pushed her into the back of the van, Miranda grasped his shoulders and wrapped her legs around his hips. Cold and hard, the metal floor scraped against her back, but she scarcely noticed it, for now he was thrusting the top of her leggings down over her buttocks, along her thighs, over her knees and ankles.

With an impatient grunt, he tore them off. Delving into the thick forest of her pubic hair, he slid a finger delicately along the moist folds of her labia to the swollen bud of her clitoris.

'God, you're so *wet*!' he whispered, as if it were the most marvellous discovery in the world.

He was stroking her now, stoking her desire for him with an unerring animal instinct, until she wanted him with every nerve. Desperate to feel him inside her, she fiddled clumsily with the buckle of his belt, then ripped apart the metal studs of his fly-buttons, and slid her hand into his pants. Strong and thick, the released spring of his penis uncoiled in her palm.

He moaned loudly. Somewhere, not too far off, a police siren screamed, but he took no notice. Instead, taking his hand from between her legs, he thrust his jeans down, then pushed straight into her, filling her up completely. There was a loud sucking sound as he withdrew, then thrust into her again.

Even at the best of times with Jack, making love had never been remotely like this. The gourmet gunman was a miracle-worker, turning her dried-up body into a turbulent river, a heaving sea. He was plunging into her, swimming between her legs with the elemental pleasure of a salmon swimming upstream.

Unable to hold back, she let the rising wave of pleasure mount in a thunderous crescendo and break, in a million ripples, through her flesh.

For the first time in her life, there was none of the, 'Are you ready?' 'Not quite, can you hang on a minute?' queries which had always been the climax of her climaxes with Jack.

Nor was there any need for him to turn to her afterwards, as Jack had done, and ask oh-so-politely, 'Have you come yet?'

He knew without asking.

She'd exploded.

And, within seconds, so had he.

Afterwards, she lay peacefully in his arms inside the dark van, kissing the thick blue cobra tattooed on his shoulder, listening to his wildly fast heartbeat slow down.

'You're amazing, Miranda!' he breathed. 'Fucking incredible!'

'Thank you. So are yo . . .'

Her voice petered out, as she realised the full implications of what had just happened. Contrary to what she had always drummed into the children on the subject of safe sex, she had not so much as mentioned the word *condom*. This stranger already knew her body inside out, but she didn't even know his name.

It was Ed, as he told her later, when, back at his house, they were curled up together between the white satin sheets of his circular, king-size bed.

Ed Baines.

'You don't want to know about me,' he said, lighting a cigarette.

'I do.'

'Honest, babe, there's nothing to tell.'

He was divorced. He had one child – a daughter – whom he hadn't seen for years. There she had it in a nutshell. That was about it.

His mother, Mabel – known to the local Bill as Mabel the Label – had been a compulsive kleptomaniac, whose speciality was working the West End and Kensington department stores. The family had wanted for nothing, thanks to her posh manner and the deep inside pockets of her off-the-back-of-a-lorry blonde mink coat. They may have lived in a rat-infested flat in the Peabody Buildings, but the lounge was furnished with a three-piece brocade suite from Maples – in an act of extraordinary daring Mabel had even arranged to have it delivered – the beds were made with the finest Debenham & Freebody Irish linen, the kitchen drawers were crammed with solid silver cutlery from Selfridges, and the larder was stocked courtesy of Harrods, Barker's and Fortnum & Mason.

As for herself, Mabel treated the shops as an extended wardrobe, and with young Ed trailing at her heels, would make regular trips *up West* whenever she needed a change of underwear, shoes or clothes.

Frank, Ed's father, had grown up in the business and was a natural born conman. At the age of ten, he was selling cat meat as sirloin steak from a stall in Brick Lane. During rationing, he made a small fortune by flogging black market 'dried egg' to regular and grateful customers, who never cottoned on to the fact that they were making their sponge cakes with wallpaper paste. No one could fault his patter. Strangers in pubs emptied their wallets so he could place bets for them on non-existent greyhounds. Lonely old ladies wrote out blank cheques for him in the hope of making a killing on the stock exchange. He could have sold bacon to the local Stamford Hill rabbis if he'd set his mind on it. Tall, debonair and dapper, few could resist his blue-eyed smile, his cheeky charm or his line in seamless chat, least of all Mabel, who cheerfully put up with his frequent affairs, his sporadic spells inside, and the occasional half-hearted clout.

Though not by nature a violent man, Frank had a burning ambition: to achieve the status of a 'Face'. Ronnie and Reggie Kray, 'Chopper' Knight and the Richardsons were his heroes. He fawned upon the Krays in the hope of making himself indispensible, but try as he might, he was never invited to join their firm. One day, a rival gang offered him the chance to prove himself in a warehouse raid. Over-anxious to please, he made the stupid mistake of turning up a day early, thus setting warning bells ringing all over London and tipping off the police.

That had been it as far as the big firms were concerned. Theirs wasn't the kind of business where you got a second chance. Convinced he'd been stitched up, Frank retreated to the roulette tables, where every penny he and Mabel had netted – including the stolen family silver – was chucked away. Club owners loved him; their eyes lit up when they saw him coming, and they plied him with drinks and offered him free life membership. And, of course, they fleeced him, time and again.

With Mabel as a maternal influence and Frank pissed, pissed off and in debt, it was not long, Ed explained, before he followed in the family footsteps; for all his tweed velvet-collared coats – nicked by Mabel from the White House in Old Bond Street – he was his parents' son; given this, it would have been a miracle if he hadn't gone off the rails, as his probation officer and social worker often said. Crime ran in his veins; he'd sucked it in with Mabel's milk and spooned it up with his stolen cornflakes. At the age of six, he was filching fruit chews by the box-load from Woolworth's. By nine, he was *at the dip*, picking pockets on the Tube. At twelve, he was taken into care after vandalising a City coffee bar. After he'd smashed up a foster home or two, he was packed off to Borstal for the first of many stays.

There the skills he had inherited from his parents were honed and refined. He emerged fitter, tougher, broken-nosed, a fully-fledged hoodlum, and a son Frank and Mabel could be justly proud of.

But, since then . . .

A shadow fell across Ed's face. Miranda kissed it away. Then she kissed his eyes and ears, his neck and shoulders. Soon, she was kissing all of him, and he was lying back, moaning with pleasure, his hands tangled in her hair.

Afterwards, he sighed deeply. His career had started off well enough: burglary, petty theft, the occasional legit stint in the print with a bit of wheeling and dealing in stolen trinkets on the side. The money rolled in, and for a time he seemed to have it made. Young, cocky and in the swing of Swinging London, he'd cruise the King's Road on Saturday afternoons in his red Triumph Spitfire and navy reefer jacket, looking for mini-skirted dolly birds with whom to dance the night away at the Valbonne.

Then he'd got a fifteen-year-old down the local laundrette pregnant. Had Val's father not been a friend of a friend of the Krays, it would have been *Goodbye, Baby and Amen*. As it was, it was goodbye, Mr Freedom. Six months later, he was doing service washes under his father-in-law's beady eye, while Val stayed home with the baby and slept all day. It was 1970. He was nineteen years old and trapped. He couldn't even buy a tie in Carnaby Street without asking permission.

After three long years of what looked to be a life sentence, remission came when Val ran off to Benidorm with her Dad's best mate, taking baby Sheryll with them. Freed from his obligations, Ed moved into this house with Frank and Mabel who, defeated by the introduction of security tags in the stores, was slowly drinking herself to death.

As for Frank – the following year he was back inside again, doing a four-year stretch for fraud. This time, the boredom and slopping out seemed to get to him. When Ed last visited him, he was shocked to see that his hair had turned white. 'I'm getting too old for this lark, son,' he had said. 'From now on, I'm relying on you to carry on the business, and take care of your mum.'

Three days later, he was dead. After that, Mabel lost the will to do anything but drink. Unkempt and incontinent, she died four years later of cirrhosis. Apart from two inspectors from the local Bill, Ed was the only mourner at her funeral.

As for the rest . . . While his contemporaries from school had progressed from TV thefts and postal order robberies to major credit card fraud, and had moved their wives and kids from the backside of London to detached splendour in Chingford, he had been content to remain alone, unfettered by family or professional ties, nicking just enough to get by and to allow him to indulge his passion for good cooking, nurtured by Mabel, courtesy of Harrods' Food Hall, and inspired by the famous Chef.

The crime world had moved on from the Ealing Comedy days when his Dad had conned money out of old ladies in felt hats and his Mum had helped herself to caviar and furs. The fun and camaraderie had gone out of it. Stunts like the Great Train Robbery and Brinksmat were a thing of the past. The big money was now in drugs, which Ed swore he wouldn't touch with a bargepole – not as a business proposition, that was. The small time had been taken over by kids – ruthless, amoral amateurs, all of them, who deftly raped old ladies, stamped on their faces and smashed their skulls to bits, all for the sake of 50p. What was wrong with them? It was hard to stomach some of the things they did.

Miranda could believe this or not: he'd never hurt anyone. That was to say, not badly. At least, not outside of the nick. Violence today had become a first-ditch resort, and the whole fucking business fucking sickened him. A growth industry crime might be – probably the only one in Britain – but he was being elbowed further and further from the grazing fields every week. Everyone was making money – coining it, as far as he could see – everyone except him. His heart wasn't in it any more. Armed robbery had never really been his bag, though he'd taken part in a number over the years. Nowadays, it was a bit like playing the stock exchange – too risky by far, considering the rewards. You needed lots of bottle, and he was afraid he was losing his. Look at the job he'd just done – what a fuck-up he'd made of that! He'd done it on the spur of the moment, out of pure bloody frustration. He'd needed the money urgently – just a couple of thousand – to pay his bookie's bills.

In the event, he'd netted more than he'd bargained for – a priceless jewel.

Here he kissed Miranda so tenderly that, had he been a mass murderer, she would happily have let him kill her on the spot.

'Do you think you could ever go straight?' she murmured, trying in vain to drag her mind away from dreams of divorce, reform and remarriage.

'I'd love to, doll. All cons would. But . . .' Sighing, he shook his head. 'I've been a villain all my life, just like you've always trod the straight and narrow. It would be as hard for me to turn an honest trick now as it would be for, well, for someone like you to rob a bank.'

Six

The Scunthorpe & Brighton Building Society in Swiss Cottage was wedged between a cut-price hardware shop and Dayvilles Ice Cream – '31 Flavours', said the sign outside. Conservative as ever, Miranda went inside and asked for a plain chocolate cone. Coming back out into the street, she caught sight of her reflection in the stainless steel door surround and stopped short with shock. Black curly hair flowed down her back, huge Chanel sunglasses hid most of her face, a scarlet oil-slick covered her lips, and her waist was cinched in tight by the belt of a calf-length Burberry trenchcoat. Was this really her? She looked more like a hooker in a French *film noir*. Ed had brought the outfit for her two days ago, arriving home from his shopping trip *up West* laden with carrier bags. Ignoring her protests that she couldn't possibly wear them, he had insisted on her getting out of bed, where she had been languishing all day, and trying them on.

The outfit, he'd declared, was just the job. The coat emphasised her tiny waist and slender figure; the long wig gave a dramatic new perspective to her high cheekbones and tawny skin, and the huge shades made any further facial disguise unnecessary. As for the high-heeled black patent boots . . .

'Mmm,' he'd purred, slipping to the floor and slowly zipping them up as he planted kisses up her calves. He hadn't stopped when he'd reached the top of the boots, but had carried on nuzzling the back of her knees, then the inside of her bare thighs, his lips slowly progressing higher and higher. After reaching the top, and lingering there, he'd pulled away and slipped the trenchcoat off her shoulders, leaving her naked but for the boots. And then they had made love, frantically and hungrily in front of the wardrobe mirror, while she swayed unsteadily on her stilettos and his jeans fell loose around his delicious hairy knees.

Just thinking about it made her shiver.

Out here in the street, the outfit was serving yet another purpose, just as he'd said it would. No one suspected that a woman who looked so deliberately conspicuous was, in reality, hiding from the police.

The shiver turned into a shudder of self-loathing. What *was* she doing? All around her, life was going on as normal. People walked by: elderly women towing their shopping trollies, teenagers in shorts or tracksuits, men in leather jackets and jeans, distracted mothers pushing prams. Less than two weeks ago, she'd been just like them: an ordinary person, unselfconsciously doing her shopping. Now she felt guilty simply for being on the street. She wished she'd never come out, but had stayed hidden away at Ed's, a concubine in self-imposed purdah.

She glanced at the solid gold Rolex which Ed had given her last night – 'Just a trinket to say thanks for the two best weeks of my life. But don't go flashing it about, doll. It'll only get nicked.' Miranda hadn't dared ask whether it was bought or stolen, she'd merely accepted it gratefully and graciously, as she had the dozens of other presents he had showered on her: the necklaces and rings, the expensive handbags, the ridiculously sexy and extravagant silk underwear. Ed's taste, nurtured by his mother along with his shoplifting skills, was immaculate. Every day with him was like Christmas – though Christmas had never been like this with Jack. Jack had given her presents, of course: Boots' bath foam; Icelandic slipper-socks; self-improvement books and cookery books; even an electric foot spa which, after being used only once, was relegated to the loft. But there had never been extravagant gifts, or even the funny, silly surprises which Ed seemed to produce so effortlessly: the tiny pink teddy bear holding a flag which said 'I love you', the real champagne bath; the dripping 'You're the greatest fuck in the world' scrawled in toothpaste across the bathroom mirror; the out-of-tune, old-fashioned love songs with which he serenaded her to sleep. Never before in her life had she felt so desired, so wanted, so excited, so loved.

So utterly, utterly terrified.

Untouched, the ice cream lolled heavily in her hand. Why on earth had she bought it when her stomach was churning like a cement mixer and her bowels felt like Semtex primed to explode? The cold brown sludge had begun to melt, and was slowly trickling down the sides of the cone and onto her hand. Not knowing what else to do with it, she walked guiltily over to the kerb and dropped it in the gutter between two parked cars. To her horror, a large dollop splashed over one of the bumpers. The car's owner was sure to be watching. He or she would call the police and Miranda would be arrested for malicious damage to private property, or littering the street.

When she saw the squad car driving towards her, she stifled a scream. Lowering her head, she swung round just in time to see its reflection flash past the building society's window. With a pounding heart, she adjusted the sunglasses Ed had forbidden her to take off. Then, taking a deep breath, she attempted to calm down. Why should she be so jumpy when she had done nothing wrong?

Not yet.

An endless flow of traffic roared past. A red Vauxhall Micra drew up in the bus lane on the opposite side of the road, and its driver, a grey-haired man in a dark suit and homburg, opened his window and beckoned to her. When she ignored him, he got out of the car and dodged across the busy road.

'Hurry up. Stop pissing about.'

'Ed, I didn't recognise you!'

'Shh! No names.'

With a firm, almost painful, grip he grabbed her by the elbow and steered her across the street. 'Where did you get this car from?' she asked as, opening the passenger door, he pushed her inside. He said nothing, just walked round the other side and got in beside her. With a sick realisation, she snapped open the glove compartment, and squinted at the things inside it. A Cliff Richard cassette, an ice-scraper, a bag of humbugs, a shopping list written in an unfamiliar, backward-sloping script. 'Oh, God, you stole it, didn't you?'

A pair of fine leather gloves landed in her lap. 'Here, put on these before you touch anything else.' With the drama of a magician producing rabbits from an empty hat, he pulled a white silk scarf from his inside pocket, and rubbed the fascia of the glove compartment clean of her fingerprints. 'Don't sound so shocked, babe. Nicking a car's nothing. Look on it as borrowed – after all, the owner'll get it back in half an hour.'

Miranda nodded, but she didn't look convinced. 'Sorry. I guess I'm just being silly.'

'You're not bottling out, are you?'

'No! It's just that . . . Well, I kind of feel . . .'

Looking bored, he drummed his fingers on the driving wheel. 'Later, OK?'

She watched him casually light a cigarette. The closeness they had shared during the past days in his house seemed to have all but disappeared. Out here in the real world, there was something rather chilling about him – just like there had been on the day of the Sainsbury's robbery. A cold sweat broke over Miranda's forehead, and her stomach somersaulted, knocking against her ribs. It was now twelve days since Ed had taken her hostage. During the intervening time, she'd discovered her husband was cheating on her, she'd committed adultery and an act of gross vandalism, received God-knows-how-much stolen property and allowed the police, and her children, to think she was probably dead. What on earth had she been thinking of?

She'd always been so boringly sane before, so down-to-earth, so rooted in routine and reality. How could she possibly have done all this? Even worse – how could she even have contemplated doing what she was about to do?

With a feeling of dread, Miranda stared across the road at the Scunthorpe & Brighton Building Society.

Ed cleared his throat. 'OK, let's run through the plan for the last time. The CCV arrives in fifteen minutes. Just before it comes, you go inside the joint and hang about – look at some leaflets or something, yeah? When it pulls up, I pull up in front of it and follow the geezers in. One'll wait by the door, the one doing the pick-up will go up to the counter and ring the bell. He goes through the screen, then comes back, this time with the dosh. That's when we make our hit. Right? I pull the knife, and I grab you from behind. I say, 'Hand over the cash, or I'll slit her throat!' or something, and you scream out, 'Give him what he wants!' Right? Then, when he hands the goods over, I'll drag you back out of the door, and into the car. You look like you're struggling, right? Then I bundle you in here, and off we go with the dosh. All sweet as a nut. Got it?'

Miranda nodded, then swallowed with difficulty. An invisible cord seemed to have tightened itself around her neck. 'Ed . . .'

'What?'

'Look, I'm sorry to ask again but . . .'

'What?'

'Promise me that no one'll get hurt.'

'I already told you, didn't I? I won't use the machete. Not unless I have to.'

'But what does that mean?'

'What it says. Trust me.'

She nodded. 'What if we get caught?'

He shrugged. 'I get ten years max, and you get off on the grounds you got forced into it. At the worst, you'll get a suspended sentence. As long as you keep your mouth shut.'

Unable to speak, she snatched the cigarette from him and dragged on it deeply. The jelly inside her bowels liquefied.

Ed stared ahead of him. 'Why did I ever let you talk me into this crazy scheme?'

'We made a deal. Remember? If I prove to you that an honest person can commit a robbery, you'll become an honest man.' Tentatively, she touched his knee. 'Ed?'

'What?'

'You will do it, won't you? You will try to go straight?'

His full lips pursed into a tight, thin, line. 'I gave you my word, didn't I?'

'Promise?'

Suddenly his expression softened. Leaning close towards her, he stroked her cheek. 'I promise, babe. I'll go so straight that you'll leave me out of bloody boredom. I'll become a . . . a judge! Don't laugh! Or an accountant. Tell you what, I'll join the Old Bill. If they won't have me, I'll become a dustman. Poor, but honest. We'll be poor but honest together. OK?' He winked at her, and held his hand out. 'That a deal?'

'It's a deal.' Their gloved fingers intertwined, and the now-familiar electricity shot up Miranda's arm, making her melt with love. She turned his hand over, pushed up the black leather glove, and kissed the inside of his wrist.

Pulling free, he stared ahead again as if she did not exist. Unlike her, he seemed able to turn intimacy on and off like a tap. 'Come on, time for you to get in there. The van'll be here any minute.'

She grasped the door handle, but her fingers felt too weak to open it.

'Come on, doll. What are you waiting for?'

She tried to move her legs, but her body was paralysed. Her throat constricted in a silent, inner scream. What was she contemplating? All her adult life she'd lived in terror of criminals. She'd never, ever, hurt anyone, or done a single dishonest thing. Now she was about to throw her lifetime of honesty to the wind. And why? Because she'd fallen in love – or was it simply lust? – with the villain who'd taken her hostage. Patty Hearst move over. She was about to ruin her life.

'Ed . . .'

'What?'

She forced the words out of her strangled throat. 'I . . . I can't go through with it.'

There was a long silence before he turned and looked at her coldly. 'But I spent a bloody fortune buying all this gear!'

'I'm sorry.' Tears pricked her eyes. 'I'm so sorry.'

'So you should be. Shit!'

'I'll pay you back. Look, I'm really sorry.'

'Stop saying that!'

'You were right when you said I wouldn't be able to go through with it. I can't. It's not me.'

Biting the side of his hand, he turned away from her, and the back of his neck flushed an angry red. She thought he was going to explode with anger. Then she realised he was shaking with laughter. Tears streamed down his creased-up face.

'Ed?'

'Oh, Christ, you're priceless! Did you really think you'd do it?'

'Well . . . yes!'

'You really thought I'd let you? Miranda! Armed robbery is big-time stuff!'

'But . . .' Confusion and anger mingled with her profound relief. 'Do you mean to say you've been humouring me all along? How could you?'

With difficulty, he stopped laughing. 'I'm a conman. Conning people's what I do best.' Putting his arm around her shoulders, he drew her towards him. 'Don't take it so bad, babe. Look, you got to understand, I never met anyone like you before in my life. You're an incredible lady. Beautiful. Classy.'

She sniffed. 'I'm just plain, boring middle classy.'

'What's wrong with that? You're classy, and natural, and honest – more honest than any other doll I ever met. That's what I love about you, and I don't want to spoil it. That bastard Jack doesn't deserve you. I certainly don't.'

'You mean, you don't want me.'

'Who says?' He tilted her chin upwards and kissed her tenderly on the lips. 'You know better than that! But, be real. What am I to you, other than a bit of rough trade? If we was together all the time, you'd get pissed off with me in five minutes flat.'

'No, I wouldn't,' she said, turning away. A hand drew her back, and his mesmerising eyes stared gently into hers.

'You don't want to get mixed up with someone like me,' he murmured. 'I'm no one. I'm crap.'

'Don't say that!'

'I'm a small time crook who's spent a third of his life inside. Which is where I'll end up again if I don't ditch this car soon. Come on! Give us one of those lovely smiles. Tell you what!'

'What?'

'Let's go out on the town tonight. A kind of farewell celebration. Blow a couple of hundred nicker on a club and a meal. A farewell meal. Then Buttons'll drop Cinders home. Home with your kids. Because that's where you really belong, Miranda, isn't it? Don't look at me like that, with those big sad eyes! You know you've got to go back sometime.'

'Yes. Yes, OK.' She reached up to push a lock of false hair away, and found her cheeks wet with tears. Ed started the car and pulled away. His fingers drummed against the steering wheel. After they had driven for a minute he suddenly patted his jacket pocket and pulled over to the side of the road.

'Shit! I'm out of fags! Do me a favour, doll – drive round the block while I run back to the shops and pick up some more. Pick me up outside the building society in five minutes sharp, OK? Got that?'

He opened his door and leapt out. 'By the way . . .' Leaning back in, he kissed her briefly on the lips. 'There's something you ought to know, just for the record. I love you. And, in case you're wondering, that's not a con, it's for real. Remember that, whatever happens.'

The next moment he was gone. Confused and heavy-hearted, Miranda slid over into the driver's seat. Not until she had travelled a hundred yards down the street did it occur to her that he had left her in sole possession of the stolen car.

As panic hit her like a football in the solar plexus, she swerved into the centre of the road. It was then that, glancing in the mirror, she noticed the white van on her tail. Above its bumper was a fluorescent orange stripe.

The police.

Guilt, like a thousand spiders, swarmed over her body and up the back of her neck. She shot forward, cutting through the traffic. The police van followed. When a green Jeep pulled out in front of her, she overtook it with unparalleled recklessness, then immediately turned left into a side street, past a low-built estate of modern houses.

She glanced into the mirror: the police van was still on her tail. Her foot crushed the accelerator to the floor. The houses sped by faster, faster . . .

Then, just in front of her, a small boy ran out into the road. Slamming her foot on the brake, she skidded to a halt, narrowly missing him.

Shaking violently, she pulled over to the side of the road. The van with the fluorescent stripe flashed its headlights at her, then overtook her. As it drove off, she read the words painted on the back doors: 'PRISM – *THE* WINDOW CLEANING SERVICE.'

Miranda's head fell forward onto the steering wheel as she burst into tears. Ed was right – it was time for her to go home. Now, before the trouble she was in grew even worse.

Back on the main road, she pulled up outside the building

society and waited for him with growing impatience. Where had he got to?

How long, she wondered after five minutes, could it possibly take to buy cigarettes?

And then she noticed the half-full pack on the dashboard.

A moment later, the armoured security van pulled up behind her. Sharp as rats' teeth, anxiety bit into her stomach. Swivelling round, she peered through the plate glass fascia of the building society.

A man in a homburg was standing in the queue.

He was going ahead with the robbery without her.

'Oh, no, Ed! No!' Her hand fumbled with the door handle, and she scrambled out into the street. Not knowing what to do, she stood helplessly by while the two helmeted security guards clambered down from their vehicle. One of them winked at her through his lowered visor. Pink faced, with large buck teeth, he looked like David's long-deceased pet rat.

Without waiting another moment, she pushed past him into the building society, and elbowed her way through the people waiting by the counter. When she tapped Ed on the shoulder he swung round so fast that he nearly hit her on the chin. He glared at her through dark, distended pupils.

'Please, don't!' she whispered.

'Get out!' he mouthed.

Both security guards had come in. One waited by the door, while the other marched up to the counter and rang the bell. The staff let him in the security door and he disappeared round a corner.

She tried to drag Ed by the arm, but he shrugged her off and wouldn't look at her. The queue moved slowly forward. She was sick with terror, dizzy with fear. There must be something she could do to stop him.

Now the guard reappeared behind the partition, the cash box in his hand. A single bead of sweat formed on Ed's forehead. 'Get out!' he hissed under his breath.

'Come with me!'

'I'm warning you, get out!'

'Not without you!'

Now he reached into his jacket and drew out the machete. Blood pounded in Miranda's ears, blocking out all other sounds. She looked around, and saw the scene as a series of frozen images: the young black assistant, counting notes behind the glass; a spotty youth in a red T-shirt, scratching his short, jet black hair; a full Waitrose carrier bag balanced between a pair of stockinged legs; the helmeted guard, poised on the threshold of the security door. It was all so ordinary, and at the same time so surreal . . .

And then her eyes collided with Ed's, and she seemed to see right to the darkest recesses of his soul. She knew then that she loved him, and would do anything for him, and would follow him anywhere.

Forgetting where she was, a beatific smile spread across her face.

The next moment a blood-curdling yell split her ear, and the knife flashed in front of her face.

'FREEZE!'

People started to scream as he tightened his hold on her throat. She could feel the blade, cold and hard and sharp against her skin. He was holding her so tight that she could scarcely breathe.

'DO WHAT I SAY OR I'LL FUCKING KILL HER!'

It felt like Sainsbury's, all over again. Except now she was on the other side. Until she spoke, she had no idea what she was going to do or say. But the words came out of their own accord,

'HELP ME! FOR GOD'S SAKE, DO WHAT HE ASKS YOU. PLEASE!'

She must have sounded convincing, because when he ordered them to the floor, they fell like skittles. The only time she had seen such terrified eyes before was on a TV documentary about calves in a slaughterhouse. Was that what she, too, had looked like when he had taken her hostage? Did these people, like herself, think they were about to be killed?

With the machete still at her throat, he inched her towards the security guard who was lying on the ground. It suddenly occurred to her that, if either of them tripped, the blade would slice right into her jugular vein.

Now his foot was on the security guard's back.

'GIVE ME THAT!'

The man's grip tightened around the handle of the cash box. His knuckles were white as bone.

'GIVE HIM WHAT HE WANTS!' she yelled. 'DO WHAT HE SAYS! DO IT!'

She could not be doing this. Jack would never believe her capable of such a thing. The guard shoved the box away. Ed picked it up. 'STAY WHERE YOU ARE – ALL OF YOU – OR I'LL . . .'

The sound of an alarm bell crashed through his voice. Ed's fingers dug into her shoulder as he dragged her backwards towards the door.

She glanced behind her: they were nearly outside. Five steps to go, now four, now three. . . . They were practically there when the second guard, who was lying beside the door, scrambled to his feet. Lunging towards them, he grabbed Miranda's arm and pulled her free.

Now it was he who was imprisoning her. 'Get behind me!' he shouted.

The blade flashed in the sunlight as Ed hesitated in the doorway. His fearful eyes met hers. With horror she realised that, like herself, he had no idea what to do.

'Go on, love, get back!'

The man was a hero. He thought he was saving her, but his grip on her wrist was condemning her to a living death. She looked from Ed to the guard, from the guard to the flashing blade. In a moment, Ed would stab him, she just knew it. She could almost hear the tearing sound as it ripped open his flesh. Wrenching free, she struggled to her feet and, tripping over the prostrate people, ran towards Ed.

She stumbled across the pavement and into the car. The door slammed, catching the hem of her coat. Ed threw the heavy cash box under her feet and pulled away at breakneck speed.

When she looked back, a crowd of people were pouring out into the street, waving their arms, pointing after them, screaming.

'You did it!' Ed yelled wildly. 'You fucking did it, Miranda!'

Pulling off the wig, she stared at her reflection in the passenger mirror. Her eyes glittered darkly back at her through her flushed, glowing skin. Her hands were shaking, and her body seemed to float weightlessly above the seat, each cell pulsing with energy. With the force of a flood-swollen river, adrenalin roared deliriously in her ears.

Seven

―――――

'Stop now, love! It's four in the bloody morning!'

Impatient as a hungry baby, Ed pulled the satin sheet off Miranda's breasts and, settling himself between her naked legs, fastened his mouth on her left nipple. Without dropping the small notebook she was holding, she gently but firmly pushed his head away and, with a well-chewed pencil, began to scribble on an already well-scrawled-upon page. Sighing with frustration, he rolled onto his back, stuffed a pillow under his head, and, with slow, well-practised fingers, began to fondle himself.

'I want you. Take a look. See?'

Preoccupied, she glanced casually at his heavy, engorged penis. Forty-eight hours ago, she would have been powerless to resist it. Now, she had more important things on her mind. 'Sorry. Just give me one minute more, darling, and I'll be all yours.'

'Every lovely nook and cranny?'

She smiled distractedly. 'Within reason.'

With growing impatience, he watched her continue to tot up the numbers. 'Why are you doing sums in the middle of the night, babe? Are you that bored with me already?'

'Just bear with me for another few seconds. OK? Hold on.'

'I am holding on.'

She giggled. 'I don't mean to that. There! Finished. Oh, it's amazing,' she murmured into his ear as, without further ado, he launched himself on top of her and firmly parted her legs with his right knee. 'Simply incredible!'

He froze, on the point of entering her, and the sharp crystals of his eyes raked her face. 'I haven't done nothing yet.'

'I meant, the figures. The ones I've been adding up.'

'Miran-dah!'

In an effort to silence her, he covered her lips with his, and, with slightly less than gentle pressure, sunk his fingers in the moist cave between her legs. For a few moments she succumbed to the pleasure of his touch. But, try as she might to relax and forget her thoughts, her mind simply would not let go.

'Ed?'

'Mmmm?'

'Please, just let me tell you one thing first! One little thing.'

This time, when he rolled off her again, he looked angry, but, failing to notice, she merely turned over to face him with the same beatific smile. 'Do you know how much we earned from the Scunthorpe and Brighton job?'

'Nope.' His erection deflating, he reached over the side of the bed and picked up his cigarettes. 'And right now I don't give a shit.'

'£46,000! And do you know how long it took us to do? Less than half an hour.'

The unlit cigarette dangled precariously from his lips. 'So?'

'Well, have you any idea what that works out as, on an annual basis?' He lit up, then hurled the spent match across the bedroom. Propping herself up on her elbows, she picked up the notebook again. 'Listen to this – calculating it on working a forty-hour week, fifty weeks a year, I make it £18,400,000!' When he failed to look impressed, she repeated the figure. 'Just think, darling, if we worked flat out, say, for two or three years, we'd be the richest people in the world!'

'Brilliant,' he said flatly. 'But aren't you forgetting something?'

'What?'

'You can't do the business every half hour, five days a week, week in, week out. Thieving's not a production line. It's not like churning out tractor parts.'

'Of course it isn't, but . . .' The notebook dropped to the floor as she rolled over to face him. 'What if we did treat it like that? I mean, what if we approached crime like a proper business? We wouldn't even have to work full time. All we'd really need to pull off is one or two jobs a week on a regular basis, and we could clean up in no time.'

A fierce blast of tobacco smoke streamed from his nose. 'Who's this *we*?'

She paused, suddenly unsure of herself in a way she hadn't been since the building society job two days before. Since then, she'd been like a love-lorn teenager on speed, sleepless, euphoric, thinking only of Ed and herself and the wonderful wealth they might achieve. 'You and me, of course.' With alarm, she noted the guarded look in his eyes. 'Listen, you told me yourself that you'd been doing badly before you met me, just making ends meet. Well, it doesn't have to be like that, does it? I mean, you proved that the other day. You were brilliant, darling. And I was good too, wasn't I? You can't deny that we make a good team. Well, just think, even working part-time, we could take – what? – over £4,000,000 a year! It'd be like winning the lottery, only better, because we could pull it off again whenever we wanted to! When we'd saved enough, we could emigrate to some wonderful tropical island. Or we could buy a fantastic mansion in the country, or . . .'

'I don't know what's got into you,' he interrupted, stubbing out his cigarette. 'You're talking a load of crap. You're a respectable lady. You don't know the first thing about being a villain. It's a tough world out there – full of ruthless bastards, doing ruthless things. I'd give you five minutes before you cracked.'

'That's not fair. So far I've done very well.'

'Ever heard of beginner's luck? Don't get carried away. You've done one job, and if I remember correctly, the whole point of you doing it was to prove to me that I could go straight.'

'Yes, well . . .'

Her voice petered out. She had been telling herself the same thing, but to no avail. Since the building society robbery, the scruples and morals which had once dominated her existence had shrunk to negligible proportions and been bulldozed aside, along with her guilt at abandoning her children, and committing a serious crime. Like a heap of broken toys swept into the corner of a room, they remained in the hazy sidelines of her consciousness, out of focus, insubstantial, and completely powerless against the flood of adrenalin which was still coursing through her like a mind-blowing psychedelic drug.

'Wouldn't it be easier for you to go straight if we first earned lots of money?' she continued, clutching at the idea as if it were a life-raft. 'I mean, it would make sense, wouldn't it? You see, darling, when I made the deal with you, I didn't know how easy robbery was.'

'Wait till the filth are knocking down the door to get you, or you're standing in the dock, and see how easy it is then. If you've got any sense at all, you won't wait for that to happen.' Ed's rugged face creased into a bewildered frown. 'This is all my fault.'

'What is?'

'This – what's happened to you! I done something shocking to you that day in Sainsbury's. You used to be honest. A real lady. Now look at you! I've corrupted you, Miranda. I'll never forgive myself.'

'Oh, darling! I forgive you! Honestly, I wouldn't have missed anything – not a single day!'

Throwing herself on top of him, she tried to kiss him

passionately, but murmuring the words, 'No, Miranda!' he turned his head away. Miranda wouldn't let him go. Soon, almost against his will, his lips melted beneath hers, and his rigid body softened – all but the softest part, which hardened against her belly.

Strong and firm, his arms slid around her, and he held her as if he would never let her go. Forcing free, she rained kisses on his eyes and his cheeks and his broken nose, and the stubbly, stubborn cleft of his chin. Her lips travelled down, over the tense tendons of his bull-like neck, stopping for a moment so that her tongue could trace the outline of the thin blue cobra which snaked across his pectorals to the hard brown aureola of his left nipple, where it ended, mouth agape.

Hours later, the chop of an axe-blade sliced through her dreams.

Waking at the same moment, Ed sprang out of bed with the speed of a wild cat and, pulling on his jeans, twitched aside the curtain, letting in the blue dawn light.

From downstairs came the sound of splintering wood. 'Shit!'

'What's happening?'

He let the curtain fall again. 'It could be the Bill.'

'But wouldn't they ring the doorbell?'

He shot her a withering look. 'Throw on some clothes, get in the cupboard and stay there. Whatever happens, don't get out! And remember – if it is the Old Bill, you don't know nothing and you haven't done nothing. I've just kept you prisoner here, all the time!'

'But Ed . . .'

Before she could say another word, he ran out of the room. Shivering uncontrollably, she clambered naked into the wardrobe and, squatting down on a pile of shoes, pulled a T-shirt down from the rail and yanked it over her head.

There was a loud crash and a dull thud, followed by the thunder of heavy footsteps.

'What the fuck is going . . .'

There was a loud *thwack*, and Ed spoke no more. She heard him groan loudly as whoever it was rained down blows. Hot, sour vomit rose up in her throat, making her gag. Sickened and terrified, she bit on her hand.

When the blows stopped, she pushed the door open a crack.

'Ed, you're out of fucking order!' barked a high, staccato voice downstairs. Someone spat loudly. Then she heard a man cough.

'What is this shit, Les?' Ed said hoarsely.

There was a short hard thump, followed by a series of fast slaps.

'What is it? It's a fucking lesson, that's what.'

'What're you talking about?'

'What am I talking about? I'm talking Swiss Cottage, that's what. I'm talking the fucking Scunthorpe & Brighton job. You've been a naughty boy, Ed. You should have known better than to have pulled a stroke like that on my plot.'

Ed coughed. 'You're off your head, Les! I don't know nothing about it.'

'Come off it! Don't try and take me for a mug punter. The job's got your fucking moniker all over it. Besides, I got contacts. You were seen.'

'Get off my back, will you, Les?'

'I give you this, Ed. You got some bottle. But you've made me angry. Ask Pete. Pete? You tell him. Am I angry or what?'

The next voice was sharp and rasping as a rusty blade. 'You better believe it.'

'Jesus, Les, why did you bring this moron along?'

Miranda heard the soft thud of a head being smashed against a wall.

'Hold off, Pete,' said the staccato voice. 'Don't go over the brink. Not yet. Look, Ed, you and me go back a long way. But something like this, well, it makes me angry.

Understand? So fucking angry that I'm shitting steam. You, of all people, doing business in my manor! You should know better than that.'

'Fuck off, Les!'

'Fuck off? Are you telling me to fuck off? That's serious, Ed. Pete? Pete, make him understand the gravity of the situation.'

'Want me to cut him, boss?'

'Cut that pretty boat? Not yet. Let's save the best for later, shall we?'

The beating continued. The sound of fists on flesh was relentless. How long was she going to sit there trembling like a coward and doing nothing to stop it? How far would Miranda let them go before, setting aside self-preservation, she did something, anything – screamed out of the window for help, or ran downstairs and physically intervened? How many times had she been shocked to read of people watching in the street as a stranger was mugged or even knifed to death in front of them? How many times had she sworn that she would never do that?

Her teeth chattering like a rattle, she crept out of the wardrobe and tiptoed over to the open doorway. Out on the landing, she peered over the top of the banister. A short, stubby man in a light grey suit was standing at the foot of the stairs with his back to her. A broad brush-stroke of red blood had been swept across the wall in front of him, descending in a rainbow's curve to the top of Ed's head. Two bare, wiry tattooed arms were holding her lover up, shaking his body against the doorframe.

'I don't know what got into you, Ed,' said the man in the suit, rubbing the tonsure at the back of his head. 'I'd have expected someone with your background to have more respect.'

'Respect? What for?'

'Give him *what for*, Pete!'

As the wiry fist landed a punch on his nose, Ed's eyes rolled upwards, and as they did he caught sight of Miranda.

He only looked at her for a split second. But it was long enough. Miranda dodged down, but not before the stubby man had swung round and seen her and pulled out a gun.

'Pete!'

Miranda scrambled into the bedroom as heavy footsteps raced up the stairs behind her. She slammed the door and leaned against it with all her strength, but whoever it was on the other side pushed it open as if there was no resistance at all. As she fell forwards across the bed, he lunged for her, grabbing her arms and twisting them up behind her. She screamed out with pain, but he took no notice, just threw her over so she was lying on her back.

Now he knelt astride her. Long, thin, lank, mouse brown hair hung down over a pallid face. Sunk in deep, dark hollows, two cold eyes glittered menacingly as they travelled down over Miranda's half-naked body. A large, blood-stained hand traced the outline of her breasts, then trailed slowly down to where the T-shirt had ridden up, just below her waist.

'Pete? Got her?' called the voice from downstairs.

'Yep.' The tip of a scummy tongue protruded through large, uneven front teeth. Terrified and revolted, Miranda began to tremble: oh God, was he going to rape her? Heaving her hips, she tried to turf him off her, but it was like trying to shift a dead weight.

'Pete? What're you doing, Pete?'

'If he touches her, I'll fucking kill the both of you!' she heard Ed shout.

There was a short pause. 'Bring her down, Pete! Bring her now!'

Licking his lips, he clambered off her, pulled her up, and twisting her arm behind her back again, shoved her downstairs. Half-way down, he let go of her so abruptly that she almost fell down the rest of the steps.

The man in the suit was at the bottom of the stairs, staring up at her with two small, brown eyes set in a pink, bloated face. Very slowly, his long, straight mouth stretched into a broad grin.

'Ed, boy! You should have told me you had company!'

Ed wiped away the trickle of blood dripping from his nose. 'You never asked.'

'Come down here, gorgeous. Come on! Come and join the fun.'

'For Christ's sake, leave her out of it! She's nothing to do with it!'

'I said, come on down!'

When she still didn't move, a hard knee prodded into her back. 'Don't you touch her!' shouted Ed.

'Hear that, Pete? The age of chivalry isn't dead!'

As she stumbled slowly down a few steps, her legs wobbling, one hand clutching the banisters, the other pulling down the hem of her T-shirt, she stared hard at Ed, trying to gauge from his expression the best way to behave. But he wouldn't meet her eyes. She could tell he was furious with her for disobeying his order to stay out of sight.

Then, from the centre of her fear came a clear, still voice, breaking through the panic, saying, *Take control.* Somehow this was her only hope. But how to do that when she was shaking so much she could scarcely stand?

Pausing on the bottom step, she took a deep breath. 'Is it really necessary for me to make my grand entrance at gunpoint?' she asked with all the sang-froid she could muster. 'A . . . a gun's such a, well, a focus of attention, isn't it? P . . . personally,' she stuttered, 'I always prefer to be the centre of attention myself. Still, Les, I'm flattered that you think me such a dangerous woman.'

'Oh-ho!' The deep set eyes twinkled more brightly. 'Oh-ho! I like it. I like it!' he said. 'A body with brains! No wonder we haven't seen you down the clubs recently, Ed.' Winking at Miranda, he slipped the gun back inside his jacket. 'What's your name, gorgeous?'

'Mir . . .'

'Liz,' cut in Ed. Miranda felt herself blushing.

123

'Ah-ha!' Narrowing his eyes with curiosity, he looked from one to the other. 'Pete? Take care of Ed for a moment, will you? Travelling incognito, are we?' he said to Miranda when Ed was being held up against the wall. 'So, tell me something – why're you wasting your time with a never-was like Ed?'

'Oh, well, I . . .' She was about to say, *Because I love him.* But sensing she would lose ground, she said instead, 'Why do you think? He's good in bed.'

Out of the corner of her eye, she saw Ed blanch. But her ploy seemed to be working, because the man called Les laughed out loud. 'You should try a real professional!'

'Thanks for the invitation. I might, when I'm ready for you. At the moment, I'm still cutting my teeth.' Gaining confidence from his surprisingly warm, infectious laughter, she walked over to Ed. 'Now, Les – it is Les, isn't it? – maybe you could explain to me why your sidekick has been cleaning the walls with my man.'

'Let him go, Pete.'

'But . . .'

'I said, let him go!'

Pete released Ed's shoulders, but when he slipped to the floor, he stood over him, fist clenched, champing with the pent-up fury of a boxer unfairly disqualified in the first round.

'Thank you, Les.'

'Think nothing of it, gorgeous.' He bobbed up and down, scrutinising her face with his small, keen eyes. 'Haven't I seen you before?'

'I don't think so.'

'I have. I'm sure I have. I'm never wrong.' The tip of a small red tongue poked out of his mouth and licked his lips. 'Been living round here long?' She glanced at Ed who answered, 'No,' very quickly. Les laughed again. 'Come on! The pair of you'll have to do better than that. Something smells. Something smells round here, Ed.'

He shrugged. 'It's no big mystery. She's married.'

'Is she? Married to the mob, eh? So it's not only other people's manors you've been sniffing about. Besides, I wouldn't expect . . .' Suddenly his dark eyes glinted with recognition. 'Hey, wait a minute! Wait a fucking minute! Come here, gorgeous! Let me have a closer look at that face.' He stared at her for a moment, then clicked his fingers sharply. 'Incredible!' he said, shaking his head. 'Fucking incredible! Pete? Come here! Don't you recognise that boat?' He jabbed his finger at her. 'Camden Town. Camden fucking Town. That's it! The Sainsbury's job the other week! Go on, you must remember! It was all over the front pages! The armed raid? The housewife hostage? *Fu*cking Sainsbury's!'

'Shit!' Scowling furiously, Ed turned away.

'I got to hand it to you, Ed. I never thought professionals still pulled stunts like that these days. I said to Pete at the time – didn't I, Pete? Remember? – whoever pulled this stunt's got to be a fucking wally, a complete nutter. I mean, taking the woman hostage! Now it's all clear. Of course! You was in it together!'

'No,' said Ed. 'I . . .'

'Darling!' It was less of an endearment than a warning, for something inside her knew that Ed couldn't afford to lose face. 'What's the point of pretending? Les is right. He's obviously a very clever man.' When she smiled at Les, he smiled back, his eyes bright with admiration for her. To her astonishment she realised that she was no longer afraid of him but, on the contrary, rather enjoying their odd flirtation. 'Well, now you know who I am, Les, perhaps you wouldn't mind explaining what you're doing here at this unearthly hour of the morning, spoiling my beauty sleep.' She jerked her chin at the shattered front door. 'Ever thought of trying the bell?'

'Miranda! Keep out of this, will you?'

'Now, Ed! Don't get shirty! The lady has obviously been dragged out of bed.' His eyes travelled up her naked legs. 'She's entitled to an explanation. The thing is, gorgeous, lover boy here's been pissing where he shouldn't have. Swiss Cottage is my manor.'

'What do you mean? How is it yours?'

'Miranda!'

'It's where I operate. As Ed well knows. And I like to know what's going on round there. Because when there's trouble, the finger points at me. I'm the one who gets fitted up by the bulls and pulled in for questioning while the real culprit – in this case, lover boy here – stays sweet. See?'

'In that case, it's me who owes you an apology. Not Ed. Because . . .'

'No!'

'Look, Ed, there's no point in pretending. You see, Les, the Scunthorpe & Brighton job was my idea.'

Looking away, Ed muttered something angry under his breath.

Les grinned. 'What is this? Ed's always been a loner. Suddenly he's part of some Bonnie and Clyde team? Incredible! Still, I should have been told. I should have been warned. It was only polite.'

'How could I fucking warn you?' Ed snapped. 'For a start, I thought you was still inside for that Nat West job in Chelsea!'

'I see! So Chelsea's part of your manor, too?'

Les gave a hefty shrug. 'That was by special arrangement, gorgeous.'

'What? Like Hoxton?' Ed's eyes blazed. 'Remember Hoxton, Les? Was Hoxton your territory, huh? Who did four years in the Scrubs for that?'

Miranda sighed impatiently. 'Oh, for heaven's sake! You're squabbling like children! I think the whole thing is ridiculous! All this talk about manors and territories. It's just London, just streets. And neither of you own any of it. My God, to listen to you, you'd think you were the only criminals who lived here, and there must be thousands!'

Les sighed. 'Gas meter bandits. Fucking amateurs, the lot of them. Business isn't what it used to be, is it, Ed?'

'Well, in that case, shouldn't you both be on the same side?' she continued. 'I mean, wouldn't it be better for you to work together rather than squabble over trivialities?'

'What, us work together?' Ed laughed. 'You must be fucking joking!'

'What? You mean, Ed and me? *Fu*cking hell! The two of us?'

'Who said anything about two?' Miranda hesitated for a moment, then added excitedly, 'You mustn't forget me.'

Eight

'I'm sorry, Ed, but I can't do this.'

Ed put his arm around Miranda's shoulder and gave it an encouraging squeeze. 'Of course you can, babe!'

She looked up into his blue eyes, her expression both adoring and apologetic. 'No, really, darling, I can't. Just thinking about it makes me feel quiet ill.'

'So don't think about it. Just get in there and get on with the business. That's what my old dad used to say – if you've got to do it, do it. And when it's over, never look back.'

Yes, but hadn't Frank Baines died penniless and in prison? Miranda bit back the words in order to spare Ed's feelings. But she couldn't help secretly feeling it might be better not to follow Frank's advice.

'Don't push your hair back behind your ears like that,' Ed continued in a monotone. 'People will notice it's a wig.'

'Sorry.' Obedient as ever, she re-adjusted the black nylon bob under which she had crushed her own long auburn locks. This was only the second time she'd been out in public since the day of the Sainsbury's robbery, and with her photograph still so often in the newspapers, Ed had thought it best that she wear a new disguise. Taking off her large, owl-like sunglasses, she glanced across the narrow shopping street. 'Look, I know I'm being stupid, but . . . Does my very first solo robbery have to be in there?' She pointed to the small newsagent's shop on the opposite corner.

'Don't point, babe, someone might see you. What's wrong with it?'

Tears of empathy pricked her eyes as she looked through the window, plastered with peeling ice cream signs and faded photographs of cigarette packets, at the middle-aged Asian couple standing behind the counter. 'I. J. Singh, Newsagents' said the sign above the door. Miranda imagined Mr and Mrs Singh at home that night, counting up their meagre day's takings; theirs was no doubt a life in which every penny counted; they must have to scrape to make ends meet.

She sighed. 'It's such a sad little shop. How can I possibly rob it? Besides, I keep thinking, what if something goes wrong and one of them gets hurt?'

Ed looked at her incredulously, then his mouth twisted into a sardonic smile. 'Want to know something? You're bananas. It's a good thing I love you so much. Tell me – how're you ever going to be a big-time villain if you won't even commit a piddling little crime like this? I tell you, if you want to hold your own with people like Les, you've got to learn the business from the bottom up.'

'I know. I know. But . . .' She shook her head, perplexed with and, at the same time, ashamed of herself. 'Look, couldn't we do another armed robbery together instead of this?'

His perfectly matched teeth glinted in the sunlight as he grinned at her, and she found herself wondering, not for the first time, what such an attractive, exciting and daring man could possibly see in a cowardly, forty-year-old housewife like herself. 'You're priceless, you are, Miranda. All this fucking useless middle class guilt! Now stop making such a fuss. We've practised the moves a hundred times. Nothing's going to go wrong. Trust me, OK? I'm going to walk away now, and leave you to get on with it. When you come out, I'll be round the corner.'

Without another word, he walked away from her. When he got to the corner he turned and winked. Miranda's confidence shot up: if Ed loved her, she could do anything. However, the moment he disappeared from sight, she felt like a small child abandoned by its mother, and a wail of terror rose up in her throat. Holding it down, she took a deep breath, crossed the road and entered the newsagents' shop, leaving her middle-class guilt outside. If she was ever to make anything of her life, she had to abandon her past self and embrace the future. In Ed's world, having a conscience wasn't a virtue, it was a liability she didn't need.

Less than two minutes later she walked out, arms crossed, head lowered, tears cascading down her cheeks. Scurrying round the corner, she ran straight into the hard wall of Ed's chest.

'Oh, God!' she sobbed. 'I feel so ashamed of myself!'

Ed raised her chin gently. 'Why? What happened? Did you get nabbed?'

'No!'

'Then what? You didn't bottle out, did you?'

'No! I did it!'

'That's great, babe! So hand over the lolly!'

Sniffing guiltily, Miranda uncrossed her arms, reached into her left sleeve and drew out a Wall's Cornetto. 'They only had orange ones, so I changed my mind at the last minute and stole this instead.'

'Let's run through the plan one more time.' Ed sank down on the sofa, put his feet up on the coffee table and crossed his ankles. 'I'm the mark walking down the street. There's this geezer walking in front of me, a businessman in a suit and tie – that's Les, right? – and suddenly his mobile phone rings . . .'

'What if it doesn't?' Miranda interrupted.

'What?'

'What if Les's phone doesn't ring at the right time?'

'Of course it's going to ring at the right time! Because I'm going to ring him, aren't I? And I'll be watching from the other side of the street, right?'

'Sorry. Of course. How stupid of me. Right.'

'So Les reaches into his jacket pocket and pulls out his phone. What he doesn't notice – or rather, pretends not to notice – is that his wallet's dropped out onto the pavement. So, I'm the mark, right behind him, right?'

'Mm-hmm.' Miranda was getting bored with rehearsing the con trick. They had already been through it five times. Far more interesting was watching the movement of Ed's lips as he sucked on his cigarette.

'And I can do one of two things – If I'm honest, I'll pick the wallet up and hand it straight back to Les. In that case, there's no ball game, we just wait till the bugger's gone and try it again with someone else. On the other hand . . .' Ed paused mid-sentence and took a swig from his glass of champagne. 'And this is where it gets interesting – if I'm not so honest, I'll wait until Les has walked on a bit, then pocket the wallet myself. A few seconds later, Les'll walk back down the street past me, but I still don't hand the wallet back to him. Now you know you're in business. The sod's as crooked as a hairpin. And that's where you step in.'

Miranda nodded earnestly. 'And I say . . .' Breaking into a grin, she threw herself across Ed's lap. "Hello, gorgeous, fancy coming round the back for a quickie?"'

Not amused, he pushed her away. 'Babe, be serious! Sit up! We're doing this for real tomorrow.'

'Sorry. I say . . . Oh God, I can't remember!'

'You say, "Excuse me, but I saw what you just did."'

Struggling to be serious, she cleared her throat, then repeated his words. 'And then, I ask you to show me what's in the wallet.'

'Good. And I say . . . I say . . .' He broke off mid-sentence, as her hand slid up his thigh and into the hot, tight space between his legs. His lips, at first pressed together in a stern expression, suddenly softened into a smile. 'I say, "Fancy coming round the corner for a quickie?"'

With a grin, Miranda hoisted herself onto his lap and kissed him tenderly. 'And I say, "Yes, yes, yes!"'

'Excuse me, but I saw what you just did.'

The man in the pin-striped suit halted underneath the Monument on Fish Street Hill, and stared at Miranda suspiciously. From the tips of his highly polished brogues to the starchy collar of his pristine shirt, he looked every inch a respectable City gent, as she'd told Ed when he'd picked him out as their mark. Never in a million years would she have suspected him of being dishonest. Yet, with her own eyes, she had just witnessed him pick up Les's dropped wallet, take a peek at the £200 inside it, then slip the slim black leather pouch inside his suit.

'I'm sorry?' His accent was Oxbridge out of Eton. Judging from the ruddiness of his cheeks and the rheuminess of his eyes, he must be fifty going on fifty-five.

She pointed to Les, who was now halfway down the street, and cleared a throat so strangulated by nerves that she could scarcely speak. 'I just saw you pick up that man's wallet. You didn't give it back to him.'

Though his face remained expressionless, he couldn't stop the tell-tale flush from stealing up his well-shaven neck. 'I was just . . . going to hand it in at the police station,' he blustered.

'Were you?' The dark semi-circles of her thickly painted-in eyebrows rose in two surprised arcs above the sensible, tortoiseshell spectacles she had chosen from Les's vast collection to be part of her disguise. 'You could have given it back to him just now. Why didn't you?' The man's thin lips parted, but he said nothing. She had felt sorry for him before, but in the face of his dishonesty, her sympathy had turned to aggression. 'Do you mind if I have a look inside it?' she said more fiercely.

Still speechless, he reached obediently into his inside jacket pocket, took the wallet out and handed it to her. Miranda opened it, then looked up at him with an expression which she imagined showed astonishment. 'There's two hundred pounds in here!'

His lips barely moved as he muttered, 'Want to split it?'

'Pardon?' Her feigned astonishment turned real. 'You don't really mean that?' Then, remembering the part she had to play, she carried on looking through the wallet's contents. When she found the piece of paper she was looking for, she took it out and unfolded it. Then her hand fluttered to her forehead in mock shock. 'Jesus!'

'What?'

Miranda pushed the thick cream vellum quickly under his nose. 'Do you know what this is?' She pointed to the scrolled italic writing. 'It's a bearer bond. Goodness, I haven't seen one of these for ages. I used to work with them all the time. I'm at—' She named a well-known city bank. 'I used to cash them in for people. Now and then I still do.'

The high forehead, surrounded with downy, receding hair, inclined in the slightest of nods. 'We ought to give it back then,' he murmured. When Miranda made no move to answer, he went on, 'What's it worth?'

Miranda had never understood why people liked fishing. Now, for the first time, she felt the excitement of feeling a fish bite on the line and began to experience the drawn out pleasure of slowly reeling it in. 'What it says – £10,000,' she said matter-of-factly.

'I see.' The line went slack as he gazed into the distance again. Then it gave another tug. 'How hard would it be to cash it in now?'

'That depends.'

'On?'

'On what kind of percentage you were prepared to offer me.'

He nodded with a slight, almost royal, inclination of his head. 'What would you want?'

'Would five percent seem fair?'

Another nod, and a barely audible, 'Fine.'

Adrenalin surged through her as his thin lips closed on her hook. 'I'll have to do it straight away, though, before the man discovers it's missing. But first, I'll need to set up a special client account. I'm afraid I'll need a bit of money for that.'

She could almost see him stiffen as he asked, 'How much?'

'To make it look legitimate – a thousand pounds. That's eight hundred, on top of the two hundred in the wallet.'

'But . . . I haven't got . . .'

'You mean, you haven't got eight hundred pounds? A man like you? I can't believe that! Can't you get it out of the bank? What's the matter? Why are you staring at me like that? Don't you trust me?'

'Well, I . . .'

'Look, I'm not the one who stole that wallet!'

'Listen, young lady, I didn't steal it! I . . . I was going to give it back!'

Genuinely aggrieved that her very first con trick was about to be thwarted, Miranda thrust the bond back in his hand and stomped away.

A moment later, he caught up with her on the corner of Pudding Lane.

Ten minutes later, outside his bank, he handed her eight hundred pounds in a plain brown envelope. Side by side, but without acknowledging that they knew each other, they walked around the corner to the building where she'd said she worked.

Before she went inside, Miranda smiled at him with a reassurance she didn't feel. 'Wait here. I'll go upstairs and open the account, then bring down the paperwork. I'll be about ten to fifteen minutes. OK?'

Emotion – was it distrust or nervousness? – flickered under his pallid cheeks. 'Don't you need this?' he said, holding out the bond.

Miranda's heart lurched as she realised how nearly she had slipped up. 'No, not yet,' she said on the spur of the moment. 'I'll take it when I bring down the paper-work. I'd like you to keep hold of it till then. Just so you know you can trust me.'

Smiling, she turned on her heels and walked into the building. Then, following the instructions Ed had given her after his recce, she walked down the corridor, up a short staircase, and went out the back way.

In the narrow lane behind the building, Ed and Les were waiting for her in a blacked-out stretch limo driven by Pete. Slipping inside, she tossed them the envelope.

'Bloody brilliant!' whooped Ed, pulling her onto his lap and smothering her with kisses. 'What d'you say, Les?'

Les popped the cork of a champagne bottle. 'Not bad! Not bad at all for a beginner. Gorgeous, we'll make a crook of you yet!'

On Miranda's instructions, Pete cruised round to the front of the building where, hands crossed tightly over his chest, her victim was still waiting for her to come back. As she stared at him closely through the blacked-out windows, her euphoria at pulling off the con-trick gave way to a sharp pang of guilt at having just stolen eight hundred pounds of his money. But then, as Ed had insisted, they'd only pick someone who looked like he could afford it. Besides, if he was fool enough, and dishonest enough, to fall for their con-trick, the punter deserved to get stung.

It had been a quiet night.

But then, all nights in the store were quiet.

Nothing ever happened when Harry was on duty. Not that he wanted it to. He was quite content to watch the box or sit and read his paper, with just the occasional patrol around the store to keep him from getting cramp.

On nights when there was nothing worth watching, and nothing to read, he'd sit and stare at the bank of video surveillance monitors stacked behind his desk. Not that the pictures on them ever changed, or even moved. It was just empty spaces – the Silver Room and the Watch Room on the ground floor, the Crystal and China Room upstairs, the Jewellery Room and the Repair Room in the basement, the downstairs corridor leading to the safe. Then there were the two outside monitors – one at the front, and one outside the staff exit, which was placed opposite his desk. Sometimes an old drunk would lurch into vision and crash out for the night on the step. And that was about as exciting as it ever got. Since the building was a modern one, there wasn't even the chance of a ghost suddenly appearing, as there'd been when he'd worked as night watchman in that old house in Berkeley Square. The Grey Man. Not that he'd ever seen him, in his gaiters and long frock coat, but there were those who'd claimed they had. Several times, though, as he'd be nodding off on duty, he'd fancied he'd heard a soft footstep, and even the clang of a sword against the stair-rail.

There was no chance of that here. At times, Harry had to admit, he got a bit bored. In all his years as a night watchman – or security guard as he was now called – nothing remotely out of the ordinary had ever happened to him. He just wasn't that sort of bloke. He had friends in the business who'd been stuck all night in lifts and held up at knifepoint and been beaten over the head with crowbars. But not him. He ought to count himself lucky. He did. Only sometimes . . .

His legs ached. Standing up, he began his last patrol of the premises, up the back stairs and onto the main shop floor, where the carpet was deep as a velvet sofa, and the silver tureens, candlesticks, ornaments and whatnots, and the onyx-and-gilt clocks and ashtrays twinkled under the lights.

Sometimes he wondered who on earth bought these things, and to what kind of grand homes they were taken. It was hard to believe that there really were people who wore £20,000 wristwatches, and ate their cornflakes out of silver-gilt cereal bowls, and drank from Lalique glass. But punters bought the stuff in quantity, so someone must use it. Since he left the store at eight in the morning, well before the customers came in, and arrived after closing time at night, he never saw them. In fact, he never saw anybody. But then, in this

business, you had to like being alone, had to enjoy the hours
of stillness and silence, the peace and quiet . . .

Somewhere far off, the telephone rang.

Harry picked up the nearest telephone, but there was
no one on that line, so he walked quickly back downstairs. The telephone on his desk by the back door was
ringing loudly. Like two black caterpillars, his eyebrows
crawled slowly together till they met in a curious frown
above the bridge of his nose.

'Hello?'

'This is the control room at Vine Street police station
here. Who's that?'

'I'm the security guard.'

'Do you have your password?'

Harry gave it.

'Everything all right at your end?'

'Fine.'

'Well, let's hope it stays that way. We had a tip-off
that there's going to be trouble.'

'Oh?' Harry's pulse began to beat faster. 'What sort of
trouble?'

'Three blokes. Believed to be armed. Be on your lookout.'

'I see! I will.' Fear squeezed at his bowels. His heart began
to pound in his chest. He hoped he didn't sound as afraid
as he felt.

'We've got a car on its way to you at the moment, to check
the situation out. Should be with you within two minutes.'

Harry put the receiver down with a trembling hand.
Armed robbers! Why, only just before he'd been thinking
. . . He sat down, his legs shaking. It just went to show,
you shouldn't count your chickens before they'd hatched.
He really oughtn't to feel so scared, what with the police
on their way. This was the point of the job, wasn't it? He
wasn't there for the nights when nothing happened, but for
the times when things went wrong.

Leaning close, he scanned the bank of monitors for something unusual. Nothing. His ears straining, he listened,

almost afraid to breathe in case he missed the forcing of a lock, or the cracking of glass. Then, suddenly, he heard footsteps approaching the back door and his heart leapt so high he could feel it beating in his mouth. Terrified, he stared at the lowest monitor, the one covering the back doorway, where a dark shape had moved into the bottom of the screen. Making out a band of black and white check, he breathed again. It was only the PC! And, would you believe it, she was a bloody woman. A brunette with glasses. So bloody brave that she was biting her nails! Harry felt furious – fancy the boys at Vine Street sending her! A fat lot of good she'd be if three hulking blokes with a sawn-off shotgun suddenly burst through the door!

She rang the bell, and he buzzed her in. The three hulking blokes burst in right after her, stocking masks pulled over their heads. Automatically, Harry looked for their sawn-off shotguns, but they weren't carrying any.

Then he noticed that the policewoman was.

What's more, she was pointing it at him.

'Mr Jenks? Your nine-thirty has arrived. Mr Jenks?'

Without looking up, the young, sandy-haired man behind the desk adjusted his tortoiseshell glasses and carried on reading through the *FT*. 'Can't you see that I'm busy, Carla?'

The willowy secretary in the doorway raised her eyebrows, and, smoothing down the pleats of her short skirt over her long, ebony muscular thighs, silently mimicked her boss's words. Ever since Alan Jenks had taken over as bank manager six months ago, he'd done his best to get up her nose. Why he felt it necessary to pull rank on her and all the other staff all the time she didn't know. His predecessor, dear old Mr Hughes, had never found cause to do it. At thirty-two, Alan Jenks was half Mr Hughes's age, barely older than she was, in fact, and, from the quick look she'd had at his CV when she'd hacked into the personnel files, not much better educated. Not only that, despite his plummy Oxbridge voice, he came from the dreariest part of Slough, where he'd attended not Eton, as he'd have everyone believe, but the local comprehensive, only half a mile from her own home.

From the way he acted, you'd think he was Chancellor of the sodding Exchequer, not a boring old bank manager in a run-down, North London sub-branch.

As he continued to skim through the newspaper, deliberately ignoring her presence, a smile crept over Carla's heavily-outlined lips.

Mr Jenks was about to get his comeuppance. Never again, after this morning, would he be able to walk into work with quite the same studiedly superior air. Little did he know it, but a large chink had just opened up in his hitherto impenetrable persona.

So what that he prided himself on never having made, or received, a single personal call within banking hours? He was human after all. He breathed, he ate, he drank, he shat. And, though there was not a card to be seen in his office, today was his birthday.

He hadn't managed to keep that a secret, had he? His friends – or was it one special friend? – had let the cat out of the bag. And Carla, for one, couldn't wait to see his reaction.

On hearing her giggle, Alan Jenks looked up at last, his humourless mouth twisting into a condescending smile.

'Is anything wrong, Carla?'

'No, Mr Jenks.'

'In that case, why are you standing there with that particular, fish-like grin? If you haven't any work to do, I'm sure I can find you some.'

Carla straightened her face. 'Your nine-thirty appointment . . .'

Folding the paper carefully into an anally-neat rectangle, he sighed with resignation. To Mr Jenks, customers weren't the friends and the life blood they'd been to dear old Mr Hughes, but an annoying inconvenience.

'I thought my nine-thirty cancelled half an hour ago. New customer, wasn't it?'

'That's right, Mr Jenks. But these . . .' She faltered. '*This* has come up at the last minute.'

'Very well. Show him in, Carla.'

'Them, sir.'

'Them. Him. It. She. And while you're about it . . .'

'Yes?'

'Does it come within the bounds of your job description to rustle me up a cup of tea?'

Carla smirked. Tea? By the time he'd seen his nine-thirty, he'd be needing something much, much stronger.

In the outer office, she nodded to the three people who'd been patiently waiting.

'You can go in now,' she said, giggling openly.

The heavily made-up woman in the black leather trench-coat winked at her from behind her huge bunch of helium balloons. 'Want to come and watch?'

Carla led them in, struggling to keep a straight face. 'Mr Jenks? Your visitors.'

The woman in the leather coat marched in, closely followed by the small fat bearded clown and the man dressed as a tall gorilla.

Not until the latter had firmly closed the office door and was standing with his back to it did Mr Jenks glance up. His eyes widened in horror, but his lips remained clamped together. He looked like a horseguard on duty, trying to ignore an uncomfortable itch.

'Surprise, Alan!'

Throwing her arms in the air, the woman let her coat fall open to reveal a tiny white corselet, stockings, and the briefest of lace panties underneath. Alan Jenks's face collapsed. Carla wished she had a camera, so she could capture his horrified expression for her colleagues.

Now, with a gesture of abandonment, the woman dropped her coat to the floor and threw herself across the desk. The short clown ran forward, and, producing two pairs of

141

handcuffs from a side pocket of his red-and-white polka-dot pants, clamped one pair expertly around Mr Jenks's wrists, and the other around his ankles.

'What the Hell is . . .' Alan Jenks began.

The woman in the corset grinned at him. 'That's just the attitude, Alan,' she purred. '*What the Hell!* I wish all our clients were as co-operative as you. I can see you must've had a singing telegram before!'

'B . . . But who . . . ?'

'Who sent us? Ah, that's our little secret! Now, just relax!' She let go of the balloons, which bobbed up to the ceiling. Then, delving into the dark crack between her breasts, she removed a small scrap of paper, unfolded it and in a high, tuneless falsetto, began to sing. '*Happy Birthday to You, Happy Birthday to You, Happy Birthday, dear Alan, Happy Birthday to You.*'

Carla clapped her hands gleefully. 'Happy Birthday, Mr Jenks! You should have told everyone. We would've got some pastries in!'

His face puce with embarrassment, he glared silently at her across the thinly-veiled buttocks laid out on his desk.

'Say cheese!'

There was a white flash as the clown crouched down in front of the desk and took a close-up photograph.

'That's for the front pages, Alan,' the woman in the corset said. 'Thirty-three today! Well, we're going to make this a birthday you'll never forget.' Clearing her throat, the singing telegram started up again to the same tune. '*Alan, don't try to run, For the fun's just begun. If you're a good boy now, We won't use our gun.*'

Swinging round, Carla saw that the gorilla at the door was pointing some kind of toy rifle at them. Well, she was sure in her heart of hearts that it was a toy, just part of the joke, but despite this she was filled with a growing uneasiness, and the colour drained from her face. Behind his desk, Alan Jenks stood up and tried to take a step,

142

but fell backwards onto the chair. Roughly, the tiny clown pushed him down on his seat.

'Come, come, Alan! Don't take it so seriously! Life's a gas!' The woman on the desk rolled over. When she stroked his cheek with one of her pale grey satin-gloved hands, he visibly flinched. 'Isn't that so, Carla?'

Carla took another look at the rifle and swallowed hard. 'What's going on?'

'Fun and games!' The woman smiled at her warmly. 'Come over here, Carla! Be a sport and join in! We've got to celebrate Alan's birthday, haven't we?' Getting up, she steered Carla around the desk and pushed her firmly down on her boss's lap. 'Coco?'

Silently, the bearded clown produced a short length of rope, and, pulling it so tight that Carla winced, proceeded to tie her hands to the handcuff chain. 'Hey, stop that!' she said. 'You're hurting me!'

But the silent clown didn't stop, he only bound her wrists more tightly so that, by the time he'd finished, she knew that what was happening was no joke after all.

'OK,' said the Singing Telegram, slipping her coat back on and swinging a large attaché case onto the table. 'Let's have no alarms set off, and no hysterics. That way, we'll all keep calm. Birthday Boy, if you ever want to see your thirty-fourth, it's time to get on the phone and order up some nice used notes for us.'

Trembling uncontrollably, Carla turned her head so that she and Alan Jenks were face to face. In his eyes, she saw the first emotion she had ever registered there: pure, unadulterated fear.

Nine

With all the reverence due to a Constable landscape, the camera panned left across a black-and-white photograph of the steel rooftop girders of Sainsbury's Camden Town store, then slid down to the blank, dark letterbox of its long shop window.

'It's now more than two months since Miranda Green, a forty-year-old mother-of-four, was abducted from this building during an armed robbery,' purred a crisp but throaty voice-over. 'She hasn't been seen since. Her car, a Morris Minor, was found four weeks later in a gravel pit outside Nottingham. It was a burned-out wreck. Inside it were remnants of her clothes, and, on the back seat, her wedding ring. Through it was threaded – in what the police describe as a bizarre, sick joke – a wizened courgette. Though ostensibly still searching for Miranda and the criminal who abducted her, the police admit they have all but given up hope of finding her alive. She has joined the ranks of those missing, presumed dead, who every day swell Scotland Yard's files.'

The shot ended at a woman, standing in front of the blown-up photograph, dressed in an immaculately-cut, yet understated, trouser suit. From beneath her glossy bobbed hair, two small, bright eyes stared myopically out through the TV screen into Ed's bedroom.

'But for me, Miranda Green will never be a mere crime statistic,' she continued. 'She happened to be one of my oldest friends. I was also one of the last people to talk to her before she was abducted, a gun held to her head.'

Here, the words Suzanne Jones flashed up, superimposed in italics across the woman's chest. As they faded away, the camera operator pulled in for a close-up. Suzanne's mobile mouth grew ever larger until, like a long, squirming, burgundy leech, it dominated the screen.

'The mysterious and possibly violent disappearance of someone whom one thought of living a very ordinary, mundane existence seems symptomatic of the uncertainty of our times. When a tragedy like this strikes home, it forces one to re-examine the assumptions on which one has based one's life. At what price has Western society embraced Modernity? And what relevance, if any, do the arts have in this violent, unpredictable age?'

All the professionalism she could muster was not enough to control the catch in Suzanne's voice, or stop the tears of genuine grief brimming in her eyes. 'Later in this *Nightfile* Special on Crime and Modernity, I'll be joined in the studio by the author Salman Rushdie, victim of the Iranian *fatwah*, novelist, historian and cultural critic Marina Warner, and George Steiner, Professor of Comparative Literature at the University of Geneva, to discuss these very pertinent issues. But first, a unique look at the other five, unheard-of victims of the Sainsbury's robbery – Miranda's husband and four children, the people who are paying a very real price for the selfish, senseless, criminal actions of one man.'

The picture cut to a close-up of a wilted jug of chrysanthemums, from which the camera pulled back to reveal the kitchen table in Huddlestone Avenue. On the right, Diana, in a huge navy cardigan, was sipping from a mug and toying with a slice of toast, while beside her David tucked into eggs, baked beans and chips. Next to them, Thomas, in his dressing gown, was staring silently at a full plate of food.

Hands encased in yellow rubber gloves, Jack stood at the sink, scouring a frying pan. Lily posed next to him, self-consciously tossing her long hair towards the camera.

146

Pinched between her thumb and index finger was the corner of a tea towel; the fastidious manner in which she held it indicating that she didn't, in fact, know what to do with it.

'Anyone want another cup of tea?' Jack called over his shoulder.

There was a chorus of Nos, followed by unprompted thank yous. The children talked quietly amongst themselves. Jack handed the frying pan to Lily, who gave it a cursory pat with the tea towel. When she'd finished, first she, then Jack joined the others at the table. By the window, poignantly empty, stood an extra kitchen chair.

'It was just an ordinary day, really,' said David's voice over the picture. 'We all got up, had breakfast with Mum, and went off to school. Afterwards, I went up to Oxford Street with some mates. It wasn't until I got home at eight-thirty that I realised something was wrong.'

From the purple and lime-green blobs of a psychedelic poster, the camera now pulled back to reveal the interior of a small attic bedroom dominated by a bulky stereo set looped with wires as thick, black and tangled as licorice straps. Back against the wall, knees drawn up to his chest, David lay back on his rumpled bed, strumming a guitar. His eyes, as large and green as Miranda's, stared at the camera guardedly through thick cigarette smoke.

He strummed the guitar tunelessly. His lips parted slightly, and a hand came into view and placed a lighted cigarette between his lips. 'When Mum still hadn't turned up by ten o'clock my sisters started to get a bit worried, you know? Then we saw the item on the News about the robbery, and we put two and two together and persuaded Dad to phone the police.' There was a long pause. The camera zoomed into his face and lingered there expectantly. David cleared his throat. 'That was that, really. The pieces sort of fitted together.'

He blinked slowly. With uncharacteristic nervousness, the tip of his tongue appeared for a moment and moistened his lips.

'David, how has your mother's . . . disappearance . . .

changed life for you?' purred a woman's voice from off-screen.

'Dunno.' He shrugged. 'In lots of ways, everything's still the same. But . . .' He hesitated. There was a short cutaway of Suzanne nodding, her face a study in commiseration, then a close-up of David. 'When something like this happens, you sort of don't feel the same about life,' he said bitterly. 'Before, you just lived and never thought about things. Now you just don't trust people any more.'

The camera cut to a close-up of spilt nail varnish, blood-red in colour, then pulled back to reveal a battered 1950s dressing table, strewn with bottles of foundation, a dirty hairbrush, a rainbow assortment of eyeshadows, half-used, open lipsticks and scrunched-up scarves. Four thin silver chains hung over its circular mirror, into which Lily blinked through heavy eye make-up, looking more like a Soho prostitute than a North London schoolgirl.

'Mum was always going on about crime,' she said sharply to her reflection. 'Every time we went out, it was always, "What time are you coming home?" and "Don't talk to strangers" and "Be careful". It used to drive me crazy. I used to think she was obsessed.' She swung round, and addressed the camera directly. 'I mean, you've got to *live*, haven't you? And besides, you just don't think these things are going to happen to you. But . . .'

For a moment she hesitated, then swallowed with evident difficulty. 'Then it did happen – to my Mum.'

In close-up, her clenched and bitten fingers writhed in her lap. Then, head cocked to one side, Suzanne nodded sympathetically. 'Has that made you rethink your mother's attitude, Lily? I mean, do you now think she was right?'

A muscle clenched defiantly in Lily's jaw, and her eyes narrowed defiantly. 'No. Not at all. Why should it? I mean, it just goes to show it doesn't matter how many risks you take, because you're not safe anywhere. What's the point of being *careful* all the time when you can get kidnapped in the middle of the day, doing something so boring and ordinary as being in a supermarket queue?'

After another close-up of Suzanne, nodding encouragingly, the camera cut back to Lily, who was now fiercely brushing her hair. 'I keep asking myself what kind of person could do that to someone like Mum. I keep hoping I'll come face to face with him one day – just so I can tell him what I really think. One of the worst things about it is not . . . not knowing what he really did to her and what she went through.' Lily put the hairbrush down, and wiped a tear away. 'Sometimes, at night, I just can't get that out of my mind.

'Being without Mum is sort of much harder than I would have expected – not that I ever thought about it before. I've kind of had to grow up and take over a lot of the things she did, and be strong for the others. I wish . . .' There was a long pause. Lily bit her lip.

'Yes?' prompted the voice off-screen.

'I kind of wish I'd been nicer to her. You know, I suppose when someone's there all the time, you tend to take them for granted. Like I can't remember the last time I told Mum that I loved her. Now . . .' Her lower lip trembled. 'Now it's too late.'

Semicircular shadows, dark as bruises, surrounded Diana's eyes as she, now, took her turn to stare out of the TV screen. 'The worst thing about Mum going is the way people react to you. I mean, they look at you as if you're some kind of *freak*. When I went back to school, some of the people I'd thought were my friends didn't even talk to me. I suppose . . . Well, I suppose they're just embarrassed but . . . It doesn't help, you know. I mean, it wasn't my fault Mum was, well . . .' Her lips trembled, then spat out the word, 'murdered. And whatever's happened to Mum, I'm still me.'

In a slow pan across the pink carpet of her bedroom, the camera followed a trail of screwed-up sweet wrappers and half-empty biscuit packets towards an overflowing straw wastepaper basket before cutting back to Diana unwrapping a Rolo and popping it in her mouth.

'I don't really like to talk about it any more,' she mumbled, huddling into her dressing gown. 'Dad says it's good for us to, but . . . I suppose I don't really want to think about it. If you let it, it's the sort of thing that could easily ruin your life. As it is, it's made me much more anxious about going out – I'm always looking over my shoulder, just like Mum used to. And that makes me really angry.' She took a deep breath. 'Incredibly angry. I mean, older people didn't grow up worrying about things like muggers and murderers all the time. Why should we have to?'

From Diana's haunted, haunting face the camera now cut to Miranda's wardrobe, where it tracked slowly across the rail of limp, lifeless garments.

'Sometimes I just go into Mummy's room and open her cupboard and just touch her things,' said a quiet voice over the picture. 'It makes me feel like she's still alive. I know she's not, because that's what the police think, isn't it? But I can't stop hoping, even though it's no use.'

Pale, pinched and unhappy, Thomas stared out of the television. Off screen, Suzanne asked, quietly and with delicacy, 'Thomas, is it very difficult to come to terms with what's happened to your mother?'

His lips parted, but he did not answer. Before the tears in his eyes could fall, he stood up and walked off-camera, saying, 'Sorry, I don't want to do this any more.'

'On the whole, the children are coping very well.' Down in the living room, leaning back in his favourite armchair, Jack squinted into the camera. 'In many ways, better than I have myself.' Here, for a split second, his narrow face broke into a self-deprecating smile, then, once again, resumed its former expression – a look at once grief-stricken, martyred and deeply understanding.

'Of course there's a work of mourning to be done for all of us, but that's a process that's time-limited,' he went on, taking off his spectacles and twiddling them by one arm.

'I think it'll be years before we can gauge the actual extent of the psychological damage to the children caused by the trauma of losing a parent in this particularly brutal way. In the meantime, I try to encourage them to talk about Miranda.'

Off-screen, Suzanne asked. 'And how do you do that?'

Jack cleared his throat. 'Once a week, after supper, we hold what I call Mourn Mother Meetings in which I urge them to express their grief.'

There was a brief shot of Suzanne nodding, then the screen was once more dominated by Jack. 'Single parent-hood is hard work, naturally, but I'm doing my best to be both mother and father to them, and on the whole I think it's working pretty well. I must say, I don't think I could have coped so well without my neighbours, some of whom have been extremely supportive. We all pull together, as it were, and take things day by day.'

'Miranda was a marvellous person but . . .' As he uncrossed and re-crossed his legs, Jack sighed regretfully. 'Despite all my encouragement, she was ultimately too afraid of life to really *live* it. The irony is, she was so obsessed with something like this happening, that it's almost as if she willed it upon herself.'

Here Jack's image exploded into a shower of sparks as Miranda picked up an onyx ashtray and hurled it into the TV screen. Then, throwing herself across Ed's bed, she burst into inconsolable tears.

Ten

A sharp wind gusted down South Molton Street, making the hanging baskets of petunias and lobelia suspended from the lamposts sway dangerously above the pedestrians. Litter and leaves swirled in low eddies. Overhead, dark clouds had gathered and begun to drop heavy spots of rain on the pavement. People scurried along between the shops, their umbrellas blowing inside out.

Feeling warm, cossetted and protected, Miranda looked down on this chaos from the window of the VIP changing room of the first floor of Browns. Then, dropping the net curtain, she looked once more in awe at her own, dazzling self, reflected in the mirror-clad sliding doors. How, she wondered, could the frumpy, washed-out mum she'd been for so many years have changed over the course of only three months into the striking peroxide-blonde, crew-cut siren she now saw?

Pleased beyond measure with her new ultra thin, ultra chic self, she shifted her gaze from her face to the dark navy wool Jil Sander trouser suit she was currently trying on. 'You don't think this jacket's a little too long for me, do you, Fran?' she asked the assistant.

The petite brunette stood back, put her hands in the pockets and regarded her critically. 'Not at all! I think it's very simple and elegant. And you're so lovely and tall, Mrs Baines, you can get away with it.' Reaching over, she plucked at the collar and pushed up the sleeve. 'My only reservation is . . .'

'Yes?'

'Well, isn't it perhaps a little too similar to the Jil Sander trouser suit you bought last week?'

'Which one?'

'The black one. You know, the one with the narrow trousers and the double breasted jacket.' Pushing her dark brown bobbed hair behind her ears, she leaned towards her confidentially. 'Wouldn't you be better off to take something a bit different?'

Miranda's armpits prickled. 'What do you mean, *to take* it?'

Fran looked surprised. 'Well, to buy it instead.'

Miranda let out her breath. 'Of course. You're right. Yes.' She bit her lip, annoyed with herself. She really must stop being so touchy. Despite ample temptation, she hadn't stolen anything from Browns – not even the new Hermès scarf she'd once found, still in its bag, left behind by a previous customer. As far as shoplifting was concerned, the store was completely out of bounds for her. That being the case, how could Fran possibly know what she got up to elsewhere? A slow flush of guilt crept up her neck, staining her cheeks red.

'Are you hot, Mrs Baines? You're not getting one of your awful migraines again? Would you like a cold drink? Or a coffee? Or maybe something to eat?'

'No. No thank you. Oh, gosh, look at the time! I really must be getting back to work soon.'

'Of course. How *is* the oil business this week?'

'*What*?'

'Last time you came in, you seemed very worried about that deal.'

'Was I? Oh yes, I remember. Well, it all went through swimmingly.'

'So the take-over bid fell through in the end?'

'Um, yes.'

'It must be a great relief to you. You really didn't need that kind of worry – certainly not in the same week that Oliver caught chickenpox!'

'No.' Miranda gazed blankly at the young woman's open, trusting face, unable to admit that she had absolutely no idea what she was talking about. Since she'd first walked hesitantly into the fashion mecca of Brown's six weeks ago, Fran had become her personal helper and fashion mentor. During her dozen-odd visits there, she'd come to look on her with adoration verging on awe. Being met at the door by Fran gave her a comforting, safe feeling, like a child being welcomed to tea by a favourite, adoring aunt. Miranda was beginning to look upon her as her closest friend – even closer than Pauline at the Sloane Street branch of Joseph, and Jane at Harvey Nichols. Fran was so genuinely friendly that one just couldn't help confiding in her. But what exactly *had* she confided? What new lies had she spun the last time she was here? She really must keep track of her fantasy life, if she was going to lead one.

Miranda pushed these thoughts aside, slipped off the Sander trouser suit and wriggled into a thigh-skimming, skin-tight black lycra Hervé Leger cocktail dress that she knew Ed would enjoy peeling off her. After that, she tried on a sleeveless Patricia Lester evening dress embroidered with beads which she'd spotted outside on the rails. Pleated into tiny folds, the royal blue silk clung to her curves like a second skin. She smiled approvingly.

So did Fran. 'Oh, yes' she exclaimed as she arranged the matching cape over Miranda's shoulders. 'Now, you could wear this for that ball at the British Embassy in Paris you're going to next week, couldn't you?'

'The ball? Mmm!'

'That is, if you don't wear your grey Issey Miyake. And look, if you've got time, there's something I think's right up your street – a new Chrome Hearts leather jacket that's just come in from the States.'

'Divine!' Miranda said, a few minutes later as she squeezed into the diminutive black patent biker's jacket and pulled up the zip. 'I'll definitely have this!'

'There's this matching bag, too.' Fran slipped the huge,

silver-studded duffle bag over Miranda's shoulder. 'But maybe you'd like to think about them both. They are on the dear side . . .'

'Are they?' she said vaguely. 'Oh, never mind, I'll take them. And the Hervé Leger. And the Patricia Lester. After all, you only live once!'

Fran went out to pack up her purchases, and, straining her neck, Miranda fastened the poppers of her cream DKNY cashmere body, then wriggled into the tight leather Moschino trousers she'd bought the previous weekend in Paris, using a stolen Amex card. A line of steel studs marched up her legs and across her buttocks with military precision. Perfect as the trousers had seemed for turning on Ed in their top-floor suite at the Georges V, she'd not yet come to terms with the way men ogled her in the street when she wore them. In appearance, she might now be head-to-toe S&M, but her self-image was still stuck somewhere in M&S.

Putting on her Raybans, she left the changing room, settled the bill in cash without outwardly flinching, kissed Fran on both cheeks and left, taking the bag and saying she would return to pick up the rest of her purchases later on.

Once outside, Miranda staggered down South Molton Street in her cripplingly-high Manolo Blahnik ankle boots, overcome with shock at the amount she had just spent.

£12,400.

On clothes.

Clothes she didn't even need.

A hefty £7,000 of that was for the Chrome Hearts jacket, and another £2,500 was for the matching bag. Compared to that, the Hervé Leger and the Patricia Lester had been real snips at £1,100 and £1,800 a piece.

£12,400. That was enough to pay off the mortgage on Huddleston Road, or to see Lily or David through university, or to sponsor six guide dogs for the blind, or to save about 100,000 poverty-stricken Third World children from life-threatening bouts of diarrhoea.

How could she have spent that much, on herself, in the

space of three quarters of an hour, particularly when her last week's purchases – all £6,570 worth of them – still languished in a pile on Ed's spare bed, their outrageous price tags yet to be removed?

Outside Molton Brown, she stopped and bought a copy of the *Big Issue*, paying with a twenty-pound note and telling the amazed vendor to keep the change. Her guilty conscience partly assuaged, Miranda wandered up and down the pedestrianised street, gazing blankly into the windows in search of more things to buy. A shopping bag from Sportsac? That would come in useful. A way-out silver necklace from Electrum? Another pair of shoes from Pied-a-Terre? Pressing her nose against the window, she looked with indifference at the strappy satin evening sandals with their diamanté buckles she'd bought in black the previous week. Maybe she should buy them in red today, or even in shocking pink. If she did, she could then spend the rest of the morning searching for a pink outfit to go with them. That would give her something to do.

As overcome with nausea as a bulimic half way through a binge, she huddled into her black sheepskin Kenzo jacket. The truth was that she didn't actually need anything. Need, however, didn't come into it. After years of scrimping, she now had to get used to being extravagant. After all, as Ed said, it was only money, and there was no point in hanging onto it when the Old Bill were just waiting to take it away. As Les had pointed out the other day, she had a duty to the economy to spend the thousands they were thieving.

Ah, duty! This was something that she could understand. With serious intent, she now strode into Cobra and Bellamy and tried on a brooch she'd been eyeing for the past few days. She *did* need something to brighten up all the chic but sombre suits she'd bought recently; this enormous heart-shaped fake ruby, surrounded by square-cut diamanté was just the thing.

Out in the street, her latest purchase stowed in the voluminous depths of her Louis Vuitton bag, she began to feel a little better about herself. The trouble was that Miranda had changed so much in the past three months that she barely knew herself. Like a plant smothered by ivy, she'd lived a stunted existence when she was with Jack. Without him hanging over her, aspects of her character which she'd never suspected existed had suddenly begun to sprout: a craving for designer labels and expensive weekends in exclusive country hotels, a penchant for staying up all night eating marshmallows and watching dreadful movies on satellite TV; passions – shared with Ed – for eating serious food in serious restaurants and for making love in public places: on a boat in Regent's Park lake, for instance, or in a darkened Oxford Street shop doorway, or under the pier on Brighton beach. This new personality, so unlike the one she had previously worn, was rather like her new clothes: she did not yet feel entirely comfortable in it, for it chafed at the seams, and tickled her armpits, and ripped open now and then to reveal a glimpse of the old, down-trodden, self-doubting Miranda, naked and trembling underneath.

For a short moment, the roller coaster of her elation slowed down, and terror seized her, a pit bull terrier at her throat. What had happened to the old Miranda? What would become of the new one, when she grew old?

Across New Bond Street, she escaped from these thoughts inside Fenwicks, where she bought herself half a dozen Chanel lipsticks and a large bottle of Issey Miyake scent before gliding up the escalators to the top floor. There was nothing she liked in the lingerie department that she hadn't already either purchased or stolen. Reluctant to leave without taking a small souvenir with her, she hung around for a moment, watching the assistant out of the corner of her eye. She had not shop-lifted at all that day, and like an addict in need of a fresh shot, her fingers were tingling with an uncontrollable craving. The moment the assistant turned away, Miranda surreptitiously slipped a size 32AA red lace bra-and-pants set from its hanger and stuffed it into the deep outside pocket of her jacket, telling herself that, though it was far too small to wear herself, she would find a use for it someday.

After stopping off in the café for a capuccino, she drifted down to the ground floor, where, on her way out, she caught sight of herself in a full-length mirror. Her eyes locked with their mirrored twins, which glinted back at her so coldly that she barely recognised herself.

She stopped short, overcome by a dizzying, stabbing pang of guilt. Frame by painful frame, last night's *Nightfile* programme replayed in her mind. What had she done to her children? How could she have put them through such pain? What the hell did she think she was doing, burdening them with her so-called death when the truth was that she had never felt so alive?

Yet how could she ever go back home when she was now a wanted criminal, and a member of a successful gang of crooks?

Oh God, she needed to talk to someone! Turning on her heels, she made her way to the public telephone, where she dialled Suzanne Jones's office number, only to be told by a plummy voice that Ms Jones was in meetings all day. 'Whom shall I say called?'

Without giving her name, she put down the receiver, but didn't take her hand off it. Then, after a long moment of hesitation, she dialled Huddleston Avenue.

Breep. Breep. Breep. When she closed her eyes she could almost see the telephone sitting on the table, and hear it reverberating around the tiled hall. Her heart pounded as she imagined the children in the kitchen, listening to its ring. Which of them would pick it up? Lily, thinking it was her boyfriend? David, answering gruffly, in what he imagined was a cool voice? Or maybe Thomas, up in her bedroom, where he had been leafing through her clothes. Since she'd left, she'd missed the children terribly, but until she'd seen last night's *Nightfile* Special, she'd managed to convince herself that they weren't missing her. Now, that comfortable, self-deluding option wasn't open to her any more.

Breep. Breep.

Suddenly her whole body ached with longing to see them. She held on, but no one answered. Of course not. At 12.30 on a weekday, the children would be at school and Jack would be at work. Yet, unable to break the connection, she continued to clutch the receiver to her ear. She was about to put it down when there was a loud click on the other end.

'Hello?'

Mary sounded annoyed and breathless, as if she'd just had to run up the stairs. Burning with sudden jealousy, Miranda slammed down the receiver and fled back to the ground floor.

Her heart still pounding, she stopped at the earring counter and she tried on a pair of cheap copper hoops. Jack and Mary had done her a favour, she reminded herself sternly. Wasn't she now much happier than she'd ever been before? With Ed, her devoted lover, Les, her new friend, no domestic responsibilities and more excitement and money than she knew what to do with, she was having an incredible time.

Of course she was.

Despite the inevitable twinges of guilt her new way of life aroused in her – and, to her shame, they were only twinges – it beat her old way of life hands down. How could one even compare travelling first class on the Chunnel to Paris on a forged passport in order to shop, with stolen plastic, at Chanel and YSL, to standing in a kitchen, listening to *The Archers* and brewing up yet another cauldron-full of bolognese sauce? Before, she'd been too afraid of muggers to go out to the corner shop after dark or even open the front door. Surely it was far better to be a criminal than to live in fear of them? Only one thing frightened her nowadays: the idea of being caught.

If only risk wasn't so addictive, she thought, as she examined the copper hoops in a small oval mirror before shifting her gaze to the reflection of a uniformed security guard who was standing close by. She was like a machine, programmed to self-destruct: now that she had started being dishonest, she just couldn't stop . . .

Taking the copper hoops off, she deliberately laid them on the counter, and tried on another pair.

As she inspected herself in the mirror again, she noticed that the security guard had turned around and, hands clasped behind his back, was staring through the plate glass window at a red Ferrari which had just pulled up in the street.

She took off the second pair of earrings, put them down beside the first pair, and plucked a pair of fake pearl studs from the stand.

'Can I help you?'

She took off her Raybans, slipped them in her pocket on top of the red bra-and-pants set, and smiled at the assistant. 'Oh, I'm just browsing.'

'Help yourself.'

'Thanks. I will.'

The assistant busied herself at the till. Miranda put the pearl studs back on the rack. Her fingers honed in on a pair of mock-tortoiseshell clip-ons.

The Ferrari drove away. The security guard swung round and looked at her.

His eyes met hers.

As she smiled at him, her fingers closed over the clip-ons. Then, as she turned around to face him, she slightly lifted her hand in order to scratch her hair. The earrings slid into her sleeve, then, as she lowered her arm, into her pocket, where they plopped out silently down.

Gathering the other earrings together, she called the assistant over and pushed them towards her.

'Thanks, but I don't think I want these.'

Her ears singing, she walked towards the security guard, stopping just past him to look at a stand of hair accessories.

She glanced at the swing doors. Two shoulder-high security devices stood sentinel, one on either side.

Would the alarm sound when she left, or wouldn't it?

Casually hoisting her bag over her shoulder, she walked towards the exit. Four steps, three steps, two more to go, now one and . . .

The security man was looking at her curiously. She heard him cough loudly. Was there an undercover store detective about?

Her blood pounded in her ears as she pushed open one of the swing doors. Forcing one foot carefully in front of the other, she stepped out into the damp, cold air.

The now familiar surge of elation hit her: Yes! She had got away with it again!

It was not until she reached the corner that she felt a restraining hand on her sleeve.

Shit, she thought. *Shit, shit, shit!*

A red stain crept up her neck and over her cheeks.

Once the police were called in, her real identity would be discovered. Her criminal career was over. The entire, illegal, exhilarating game was up. In all probability, she'd never see Ed or Les again.

Miranda cursed herself for having ruined everything for the sake of a pair of worthless earrings, a bra that didn't fit and a cheap thrill.

'Hold on a minute, lady,' said a voice in her ear.

Turning her head, she found herself held not by the security guard but by a tall black youth in a grey track-suit. Beneath his drawn-up hood, his eyes squinted at her suspiciously. Then the colour drained from his lips, and his mouth dropped open.

'Shit, fuck and corruption, I was right!' he gasped. 'Well, if it isn't Mrs G!'

'I thought at first you was a ghost,' he said, as he sat across a table in Fortnum and Mason's Fountain Room, licking the capuccino foam from his lips. 'What happened to your hair? Did it fall out after you were held up in Sainsbury's? Did you go blonde overnight with shock?'

Two steely-haired women lunching at the next table glanced at them curiously.

'Please, keep your voice down, Justin!' Miranda muttered.

'Afraid you might be recognised after being on the telly last night?' Justin's sturdy fingers plucked up the long-handled spoon beside his plate and dipped it into his Banana Split, then he slipped a mouthful of chantilly cream between his full, firm lips. 'Don't get me wrong, Mrs G. You're looking good. Quite sexy, actually. To tell the truth, you look a hell of a lot better now you're dead than you ever did when you was alive.' His large, brilliant white teeth bit through the tail of a fan-shaped wafer, and he looked defiantly into her eyes. 'Well?'

'Well what?'

'Spill the baked beans. Where've you been hiding?'

She hesitated. 'I don't think that's any of your business.'

'No? When the mother of my best friend disappears and everyone thinks she's . . .'

'Look,' she interrupted. 'Let's just say I decided to take a sabbatical.'

'A what?'

'Don't they teach you and David anything at that school?'

'I'm not at school no more. I left.'

'Why?'

He shrugged. 'I couldn't see the point in staying on for another year. I'm working now.'

'Justin, that's marvellous! At what?'

'Working at finding a job.' He sniggered.

Miranda sighed. 'Look, a sabbatical means time off. Unpaid leave. A kind of long holiday from normal life.'

'So where are the postcards, then?'

'What postcards?'

'People on holiday send postcards. *Having a brilliant time. Wish you were here, love Mum.* Know what I mean?' Putting down his spoon, he looked at her wryly. 'You know, I used to like coming over to your house. It was nice there. Cool. Really kind of relaxed, know what I mean? You always had time to listen when I wanted to talk, and there was always something to eat, and you never minded what mess we made, or how loud the music was, or how often I stayed the night. I always felt welcome and I want you to know I appreciate that. But now . . .' He shook his head. 'It's not the same. Everyone's moping about. And Mary . . .' He hesitated.

'Is she there a lot? Don't look so embarrassed, Justin. I know she's having an affair with Jack.'

He popped a glacé cherry into his mouth and swallowed it whole. 'Man, I can't understand it. I mean, just look at her! Who in their right mind would touch her?'

'Obviously Jack doesn't feel the same way.'

'It's not just what she looks like. She never leaves you alone. She's in and out of everyone's rooms, all day long. Always with some stupid excuse. You'd think it's her house, the way she bosses Lily and Diana about. What you grinning at, Mrs G? Honest, I don't know how you can bear it, knowing she's screwing your husband and looking after your kids.' His nostrils flared with anger. 'I don't understand how you could leave like you did! The house is like a *morgue* now. Your kids think you're *dead*, for Christ's sake! How could you do that to them? Don't you care about them any more? Jesus, you haven't even asked if David and Lily passed their GCSEs!'

She hung her head. Tears of shame splashed onto the tablecloth. 'How are they all, Justin?'

'You must've seen the programme. How d'you think? David doesn't ever talk about you. Thomas doesn't talk about *anything*. Lily's out most of the time with her new bloke. And Diana, well, we've never said much more than *hello* to each other.'

'How's Jack?'

He sipped his coffee. 'Jack is . . . Jack is Jack. Same as ever. More cheerful than usual, if anything, now that he's got something real to be miserable about.' He scraped the sides of his empty sundae dish, then pushed it away. 'You haven't got a fag, have you?'

'You shouldn't smoke. It's so bad for you, Justin.'

'Don't start all that shit, man.'

'Sorry.' She opened her bag, took out a packet of Sobranie and the gold and mother-of-pearl lighter Ed had given her, and pushed them across the table. A cigarette clamped between his teeth, Justin examined the lighter with curiosity, flicked it open, then gave Miranda a long, appraising look.

'You know, you're quite something, Mrs G. All the years I've known you, you've been pretending to be this mousey little housewife. And all the time you must've been running deep, know what I mean? Because look at you now! You've changed. Want to know something? I like you better like this. You're not so nice or nothing, but you're more, well, more interesting. If you was twenty years younger, I could really fancy you.'

She laughed. 'Thanks a lot.'

'Don't take that the wrong way. It's a compliment.'

'Sure.' Resting her chin in her hand, she smiled at him across the table. 'So, what are you going to do, now you know that I'm alive?'

'I dunno.' His eyes were withdrawn, thoughtful, objective. He dragged deeply on the cigarette and blew out a perfect smoke ring. 'It depends. Know what I mean?'

'No, actually I don't know, Justin. I suppose it means that you want something from me. Money? How much?'

'Don't insult me, Mrs G! You know me better than that.' Elbows on the table, hands clasped, he leaned towards her. 'I'm curious. I want . . .' He paused. '. . . information. I want to know what happened that day in Sainsbury's. And where you've been holed up for the last three months.'

Her fingers shook as she lit herself a cigarette. 'Believe me, you're better off not knowing.'

'Look, you can trust me.' He grinned. 'You might as well, because you haven't got much choice, have you? What's your game?'

She hesitated for a moment, then beckoned him close. 'Robbery,' she whispered.

His eyes widened. Suddenly he looked like a young child watching a conjurer. 'What, burglary? Hold-ups? Banks and things?'

'Banks and . . . con-tricks and . . . building societies and . . . jewellery shops.' She took a deep breath. 'Last week it was a warehouse raid in Hendon. You might have read about it in the papers.'

He stared at her open-mouthed for a moment, then his shocked face broke into a grin. 'You know, I almost believed you for a minute!'

'But you don't?'

'Think I'm stupid? Someone like you, a robber? Never!'

She should have felt relieved. Instead, she felt unaccountably annoyed. 'Why is it so impossible?'

'Come on, man! You're David's mum! You're not a criminal type.'

'What exactly is a criminal type, Justin?' she snapped. 'Have you ever met one?'

'Of course. All the time. Well, one or two . . . dealers and stuff, know what I mean?' His voice trailed away. 'You're not on the level?' When she nodded, he whistled softly through his teeth. 'What's got into you? You seemed to have everything a lady could want before. I always used to think to myself, what a life!'

She sighed. 'I suppose that's what it looked like from the outside. But inside, Justin, well, I felt like I was suffocating. I hated myself for having done nothing with my life, and I hated how I was with the children, and I hated how things were with Jack. I wanted so much for things to change, but – I don't know – somehow I couldn't change them by myself. And then . . .'

'Yes?'

'Well, a door sort of opened up and . . . and I was dragged through it and . . . And suddenly an opportunity was there, a chance for me to have a career at long last,

166

the kind of career I'd never have thought of in a million years. And so, for better or worse, I took it. And here I am. My life has completely changed. And do you want to know something?' She pushed her Raybans down to the tip of her nose, and looked earnestly at him across the bridge. 'I'm good at what I do. Really good at it. After years of being a nobody, I'm successful at last. You can't imagine how wonderful that feels.'

He shook his head slowly. 'You've flipped, Mrs G.'

'Maybe.' She stubbed out the half-smoked cigarette butt. 'It doesn't feel like that. More as if I've come to my senses. As if I was dead for years, and now I'm living, really living, at long last.'

'Too right. Living on the edge.'

She nodded. 'It's exciting.'

'It's against the law.'

'So's ganja, or Ecstasy, or whatever drugs you and David are currently poisoning your minds with.'

'That's different! It's part of the culture, isn't it? Besides, I don't rob people.'

'Well, I don't rob people either – not individuals, only big businesses, shops, organisations that can afford to lose the money.'

'What if you get caught?'

She laughed. 'I won't.'

'What if you do? What if, well, what if someone got hurt?'

'That's impossible. We don't use real weapons.'

His eyebrows went up again. 'We?'

'I mean, I . . . I don't . . . I . . .'

She drew in her breath. Justin was staring at her in a most disturbing way. With an odd, stirring sensation, she realised that, in all the time she'd known him, this was the first time they had ever been out alone together. A blush crept up her neck as she remembered all her wild, erotic dreams about him. Confused, she signalled for the bill, then silently fiddled with the bowl of sugar lumps.

Justin put his hands over her restless fingers. His palm was smooth and warm. 'Mrs G,' he said gently. 'Look, you've already told me enough to get you put away for half a century. You might as well come clean and tell me the rest.'

The sound of whistling emanated from the front room, where Ed was ripping open one of twenty large cardboard boxes stacked up against the wall. He looked up and smiled at Miranda when she came in, but a moment later he turned ashen.

His fist clenched around his Swiss army knife. 'Who the fuck is this?' he snapped.

Suddenly Miranda knew that she should never have risked bringing Justin home with her. 'Darling, this is Justin. He's an old friend. A friend of my son David's.'

'*So what the fuck is he doing here?*'

Justin gave him a cocky grin and held out his hand. 'Nice to meet you too, Ed.'

Like two ice-cold darts, Ed's eyes flicked from Justin to Miranda. '*Are you out of your fucking mind?*'

'I . . . I'm sorry. Look. I bumped into him while I was out, and he recognised me.'

'What've you told him? *What, Miranda?*' She bit her lip. 'Jesus! You've told him everything, haven't you? *Haven't you?*'

She spread her hands. With another loud '*Fuck!*', he hurled the open penknife across the room. She flinched as it grazed past her and lodged in the wall. Ed snatched up his cigarettes from the coffee table.

'*You bloody idiot!* I should have known this whole idea was a disaster! I should have thrown you out on that first day!'

'Excuse me!' Now it was her turn to get angry. 'I didn't exactly choose to come here in the first place, did I? It wasn't exactly of my own free will!'

As he lit the cigarette, his hands shook with rage. 'Don't

you realise what you've just done? Have you any idea how long we could all go down for if we get caught? Les will hit the roof! *Jesus Christ!*'

'Look, I'm sorry! I really am. I suppose you're right but . . . It'll be all right, darling, I promise. Justin won't tell anyone about us. He's given me his word.'

'Well, that's all fucking right then! And I suppose you believe him?'

'Of course! Look, I've known him practically all his life. I told you – he's David's best friend.'

'And you're telling me he's not going to tell David? He'd better bloody well not tell David!' He pointed threateningly at Justin, his face distorted by anger. '*I'm warning you!*'

'Don't shout at him like that!' She was trembling. This was a side of Ed she hadn't seen since the day he'd taken her hostage: furious, violent, unreachable. Terrified, both for herself and for Justin, she clutched the boy's hand. 'Leave him alone. It's not his fault. He's only a child, for God's sake!'

'A *child*? He's six fucking feet tall!' As he calmed down slightly, he perched on one of the boxes, and, with an exasperated sigh, covered his face with his hands. 'How old are you?' he said at last, peeking at Justin through open fingers.

'Seventeen. Well, sixteen-and-a-half. Look, Mrs G's right, I won't grass on you. Honest.'

'Why? What do you want? Money? How much?'

'Nothing.'

'Listen, mate, only a fool wants nothing in this life.'

'Well, I don't want money.'

'Then what?'

'I want . . .' He cleared his throat. 'I want in. To your gang.'

'*You* want *in*? To the *gang*?' Ed snorted contemptuously. 'What do you think this is, *The Lavender Hill Mob*?'

Miranda sat down beside him. 'I told him it was impossible, darling, but he insisted on asking you himself. Anyway,

'I couldn't let you do it, Justin. You'd get into terrible trouble. I'd never be able to face your mother if you did.'

'You won't have to face her anyway. She thinks you're dead, right?'

'Justin . . .'

'Think about it, Mrs G. What else am I going to do with my life?'

'For heaven's sake! You've got a good brain. You could go into business if you made up your mind to, or even become a lawyer or a social worker or . . .'

'Shit, man, I want to do something *worthwhile*. Be reasonable. Look at it from my point of view. I've got three GCSE passes – woodwork, maths and English. If even white university graduates can't get a decent job nowadays, what am I going to get? Shiftwork at McDonalds? I got ambition, Mrs G! I want a Porsche, and a flat in Belgravia! I want to buy my mum a house in Antigua! I want to be a millionaire!' Ed gave a short, but desperate laugh. 'I'm serious, man!' Justin turned on him earnestly. 'I could learn things from you two, know what I mean? Don't you want to help a young person get on in life? It wouldn't be forever, just till I'd learned enough to go it alone. Look on it as an apprenticeship. A kind of Youth Training Scheme.'

'Justin, crime's a dangerous business.'

'That's why I got to learn it right, Mrs G. From the experts.'

'Jesus wept! I can't deal with this shit!' Ed stood up, shaking his head, and pulled his penknife out of the wall. Like a butcher cutting open the belly of a carcass, he ripped open another cardboard box. From the white, polystyrene shell within it, he extracted a large pale grey machine.

'What's that?' Miranda asked.

He shrugged. 'It's a laser printer.'

'Hey, are you a forger?'

'No, you berk.' He upturned a large plastic carrier. A snakes' nest of leads and wires came tumbling out. After untangling the wires with difficulty, he tried to fit one of the plugs into the back of the machine. 'This won't go in! Where's the bloody handbook?'

Justin watched them for a moment, then turned his attention to the rest of the boxes. 'Are all these part of your haul from the Computa Land raid? What'd you get? Hey, laptops!' Excited, he read the printing on the boxes. 'Toshiba! State of the art, man! Colour screen. 320 megabites!' Now he too began ripping open boxes, unpacking discs, bags, spare batteries, salivating over the machines. 'Man, what I could only do with a set-up like this!'

'Oi, get your filthy hands off! A computer's a delicate instrument. You'll ruin it. I said, hands off! I want to try it out.' Frowning at the tangle of wires on the floor, he picked another lead up and tried to force it into the back of a monitor.

Justin cleared his throat. 'Need any help?'

'Nope.'

'That's not the right . . .'

'Look, just keep away, I know what I'm doing!'

'Sure. OK. Don't bite my head off, all right? What a great set-up! All you need now is a modem and you'll be in business.'

'A what?'

'A modem.'

'Justin, these machines aren't for playing games on.'

'A modem ain't for playing games either, Mrs G, it's for surfing on the Internet.'

Ed dropped the lead he was holding, and struggled to fit another plug into the back of the monitor. 'What's a sodding internet?'

'Where've you been living, man? It's the future, the electronic highway. It's e-mail! Information access! The key to the universe! Cyberspace!'

'This doesn't bloody well fit!' Exasperated, Ed threw down the lead, and glared at Justin. 'Cyberspace, internet . . . What is this? Science fiction?'

171

Justin picked up the lead. 'Here, I'll do that!'

'You? You won't be able to. It's not possible.'

'Not the way you're doing it.' Justin examined the plug carefully. 'No wonder you can't get this into the monitor, it's for linking up a laptop with a CD-Rom. The pins are all bent now. I'll straighten them out for you, if you like. Got a small screwdriver anywhere?'

With a show of impatience, Ed handed his army knife over, and sat down beside Miranda on the cardboard box. Deftly, Justin began to fiddle with the plug. 'The Internet's like a master key, man. With it, you can get in and out of almost every organisation in the world!'

Miranda looked up, suddenly interested. 'Like what?'

'Anywhere. You name it, the Internet will get you in. With a few basic hacking skills, you can access the files, see what's cooking, shift a few numbers about, move some decimal points. Transfer funds . . .'

'Really?'

'With a bit of know-how you can make yourself a fortune. Best thing is, no one gets hurt, because none of it exists.'

'Listen, something either exists or it doesn't.'

'Not on the Internet, Mrs G.' He put down the knife, and, with a satisfied smile, fitted the straightened plug into the printer. 'It's not real, see? It's just cybernetics, electricity, numbers on a screen. Know what I mean?'

'Sounds like a load of bollocks to me.'

Miranda squeezed Ed's hand. 'And do you know how to do all this, Justin?'

'Sure. Well, I mean I've read about it. There are lots of books by hackers. And . . .' He glanced at Miranda. 'David's got a modem.'

'Has he?'

'He bought it in a car boot sale in Highgate. Him and me have messed around a bit with it, up in his room. Don't look so shocked, Mrs G. What did you think we were doing all the time, playing SuperMario?'

'Do you mean to tell me you've both been stealing?'

'We've just been messing, right? Having fun. The only time we ever stole was once, when Mum was really short of money, and we accessed the health authority computer and added a couple of noughts to her wage packet.' He laughed. 'Know what she did when it came through? Phoned them up and told them they'd made a mistake! Nearly got us bloody arrested!'

Having neatly arranged the lap-top and printer on the coffee table, he flicked a switch. A panel of lights flashed on top of the printer. 'Hewlett Packard,' he murmured. 'Good stuff. So what you going to do with this set-up, then? Print your own fivers?'

'Forging's too much trouble. We'll flog it off. We should get a couple of hundred nicker a piece.'

'That's a pity, man. You could really earn some dough with a set-up like this. Want me to load the software in?'

'What's *software*?' asked Miranda.

Justin pursed his lips and whistled, and then he turned to Ed. 'I presume this has got Windows preloaded? Or is it still on disc?'

There was a long pause. Ed looked embarrassed.

Justin shook his head in disbelief. 'Where am I, Hackney or Jurassic Park? Let me tell you something, Mr Ed-whatever-your-name-is: never mind my apprenticeship in your line of work, it's you who needs to learn a few tricks from me.'

Eleven

Jack lay back on the pillows sipping the tea which he'd trained Diana to bring up to him every morning before she left for school. Strong and hot, the liquid coursed down his throat, starting the cycle of peristalsis which began somewhere just below his tonsils. With primitive satisfaction he felt his bowels contract. In precisely ten minutes' time he would have to get up and go to the lavatory to expel their contents. Until then, he had time to relax in the comfort of his bed.

While he waited for the tea to take effect, he picked up *The Dictionary of Psychotherapy* from his bedside table. Outside, the sky was a leaden grey. Rain spattered against the window, and rattled the loose sash. It had been like this for days. The choked gutters out in the street had, even yesterday, become overflowing sewers, the garden lawn – the ex-lawn, to be more accurate – a muddy swamp, and Miranda's herbaceous borders, overgrown and neglected since her – he searched his vocabulary for the right word – her disappearance, wet bogs where only slugs and snails flourished.

Shivering, he pulled the duvet up over his chest. With a pang of guilt, he imagined his four children waiting at their respective bus stops, clutching their sodden satchels, anorak hoods pulled up over their damp hair, umbrellas – if they'd remembered to take them – blowing inside out. Maybe he should have got up early and driven them to school, as

Lily had asked him to. Without question, Miranda would have done so, were she still here.

But Miranda wasn't here. Only her ghost remained to reproach him, and, luckily for him, Jack didn't believe in ghosts, only in guilt trips of the psyche. And since he did not believe in guilt trips, either – not as a motivating force for himself, that was, only as a psychological phenomenon – the pang was immediately dismissed and turfed out. The fact was that the rain wouldn't melt the kids, nor would it result in them catching colds, 'flu or pneumonia, even though Miranda had always, irrationally, insisted that it would. Being overprotective towards children only damaged them, as he'd often warned her. As David, Lily, Thomas and Diana had already had to learn since June, the world was a tough place, and Life – Jack forgave himself in advance for the cliché – was no bed of roses.

Nor, he reflected, was Miranda's rose bed any more.

He took another long gulp of tea. From somewhere below his bellybutton came an ominous gurgle. He glanced at his watch: seven minutes to go.

Lacking his usual deep concentration, Jack flicked through the psychotherapy dictionary, starting, as always, with the As. *Alienation. Ambivalence. Anal Stage.* His stomach rumbled again, this time with hunger. Had the kids, he wondered, left him a Pop-Tart for breakfast, or had they, with the blind ego-centred selfishness of childhood, scoffed the lot? He hoped not. Pop-Tarts, as he'd discovered when Mary had first brought around a packet one morning, though admittedly not as nutritious as Miranda's home-made organic muesli had been, seemed to be acceptable fare to all of them. They certainly dispensed with the ritual of morning arguments about what the kids would or wouldn't eat, and they also absolved him from having to get up in order to provide them with a hot breakfast. The kids simply popped them in the toaster themselves, then waited the required three minutes, thus leaving him extra time for a lie-in.

He returned to the dictionary. *Basic Id. Behaviour therapy. Compensation*. Ah, yes. His eyes alighted on *Competence*, and, while he skimmed through the definition – *Adequate and appropriate practice on the part of the therapist* – he reflected how efficiently the household had been running since the introduction of his new regime: the convenience food which the kids all ate uncomplainingly, the housework rota which had enabled him to sack the weekly cleaner; the long line of new dirty washing baskets on the landing – one for each colour – which made washday such a painless affair; the rule that each individual wash up their own fork, knife, glass and plate after every meal; his unilateral decision to change the bed linen once a month, not once a week as Miranda had slavishly done. These small improvements, and many more like them, had made such an accumulative difference that the total effect was nigh revolutionary: the house was tidy, clean and orderly all day long for the first time in living memory; and he was actually saving money, money which could be spent on frequent takeaways, thus minimising the need for cooking and shopping. When cooking a meal became unavoidable, there was always Mary, so anxious and eager to step into, as it were, the breach.

As he'd always told poor, disorganised Miranda, it was amazing how little time and effort it took to run a house and care for four children if you approached the job in a cool-headed, business-like way. Sadly, there had been two things that his wife – his late wife, he corrected himself – had never been able, or rather willing, to master: the twin arts of delegation and organisation. But then, as he'd said in the *Nightfile* documentary, running the house hadn't been so much a job as a vocation for Miranda – no, a flight from reality, an escape from the truth. Why, she'd jealously guarded the minutiae of her maternal role, at the same time complaining that the role oppressed her! A classic double bind, if ever there was one.

Poor, poor Miranda. The whole affair was really quite tragic. As he'd told Mary last night after their bout of *soixante-neuf* on her living room sofa – Brian had been out at the Irish Club in Camden Square, and Seamus had been next door with Thomas, watching the *Natural Born Killers* video for a school project on violence in the media – he had to congratulate himself on the way he'd taken over her role.

Of course, the children all missed her. He'd go so far as to say they were still deeply upset. Thomas was increasingly withdrawn, Diana and Lily were still often tearful, David seethed with anger that masked his transparent self-blame. But all this, Jack knew, was a completely natural part of the grieving process. For all her faults, her paranoias, her lack of *joie de vivre* and her neurotic tendencies, Miranda had been their mother, and thus emotionally significant to them. However, by encouraging them to talk openly about their grief in an emotionally supportive environment, he liked to think he'd averted the worst effects of what was bound, out of natural filial attachment, to be a traumatic event.

Since the children had so clearly benefited from his Mourn Mother Meetings – he only had to re-watch his video of the *Nightfile* Special to see that – why, Jack wondered, had they suddenly and unanimously voted the other day to end them forthwith? 'It's all so bloody miserable!' Lily had complained, while the others nodded agreement. 'And sort of tacky and artificial.' To which Thomas had added, 'The whole thing was your idea, not ours. If I want to mourn Mum, I'd rather do it by myself, in my own way.' Try as Jack had to explain to them the benefits of sharing their feelings, they had remained stubbornly adamant. As David had bluntly put it, 'Sharing's crap.'

Even though Jack's tea was now cold, it still retained its purgative properties. As he drank, the muscles in his lower abdomen contracted in preparation for action in – what? he checked his watch – five minutes' time. Turning to the Gs in the dictionary, he read through *Grief*, carefully avoiding the entry on the *Good Enough Mother* on the opposite page.

178

> **Grief:** *A normal, time-limited reaction of intense sorrow following the loss of an emotionally-significant person through death or separation . . . For Freud (1917), the grieving process allows ties with the lost object to be broken through the withdrawal of libido.*

As he read the last four words, Jack's bowels churned into action, a minute early. Dropping the dictionary on the floor, he threw on his dressing gown and headed for the bathroom. Freud, he reminded himself as he perched straining on the lavatory seat, had not always got things 100 per cent right. Or maybe, on reflection, he had. After all, his emotional ties with Miranda had broken coming up to three years ago, at about the time he and Mary had first got together. And his libido had certainly withdrawn then. From Miranda.

Sometimes, recently, he'd even had the feeling it was withdrawing from Mary, too. In fact, from the very moment when Suzanne Jones and her film crew had walked through the front door, he couldn't help seeing Mary in a new, unflattering light. Like a blister forming on a toe, an uncomfortable question had begun to shape itself in his mind: what was it, apart from sex, that he saw in her? Besides, there wasn't quite the same *frisson* to their fucking now that they were free to do it every day. Maybe it was time to move on . . .

An uncomfortable, heavy feeling weighted Jack's slumped, down-sloping shoulders. Was it so awful that he didn't miss Miranda? And was it immoral of him to have enjoyed the fifteen minutes of fame her disappearance had brought him? Never in a million years would he have wanted her to have been murdered, as she obviously had been, but since it had happened . . . Really, there was no reason why he should blame himself. The whole, tragic, yet, given Miranda's neurosis about crime, somehow poetically appropriate, event had been completely beyond his control. His secret desires and wishes – his wishes to be, yes, free of her – hadn't affected her fate in the least; Good God, he hadn't willed her murderer into existence!

What was the Freud quotation? 'Conscience is the internal perception of the rejection of a particular wish operating within us.'

Red in the face, Jack strained again. The sound effects echoed through the empty house. He reached for the lavatory paper, tore off a wad and blotted the beads of sweat from his brow. What was he meant to do, mourn for Miranda for ever, for Christ's sake? Take a vow of celibacy as penance because he'd fallen out of love with her long ago? How ridiculous! For all his faults – for a split-second, he tried to think of one – he was no hypocrite.

In that case, why did he feel so inappropriately guilty whenever he fucked Mary nowadays? Surely one couldn't be unfaithful to a dead wife, only to a living one? Why did he feel so . . . so . . . ?

So haunted.

A shiver ran down his spine.

Yes, haunted. Almost as if Miranda, mild and malleable in life, had in death turned into an evil vampire intent on sucking him dry. Sometimes, when he was alone in the house, he half expected her to appear before him, her stubby fingernails grown into pointed talons, her hair a Medusa tangle, her eyes yellow with anger, blood trickling from her lips, her skin bone white. Miranda, transformed by death into an unearthly, vengeful presence . . .

Downstairs, someone rang long and loud on the doorbell, making him jump off the seat. When he sat down again, his heart was beating wildly. What *was* the matter with him? Who could it be at ten past nine on a Monday morning? The children had gone to school – besides, they all had keys. That left only the milkman or the postman, or one of the army of spotty-faced, unemployed youths who lugged plastic crates of tea towels, ironing board covers and sponges from door to door in the hope that someone would buy them out of pity.

The bell rang again, insistently.

Jack sat resolutely still. If it was the milkman or postman or a man wanting to read the electricity meter, they'd come back. If it was one of the unemployed, too bad. In his opinion, the state, not individuals, had a duty to support them. Besides, Miranda might have been taken in by their pathetic hard-luck stories – he knew this from the number of plastic bags of thin yellow dusters she'd left, as a legacy, in the under-the-sink cupboard – but he certainly wasn't going to cut short a good crap in order to run downstairs and buy an over-priced car-cleaning kit from someone who was, in all probability, a conman.

The bell rang for a third time, making him jump again. It was a good thing he didn't believe in meaningful coincidence, otherwise he might have found it odd that someone had unexpectedly rung the bell just when he was thinking of Miranda. Even so, he shifted his buttocks anxiously, and pulled his dressing gown closed over his pale, concave chest.

Then, to his horror, the latch on the front door clicked.

Jack froze as footsteps clattered across the tiled hall floor. Whoever it was down there – he, she, it – flung open a couple of doors then started up the stairs with a slow, deliberate tread.

His thin bare thighs trembled as the intruder reached the half-way landing and stopped, panting loudly. Then, with renewed vigour, it charged up the rest of the stairs.

The bathroom door crashed open with such force that it bounced back on the rubber doorstop and slammed closed.

When it opened again, the unearthly, vengeful presence strode in.

She was just as he had imagined her. Her eyes were sunk in purple hollows, her skin was deathly-pale. Medusa curls snaked over her broad, black-clad shoulders, stopping just short of her waist. Arms akimbo, she glared at him furiously.

Jack gasped, then breathed again. 'Hello, Mary, love.' Though he tried to sound calm, his voice was tremulous.

181

'What the bloody hell do you think you're doing?' she shouted.

He swallowed. 'Just having a crap.'

'Oh, for Christ's sake, Jack, I'm not stupid! I could smell that a mile off! I mean, what the hell do you think you're doing, sending me *this*!'

Raising her fist, she shook something small, red and lacy at him.

'What's that, dear?'

A moment later, a tiny lace bra and g-string landed in his lap. 'Posting them to my own home, Jack! Right under my Brian's nose! Blimey, my Seamus could've opened the packet! What a nerve you got! What the bleeding hell were you thinking of?'

'But, Mary, love . . .' Genuinely perplexed, he examined the garments.

'Don't you *Mary love* me!' Mary stood on tip-toe and examined her purple eye socket in the over-the-sink mirror. 'God Almighty! Look what the bastard did to me!'

'What?'

'What do you think this is, eyeshadow? He clocked me one, didn't he?'

Jack's buttocks sank down into the bowl. 'Do you mean he hit you? Good God, Mary! The bastard!'

Her good eye narrowed. 'He's not the bastard round here! I'm only sorry that the bloody coward didn't come round here and hit you. Specially after he'd read that note!'

'Note? What note?'

Her hand delved into the deep cleavage framed by her dressing gown, and came out holding a screwed up piece of paper which she smoothed out. '*For my favourite muff, Muffin, with lovey-wovey from Jack-the-Mule, your bucking bronco next door.*'

'Here, let me see that!' Jack peered short-sightedly at the typewritten note. His small mouth opened and emitted a short, horrified laugh. 'This is . . . incredible! Believe me, I've never seen this before!'

'Aw, stop pissing about, Jack! I'm not in the mood for it.'

'Whoever sent it to you, it wasn't me. This parcel . . . these, these things . . . Look, have you thought that they might have been meant for someone else, not for you?'

She drew in a long breath. Jack felt the air in the room implode. 'AND WHAT DOES THAT MEAN?'

'Only that . . . that . . .'

Hands on his shoulders, she towered over him, a pastel King Kong. 'Have you been messing around with someone else, lover boy?' Her voice was a menacing whisper.

He shrank back. 'Good grief, no, Mary!'

She sniffed. 'I bloody well hope not. Because, if you have . . .' The ten, vicious daggers of her fingernails bit through his dressing gown and into his flesh.

Jack swallowed. 'How could you think such a thing? My God, Mary! I had no idea you were so insecure!'

She let go of him suddenly. 'Aw, don't give me any of that psychology crap!' she snapped. 'Keep it for your students.'

He looked at her warily as she returned to the mirror and ran her fingers through her hair. This was not the warm-hearted, simple, adoring Mary he had always had the hots for. She had changed – changed into a terrifying monster. 'I just don't understand . . .' he ventured, reaching for the lavatory paper. 'I mean, who could have . . .' He stopped, warned off by the dangerous glint in her reflected eyes.

'*And* they're the wrong size.' Her voice was cold and accusing.

'Sorry?' He wished she'd leave, so he could wipe his bottom in private.

'So you should be. The bra and pants – they're the wrong size. About ten sizes too small.'

'Sorry.'

'Maybe you did mean to send them to someone else!'

'Really, Mary, I didn't . . .' Her eyes glinted again. 'The, er, the shop . . . they must have got muddled up . . . you see, I, er, ordered them by . . . by telephone.'

He'd landed in the shit by some strange quirk of fate. Why, he wondered, was he digging himself in deeper? To his surprise, the lie, unlike the truth, seemed to convince Mary, who suddenly smiled at him lovingly in the mirror.

'Aw, Jack, love!'

'Hmmm?' He forced his trembling lips to smile back.

'If you'd wanted to give me a sexy pressie, you should have done it here!'

'Yes, well . . .'

'As it is, you gone and messed things up right and proper, haven't you?'

'Have I?'

'Or maybe . . .' She paused, smiling at him hopefully. 'Maybe that's what you wanted to do, all along?'

'Wh . . . what do you mean?'

'If you wanted me all to yourself, love, you just had to say so.'

'Well, I . . .'

Mary leaned down and stopped his words with her hard, wide mouth. Her breath smelled of over-boiled brussels sprouts.

'I'll just pop home and get my things, shall I?' she murmured. 'My bits and bobs. Clothes. Make-up. My Joan Collins workout video. Seamus. Stuff like that. I'm moving in, Jack. We'll be together all the time from now on. That's what you wanted, isn't it?'

He tried to protest, but a large, stale, dry Danish pastry seemed to have materialised out of nowhere and lodged itself in his throat.

'What about Brian?' he croaked eventually.

'What about him?' Her lip curled with derision. 'It's nothing to do with him what I do from now on, is it, love? Not when the bastard's just thrown me out.'

Twelve

The main building of the Balls Pond Road University jutted above the surrounding Victorian terraces like a large, up-turned egg box. Stained with rain and dripping limescale stalactites, its pre-cast concrete panels were interspersed with windows so grimy that they gave the appearance of blocking out the surrounding urban scenery, rather than letting it in.

'It's horrible. I wish we hadn't come here,' Justin muttered, as he and Miranda stopped for a cigarette in its dark angular shadow. 'Someone's bound to spot us. They can hardly miss us, can they, dressed like this?' He plucked at the lime-green track suits he and Miranda were wearing, and pointed to the words 'Clean-o-Serve' emblazoned on his chest. 'I always thought big-time crime was supposed to be glamorous. I feel like one of them geezers who unblock the drains.'

Miranda patted her grey, curly wig, and sighed impatiently. 'This isn't a fancy dress party. "Clean-o-Serve" happen to have the cleaning contract here, so wearing their uniform is about the best way to look inconspicuous, as I've told you before. Now do stop complaining, Justin. Don't be so jumpy. You've got stage fright, that's the trouble.'

'I haven't!' His eyes blazed at her above a burst of smoke which poured from his nostrils. 'I'm just . . . well, concerned. I mean, what if you-know-who turns up while we're taking care of the business?'

'Look, I've told you a million times, it's only seven-thirty in the morning, and Jack never gets into the office until ten. He's never early, just always punctual. I should know – I lived with him for nineteen years.'

Justin nodded, but he seemed doubtful. Feeling guilty, Miranda removed the pebble glasses which were part of her disguise and looked at him with a heavy heart. Just what had she got him into by agreeing to let him take part in this crime? In the past twenty-four hours, he'd lost all his ebullience. His head hung low, and his massive shoulders were bowed with resignation. He had all the cockiness of a convicted killer awaiting his fate on Death Row.

'I know what the trouble with you is.'

He flicked the half-smoked cigarette stub into the gutter. 'What?'

'You don't want to go through with it.'

His trainer-clad foot kicked at the pavement. 'Who says?'

'Look, if you've changed your mind, no one's going to force you. It's not too late to call the whole thing off.'

'Come off it!' His eyes widened. 'Les and Ed have flown to Switzerland because of what I said I could do! They already think all I'm good for is flogging disco-biscuits down the clubs, Mrs G. This is my one chance to prove myself! If I back out now, I'm finished before I've started. Know what I mean?' His chin jutted towards her in a defiant gesture. 'You think I'm scared, don't you?'

She sighed. 'Look, you don't have to pretend to be *macho* with me.'

'I don't *have* to pretend, man! It's just that . . . Well, this is my first crime, right? I just want to get on with it.'

The bottles of cleaning fluid in his bucket rattled loudly as the two of them pushed through the revolving doors into the lobby. To Miranda's relief, the security guard on the reception desk nodded them through without a second glance. As they trudged down the corridor where Sellotaped notices fluttered like Buddhist prayer flags from the walls, a feeling of depression descended on her. She began to wish she hadn't insisted that they use Jack's office for their first computer fraud – hacking into the university's deposit account and transferring the money to a secret account in Switzerland. Did she really want the finger of blame to point at Jack when the theft was discovered? Just why was she so set on revenge?

In silence, she led Justin up the concrete staircase. If only Ed had come with them, she might feel more confident. It was just like him to insist she was able enough to pull the job off without him beside her. 'I got to keep an eye on Les in Cuckoo-clock Land,' he had said just before he'd left for the airport. 'We don't want him scarpering off with the dosh. Besides, I know you can do it, babe. And just think how proud of yourself you'll feel when you get home.'

With a heavy heart, Miranda pushed through the swing doors on the third floor and entered the Psychology Department. Under the nameplate on Jack's door, someone had scrawled 'This is a Jung-Free Zone'. Posting Justin between the lift and the staircase to keep watch, Miranda pulled on her rubber cleaning gloves, picked Jack's lock with a piece of plastic and went inside.

A hollow pit opened up inside her when she saw the framed photograph of Jack and the children. Unable to stop herself, she picked it up, and kissed the children's faces. There stood Diana, dark hair blowing across her hollow face, shielding her eyes from the sun. David, impassive behind dark glasses, his pressed-together lips giving nothing away. Lily, looking like a model with her flaxen hair pulled back in a side pony-tail, a confident smile on her pouting lips and a bare, sun-tanned arm slung protectively around Thomas, whose sad eyes belied the happiness of his smiling mouth. Behind them all stood Jack, his eyes screwed up in the sunlight, his small mouth smiling smugly, as if he were saying to her, *They're not yours any more, they're mine*.

A pain – it felt like severe heartburn – stabbed through her chest. When and where had this new photograph been taken? And who had taken it? Suddenly she wanted nothing more than to go home and see her children again. But she couldn't go home, however much she wanted to. She'd travelled much too far to turn back.

'Ok, let's get on with it,' Miranda said abruptly, putting the photograph down. 'Gloves, Justin!' she snapped as he reached out to turn on Jack's computer. 'Unless you want to leave your fingerprints all over the keys.' Impatient to get it over and done with, she watched him wriggle his hands into the thin rubber sheaths. 'How long is it going to take you to do this? This place is giving me the creeps.'

He bent over the keys, and mumbled something about it not being that easy.

'But you can do it, can't you?'

'Course. I think so.'

'But you said . . .'

'Yeah, I know what I said! Give me a break, Mrs G, and stop going on at me! I need to concentrate. There's a long way to go. It's a big world out there in Cyberspace. We'll have to wait till Les and Ed do the pick-up from the Swiss account to know if it really works.' Turning away from her, he began to tap into the system.

Miranda watched the screen closely. 'GREENJAC.@edu. balls,' she read. 'What does that mean?'

Justin glanced up angrily. 'I wish you wouldn't hang over my shoulder. You're making me nervous. Blast! I've got to go to the loo again.'

'Oh, for God's sake!'

'Sorry. It's my stomach. I can't help it. I'll be back in a jiffy. I saw one just down the corridor when we was coming in.' Opening the door, he went outside, but a split second later he was back, a look of pure panic on his face. 'Jack!' he hissed.

'What? Where?' He jerked his head towards the corridor. 'But it can't be! It's not even eight o'clock yet. He never comes in this early!'

'Well, he has today!'

'Shit!'

His eyes were at once terrified and helpless. 'What're we going to do, Mrs G?'

Miranda looked round for a hiding place or an escape route, but there was nothing. Desperate not to be seen, she grabbed Justin's hand and yanked him into the dark shadow behind the open door.

A moment later, Jack swept into the room, throwing his raincoat over a chair, and hurling his briefcase onto the floor a few inches away from where they were hiding. He sank down on his chair, face to face with the glowing computer screen. For a moment, he stared at it blankly, then, pushing the keyboard to one side, he covered his face with his hands. 'Shit!' he said.

With a deep sigh, he lifted the telephone receiver and dialled. 'Mary?' he said when the other person answered. 'We've got to talk. I . . .' His decisive words were immediately cut short as a vicious voice poured out of the earpiece. 'Mary, will you . . . Will you . . . Will you . . . No, hold on a minute, love, that's not what I said at all! You're twisting it completely. What I said was, if the relationship wasn't working *for you* . . .' Cupping his hand over the receiver, he muttered an expletive under his breath. 'Of course I don't want to end it – darling,' he carried on a moment later. 'No, I never said that. I never said . . . *Will you listen*? I never . . . No, I did *not* say I wanted you to move out. You . . . Of course we couldn't manage without you! Yes, I know that . . . It's just that . . . Why are you being so bloody unreasonable? Oh yes, you are! Can't you get it through your skull that I *was* at a lecture last night? Look, I can't sit in front of the television with you all the time. I need stimulation . . . No, I'm not talking about that kind . . . For Christ's sake, I'm *not* lying! I never lie. What? How dare you! I did *not* lie to Miranda! I may not have told her everything but . . . Well, it'd have made her unhappy to have known! You can hardly compare that to . . . Mary, Mary! You don't seem to understand that truth is not an absolute!'

There was a loud click as Mary hung up on him. Seething, Jack slammed down the phone and tore at his thumbnail with his short, terrier-like teeth.

From just outside the door came the sound of someone clearing their throat.

'Dr Green? Dr Green?'

Widening his eyes at Miranda, Justin mouthed the word, *Help*!

'Sorry,' the woman's lilting voice continued. 'Am I disturbing you?'

'What?' Miranda shrunk into the shadow as Jack's eyes focused on the doorway. 'No. Sorry, I . . . I was miles away. Looking over some, er, some notes for this morning's lecture.' His small mouth stretched into the kind of cool but interested smile which Miranda remembered from the distant past. 'It's, er, Gwen, isn't it?'

'That's right. Well, almost. I'm Gwyneth. Gwyneth Barton. First year, Psychology. Look, shall I come back later when you're not so pressed?'

'No, no! Come in.'

'Are you sure? I know it's very early. But . . .'

'Please.'

A pretty, porcelain-faced doll – she looked barely older than Lily – stepped nervously into the room, running her tiny hands through her mop of black curls. Through the crack in the door, Miranda caught a glimpse of a pair of sturdy thighs encased in tight brown leggings, and a black clinging jumper which outlined two high, round voluptuous breasts.

Jack had clearly seen them, too, because his face suddenly lit up with an interested, welcoming expression. 'Please, make yourself comfortable. Draw up a pew.'

'Thanks.'

Dragging her feet, the young woman came in, sat down on the moulded plastic chair near Jack's, crossed her legs tightly and folded her hands in her lap. Clearing his throat, Jack turned his chair towards hers, and, like a lepidopterist

190

spearing a butterfly, fixed her with his small, dark eyes. 'So, what can I do for you, Gwyneth?'

'It's about my last essay, Dr Green.'

He raised his hands in protest. 'Jack, please!'

'OK, Jack. You've probably forgotten. It was on the social effects of housing policy during the last Labour government.'

'Oh . . . yes.' Picking up a pencil, he tapped it gently on the desk-top. 'Of course I remember! It was very interesting work, Gwyneth.'

There was a pause. 'You gave it a D minus.'

The tip of the pencil snapped off and shot across the desk. 'Interesting,' Jack repeated. 'But, I'm afraid, essentially flawed.'

There was another pause. 'How?'

'What?'

'I wondered if you could explain how it was flawed. You only wrote, "Not up to the required standard" on the bottom.'

'Did I? Yes, well . . .' Crossing his legs, he leaned back and adjusted his glasses. 'I'd need to have another look at it first.'

'Only, you see, I find it curious that you gave it such a low mark.'

'Ah-ha! You're questioning my academic judgement?'

'No. More your . . .' Lowering her head, she mumbled something.

'My . . . ?'

'Your memory. You see, the gist of my argument came from an academic paper published last year in *Social Psychology Today*.'

'Yes? Whose paper was that?'

'Actually it was yours.' She paused. Jack's face froze. 'So you see, that being the case, I just can't understand why you gave me such a low mark. Naturally, you must agree with your own argument so . . .' She cleared her throat. 'I can only assume something else was at stake.'

A muscle began to pulse in Jack's neck. Leaning back, he

clasped his knees. 'Something else?' he threw back at her.

'I wondered if it . . . if it had anything to do with the fact that I'm . . . that I'm a woman.'

'Now Gwyneth, really!'

'Or . . . Or . . .'

He leaned forward, genuinely curious. 'Yes?'

'That I'm Welsh.'

'Welsh,' he repeated. He nodded slowly, tried in vain to supress a smile. 'Let me get this clear – you're accusing me of bias in my marking. No, let's be more accurate, of sexual and/or racial prejudice. Political incorrectness, as it were. You're saying that I'm Welshist. I mean, an anti-Welshist. A Welshophobe. A . . . a . . . a . . . how shall I put it? – an Anti-Celt.'

'I'm not accusing you of anything. I only said, I *wondered*.' She continued staring at him while a strange, rasping noise, like the sound of sandpaper on wood, began in the back of his throat. 'You're laughing at me. Does this mean you consider racial prejudice a laughing matter?'

The laugh stopped abruptly. 'No, no! Not at all! Miss – Ms Barton – Gwyneth . . .' Just then, the telephone rang, so he snatched up the receiver gratefully and pressed it to his ear. 'Dr Green here . . .' Scowling, he turned away from the student. 'No . . . No, *no*. I can't. Not now. Because. *Because*. *Yes*, I have someone with me. Well, I am at work. That's right. No. No, it's not . . . I shall have to call you back on that one. Look, *I said* I shall . . .'

Click.

Jack replaced the receiver in slow motion, then drew a deep breath and stared into space. After a few minutes, Gwyneth Barton leaned forward and tapped him on the shoulder. 'Look here, are you all right? Is anything the matter?'

'No . . . I . . .' He turned towards her, looking tired and haggard. 'I'm sorry,' he said in a broken voice. 'I . . . I can't cope with this now. You see . . . .'

Miranda watched a single dewdrop tear trickle pitifully

down his cheek. She knew that tear well. She had seen it herself, and fallen for it, many times before, as Jack sought an easy way of extricating himself from difficult situations by turning the guilt tables on her. Now she wondered why she had been taken in by it for so long.

'I'm sorry. It's just that . . .' He smiled a watery smile. 'No, no, you haven't come here to listen to my problems. Carry on with what you were saying.'

'Oh, please!'

'Well, if you insist. You see, things have been rather difficult . . . personally speaking . . . since my wife . . . my wife . . .'

'Yes?'

'I thought one of the second years might have told you. She was . . .' He cleared his throat. 'Kidnapped. Murdered. Towards the end of last term.'

'Oh!'

'Yes. Well . . .' He spread his hands in resignation. 'One must struggle on, despite the grief. It's hardest, of course, for the children. One does one's best to do everything for them, of course, but being a single parent to four children . . . *having to do everything myself* . . . now I'm *on my own*. Well, the situation is . . . But enough of my problems. Let's get back to that essay of yours.'

'Oh, no! I couldn't possibly . . . I mean, it's trivial compared to . . . Murdered, you say?'

He nodded mournfully. 'You probably read about it in the papers. She . . . Look, I say, do you fancy a drink?'

'But it's only breakfast time! The bar won't be open for hours!'

'Yes of course! I meant, coffee. In the canteen. Tell you what, I'll treat you to their special fry-up!'

'No, I couldn't possibly let . . .'

'Please. It'll be my pleasure. I know how hard up you students are. You know, I've been keeping it all bottled up for so long, I can't tell you what a relief it'll be to talk to someone sympathetic about it – Gwyneth.'

'Oh, of course, Dr Green!'

'Do you know,' Justin said, letting out his breath when they'd gone, 'In all these years, I never knew that old Jack was a doctor.'

Miranda scowled. 'The bastard's got a PhD – in bullshit. Now, we'd better hurry and get this money transfer over with before he comes back. And don't let me forget – there's something else I want you to look up on the computer. Personnel files. Student addresses.'

Jack seemed to be having much too good a time for Miranda's liking. And she had just had a brilliant idea.

Thirteen

'Yes, that's right, £2,000. Half now, and half on completion. No, no, I'll get it to you, you don't have to worry. What? No, there's no need for you to know who I am. Let's just say that I'm someone who's suffered from the same kind of . . . how shall I put it? . . . oppression, as you have. Frankly, the whole thing's a cinch. But, once you've started, you've got to carry it through without giving the game away. OK? Think you can do that? Great!'

Miranda turned off her mobile phone, and threw it down on the duvet. As she passed the mirror in the hallway, she stopped to look at herself and tried to wipe the smile off her face. It was no good. The moment she entered the kitchen, Ed knew she'd been up to something.

'Who was that?' he said, without looking up from chopping the shallots.

'Who was what?' she murmured, slipping her arms around him from behind.

His knife battered down on the chopping board. 'The geezer on the blower.'

She rested her cheek against his back. 'No one. I mean, no one much. A student of Jack's, actually. I'm fixing up a little surprise for him.'

He swung round, and looked at her curiously. 'Well, I hope you're being careful.'

Miranda laughed. 'You sound like me, talking to the children.'

His face creased into a frown. 'I'm being serious, love. You don't want to land yourself in a trap. What sort of surprise, eh?' Miranda was silent. He shook her gently by the shoulders. 'I'm waiting for an answer.'

'Really, it's nothing much.'

Dissatisfied with this brush-off, he pulled her towards him and nuzzled the base of her throat. 'You know, I'm worried about you, angel,' he murmured between kisses. 'Since that business in Jack's office, you haven't been the same.'

'Of course I have,' she lied. Then, drawn inexorably to the truth, she couldn't help adding, 'What do you mean?'

'I don't know. You're acting funny. Different. Distant.' She tried to push him away, but he held on to her tightly. 'What's the matter? D'you want to go back to him?'

Miranda attempted to laugh. 'Don't be ridiculous!'

'So what is it? Are you sorry about all this? About getting tied up with me?'

'No! It's just that . . .' She stopped, unable to express her feelings about Jack, even to herself. Why should seeing Jack have upset her so deeply when she was in love with this handsome, thoughtful man and life was so exciting? Why did she feel so . . . yes, so horribly jealous at the thought of Jack having a life of his own?

Tenderly, Ed ran his fingers lightly down her face. 'Want to know something, Miranda? I've had enough of this game. Let's cut our losses and get out now, while we still can.'

She looked at him in astonishment. 'But why, darling? We've been doing so well since we've been working with Les! My God, we must have pulled off ten jobs in the last couple of months. Just think of what we've earned!'

'Yeah, but . . .' He shrugged. 'We're pushing it, babe. Pulling off too many jobs, too soon, in too small an area. Taking too many risks. The bulls are going to get suspicious if we carry on like this. After all, they're not *that* stupid. And another thing – I don't like working with Pete and Les. I don't trust them – Les in particular. Yeah, I know you like him, but I know him better than you do. He's

196

all sweetness and light and smiles at the moment, but, believe me, it doesn't take much to push him over the edge. Besides, he's around too much – you and I aren't hardly ever alone any more.'

He kissed her again, more deeply. 'Look, I never had what you'd call a normal life before, Miranda. I suppose I never wanted one. But now . . .' Cupping her chin, he stared down at her, and she felt herself drowning in the swimming pools of his eyes. 'I want to *be* with you. I don't want the only time I get to see you to be when we rub shoulders in the dock. I don't want to spend the next fifteen years of my life doing bird. I want a normal life. An ordinary life. A good life.'

'But we do have a good life,' she protested weakly.

'Call this good? Robbing, thieving, living from day to day? Mixing with scum? Haven't you had enough of it yet?' When Miranda failed to answer, he kissed her again. 'You know, you and me could even have a kid together.'

Miranda's heart skipped a beat. She thought of the photograph of her children in Jack's office, and tried hard to smile. 'Darling, I'm too old. I'm nearly forty-one.'

'That's not old! Women of your age have kids all the time. You only got to read the papers.'

'Yes, but . . .' She was almost speechless. How could Ed suggest such a thing when he knew how she had just abandoned four innocent children? The knot of guilt buried deep inside her swelled and twisted in her gut. 'I . . . I like things how they are. Just you and me. Having a baby, well . . . I don't know, it'd change things. You had a child once before. You know what it's like. It's a big commitment.'

He let go of her abruptly. 'So what are you saying? That you're not going to stick around long? That you're going to piss off like Val did?'

'No. It's not that.'

'Then what? Don't you love me?'

'Of course I do.'

'So what's the problem?'

Like everything in life, it was all so simple to him. She

turned away, unable to put her feelings into words.

'Kids are such a tie, darling. You've no idea how much time they take . . .'

'Time's the one thing we've got.' He sounded testy. 'What else are we going to do for the rest of our lives?'

'You simply can't imagine how much work they are. The cleaning, and washing, and ironing and the endless boring old cooking . . .'

'I can cook, can't I? Didn't I do you a lovely dinner last night?'

'Wonderful. But you try getting a picky five-year-old to eat *foie gras en croute*.'

Refusing to be put off, he pulled her fiercely back towards him. 'I love you, Miranda,' he murmured. 'I never felt like this about anyone before. Let's get out of this business now. While we're on top. Before we get so tied up with Les that we can't get out of it. Before we burn up every penny we've got. Remember what I promised you before we done that first job – that I'd go straight? Well, we got enough stacked away now to last us if we're careful. We could get on a plane tomorrow and be out of here.'

What about my children? she thought bitterly. She should have felt excited at the prospect of life abroad with him, but instead she felt depressed. 'Where would we go?'

'Spain. Rio. Mexico. Paraguay. Anywhere in the world you want to. As long as we're together. That's what matters, isn't it? We'll buy a little house somewhere. Tell you what, I'll start a business!'

'Oh, yes?' She laughed. 'What kind of business?'

'I'm telling you, I'll start a legit business. We'll have a normal life. We'll do normal things, like normal people do – go to the supermarket, take up DIY, have babies and argue over what to watch on TV. Well? How about it?'

She knew what it was costing him to make this offer. So how could she say, without sounding cynical, *Thanks, but I've been there before, I've done all that*? His stubbly

198

cheeks grazed the side of her neck, sending a shiver of desire through her, but for once, she resisted it.

'I'm sorry, it's not what I want,' she said, pulling away.

'What *do* you want, then?' Grabbing hold of her arm, he spun her around to face him. Beneath the anger in his eyes she saw a deeper hurt. 'To carry on like we are, thieving and robbing with toe-rags like Les until we push things that bit too far and get nailed? To live the rest of your life on the run?'

'I don't know, Ed. Please, stop going on at me! I just don't know!'

His face pale and pinched, he glared at her for a moment. 'Well, let me know when you've made up your mind.'

Then, grabbing his jacket and cigarettes, he left the room. A moment later, she heard the front door slam.

Looking like one of Mary's gnomes, dressed by Armani, Les perched on the back seat of the white stretch Cadillac and filled two cut-glass flutes with champagne. One he handed to Miranda, the other he raised himself. 'Cheers, gorgeous!'

Their glasses clinked. Sinking back into the soft white leather beside him, Miranda sipped the fizzing liquid and stared out blankly at Belgravia's broad, white wedding-cake streets. After lunching at San Lorenzo's – each of the four courses accompanied by an appropriate vintage wine – the last thing she needed was another drink. Still, with Ed having stayed out all night and not yet come home, Miranda could think of no good reason to remain remotely sober.

'OK, come clean, gorgeous.'

She looked up sharply. 'What are you talking about?'

Les raised the thick semicircles of his eyebrows. 'We done all the small talk over the Parma ham. It's not every day you get on the blower and ask me out for lunch. I figured it wasn't for nothing. That something must be up. That's why I got this charabanc for the afternoon. Thought you might need cheering up.'

'That was sweet of you.' She stretched her long legs out

along the thick, pink shag-pile carpet. 'Well, I have cheered up.'

'Seems like it.' He plucked a chocolate bar from the stack on the walnut-veneered windowsill and tossed it into her lap. 'Here, have a Kit-Kat.' Taking out his platinum lighter, he lit up a short, fat Havana cigar. 'Got problems with the man? Oh, don't worry about Pete,' he said, when she glanced at the back of the driver on the other side of the glass partition. 'This thing's soundproof. You got to talk to him through here.' His pudgy fingers flicked a switch on a small, gold-plated microphone. 'Just drive around, will you, mate?' Pete nodded discreetly without looking round. Les flicked off the switch. 'I happen to know that lover boy spent all last night playing Blackjack at the Victoria Club.'

'Oh!'

'Don't look so surprised, gorgeous. Didn't you know he can't resist a flutter? Oh yes, our Ed's a real chip off the old block – up to and including carrying on when he ought to stop. Losing must run in the family. So, had a lover's tiff, have you? Has he been treating you bad?'

'Not at all.' She paused, torn between her desire to confide in someone and loyalty to Ed. 'Have you ever been married, Les?' she asked eventually.

'Sure.' The word was like a shrug. 'I tried it once or twice. Maybe it was three times. Somehow I never got on with it. Maybe I always picked the wrong girls.'

'What were they like?'

'What do you think? Blonde and beautiful.' The cigar waved near her face as he traced an exaggerated hour-glass with his stubby fingers. 'Don't ask me what went wrong. In the good times it was spend, spend, spend, and we had a good laugh together. In the bad times . . . who knows? Maybe I didn't always treat them proper. Maybe I was away too much. And maybe I was too hard on them when they got out of order. The thing about women is, they can never get it through their thick skulls that business comes first. If you've got to work, you've got to work. Understand me?' He sighed. 'They all pissed off in the end. The last one – Rita – did a bunk while I was doing a stretch for GBH. She ran off with the bastard who grassed on me. Now they're living it up in fucking Acapulco. Only thing that stops me going after them is, I hate Mexican food.'

Miranda smiled. 'Are you seeing anyone at the moment?'

'There's a couple of small fish for when I fancy a nibble.' He turned towards her. 'I'm waiting for the big fry.' Without taking his eyes from hers, he reached for her hand and lifted it to his lips. His meaning was unmistakable. A hot flush crept up her neck.

'No, Les. Please.'

He kissed her hand again. Ugly as he was, a sharp tingle of desire passed down her spine. 'Haven't you had enough of that has-been yet?'

'Don't say that.'

'Look, I've got nothing against Ed. He's a nice enough bloke. But for a woman like you? Pah! You're wasting your time with him, gorgeous. Running to stand still.'

His words rang a chord in her. Even framing the question in her mind made her feel disloyal. Still, she asked it: 'What do you mean?'

He shrugged. 'He's a small man, Miranda. A small man, with no ambition. Understand? He won't ever amount to anything, or go anywhere. Why, he won't even leave his Mum and Dad's old house in that piddling little street, full of those piddling little trinkets and souvenirs!'

'But he does want to get out. Now,' she said quietly.

'What, and leave the business? With *you*?' A laugh burst from his lips. 'No bloody way!'

'What's so funny?'

'Forget it! Take it from me – Ed's got more chance of going straight than you have.'

Both his words and his tone shocked her. 'That's ridiculous! Why?'

He waved his cigar emphatically. 'Because, gorgeous, trapped in that respectable middle-class body all your life

201

was a crook's brain, and you only just discovered it. You was born for ducking and diving! You're not going to give it up now! Blimey, you only just started! Believe me, you'll be picking the undertaker's pocket on the way to your funeral.' When she started to protest, he interrupted her immediately. 'And I'll tell you why, gorgeous – you're already addicted. Crime's a drug, see, like coke, or horse. Once you done it once, you want to do it again. And again. And again. Only every time you go a little bit further, take a little bit more. It gets in your blood. Like sex, only better, because it's more dangerous. It makes AIDS look like a dose of the runs.'

She digested this in a stunned silence while he relit his cigar.

'Look, we all got fantasies about getting out. Even I kid myself I'm not going to be on the pavement for ever. I'll tell you something. I never told anyone this before. There's this hotel in the south of France, outside Cannes. Very exclusive. Big white building, marble bathrooms, pine trees, gravel drive, perched on the rocks, overlooking the sea. Beautiful joint. I stayed there on my second honeymoon – or maybe it was the third. Me, the wife, her sister and brother-in-law, her Mum and Dad, the lot. Did we have a ball! If I tell you, we made such a racket that they threw us out before we could scarper without paying the bill!' He grinned. 'Well, I swore that one day I'd get out of this business and buy that place. At times, I still dream about it. But it's a dream. I know now I'm never going to get out. See what I mean?'

Not wanting to hear him, she stared out of the window.

'Want to know what you and I like about this business?' he went on relentlessly. 'It's a joke. A big fucking joke. It's as simple as that. There's the money, of course. But there's got to be something else in it, see? It's got to be a laugh. If it was just for the money, you might as well work in a fucking bank.'

They stopped at some traffic lights. A neat crocodile of schoolboys in corduroy plus-fours straggled across the road in front of them. One had a shock of red hair, just like Thomas's. Miranda's heart lurched. For a moment, she was aware how far off-track her life had skidded.

'I'm telling you, gorgeous. The joy of this business is you can get away with anything. Anything. *If.*'

She turned towards him. The full force of his energy hit her like a wave.

'*If* you do it in the right spirit. You only need one thing to succeed.'

'What's that?'

He spread his hands. 'Bottle! Understand me? Bottle! And you've got it, babe. If you've got bottle, you can get away with anything.' As the car cruised down Knightsbridge, he pointed out of the car windows at the exclusive boutiques. 'The world's your oyster. Anything and everything in it belongs to you.' When she laughed, he grinned back, 'Go on – test me! Try me out. Name me something, anything, and I'll get it for you. Right now. This minute. Anything you like.' Like an overgrown child, he bobbed up and down on the edge of the seat. 'Here, Pete, pull over,' he said, suddenly grabbing the microphone. When the Cadillac stopped, he opened the electric window and pointed out. 'See that?' he said.

She looked at the huge red-brick building on the other side of the road. 'What, Harrods?'

'That's right. Harrods. The greatest department store in the whole fucking world. They sell everything you can think of, right? So what do you want? A pair of shoes? A four-poster bed? A pound of apples? Ruby bracelet? A box of chocolates? The deeds of a house? Name it and it's yours!'

She laughed again. 'I can't think of anything!'

'Sure you can. How about a set of encyclopaedias? A canteen of silver cutlery? Another Rolex to add to your collection? A pearl necklace? A three-piece suite? How about a microwave?'

'Look, I . . .'

'I said, name it!' She caught her breath at the edge of barely-suppressed anger in his voice. 'What's it to be?'

'Well, I . . . I don't know. Anything . . .' She glanced out of the window at the passers by. 'A . . . OK, a coat!'

'A coat? That's too fucking easy. How about a fur coat?'

'But I've never owned a fur. It's cruel.'

'What's cruel about a dead animal? Are you telling me Ed hasn't bought you a fur coat yet? Now, that's what I call cruelty! OK, that's settled it! Now we're getting somewhere. What sort of fur?'

'Look, I really don't . . .'

'Chinchilla? Fox? Beaver? Mink? Yeah, mink'd look nice on you. What colour shall I get you? White? Blonde? Black? Pink? Brown? Hurry up, or we'll get clamped while you sit here making up your mind.'

She sighed, defeated. 'OK. Cream. A cream mink coat.'

'Size?'

'Twelve.'

'Good, we're in business! Now comes the fun part. How shall I steal it?'

'What?'

His lighter flame leapt as he re-lit his cigar. 'Any mug can walk into Harrods and walk out with a mink. You want to make hoisting *fun*. You want to turn an everyday, run-of-the-mill transaction into something out of the ordinary. A work of art. So name your method.'

'I don't understand.'

He bobbed up and down impatiently. 'How do you want me to nick it, Miranda? On my hands and knees? Blind-folded? Armed or unarmed? Walking backwards? Singing? Come on, think!'

Nerves – or was it excitement – stirred inside her. Again she looked out of the window, searching for inspiration. 'On wheels,' she said impulsively.

'Wheels? I like it. Mink coat, cream, size twelve, on wheels. Now you're talking! What wheels? Bike? Kid's trike? Car? Rollerblades?'

'A motorbike.' Anticipating his next question, she quickly added, 'A Harley-Davidson.'

He slapped his knees. 'Didn't I tell you you were born for this game? OK! Pete?' He switched on the microphone again. 'I'm getting out mate.'

'Sure, boss.'

'Pick me up on the corner of Cadogan Square in . . .' Pushing up his sleeve, he glanced at the heavy gold watch strapped to his plump, hairless wrist. 'twenty minutes. Three forty-seven. Got that?'

As Les climbed out of the car, Miranda touched him lightly on the shoulder. 'Good luck.'

He grinned. 'You don't have to wish me good luck, gorgeous – you're coming with me.'

Tight as handcuffs, his fingers encircled her wrist as he pulled her out of the car and into the road. Still holding her, he raised his free hand, and, with a thumbs up sign, stopped the lanes of fast traffic so that they could cross over. As the cars screeched to a halt in front of them, Miranda felt the sickening, thrilling, delirious terror of being totally out of control.

Round the corner, in Hans Crescent, he stopped by a motorbike stand. 'That's what I call convenient! What've we got here? A Suzuki. A BMW. A Kawasaki.'

'There's no Harley.' Try as she might, Miranda could not suppress the note of relief in her voice.

Les raised his eyebrows. 'You're a reasonable woman. The BMW will do, won't it?'

With a quick glance over his shoulder, he went over to the bike, and, taking a small penknife from his pocket, casually prised open the fibreglass container on the back. None of the scores of passersby took the slightest bit of notice.

'Incredible!' he exclaimed, openly rifling the contents. 'Two helmets. With visors, no less!' He held one out to her. 'Safety first. And what's this down here! Oh-ho! A spare key? Someone's been a silly boy, haven't they? And more . . . Gloves? Save me leaving my dabs all over the place. Don't you touch anything. Hear me? Just cling on to my waist.'

He settled in the saddle, his short legs dangling a foot above the ground. Miranda pulled the visor low over her face and climbed on behind him, her tight leather skirt riding high up her thighs.

'Now,' he mumbled through the helmet. 'How the bleeding hell do you get one of these things started?'

'Don't you know?'

'Haven't got a clue. Never driven one.' His foot stretched towards the ground with difficulty, then he kicked out at one of the pedals a couple of times. At first there was nothing. Then, without warning, the massive machine between Miranda's legs throbbed into life. 'Here we go! Whoa-hey!'

He sounded like a child on a funfair ride. With a precarious wobble, the bike lurched into the street. A car screeched to a halt behind them as, without warning, they shot across the road.

'Watch where you're fucking going, mate!' Les jeered.

More terrified of being killed in an accident than caught by the police, Miranda shouted in his ear, 'Pull over. This is suicidal!'

Les turned around, raised his visor and grinned at her. 'Yeah, but think about it, gorgeous – what a way to go!'

By the time they'd circled the back of the store, he'd just about got the hang of the controls. Then, suddenly mounting the pavement, he shot towards the glass entrance doors of the store. Crouched behind his shoulders, Miranda screwed her eyes shut.

'Excuse me, love! Mind out, madam!'

The tourists crowding through the glass doors threw themselves out of the way. There was a loud thump and the bike shuddered. When Miranda opened her eyes again, they were inside Harrods sailing between two astounded security guards.

'Hey! You can't do that!'

'Who says?'

Gasping and shrieking, people scattered in front of them. 'Shades, anyone?' Les shouted cheerfully over his shoulder, as they cruised past the sunglasses display. 'No? What's this coming up?' He slowed down to read the sign over a small archway. 'Room of Luxury? Now, that sounds just up my street.'

Steering the bike in a wide zig zag through the yelping customers, he drove on across the thick carpet, then slammed on the brakes by a display of Louis Vuitton luggage. 'Grab that little black bag for me, will you, gorgeous? I've been looking for something just like that.'

As she turned to pick it up, she saw the security guards closing up on them. 'Move!' With a jolt, the bike shot forward into the Egyptian Hall, and crashed straight into a pile of huge ceramic pots. The next moment it crunched forward over the broken china and into the Food Hall, where Les pulled up beside a glass cabinet of Belgian chocolates and, leaning over the counter, helped himself to a handful of marzipan strawberries.

'Here!' he said, popping one under Miranda's visor and into her mouth.

'OK! Stay right where you are!' shouted one of four security guards who suddenly closed in on them.

'What's all the fuss about?' Les shouted through his helmet. 'I'm just doing my shopping! I'm an account customer!' Then, with a cry of 'Out of my way, toe-rags!' he accelerated between their outstretched arms, drove through the glittering black and glass cavern of the Perfume Hall and cruised towards the lifts.

'Going up!' As the brass gates slid shut on the huge bike, two middle-aged tourists in green loden coats and Tyrolean hats, flattened themselves against the side wall.

'Morning, madam. Morning, sir,' Les said cheerfully. 'You speaka di English? Yes? This Buckingham Palace, yes?' Terrified, they shook their heads. 'No? What? You mean, this not Buckingham Palace? Gorgeous, did you hear that?'

Laughing, she tapped him on the shoulder as the lift gates opened. 'Look, drive, will you? It's the first floor – Ladies Clothing. We're there.'

Hopping on one foot, he backed the bike out of the lift, straight into a pair of plaster mannequins in evening dress. 'Sorry girls!' he said as they toppled over, arms and legs splintering apart. 'Now for that mink!'

In the centre of a large, low room full of designer clothes, two young assistants were hanging dresses on a stand. As Les roared to a halt beside them, they looked up with extraordinary sang-froid.

'Sorry to bother you,' he said in a mock-posh voice. 'But can you beautiful young ladies direct us to the fur department? My wife wishes to purchase a mink coat.'

Without batting an eyelid, they glanced at each other. 'I'm sorry, sir, we don't have a fur department,' said one of them calmly.

'WHAT? You're having me on!'

She shook her head. 'The Fur Salon closed ages ago. It was a policy decision.'

'You've got to be joking!'

'So, if you're from the Animal Liberation Front, you're a good five years too late.'

'No, I'm not from the fucking Animal Liberation Front!' His eyes blazing, he swung round and glared at Miranda. 'Would you believe it? A place like this, held to ransom by a bunch of raving lefty loonies!'

Remembering her own days of handing out anti-fur leaflets from a Friends of the Earth stand in Kentish Town Road, Miranda bit her lip. Now was definitely not the time to mention it.

'Fucking incredible!' With the entire department now watching them in a stunned silence, they sped off towards Lingerie, then swung left into something called the Circle Café.

'Fancy a bite?' Miranda said as the diners scattered before them, knocking over chairs and up-turning tables.

But Les was inconsolable. 'I don't like it,' he yelled as, grabbing a large Danish pastry from someone's plate and cramming it in his mouth, he swung right out of another doorway, into yet another department full of clothes.

'But I didn't even want a fur coat!' Miranda shouted over the roar of the engine. 'Honestly! I'd much rather have something else.'

'Oh-ho! Look at this bunch of wallies!'

Shoulder to shoulder, ten security men were advancing towards them. With a thunderous rattle, metal shutters slammed down over the department doors, trapping them in the room.

'Whoa-hey!' Circling the bike between the racks of clothing, Les whooped with delight.

'Quick!' Miranda laughed. 'Over there!'

He swung the bike round in a figure of eight and, revving the engine, shot towards the wide, carpeted staircase in the corner.

'See that?' Les pointed to a sign painted on the wall. '"Second Floor: Homewares. Travel Goods. Pets". *Pets*! If you can't have a dead fur, you might as well have a live one. What do you say?'

The bike juddered precariously as, accelerating at full speed, they forced it up the stairs, with the security men hard on their heels. As they lurched over the top, almost out of control, the front wheel hit a large round table upon which stood a high stack of Wedgewood cups and saucers. For a moment, the pyramid wobbled. Then, with an enormous crash, it collapsed in on itself like a house of cards.

'Whoa-hey!' yelled Les. Circling the bike round, he headed straight for a long display stand covered with dinner plates. 'Whoa-hey!' With a loud thump, the front wheel hit the stand. The legs gave way, and the plates fell down, smashing with a thunderous noise.

'Whoa-hey!'

Hotly pursued by the guards, they shot through a doorway marked Crystal and Glass. Miranda felt a rush of utter naughtiness flood through her veins. Grabbing a brass candlestick from a table display, she held it out at arm's length as Les drove through the department. Vases, champagne flutes and punch-bowls disintegrated behind her in a shower of diamond sparks.

Books, Kitchenware, Electrical goods. Somewhere along the way, they picked up a stainless steel egg whisk for Ed and lost the security guards. Now, suddenly the air was filled with the chirping of birds. Slowing down, Les turned the bike into the glass-walled partition of the Pet department. Startled by the noise, a white angora rabbit scurried to the back of its cage.

Clambering off the bike, Miranda walked around, looking in the cages. 'Oh, look! What an adorable little King Charles spaniel puppy!'

'Like it? It's yours!' Leaning the bike against the central aviary, Les leapt over the barrier with surprising agility and, taking a steel comb from his inside pocket, forced the padlock of the cage. Grabbing the yelping puppy, he handed it to Miranda. 'Now, let's clear out!'

'Hey!' Clad in green overalls, a young male assistant came running towards them. 'You can't take that dog!'

'Why not?'

'B . . . but you haven't paid for it!'

Les winked at him. 'Put it on the account.'

'But all animal purchasers have to be vetted!' he wailed as they drove away with the puppy zipped firmly into Miranda's jacket.

To the sound of an alarm bell ringing in the distance, they cruised back the way they'd come, searching for a lift. When three security guards appeared in the doorway in front of them, Les turned the bike full circle, and headed for a sign saying 'Escalators'.

'No!' Miranda screamed. 'We'll never do it!'

'Course we will! COME ON, PUNTERS! MIND OUT THE WAY!'

The bike shuddered violently as, shoulders hunched and

neck lowered, Les forced it down the moving stairs, closely followed by the security guards. The puppy squirmed with fear inside Miranda's jacket. Then, suddenly, she felt something hot and wet against her skin.

'The bloody thing's peed on me!' Letting go of Les for a moment, she lifted the struggling creature out. When they reached the first floor landing, she handed it to a startled passer-by.

A line of security guards were waiting for them downstairs, barring the exit.

'Oh, God!' wailed Miranda. 'We'll never get out!'

But as Les shot towards them, yelling, 'Geronimo!' they broke ranks and scattered in all directions. A moment later, the heavy glass doors thumped closed behind them, and they shot off down the street.

By the time she got home that night, Ed was sitting on the stairs waiting for her. His arms were crossed over his chest, and his face was set and grim. Dishevelled and glowing, she threw herself into his arms hoping he wouldn't notice her guilty expression. 'Darling, thank goodness! You've come home!'

'So, I see, have you.' Peeling her away like a plaster, he held her at arm's length and looked at her critically. 'You've been drinking,' he said flatly.

'Yes. A little bit.' She giggled.

His face creased into a suspicious frown. 'Who've you been with, Miranda?'

'Only Les. We had lunch at San Lorenzo. And guess what? We sat next to Princess Diana!'

'And?' He shook her by the shoulders. 'Look at the mess you're in. It's seven-thirty, Miranda. Where have you been since then?'

'Hey, let go of me!' Wrenching free of him, she smiled slowly. 'Are you jealous?'

His eyes narrowed. 'Should I be?'

'Of course not!'

He grabbed her arm. 'So why are you smirking like that? What've you been up to, Miranda? Something happened, didn't it? Did that bastard try and seduce you? If he did, I'll kill him!'

'No! Of course not! Well . . .' She hesitated. 'Only psychologically.'

'What the hell's that supposed to mean?'

'Let go! You're hurting me.'

The tip of his nose wrinkled in disgust. 'You smell like a car park staircase.'

'Yes, I do, don't I? The puppy peed on my shirt.'

'What puppy? Miranda?'

Suddenly angry, she pulled away from him again. 'God, what's the matter with you? You're the one who stayed out all last night! I was just having fun.'

'What kind of fun?'

'*Fun*. We went . . .' She failed to control a grin. '. . . shopping. In Harrods.'

'And? What was such fun about it?'

She thought back to the trail of wanton destruction they'd left behind them, and the thousands of pounds of damage they'd caused, and suddenly she didn't know. A bleakness descended on her, quenching the flame of her elation like a wet towel. 'If you want to know all the details, you'd better watch the News at Ten,' she snapped. 'I'm going to have a bath.'

'Miranda . . . Miranda!'

'No! Why do you always have to bring me down?'

'Miranda!'

She was halfway up the stairs before he caught up with her, grabbing her by the shoulder, forcing her round. 'Let go of me, Ed! You're hurting me.'

'First, I want to know what's going on with you and Les.'

'I told you – nothing. OK?'

'No, it's not OK.' His fingers dug into her shoulders. 'I don't like the idea of you two hanging around together. I don't trust him. He's up to something.'

'Why do you say that? Can't you accept that he just happens to like me? We're friends.'

'Friends!' He shook his head, despairing of her. 'Don't act like a fool, Miranda! Men like Les don't have friends! As far as he's concerned, the world's divided into two sorts of people – people that he uses and people that he screws. For some reason, it suits him to use us now. But the moment he wants to, he'll screw us blind.' Ed's pupils glittered at her darkly. 'That is, if he hasn't screwed you already.'

Without thinking, Miranda slapped him hard across the cheek. The next moment, he grabbed her shoulders and glared wildly into her face. She had never seen him look so angry. 'Don't you ever, ever hit me again!' he spat. 'Understand?'

Furious and shaken, she pulled free and ran upstairs.

Fourteen

'Fancy a cup of tea, love?'

'No, thanks, Mary.'

'Coffee?'

'No.'

'Cocoa?'

'*No.*' Jack turned a page of *The Psychology of Love*, and added, begrudgingly, 'Thanks.'

'Sure there's nothing I can get you?'

'No.' Only earplugs.

'Not even a little nightcap?'

A little nightcap. At – he glanced at his watch – only ten past nine? Was Sunday night really passing as slowly as the rest of the weekend had? On second thoughts, a nightcap wasn't such a bad idea. But not a *little* one. A pint glass, perhaps, of whisky or brandy, enough to knock him out for the rest of the evening. And saying yes might be worth it, merely to get Mary off his back.

And to get her slippers out of the living room. Every time he glanced at the television – and how could he help glancing up at it, when it was there all the time, shouting away at him like a loutish intruder? – there they were, planted on the coffee table, directly in his line of vision: two fat, pink shapeless pigs with red snouts and pointy ears, their grubby fake-fur bodies matted into grubby clumps. In the four weeks since Mary had moved in, Jack had grown to hate them with a vengeance. The mere sound of their suede soles slurping across the kitchen lino or slapping up and down the stairs was enough to give him a migraine.

What, he wondered, had happened to those delectable fur-trimmed silver mules that she used to clip-clop around in when she lived next door? What, for that matter, had happened to her adorable pudgy little feet with their red-lacquered nails? Nowadays he only glimpsed them in short flashes between the pink pigs being kicked off – and invariably left right in the middle of the bedroom floor, where he was bound to trip over them when he got up to go to the lavatory in the middle of the night – and her woolly bed socks being pulled on. Even then, her toes were adorned with corn plasters and her heels smeared with Vaseline, and her feet failed to turn him on as they used to.

'OK, I'll have a vodka.'

'With lemonade?'

'Neat.'

The pigs dropped to the floor, and, as Mary stood up, the sofa heaved a sigh of relief. No sooner had she shuffled off to the kitchen than Jack grabbed the remote controls and pressed the mute button. The quiz show compère on the box carried on gesticulating at him, unaware that he'd been silenced. Jack closed his eyes against the garish glare, leaned back and enjoyed a moment of relative peace and quiet, with just the sound of Diana's laughter in the distance, and the fast dull, bass throb of rap music emanating from David's room. Then, picking up his book again, he attempted to get to grips with the chapter he'd been trying to read, 'Love as Attachment: The Integration of Three Behavioural Systems'.

But after skimming the first couple of sentences, he found himself staring at the TV again. It was Mary's fault. She'd destroyed his powers of concentration. As he'd learned since she'd moved in, she could bear neither stillness nor silence. Nor, it seemed, emotional intimacy. If the two of them ever had a quiet moment alone – and with four children in the house, five, including Seamus, such moments were inevitably rare – Mary would fill it: with Radio 2, daytime chat shows or Australian soaps; with endless and unnecessary hoovering and spray polishing; with lavatory scouring and sausage-frying; perhaps worst of all, with her seamless, meaningless talk.

It was an obvious case of displacement activity. What dark secret in her past was she avoiding? There must be a dark secret, he could think of no other explanation for her frantic behaviour, except one which was laughable: that she was, for some strange and unaccountable reason, avoiding him.

Shlupp, shlupp, shlupp. After what seemed like a long time, the pigs waddled back into the living room. Without looking up, Jack held out his hand for his drink. The sofa creaked with exhaustion as Mary sat down next to him, then leant forward and took charge of the remote control. The TV volume shot up again. Jack knocked back his drink. Mary chuckled at an animated butter commercial. Jack gritted his teeth. There was no avoiding the unavoidable: it was time to move on and get out. Or rather, since this was his house, to get Mary out. Had he been a snob, he might have said that Mary wasn't intelligent enough for him. But since he wasn't – Good God, hadn't he always voted Labour? – he justified his sudden change of heart by telling himself that he and Mary had simply outgrown their mutual attachment.

After all, Mary was a marvellous woman. The salt of the earth, as that detective had said the day Miranda disappeared. In small quantities, a dose of salts did wonders for the constitution. However, a four-week, unadulterated diet of it had left him parched, craving, as it were, a long drink of designer mineral water.

He stared glumly into his vodka. If he was honest with himself – and when, he asked himself, wasn't he – he had to admit that Mary was holding him back. He'd learned in the past weeks that she wasn't the only woman in the world. Single men – yes, even widowers with four children in tow – were, it seemed, socially at a premium in North London.

In fact, there seemed to be plenty of unattached, attractive females, desperate for him to ask them out. Gwyneth Barton, for one, with her breasts as soft as Bath buns and her surprisingly muscular mouth, who'd unexpectedly approached him in the students' union bar on Thursday night, and asked him to come with her to the university film club, where they'd enjoyed a quick snog in the back row during the last reel of Kurosawa's *Rashomon*, and a further long, passionate clinch in his office when she came back with him to collect his briefcase.

Then there was Suzanne Jones, who'd kept in intermittent touch since making the documentary, and then telephoned him at work last week to ask him to a dinner party next Saturday night. 'Just a few very close friends are coming: the Mortimers, Salman and Melvyn Bragg.'

Jack bit his lip. What he'd give to go, just to be able to casually drop those names in the office! But, because of Mary, he'd had to invent some lame excuse. Mary never let him out of her sight on weekends, and he could hardly take her along to a dinner party like that, could he? Not that he was ashamed of her or anything childish like that, he was only thinking of sparing her feelings; after all, he didn't want her to suffer the embarrassment of feeling so out of place.

Still, Suzanne's invitation, and his grope with Gwyneth, had made him pause and think. Given that opportunities like these were opening up to him now that he was free of Miranda – opportunities to expand his intellectual horizons, widen his network of contacts and chase skirt – he'd be selling himself short if he were to settle down with the first woman who came along, particularly a woman whose cultural high spot every week was playing the National Lottery.

With great determination, he returned to *The Psychology of Love*. Skipping to the tables, he skimmed over their headings: 'Comparison of the Features of Attachment and Adult Romantic Love'. 'Adult Attachment Types and their Frequencies'. 'Attachment Style and the Experience of Love'. Ah, yes! Pausing here, he perused the listed categories morosely, as if they were symptoms of some incurable disease.

Happiness.

Friendship.

Trust.

Fear of Closeness.

Acceptance.

Jealousy.

Obsessive preoccupation.

Sexual attraction.

As if it had a life of its own, his right hand slid along the back of the sofa and dropped down past Mary's shoulder onto the wide shelf of her breasts, where his thumb and index finger sought her nipple through the loose weave of her mohair jumper. His penis gave an involuntary twitch. Pulling her head round towards him, he plugged his tongue into the electric socket of her mouth. As always, a series of shock waves passed through his body. What was it about her, he thought angrily, that still turned him on? He didn't love her – not in the conventional sense of the word. Nor, if he was honest, did he even like her very much any more. Since she'd moved in after the red bra-and-pants fiasco – he still couldn't understand who'd sent them, he'd probably never get to the bottom of it – he'd seen aspects of her which he'd never dreamed existed, not least her bare backside oozing out of a high-cut fuchsia leotard as she bent double in front of the TV during her thrice-weekly workout to her exercise video.

What had seemed attractive, even thrilling about Mary when he'd only been able to see her for the odd, snatched hour a few times a week now bored, even revolted him: her earthiness; her relentless cheerfulness; her long painted fingernails – false, as he had discovered the other day when he'd found one in his bowl of All Bran; her permed and dyed curls, which, when she washed her hair every morning, came out in handfuls, coating the bath and clogging the drain.

And yet . . . Unable to resist her despite all this, he nose-dived into her cleavage and breathed in her heady, musky scent. 'Oh, Muffin!'

'Oh, Mule! Naughty boy! Get your hand off! We shouldn't! Not with the children still up and about. Ooh! Come here!'

He winced with reluctant pleasure as her hand expertly unzipped his jeans and wormed its way into his Y-fronts. Sighing with ecstasy as her false talons grazed his erection, he pulled up her jumper, and fought to undo her bra.

'Dad, have you seen my . . . ? Oh, for Christ's sake!'

Lily stood frozen in the doorway, her eyes burning in a pale, pinched face. As Jack pulled himself upright, Mary attempted to remove her fingers from between his legs, but they were trapped between his balls and his straining pants.

'Sit up a sec, will you, love?' He let out a yowl of pain as, grabbing hold of her wrist, she yanked her hand out. 'Sorry about that, Lil. Me and your Dad got carried away.'

Lily's hair flicked over her shoulder with the violent crack of a matador's cloak. 'My name's Lily, not Lil.'

'Really, Lily, there's no need to be rude to Mary. Haven't you heard of knocking before you come into a room?'

Her furious eyes burned brighter. 'Well, excuse me for existing! I was under the false impression that this was my home!'

'*Our* home.' Suddenly aware that his penis was hanging out, Jack pulled his shirt down over his open fly. 'We're a family. And families must co-exist harmoniously together. And harmonious co-existence means co-operation and compromise, as I've told you a hundred times.'

'Well, maybe you and Mary could *compromise* by *co-existing* in your bedroom when you next fancy a quick grope. For Christ's sake, it's bad enough having her living here without coming into the lounge to find you two working your way through the *Karma Sutra*. It's disgusting!'

'You find the idea of your father having sex disgusting, do you?'

Immediately, he realised it had been a mistake to throw this at her. Her eyes burned into him like acid. From whom had she inherited her murderous temper? he wondered. Not from him, that was certain. Nor from Miranda – unless she had kept hers hidden all those calm, quarrel-free years.

'Fuck off, Dad!'

'Ooh, Lily! Wash your mouth out! Speaking to your Dad like that!'

Lily's face darkened with scorn. 'He's my father and I'll say what I bloody fucking well like to him! It's none of your bloody fucking business!'

'Look, don't swear at Mary! I understand that you're upset, but your mother wouldn't have liked rudeness.'

'And I suppose she would have liked to see you two at it like rabbits on her sofa?' Lily's lips trembled. 'For Christ's sake, Mum's only been gone for about six months, and look at you! Anyone would think you were glad she'd been murdered! Christ, she must be turning in her grave . . . That is, if she has one . . .'

Bursting into tears, she fled, slamming the door behind her.

Ashamed of himself, Jack covered his face with his hands. He'd just been faced with a classic Oedipal situation, and, instead of handling it well, he'd blundered. To blunder was so unlike him. Was he losing his grip?

Next to him, Mary adjusted her bra straps through the stretched neck of her sweater, then heaved the two pink pigs back onto the coffee table. 'Never mind, love. It's probably just her time of the month. Don't let it get you down. Tell you what, there's an *Are You Being Served?* special repeat in a minute. That ought to cheer you up. As for the other, we'll get in the mood later, eh? As long as she knows the Mule is on his way, Muffin can wait.'

The following morning, anxious to avoid Lily, Jack got up early and crept quietly towards the bathroom. As he was about to push the door open, Lily came out, her wet hair twisted up in a high towelling turban, her body barely covered by a skimpy towel.

'Look, love . . .' he started in a brave attempt to make peace with her.

There was a short, hostile sigh. 'I'm not interested.'

'But . . .'

'The subject's closed.'

'But I haven't even mentioned a subject.'

'All subjects are closed from now on,' she snapped, trying to brush past him.

'But Lily . . .'

When he gently but firmly clasped her bare shoulder, she swung round and glared at him with the hauteur of a high-ranking medieval princess molested by a hump-backed, warty serf. 'Don't you dare touch me!' His hand recoiled, as if from a burning-hot faucet. 'Just leave me alone, will you? Can't you stop prying into people's minds for once? Just accept that I don't want to talk about last night. All right? OK?'

Jack shook his head sadly. 'Avoidance will only lead to depression, love. Believe me, if you have a problem, you'd be far better off to share it with me.'

Her head cocked to one side, she smiled at him coldly. 'It's not me who has the problem, Dad. And the only thing I'm likely to *share* with you in future is this bathroom. So take it or leave it. If you don't want it, I'm sure the others do.'

'Anyone know what's eating Lily?' Jack casually asked David, Diana and Thomas when, half an hour later, he went down to the kitchen. There was a grunt from David.

After glancing up at her father with a brief, astonished look, Diana stared down miserably into her mug of tea. 'Thomas? Any ideas?' Jack persisted.

'I dunno.' The mop of wiry curls trembled as Thomas looked up from his scorched Pop-tart. 'Use your imagination, Dad.'

David snorted. 'Dad doesn't have an imagination. He doesn't believe in them, do you, Dad?'

'I don't know what you're talking about.' Puzzled by the hostility he felt coming from his children, Jack squeezed a Pop-tart into the toaster. Looking round, he noticed that none of yesterday's washing up had yet been done. 'Really! Does no one feel any responsibility towards the family unit? Who was on kitchen duty this weekend?' When this question met with a wall of silence, he examined the rota pinned to the fridge door. 'Saturday, Lily and Diana. Sunday . . .' Seeing Mary's name written in the Sunday square, he went silently back to the toaster, and stared down into its orange glow.

'Dad?'

'What is it, Diana?'

Diana pushed back her hair from her sallow forehead, and looked up at him warily with her dark, moist eyes. When she spoke again, there was a tremor in her quiet voice. 'You know, this whole thing hasn't been easy for any of us. We find it really hard to . . .'

'Come on, Diana!' he interrupted. 'How hard is it to spend a few hours a week helping to keep the place clean?'

After she, too, had fled from the room in tears, Jack escaped the chill, haunted feel of the house and rushed gratefully off to work. On his desk, he found an envelope marked Private and Confidential, inside which was a short note from his Head of Department, Jonathan Howes, asking to see him in his office at 11.15 that morning to discuss 'an extremely important and sensitive matter.'

Jack's lips curled into a tight, self-satisfied smile. At long last, he'd had the call.

Promotion.

Fifteen years was far too long to have remained stuck in the same old senior lecturer's job, even if the poly had recently been granted university status. Yet, with Jonathan being a scant five years his senior, there had seemed little prospect of moving up in the teaching hierarchy there. He'd thought of changing jobs, of course: eight years ago he'd even applied for a post as Reader at the LSE. When he'd failed even to get short-listed, he'd decided to bide his time at the Balls Pond Road and wait for either Jonathan or the Dean to make a move.

Just last week, he'd heard on the grapevine that the Dean was taking up a job offer in Sydney. Jonathan was no doubt applying for the Dean's job, and he would then be the natural candidate to step into Jonathan's shoes.

His low spirits soared at the thought of the impending increase in his status and salary. Though worldly success, *per se*, was a hollow thing which meant nothing at all to him, he couldn't but be excited at this sudden up-swing in his prospects. Promotion *and* Gwyneth Barton . . . Life was definitely looking up! And how much more interesting it would be to be introduced to Melvyn Bragg as a university *Head of Department* instead of a plain old senior lecturer. Once he got rid of Mary, that was.

The moment his ten o'clock tutorial was over, he scooted upstairs, two at a time, to Jonathan's office. On the second-floor landing, he bumped into a small, muscular figure in a short, skin-tight black lycra dress.

'Well, hello, Gwyneth!' he said jauntily, glancing quickly at the nipples outlined by the clinging fabric.

Her face grim, she froze on the stair above him.

'Have a good weekend, did you? Go out much? No? Me neither. Just a long, busy weekend looking after the kids. How's it going? Gwyneth? I say, is anything wrong? Gwyneth?' Noticing her stony expression, he laid his hand on her wrist.

'Don't you touch me!'

Her yell echoed up and down the concrete staircase. Jack quickly withdrew his hand. A long-haired youth from the second year, coming down behind her, stopped and stared at them.

'Gwyneth? Is everything OK?' Jack said, smiling at her quizzically.

'Stay away from me, you bastard!' she shouted, pushing roughly past him and fleeing downstairs.

Deeply embarrassed, Jack smiled at the youth sadly and shook his head. 'The great question which I haven't been able to answer, despite all my research is *"What the bloody hell is it that women want?"*' he intoned, misquoting Freud.

The youth grinned at him conspiratorially. 'Yeah. Fuck PC, Jack! That's what I say.'

'Sexual harrassment?' Jack repeated. 'Me?'

'I'm sorry, Jack. It's even more serious than that.'

'I don't believe it!' Jack ran his fingers through his hair, causing a snow shower of dandruff to fall onto his shoulders. 'I don't understand, Jonathan. Who on earth could have made such a ridiculous allegation against me?'

Sitting down at his desk, his head of department picked up a letter from his in-tray, and scanned it with his mournful, bloodhound eyes. 'Her name's Gwyneth Barton.' Jack's jaw dropped. 'One of your first years, as I understand. Know her?' He nodded slowly. 'Well, this letter from her was on my desk this morning. She claims . . . let's see . . . she claims that you went and sat right next to her in the film club last week, and persisted in chatting her up. That you then got her to come back to your office with you on some false pretext – something about handing her back an essay – and . . .' He paused to clear his throat. 'And that you then locked the door and indecently assaulted her.'

'*What?*'

225

'She also claims that you threatened that if she didn't sleep with you, you'd mark down her grades.'

'You're joking!'

'I'm afraid not, Jack.' Putting down the letter, Jonathan looked up. 'I presume she's making the whole thing up?'

Jack felt as if he had just witnessed a terrible accident. And he was the victim of it. He could feel the blood drain from his limbs and rush to his cheeks. 'It's . . . it's preposterous, Jonathan!'

'I knew it, Jack.' Jonathan smiled sympathetically. 'It's all a pack of lies, isn't it? Every bloody word?'

'*Of course it is!* Yes! I mean . . . Well . . .' His voice gave out.

Above the thick brown splash of his moustache, the tip of Jonathan's long nose twitched. Suddenly he seemed to bear an uncanny resemblance to Jack's old headmaster – a severe and formidable man prone to swiping at his pupils' heads with a wooden ruler. 'Well, what?'

'Well . . . I mean . . . Of course it's lies. Absolutely. But . . . well, not all of it. Not exactly, if you see what I mean.'

Jonathan blinked. 'What exactly do you mean by *not exactly*, Jack?'

'What?'

'Did you assault this girl, or threaten her, or didn't you?'

'No! For God's sake, Jonathan! What do you think of me? Of course I didn't!' He paused, trying to gather his thoughts. 'It's an incredible interpretation of what happened! A . . . a travesty of the truth!'

'So something did happen, then?'

Bewildered, Jack spread his hands. 'It was just . . .' He shrugged. 'You know!'

'No, Jack, I don't know. Look, I'm not being nosey, but I've got to find out. These are serious allegations. After all, sexual harrassment contravenes our Equal Opportunities policy. And, if there was an actual assault, we're talking gross misconduct, and dismissal, and a possible criminal investigation.'

Jack gulped at the air. Oxygen seemed to be in short supply. His armpits felt hot and sweaty under his old corduroy jacket. He tried to think back to Friday night, and what had happened, but his thoughts were suddenly confused. 'The stupid girl must be deeply disturbed to make up a story like this. She *is* deeply disturbed. I mean, Jonathan, get this: she came to me a couple of weeks ago, complaining that I'd given her too low a mark for her essay because she's bloody *Welsh*, for Christ's sake.'

There was a long pause before Jonathan said anything. 'I'm *bloody Welsh*, too, Jack.'

'Oh, Jesus! I know you are! I didn't mean it like that. What I meant was, it was a ridiculous allegation, as she soon realised once I'd bought her breakfast and we'd had a chat.'

'You bought her breakfast?'

Jack looked up at him sharply. 'So what? Are you insinuating that I was trying to bribe her with canteen fried eggs? Give me a break! Anyway, it was all perfectly friendly in the end. I didn't see her after that – I mean, I saw her around, but I didn't *see* her, if you know what I mean. Then on Thursday I ran into her . . .'

'Literally ran into her? You made physical contact?'

'Of course not *literally*! We met, by chance, in the bar and . . . well, she asked me if I'd like to come to the film club and see *Rashomon* with her and . . .'

Jonathan picked up a pencil. 'Let me get this straight – you claim that she asked you?'

'I'm not *claiming* anything. It's a fact. She did. Yes, I'm almost sure she did. Well, we went to the film club together. And . . .' He watched as Jonathan wrote something down on a piece of paper.

'And?'

Jack shrugged. 'You know! She's an attractive girl and . . . well, we were sitting kind of close together and . . . OK, so we snogged a bit. Don't look at me like that.

Snogging the students isn't a disciplinary offence, is it? If it was, there wouldn't be a male lecturer left in this college. These things happen, for Christ's sake! I happen to know they've happened to you!'

'Hold on, let's not get personal here, Jack.' Jonathan bridled. 'That was a long time ago. And it was a completely different kettle of fish. Chrissie and I loved each other! It wasn't a casual fling. I left my wife for her, and married her, didn't I? Then what?'

'And then, well, I had to get something from my office and she tagged along with me. And then . . . well, we kissed some more. Look, it got pretty amorous, but nothing serious happened. We didn't screw or anything. She certainly wasn't reluctant, I can tell you!'

'Did you touch her?'

'Of course I bloody touched her!'

'Where?'

'What?'

'Where did you touch her?'

'In my office. I just told you.'

'I mean, where on her body?'

A wave of self-righteous indignation flooded through him. 'That's none of your bloody business! Christ, I'll kill that bitch! What's she trying to do to me?'

Jonathan stood up. 'I'd be careful what you say, Jack. It won't do you any good to talk like that. I don't have to tell you, you're in deep shit here. I know how upset you must be about what happened to Miranda, but if you used force on this Gwyneth Barton girl, mitigating circumstances are not an excuse.'

'I did *not* use force! She was willing. More than willing! And anyway, all we did was kiss and cuddle a bit.'

'Kiss and cuddle,' Jonathan repeated slowly, writing the words out. Then, sighing deeply, he tapped the end of his pencil on the desk. 'Oh dear, oh dear! I'm afraid that her version of events doesn't tally with yours at all. I really don't know what to say, Jack. Frankly, this is a bloody awkward situation you've dropped me in. I'm sure . . .' His voice faltered '. . . that you're telling the truth and that this girl is following some private agenda. After all, we all saw *Oleanna* at the Royal Court. Still . . .' He drew himself up. 'I've a duty to take seriously any allegations made by a student against a member of staff, so much as I'd like to clear the matter up right now and throw it out, I'm afraid I'll have to refer it to the Dean.'

'I see.' Jack tried to stand up too, but a ton of invisible bricks seemed to have dropped into his lap.

Jonathan cleared his throat. 'Until we set a full investigation in motion, I suggest that you, well, er, that you take some time off.'

Jack stared at him in silence for a moment. 'Are you suspending me?' he said bitterly.

Jonathan raised a hand. 'Nothing of the sort. Let's just call it sick leave, shall we? Go home, Jack. Things have obviously been getting too much for you. Take it easy while you have the opportunity. I'm sure you could do with a rest.'

Shocked, confused, unable to face having to explain the situation to Mary, he spent the rest of the day wandering through the rain-drenched streets of North London. Everywhere he went, the shop windows sparkled with red and green tinsel. In the pubs, of which he visited three or four, paper chains and lurid foil lanterns hung overhead. After a while, he realised with alarm what all this signified: that it was late November, only four weeks away from Christmas. In the past, he'd always looked on the drawn-out, over-commercialised festivities with indifference bordering on contempt, content to let Miranda organise everything at home. This year whatever did or did not happen – the present buying, the decorating of a tree, even galvanising the kids for the ritual pre-lunch walk up Parliament Hill on Christmas Day – would be entirely up to him. How would he cope with it? With Miranda gone, Mary in her place, the children being so difficult, and himself suspended, what kind of Christmas was it likely to be?

Rain seeped through the soles of his shoes and up his trouser legs. By the time he returned home in the late afternoon, it was dark and he was icy cold. On opening the front door, he heard the warming sound of his children laughing in the kitchen. But when he shuffled in to join them, and they saw it was him, they immediately fell silent. Seated at the kitchen table like four conspirators, a pile of crumpets, a pot of jam and a half-wrapped, crumb-strewn packet of butter between them, they stared meaningfully into each other's eyes.

'Hello,' Jack said with as much cheerfulness as he could muster. 'Anyone fancy making me a cup of tea?'

Diana looked at Lily, who looked at David, who looked at Thomas, who looked at Diana, who pulled off a morsel of crumpet and buttered it carefully.

'Lily?'

She sniffed. 'Will someone please tell Dad that I'm not talking to him?'

'Diana?'

'Sorry, Dad. Can't. The smell makes me sick.'

'The smell of tea?'

'Yup.' Putting the crumpet in her mouth, she chewed on it deliberately.

'David?'

'What?'

Jack turned away. Sometimes his eldest twin looked so like Miranda that he could barely look at him. 'Make me a cup of tea, will you?'

'Got to do my homework.' He pushed back his chair and stood up. 'Justin's coming over later. We're going out.'

Pushing back his dripping wet hair, Jack went over to the sink, and, fumbling with his numb fingers, filled the kettle himself. 'Seamus and Mary not in?' he asked carefully. No one answered. 'Anyone know where they are?'

Lily smiled coldly. 'Don't know. Don't care.'

'Maybe she's gone home to fry some sausages for Brian.'

'Where're you and Justin going to, then?' Thomas asked David.

'To the pictures.'

'Can I come?'

'Not with that muck spread all over your face.'

'It's not muck, it's foundation!'

'David! Leave Thomas alone. He'll stop wearing make-up when he's ready to.'

'No, I won't, Dad.'

'Of course you will.'

'No, I won't!' Thomas's vehemence took Jack by surprise. 'I'll never stop. I'm a proper trans-social.'

'Get your terms right, Thomas. The word's trans-sexual.'

'I don't care what it is. I . . . I'm going to have an operation when I'm grown up.'

'What, a brain transplant?' David guffawed. 'Good idea.'

'Oh, leave me alone!' Thomas's small mouth puckered up. 'Why do you all hate me so much?'

'Stop teasing him, David!' Lily shouted. 'Stop it, everyone! Can't you see Thomas's really upset? Of course we don't hate you darling,' she went on, getting up and putting her arms around him defensively. 'We all love you! Everyone loves you.'

'Of course we do.' Glad to be on more familiar territory, Jack came over to the table, and put his hand on Thomas's heaving shoulder. 'David, Lily, Diana, myself, Mary . . .'

Lily froze. 'What's *she* got to do with it?'

Jack took a deep breath. 'I don't know why you've all suddenly taken against Mary. You used to like her.'

David muttered, 'That was before she moved in.'

'Well, she lives here now, and it's about time you all started to accept her.' Jack tried to keep the note of gloom out of his voice. 'I know that, well, that she's not your mother, but she is a part of our lives now.'

Forgetting she wasn't talking to Jack, Lily rounded on him angrily. 'She may be part of your life, but she's certainly

231

no part of mine! It's unbearable here now. If you must know, I'm thinking of moving out after Christmas.'

'What?' Jack shook his head. 'Don't be ridiculous! Where would you go?'

'I might move in with Sol.'

He looked bewildered. 'Who or what is Sol?'

'He's my boyfriend. You'd know that if you took any interest in me.'

'You mean the waiter at the Café Rouge? I thought his name was Derek?'

'Derek and I broke up *yonks* ago. In September, as a matter of fact.'

Jack nodded slowly. 'Aren't you much too young to be thinking of moving in with someone, Lily?' he said carefully. 'You're still at school. You've only just turned seventeen.'

'So what?' she said, fixing him with an unflinching, cold stare. 'I do know the facts of life, Dad – thanks to you and Mary.'

Suddenly Jack realised he was shivering violently. Turning on his heel, he left the kitchen, and went upstairs. Miranda's ghost stood on the upper landing, smiling down. Pushing past it, he stumbled into the bedroom he now shared with Mary and, still in his wet clothes, collapsed on the bed.

Gwyneth Barton kneeled on the floor in front of him, licking his toes. The pleasure was delectable. Then, suddenly, without warning, she sank her teeth into his big toe.

Jack screamed.

Pulling back, she smiled up at him. Blood was dripping from the corner of her mouth, and there was a column of bleeding flesh hanging like a cigarette from her lips. Taking a deep breath, she spat it out. '*Truth can stand on one leg to be sure, but with two it can walk and get about,*' she quoted. 'Come on Jack – who said that?'

'Gwyneth! What have you done?'

The next moment, she lunged at him again. In a state of shock, he felt the sharp ivory of her teeth sink into his thigh. A moment later, they met in the middle of the muscle with a soft click. There was a loud rip as the tendon tore away from the bone, then a squelchy sound as she sucked it into her mouth like a strand of spaghetti.

'*The only antidote to human suffering is physical pain,*' she slurped, the end of the tendon still dangling from her lips.

'Aaaagh! Stop! Why are you torturing me?'

He tried to fight her off, but, despite her diminutive size, he was no match for her. Teeth bared for a third time, she lunged towards him. This time, she seemed to be heading straight for the crux, or rather the crutch of the matter, to the terrified, shrivelled sausage hiding in his lap.

Transfixed with horror, he watched her mouth move closer and closer, the red, bloody, hungry lips gaping wide. Then she came down on him. For a short delicious moment, his penis was embalmed in the warm silky wetness of her mouth. Then an indescribable pain shot through him. Screaming hysterically, he looked down in horror at the bloody stump between his legs. She had bitten off the root of his manhood.

'Give it back! Give it back!' he yelled.

But it was too late. The sausage was swallowed.

'Give it back! Give it back!'

'Jack! Jack!'

'GIVE IT BACK, BITCH!'

'Wake up!'

'GIVE IT BACK!'

'Jack!'

It was Mary's voice. Sweat pouring off him, he groped instinctively between his legs. When his hands closed on the soft, squelchy mass there, he gave it a small tug. Finding that it remained attached to his body, he burst into tears of relief.

'Oh, thank Christ!' he whimpered into the pillow. He rolled over and opened his eyes a crack.

Two strangers – burly, clean-shaven men in grey suits – were standing at the end of his bed.

'Dreaming, were you, Jack?' said one of them. 'About giving it back?'

He tried to sit up, but a hammer-like, throbbing sensation crashed through his head and he collapsed back on the pillows, screwing his eyes closed. When, tentatively, he opened them again, the men were still there.

'God, I feel terrible,' he moaned.

Mary's red talons reached towards him and patted his hand. 'So you should, love. You've got a bad dose of 'flu. You should never have let yourself get so wet the other day! You've been out of it completely with a temperature of 103! Delirious. Imagining things.'

He jerked his chin at the two strangers standing at the end of his bed. 'Am I imagining them? Or do they exist?'

Mary snorted. 'They exist all right. They're police officers. I told them you were sick, but the buggers didn't believe me. They insisted on coming up to see for themselves.'

'Detective Inspector Knowles,' said the taller of the two, flipping open his identification. 'Fraud squad. Sorry to bother you like this, but we were hoping you could help us with our enquiries.'

'Oh Christ!' Jack sighed deeply. 'Don't tell me – the stupid girl went to the police and reported the rape?'

Mary's face darkened. 'What rape? Jack?'

The detective raised a curious eyebrow. 'I don't know anything about a rape, Jack. We've come about the theft.'

'What theft?' Jack frowned. 'I haven't reported anything missing.'

The detective smiled knowingly. 'That's right, Jack, you haven't. But the Balls Pond Road University's accounts department has.'

Fifteen

The paintwork of the Mercedes saloon warmed Miranda's fingers as she leaned against it, watching her fast breath explode in the freezing air. The silence of the countryside deafened her. Gradually, as her ears grew accustomed to it, she began to hear sounds: the cry of a lone rook; the distant bleat of a sheep; the soft, moist cracking of twigs in the hedgerows; the rustle of an unseen bird.

She folded her arms, and, standing on tiptoe, peered over the top of the nearest hedgerow. Wide, flat fields stretched away into the distance to where the cold mist drained the bare earth of its colour and bled it into the sky. To her right, at the top of a small hill, a group of trees stood out blackly against the mist, their bare branches reaching upwards in a gesture of surprise. It was all so peaceful, so idyllic . . .

'Don't hurt me! I b-b-beg you!'

'Just shut up and do what I say, or I'll plaster your brains all over this field!'

She glanced quickly over her shoulder, to where the cash-carrying security vehicle was parked, blocking the narrow lane. The driver's door was gaping open, revealing the thick rivets on the inside of the armoured window and a rolled-up tabloid newspaper on the dashboard. His face grotesque under a tight stocking mask, Justin stood in the back, dressed in a plain navy anorak, throwing bags of money out to a similarly attired Pete, who in turn was loading them into the back of a green transit van.

Eyes wide with fear, the driver of the CCV and his fellow guard stumbled through an open farm gate and into a field, urged on by Les and Ed, who, masked like the others, strutted beside them, chests puffed out like cock turkeys, sawn-off shotguns clasped in their gloved hands.

Miranda shivered. Huddled into her waxed jacket, she followed slowly after them. Her part in the robbery – coaxing the men out of their cab on the pretext that 'her' Mercedes had broken down in the lane and blocked their route – was over. The rest of the job was up to the others. Nevertheless, her heart still pounded wildly inside her, pumping adrenalin to every cell. Though there wasn't much chance of being caught red handed in an isolated spot such as this – as Les had said when they'd planned it, the job was guaranteed sweet as a nut – she wouldn't be able to relax until the whole thing was over and they'd dumped the Transit and made off in their second getaway car, the Ford Granada parked in a derelict barn a mile away.

Leaning against the wooden gate, she watched Ed push the terrified driver to his knees.

'Wh-what are you going to do to us?'

'Shut up. Keep still.'

The barrel of his shotgun pointed at the driver's head while Les took a length of rope from his pocket, and tied the man's hands behind his back. After a moment of apprehension, Miranda took a calming breath and looked away. There was no need for her to worry, because Ed's gun wasn't loaded. What happened now was just a matter of routine. Within a few minutes, the CCV's former occupants would be safely trussed up, and the five of them would be on their way, tens of thousands of pounds richer. By tomorrow, the guard and driver would have recovered from the shock of being held up, and no one, except the van's insurers, would be any the worse off.

There was a soft rip, as a length of electrical tape was unwound from the roll and placed over the driver's mouth. 'OK,' said Ed's voice. 'Now you – get down!'

A moment later a sudden shout from the field made her swivel round and run back towards the gate.

'You bastards! HELP! POLICE!'

'SHUT UP!'

'SOMEONE HELP!'

Back in the field, the bound and gagged driver was lying on the ground, his eyes bulging with terror while Les, his sawn-off shotgun clasped in one hand, leaned over the crouching, kneeling second man.

'*Fuck!*' Les called to Ed. 'Did you see that? This piece of shit spat all over me!' His face purple with rage, he leaned over the now-cowering figure. '*You just made a bad mistake, sonny boy! No one fucking spits at me!*'

With the practised ease of a number one seed on Centre Court, he swung his shotgun to one side, then brought it forwards in a perfect backhand shot. With a loud crack, it thudded into the side of the security guard's head, sending him toppling sideways onto the grass.

Still trembling with rage, Les hung over him. 'Who do you think you are? A fucking hero?' Now his small neat feet danced around him, kicking out as if he was kicking a football, his boot landing blow after blow in the man's ribs.

'Ugh! Ooof! Argh!'

The comic-book sounds flew across the field. Horrified, and yet at the same time gruesomely fascinated, Miranda watched Les lay into the body. This, then, was what the business was all about. It was as if, up till now, all the jobs she'd been involved in had been play-acting, a mere dress rehearsal for the real thing. For the first time in months it dawned on her that she was a real criminal, committing real crimes, inflicting real pain on real people. She, who had never once slapped her children, so repulsed was she by the idea of violence towards others, was standing by while one man kicked another into pulp. If the security guard was killed, she would be responsible: not even a guilty bystander, but an accessory to a cold-blooded murder.

Slowly at first, then faster, she began to run across the field towards them, but a moment later, a strong hand caught her from behind.

'Keep out of it!'

She swung round, and found herself eye to eye with Pete. Yanking her arm free, she carried on running, but as she got near to Les, Ed, too, grabbed her by the arm and pulled her back. 'Leave him, Miranda.'

Shocked and bewildered, she stared at him uncomprehendingly. 'But why's he doing it? *Stop it!*'

Had Les heard her? If so, he took no notice. The next moment, he brought his boot down smack in the middle of the guard's face. There was a loud squeal like the sound of a stuck pig, then blood spurted up in an ornamental fountain, showering the grass with scarlet rain.

'*Oh Christ!*' Miranda tried to tear free, but Ed wouldn't let go of her. 'Do something!' she shouted at him.

Ed hesitated. Hard and bruising, his fingers dug into Miranda's upper arms as he hissed, 'Shut up, for Christ's sake!'

'But he's going to kill him!'

'I can't interfere!'

Miranda hid her face. 'Please! Please! I can't stand it! Do something! *Stop him!*'

The driver was moaning, sobbing, clutching his mangled face in a vain bid to protect it as Les stood over him, seething, frenzied, kicking randomly at his arms and legs and head. With a loud thud, the guard's right arm bent back at an odd, obtuse angle.

'That'll fucking learn you!'

'Lay off him! I said, lay off!' Releasing Miranda suddenly, Ed ran forward, grabbed Les's arms from behind, and jerked him backwards away from the bloody mess on the ground. But it was too late – the mess rolled over limply and landed face down in the grass.

Panting, Les stared at it for a moment, his fists clenched. Then he glanced down at his feet. 'Shit!' he said, swinging round and grinning up at Ed. 'Look at the state of my fucking boots!'

With the same distaste he would have shown had he stepped in dog shit, he began to wipe the blood off onto the grass. Bound and gagged on the ground, the CCV's driver stared at him with eyes that bulged like a Pekinese's.

'*What are you fucking staring at?*'

The driver shook his head wildly.

'Ready!' called Justin, running into the field. When he caught sight of the body, he stopped short, wide-eyed, and covered his mouth. '*Jesus Christ!*'

'Come on,' Ed snapped. 'Let's get out of here.'

Les wiped his hands on his flack jacket. 'And a happy Christmas to both of you,' he called over his shoulder as he swaggered out of the field. Back in the lane, he watched Justin vomit into the hedgerow. 'That'll give Forensic something nice to put in their handbag!' he chuckled to Pete.

Pete laughed. 'What about the car, boss?'

Les tore off his blood-stained jacket and climbed into the driver's seat of the van. 'You know the plan, mate. Change the plates, then take it back to Chingford. Col'll know what to do with it. We'll see you back in Hackney. And while you're at it, torch this jacket for me. Here, you!' he called to Justin. 'Wipe that filth off your face and get in the van!'

'Hurry up,' Ed yelled. 'Move it!' Grabbing Miranda by the wrist, he bundled her into the front seat next to Les, then got in the back with Justin.

Les tore off his face mask. The Transit's tyres screeched as he put his foot down and pulled away. 'Get that wig off, gorgeous!' he said, jerking his chin at Miranda.

For a long minute no one spoke. Then Miranda exploded. 'We can't just leave them there!'

Les glanced across at her, genuinely surprised. 'What do you want to do? Stop at the next house, and ask them to call an ambulance?' His laugh grated on her like jagged metal. '*Fu*cking hell!'

'He's only bruised, babe,' Ed said from the back.

Miranda swung round and glared furiously at him. 'How do you know? He looked like he was unconscious! For all we know, he's dying!'

'Jesus Christ, what a fuss to make about a bit of blood!' Les wiped his nose on the back of his hand. 'The point *is*, the point *is*, gorgeous, that we just pulled off our sixth job this month, and got away with – what?' Glancing over his shoulder, he took a quick look at the sacks of money. 'A hundred thousand quid? It's going to be a fucking good Christmas!'

A band of steel tightened around her chest. She was so shocked by Les's absolute indifference to what he'd just done that she could scarcely breathe. It was as if the whole thing had never happened. 'Why did you do it, Les? We've never had any violence before! We all agreed to that when we started! Why'd you have to go back on it?'

Les swivelled round and looked at her as if he didn't understand the question. 'He asked for it, gorgeous! He fucking spat at me! If he hadn't, it'd never have happened. He knows as well as I do, you got to play by the rules.'

'Rules? What *rules*?'

He shrugged. 'The cunt should have shown more respect. Isn't that right, Ed?' he added, glancing in the mirror. Ed didn't answer.

'Respect? For us?' Miranda laughed bitterly. 'Jesus! You might have killed him. And for what? For trying to do his job. Is that fair?'

He snorted. 'What the fuck's *fair*?'

Miranda turned away from him. 'Ed?'

Ed cleared his throat. 'You didn't have to have laid into him so bad. It wasn't really necessary, was it?'

'*Necessary?*' Les slammed on the brakes, sending the three of them flying forwards. 'What is this shit?' Turning around, he glared at Ed. His eyes were poisonous splinters in a septic-red face. 'You know the trouble with you, Ed? You're fucking pussy-whipped.' Writhing in his seat, he turned on Miranda. 'Let me tell you something, young

240

lady,' he shouted, spraying her with spittle. 'I've been on the pavement for forty fucking years, since I was ten years old and started at the dip. I've pulled more strokes in my time than you've had hot dinners. No one, but no one, tells me how to work, least of all a fucking amateur piss-artist like you. Understand? This is armed robbery, not the Women's pissing Institute. If you wanted to keep your hands clean, you should have stuck to flower arranging. Isn't that right, Justin?'

Justin didn't answer. Eyes screwed resolutely shut, he leaned against the side of the van, his hands clenched in his lap.

'I sent a bloke into Morpeth's yesterday to check out the stuff and take the pictures,' Les said later that night, as he, Ed and Miranda sat together in Ed's living room. 'He said the diamonds are something else. They got more fucking carats than you'll find in Tesco's. Worth a fucking fortune!'

'How much?'

'For the necklace and bracelet? About three and a half million.'

Ed whistled through his teeth.

'They brought them over here, hoping some punter'd buy them for Christmas.'

'What if they do?' Ed leant back on his sofa, his arms folded behind his head.

Les laughed. 'No chance! What mug's going to walk in off the street and shell out that kind of dough on a handful of stones? Only the fucking Arabs, and they're all back home soaking up the sunshine. I reckon we'd be safe to get some copies made up over Christmas, and pull the job off just before the New Year.'

'What do you think, love?' As he reached for his cigarettes, Ed glanced across at Miranda, who was curled up in a chair in front of the television. Getting no response from her, he turned back to Les. 'Who's going to make up the jars?'

'There's this bloke down in Bermondsey – Pete Brown. Know him? He restores old chandeliers. A real expert. He can cut glass to look like anything. And he's as crooked as a camel's back.'

Turning away from the television for a moment, Miranda gave an irritated sigh. 'Do you really think you can fool the staff of one of the oldest established jewellers in the country by switching diamonds for a string of cut-glass beads?'

Les plucked a stained teaspoon from an old mug on the coffee table and scooped a dollop of caviar out of a large blue tin. 'Why not?'

Miranda turned away again. 'You're mad!' she snapped.

'I told you before, gorgeous, you can get away with anything if you have enough bottle. It's all a matter of style. Besides, you only got to fool the punters for a couple of seconds – just until we get away.'

Ed drained the last drops from the magnum of Bollinger he'd been drinking all evening, then wiped his lips with the back of his hand. 'So how're we going to do the switch?'

Like Pavarotti in mid-performance, Les pulled a white handkerchief from his pocket and blotted the beads of sweat from his forehead. 'A piece of cake, mate. Miranda and me dress up as customers. The only Arabs in London. I can wear my Armani – the one I got down Brick Lane the other day. She can have some black shmutter draped over her head. First, I go in and get their trust, by buying something in cash. We'll look on it as an investment. Next time we go in, we get them to leave us alone with the goods and do the switch!'

'What about the surveillance cameras?'

'Come on, Ed! Where's your respect? Don't you think I've thought of that? We cut the power. Simple! That's where you and Justin come in!'

'Yeah, but won't they have an emergency supply? A generator or something?'

'Ye of little faith, Ed. If they have, I'll get it taken care of. Trust me – I got contacts everywhere.' As the overflowing spoon slipped between Les's lips, he swallowed hard, then winced. 'Yuk! What is this muck? It looks like tea leaves.'

'For Christ's sake, it's the best Beluga!' Ed moaned. 'You're meant to treat it with respect, not gulp it down!'

'I fucking paid for it, mate! I'll have it with OK Sauce and beans, if that's how I want it. The truth is, I can't stand the stuff. I wouldn't touch it if I wasn't bloody starving! Isn't there anything better to eat? Here, gorgeous, knock me up a ham sandwich, will you? And while you're out in the kitchen, fetch me another beer.'

Without saying a word, Miranda uncurled from the chair, relieved to have a reason to leave the room. At the kitchen counter, she picked up the breadknife and ran her index finger dangerously along the jagged blade.

'Miranda? Are you all right?'

'Sure.' Her body froze as Ed's warm, muscular arms encircled her from behind.

'I've been worried about you.' When he kissed the back of her neck, she shrunk away from him, like a child trying to escape the clutches of an over-effusive aunt.

'You don't have to worry. I can look after myself.'

'Uh-huh. About today . . . Look, babe, sometimes these things just happen.'

She nodded without conviction. 'Do they?'

'You got to accept it. It's like my Dad used to say – if you can't stand the heat, get out of the kitchen.'

The cliché sickened her. Swivelling round, she glared at him with sudden hatred. 'Look, I'm perfectly all right! Just let me be, OK?'

The moment he went out, she picked up the serrated knife again and stabbed it into the breadboard. Then, her head bowed with remorse, she burst into tears. Why was she blaming Ed for the mess she'd made of things, when it was her responsibility? If she had a right to feel angry, it was only with herself. For how could she have left her old way of life for *this*? How could she have abandoned her children and put them through so much pain in order to throw in her lot with people like *these*?

What had she been thinking of? Until now, the whole thing had seemed like a wonderful game. It was as if she'd climbed aboard a big dipper, and carried away by the first thrill, had stayed on for a second, then a third, ride. Now, the n'th time around, the machine had gathered momentum under her and was propelling her forward towards disaster at breakneck speed. Sickened and reeling she might be, but there was no getting off. She had trapped herself, more firmly than she'd ever been trapped by domesticity.

As she split a baguette open, she thought with longing of the children, and a hundred *if onlys* rattled tortuously through her head. If only she'd gone straight to the police when Ed had first freed her . . . If only Suzanne had been in when she'd 'phoned . . . If only she hadn't gone back home just at that particular moment and discovered Jack and Mary in the kitchen . . . If only she'd never fallen in love with Ed – whatever that meant. If only she'd had some sense right at the beginning! If only she could persuade herself that what had happened that very morning had been all Les's fault! But it was she, Miranda, who had planned the job. She, Miranda, who'd insisted, against Ed's wishes, on getting mixed up with Les in the first place. Without her, the injured security guard wouldn't be lying in intensive care in some hospital, as he undoubtedly now was – if he wasn't already dead.

Out in the hall, the telephone rang. Quickly drying her eyes, she went out and picked it up.

'Mrs G?' said a shaky voice on the end of the line.

'Justin?'

'You OK?'

She hesitated. 'Sure. What about you?'

'Yeah. Well, sort of. Know what I mean?'

'Mmm.'

'Actually, I feel pretty terrible, if you want to know.'

'Me, too.'

'Kind of . . . well, guilty.'

'Mmm.' In the long pause that followed, she heard the sound of voices and a Wet Wet Wet record in the background. 'Where are you?'

There was a short, awkward pause. 'Just out,' he said. Miranda's armpits prickled as she guessed with a sick feeling just where that 'out' was: the house in Huddleston Avenue. Her throat constricted as she realised how easily she could ask Justin to call one of the children to the telephone. Just to say hello, to let them know that she was alive, and thinking of them . . . Or, she could come clean, tell them everything, go to the police and take the consequences . . . How much worse could prison be than the present living nightmare she had landed herself in?

Silenced by fear and temptation, she strained her ears, trying to pick out a single familiar voice from the faint wallpaper of sound at the other end of the telephone.

'Mrs G?'

'What?'

'I . . . I never thought it would be like this.' Justin, too, sounded choked. 'Like today. I mean, I suppose I knew, but I never really took it in. It wasn't real. Know what I mean?'

'Yes, I do.'

'It's made me wonder what the hell I'm doing. And I'm . . .'

'Not now,' she interrupted him stiffly. 'We'll talk about it when I see you. Come round tomorrow morning as usual. OK?'

Back in the living room, she slammed a plate of sandwiches in front of Les, who picked one up and stuffed it in his mouth.

'I know that ten or twenty grand's a lot to shell out – thanks, gorgeous – but just think what we'll get in return.'

'Will you be quiet?' The armchair sighed as Miranda sat down in it and, grabbing the TV's remote control, turned up the sound. 'The *Nine O'clock News* is just coming on.'

Les stopped and looked at her curiously, his mouth half full. 'What's up? Want to make sure we haven't hit the headlines? Worried you've got a stiff on those lily-white hands?'

'Just shut up, will you?' Leaning back, she bit her nails as the blue-and-grey BBC logo flashed up on the screen.

'*Tory minister resigns in new adultery scandal. Pandemonium on the Stock Exchange as the pound hits an all-time low. A commuter train collides with a milk-float outside Harlow, killing ten. And the Princess of Wales flies to New York again for Christmas – "I'm just visiting," she tells her fellow travellers on the plane.*'

'Told you we wouldn't be on,' Les scoffed. 'Jobs like we did today are a dime a dozen. I'll bet you a crate of bubbly that it doesn't even get a mention in the local village rag!'

Hung over on too much champagne, Ed stumbled into the kitchen at midday the following morning to find Miranda sitting silently at the kitchen table, scanning the newspapers, and Justin clearing up the mess of the night before. 'Morning, babe,' he mumbled as, pulling his Liberty silk dressing gown closer around him, he reached for his cigarettes.

The anger which had been growing inside her since she'd awoken at five suddenly exploded. 'Must you smoke this early?' she snapped.

He looked at her in surprise. 'What's bitten you?' He lit up, then threw his lighter across the table. 'You're not still going on about what happened yesterday? Give me a break!'

Miranda chewed on her thumbnail, like a dog gnawing at a bone. 'I don't want to work with Les any more,' she said eventually.

Ed stretched his bare legs out lazily. His mouth twisted into a sardonic smile. 'That's funny. Only the other week I said the same thing and you was the one insisting that you wanted to carry on. Les was your big buddy then.'

'Well, he isn't now.' With a small shiver, she gathered the

246

soft folds of her own dressing gown under her chin. 'I want out of our partnership. As from today.'

Justin hovered sheepishly behind Miranda's chair. 'Me, too, boss.'

Ed nodded. 'Crime binge over, is it? Heat got too high for you both? Well, yesterday certainly sorted the men from the boys.'

'As far as I'm concerned, kicking someone unconscious is nothing to do with being a man.'

'Don't go all sanctimonious on me, Miranda – it's bad taste. You're a bank robber now, not a member of the moral majority.'

'I know, but . . .'

'I told you when you started out this was a tough business.'

'Beating that man up wasn't tough, Ed, it was just sadistic!'

'Well, Les's a sadistic bastard. You knew that from the start. Don't say I didn't warn you about him.'

'I'm sorry. I should have listened to you. He . . . he was just so cold after it happened! It was horrible. I don't think he's got any feelings at all.'

'Yeah, well you don't survive long in this business by having feelings.'

'You're not like that.' Miranda tried to take his hand across the table, but he snatched it away. 'You're not.'

Ed raised his eyebrows, and inhaled deeply. 'Don't kid yourself. I'm the same as what he is. When the chips are down, I'll do whatever's necessary to save my own neck.'

'I just don't believe that, darling. I know you too well.'

'I wouldn't count on it. Make me a capuccino, will you, Justin?'

'Sure, boss.'

While Justin got out the coffee and fiddled with the knobs of the chrome Pavoni, Miranda plucked a croissant from the paper bag he had brought with him earlier and picked half-heartedly at its crust.

Ed drummed his fingers on the tabletop. 'Well, this is a fine time to discover you've both got scruples. You do realise that we're in it up to our necks?'

'What're you saying, boss?'

Ed shrugged. 'Les's a powerful man. The nearest thing round here to a face. You can't just pick him up and drop him like some bit of dirt you found on the street. A man like that expects some loyalty. Besides, we're in the middle of planning a job, aren't we?'

'The Morpeth diamonds?' Justin handed Ed his coffee.

'Well, I'm not going through with it.' Miranda was resolute. 'I'm never working with that bastard again!'

'You may not have any choice.' Ed looked at her with a glum expression.

'What do you mean?'

He shrugged. 'He won't want us to back out.'

'So what? How can he stop us? He doesn't own us.'

Ed shrugged. 'You've seen what he can do when his back's up.' He sipped the capuccino. A moustache of white froth frosted his upper lip. 'Anyway,' he added in a mumble, 'we've got to go through with the job.'

'Why?'

When he put the cup down, it rattled against the saucer. 'We need the dosh.'

Miranda laughed. 'Don't be ridiculous! We must've got lots of money left.'

Ed cleared his throat. 'We're skint.'

'That's impossible, boss. How can we be after what we've been earning?'

'Earning's easy, Justin. It's hanging on to money that's the tricky part. The lady here's got expensive tastes. Besides . . .'

Miranda looked at him sharply. 'What?'

'There's something I haven't told you. Remember when you and me had that tiff the other week? Well, I spent the night down the Victoria Club. Gambling. And I blew it.'

248

'What do you mean?'

'I lost the lot. On blackjack. And roulette.'

Miranda stared at him, incredulous. 'You're kidding!'

''Fraid not.'

'It's impossible! You couldn't have gambled everything away? Not in one night?'

'It was a long night.'

She lapsed into a stunned silence. Coming up behind her, Justin put his hands on the back of her chair. 'What about the money you was keeping for me, boss?'

'Yeah, well there's not much of that left, either.'

Justin's lips trembled. 'What do you mean? There was sixty thousand quid!'

'Well, I had to do something to win back some of the money I'd lost, didn't I? So I put yours on a dog.'

The colour drained from Justin's cheeks, 'You did *what*?'

'I tell you, Justin, I'd have been mad not to! Right-on-Time, in the seven-thirty at Wembley. The odds was forty-to-one, and the race was fixed – the bitch was on steroids and all the other dogs was on Valium. If she'd have won, Justin, you'd have been a millionaire!'

'*Jesus Christ!*'

'No use appealing to him, son. If He was on your side, He'd have stopped the fucker from catching the electric hare, biting through the cable and going up in sparks.'

The chair shook as Justin tightened his grip on it. Then, letting go suddenly, he lunged across the table towards Ed. 'You stupid bastard!'

'Stop it, for God's sake!' Miranda leapt up, prised them apart and stood between them, a hand on each of their chests. 'Justin, that's not going to help! Oh, God, Ed! I just can't believe that you've been so . . . so idiotic! We can't have *nothing* left! What about the money we took yesterday?'

He shrugged. 'Ninety grand may sound a lot, but it's not going to keep us going very long after the five-way split.'

Sitting down again, Miranda stared out of the window at the small, overgrown backyard. 'OK,' she said eventually, 'We'll go ahead with the diamond robbery. Only . . .' She sighed wistfully.

'What, Mrs G?'

'I wish we could cut Les and Pete out and do it by ourselves.'

'Wish away, babe.'

'It seems such a pity. I mean, the three of us could easily manage it, couldn't we?'

Ed shrugged in reluctant agreement. 'Sure.'

'Then, when we'd sold the diamonds, we'd only have to split the money three ways.'

'We'd be rich, Mrs G!'

'Yes, we would, Justin. Think about it, Ed – you said you wanted to get out of the business. Well, here's your chance.'

'It's not on.' Ed lit another cigarette. 'You're talking dreams. Besides, I'd never be able to hold my head up again. After all, the job's Les's idea.'

'Ah, honour among thieves!' Miranda looked at him with a half-serious expression. 'What'd he do if we stole his idea? Sue us for breach of intellectual copyright?'

'He'd fucking kill us, that's what he'd do.'

Miranda drew in her breath sharply. 'That's true.'

'Not if he couldn't find us, he wouldn't.' Both Miranda and Ed turned in surprise towards Justin. 'I mean, if we was holed up somewhere, out of reach,' he continued. 'You know – somewhere he'd never find us. The Bahamas, or Jamaica, or L.A. I wouldn't mind a little holiday in the States, myself. I've always wanted to see Disneyland.'

Ed snorted in derision. 'For Christ's sake, grow up!'

Miranda put her hand over Justin's. 'He's not wrong, you know, Ed. We could pull the job off, and be out of the country before Les realises we've done it.'

'And then what? I'll tell you something – it'd have to be more than a holiday. Once you were gone, that'd be it.

You'd never be able to come back here again – never.'

'What? You mean, I'd never be able to queue in the pouring rain for a night bus down Holloway Road again? How would I survive?' Justin grinned at Miranda. 'I'll just have to buy myself a beach house in Antigua, send for my Mum and then . . .'

Miranda's heart sank as his words flattened the small bubble of hope which had been growing inside her. Leaving Britain for good would mean leaving her children. She would never, ever see them again. True, she didn't see them now, but at least she was near at hand. If something went wrong, she could be with them in less than half an hour . . .

She hung her head. Who was she fooling? The reality was that she couldn't be with them. By now they'd have rebuilt their lives without her. Even if she went back to them, and owned up to everything, they wouldn't want her once they knew what she'd done. She had to resign herself to never seeing them again. They were better off without her, just as she was better off without them . . .

She looked up sharply as the doorbell rang. She, Justin and Ed exchanged looks, like three conspirators.

'Anyone expecting a visitor?' Ed said softly.

They waited in silence till it rang again, this time with a terrifying persistence.

'Shit!' Justin's eyes were wide with fear. 'Do you think it's Les?'

Miranda frowned. 'Why? He never usually turns up here before late afternoon!'

'Then,' Justin's eyes grew larger, 'do you think it's the police?'

Ed shook his head. 'If it was, they'd have been in here with a crowbar by now. Shit! There it goes again.'

'M-maybe it's the milkman,' Justin stuttered.

'Very clever. We don't have milk delivered.'

'Yeah, well, maybe he's trying to drum up more business.'

'Look, ignore it, OK?'

251

Stock still and silent, they waited. After a long pause, the bell sounded again. This time, whoever it was kept their finger on it.

'I'll get it.' Ed got up, opened a drawer, took out a small pistol and shoved it into his dressing gown pocket. 'Justin, you stay in here. Miranda, get out of sight somewhere.'

Upstairs, she dropped down onto the floor of the landing. After a moment, she heard the front door latch click. Then Ed said in a gruff voice. 'Yeah? What do you want?'

There was a short pause. 'We want to see our mother.'

Her heart seemed to stop. Lily sounded nervous, but at the same time determined. Miranda felt the free will drain out of her. Suddenly she was no more than a puppet, yanked back to reality by a single pull on an umbilical string.

'Sorry?'

'We want to see our mother.'

'Who's she?'

He must know that they were her children. She knew he knew it, and she hated him for being so cold to them. Her heart soared with pride when Thomas's high voice retorted, 'It's no use you pretending that you don't know her, because we know she's here.'

'Sorry, kids, I haven't got a clue what you're talking about.'

'Yes, you do.' Lily's clear voice rang with that high petulant note she remembered so well. 'She *is* here, and we want to see her!'

'I don't know nothing about her. What's her name?'

How could he play with them like that? When Lily next spoke, she sounded near to tears and less sure of herself. 'Miranda. Miranda Green.'

'Never heard of her. Now, piss off, will you?'

'Please!' Thomas shouted. 'You've got to let us in?'

'I said, piss off!'

'Justin's here, too! We . . . we followed him here! We saw him come in!'

252

When Ed eventually spoke, his voice was shaking with suppressed fury. 'Look, love, you've got the wrong house. Now, clear off, both of you.'

'Not until you let us speak to her. If you don't, we'll . . . we'll call the police. Hey, don't shut the door on us! Ow! That's my foot!'

'Hey, stop it! Don't you hurt my sister! Let go of the door! Let us in! MUMMY!'

'I said, clear off!'

Miranda jumped up, remembering the gun.

'Don't you push me!'

'Stop! My foot's caught! MUMMY!'

'Leave my sister alone! Mum! Mum!'

'Stop it! Don't you touch them!' Unable to stand any more, she flew downstairs, pulled Ed roughly away from the door and yanked it open. When she saw Thomas and Lily outside, she burst into tears.

The two of them looked at her as if they did not recognise her.

'Mummy?'

'Mum? Is it really you?'

'Oh, darlings!' First Thomas, then Lily, fell into her arms.

'Oh, Mum! Mum, you're not dead! You're alive!'

'Yes, Thomas, I'm alive.' Burying her face in his hair, she breathed in the fresh clean scent of his shampoo. 'Oh, God,' she sobbed, 'it's so wonderful to see you!'

Suddenly Lily pulled away from her, and stood back, glaring angrily at Ed. Narrowing her eyes, she scanned down his body from the open neck of his dressing gown to his bare feet.

'Who's *he*?'

'He's a . . . a friend of mine.'

'Some *friend*! He tried to stop us coming in. He didn't want us to see you. Mummy, who *is* he? And Mummy, *what are you doing here*?'

'Darlings, it's a very long story.' She squeezed them both

253

tightly again. 'Oh, I can't tell you how wonderful it is to see you both! Hush, Thomas, don't cry. I'm quite all right, you can see I am. Look, come in, come in!'

She led them in to the kitchen, an arm wrapped protectively around each of their shoulders. When Ed scowled at her, she shrugged helplessly. They were her children. What was she supposed to do?

'Where are David and Diana?'

'They don't know we've come. They're at school. It's the last day of term today.'

'Is it? Why aren't you both there?'

'Why do you think?' Lily retorted. 'We had to come and see you. Hello, Justin.'

Justin backed towards the door. 'I never told them nothing,' he said quickly to Ed.

'*No?*'

'Honest.'

'*So how come they're here?*'

Thomas raised his tearful eyes to Miranda. 'I overheard him talking to you on the phone last night, Mum. I heard you tell him to come over in the morning. I just couldn't believe it was you. I thought I must have made a mistake. So I told Lily, and we decided to follow him.'

'And I decided not to tell the others, in case it was a mistake.'

Ed turned on Justin. 'You phoned from their house? On their line? *Bloody idiot!* Why the hell didn't you go outside and use your mobile? What the hell do you think I bought it for you for?'

Justin winced. 'Flat battery. Sorry, boss.'

'*It's a bit fucking late to be sorry!*'

'Look, what's done is done.' Miranda blew her nose, and smiled at Thomas and Lily through her tears. 'Anyway, I'm glad they're here. I'm so glad, I can't tell you.'

She wiped her eyes and turned away, overcome with emotion. What had seemed impossible five minutes ago had just become reality. Now, with Thomas and Lily in front of her, she asked herself how she could ever have left them, even for a day. They were her flesh, the most important thing in her life.

Ed slammed out of the kitchen and thundered upstairs, Justin trailing at his heels. 'Boss? *Boss!*'

Miranda blew her nose. 'Sorry, darlings. Ed's just a bit upset. He'll calm down in a minute.'

'Who *is* he, Mum?'

'He's . . . Well, he's a friend, Thomas.'

'A *friend?* Of *yours?* And I suppose Justin's a friend of *yours* now, too?'

'Don't sound so surprised, Lily. You're not the only one who has friends. Look, you may as well know, this is Ed's house, and, well, I've been . . .' she searched for an appropriate but non-committal expression, 'staying here for a while. But let's not talk about me! Not yet. I want to hear about you two. Take off your anoraks, both of you, and sit down.'

Still sobbing quietly, Thomas sat down at the table. With her curtain of long hair, perfect skin and almond-shaped eyes, Lily looked much the same as she remembered her, but Thomas looked thinner, sadder, taller. His red hair had grown longer and even more unruly, and the freckled cream of his cheeks had a sallow look, as if it had been washed with a thin tint of yellow paint. Around his eyes were dark blue smudges of mascara. With a swollen heart, Miranda reached over and wiped them away with a fingertip.

'Would you like something to eat or drink? No? Lily, what about you? Tea? Toast? Look, there's a couple of croissants left. And we've got some lovely real French black cherry jam somewhere. How about some hot chocolate or something?'

'We don't want anything.'

'Oh, go on, have something, you must be so cold. It's bitter outside.'

'No.'

'You could have . . .'

'Stop it, will you?'

'Stop what? What is it, Lily?'

Lily's eyes blazed like blue gas jets. 'For Christ's sake, Mummy! You ran off and left us! You can't just charge back into our lives and start ordering us about again!'

'But I wasn't! I just . . .'

'Oh, leave me alone!'

Bursting into tears, Lily ran from the room. Miranda kissed Thomas on the forehead.

'Wait here, darling,' she said. 'I'll be back in a moment.'

She found her daughter sitting crying at the bottom of the stairs, and held her arms out to her.

'Go away!' Lily wiped her wet face on her anorak sleeve. 'I hate you! I hate you! I hate you! I never, ever want to see you again!'

'Oh, darling!'

'Don't *darling* me!'

'Lily . . .'

Raising her head for a moment, Lily shot her a look of pure animosity. Miranda went cold as she realised this was what she had done – made her daughter hate her. For a moment, she'd been so carried away by the pleasure of seeing Lily and Thomas that she'd forgotten the reason for her absence.

From upstairs came the sound of Ed and Justin arguing.

'*Justin, you're a fucking piss-artist!*'

'*Look, Ed . . .*'

'*Don't talk to me! I'm not interested in your excuses . . .*'

'I just can't believe that you've been alive all this time, and you haven't even bothered to phone us!' Lily sobbed.

'I'm sorry, darling. I . . . There were reasons why I couldn't.'

'Or that you left us – to live here with *him*!' She looked up at Miranda through narrowed eyes. 'You're not really living with him, are you?'

Miranda took a deep breath. She had forgotten how

intimidating her eldest daughter could be. 'As a matter of fact, I am.' Sitting down on the stairs beside her, she tried to take her hand.

Lily snatched it away and edged across to the banisters. 'You mean,' she sniffed. 'you rent a room here?'

She hesitated. 'Yes. And . . .'

'And what?'

'And . . . well, we're lovers.'

Somewhere on the upstairs landing, Justin was rapping on a door. '*Ed . . . Ed . . . Please listen, boss!*

Lily laughed coldly through her tears. 'You're joking!'

'Joking? Why should I be?'

'You mean, you actually have sex with him?'

Once again, Miranda hesitated. 'Isn't that what lovers usually do?'

Lily shuddered. She looked like a slice of lemon had just been placed under her tongue. 'How . . . how revolting!'

Automatic as a pilot light, a spark of anger ignited inside Miranda. She bit her lip. 'Actually, there's nothing revolting about it,' she said as calmly as she could. 'In fact, I enjoy it very much.'

The bedroom door opened, then slammed. Barely muffled, Ed's angry voice echoed through the house.

'How can you?' Lily said. 'With *him*? After someone like Daddy.'

'Very easily, actually.'

'Jesus, Mummy! Why?'

'Because . . .' Miranda's face relaxed into a smile. 'I suppose it's because I love him, Lily,' she said quietly. 'Don't look so disgusted. It happens to be true.'

Lily sighed impatiently. 'Aren't you a bit old for all of that?'

'It seems not.'

'You can't possibly love him!'

'But I do, darling. Ed may be a bit – well – different from Daddy . . .'

'Huh! You can say that again!'

'But when you get to know him he's a remarkable man. He's kind, and thoughtful, and interesting, and intelligent – don't roll your eyes like that, darling.'

'Face it, Mummy – he's a . . . a common yob!'

'Lily!'

'Christ! I never thought you of all people, my own mother, would be into rough trade!'

Suddenly it was as if the last six months had not existed. She was back in the same old parent-child battle, a foot-sore soldier fighting wearily on the losing side. 'How dare you talk to me like that!'

'Why shouldn't I? You're the one who ran off and left us! You're the one who let us go around believing you'd been murdered! Have you ever stopped to think what it's been like for us? Can you imagine what we've been through? Or don't you care?'

As her neck drooped, her hair flopped in thick strands over her red, wet face. She looked distraught. Gripped with guilt, Miranda began to cry too.

'Oh, darling! You're right. I'm so, so sorry. I never meant to hurt you but . . . Oh, it's all unforgivable.'

'Yes, it bloody well is!' Lily looked up. Streams of black eyeliner were running down her cheeks. Miranda reached out to brush them away. 'No, don't touch me! Don't you dare come near me!' Shoulders shaking, she continued to sob loudly into her sleeve. 'Life at home's been unbearable without you!'

Miranda's heart turned to jelly. 'Have you really missed me?'

'What do you think? It's just been horrible there! Everything's gone to pieces. First, Daddy sacked Mrs Weaving and made us do all the cleaning. He ran the place like a bloody prison camp. Nowadays, no one but me does anything. The place is a real pigsty! And there's never anything decent to eat in the fridge, only the crap Mary brings in. Can you imagine, she's actually living with us now, Mum, actually living in *our* house. Sleeping in *your* bed. With Dad! Having the same old rows with him that you used to have. She's driving us all bloody crazy. As for the others, they come to me all the time, expecting me to cook things for them and . . . even iron their clothes! Just because I'm the eldest girl! And as for Dad – he's falling to pieces! He's been *suspended* by the university! Can you imagine, they've accused him of attacking someone or something and . . . and . . . I don't know, embezzling the university funds! Now he's home all the time, just hanging around, nagging us to economise. He's even made me give up my jazz dancing lessons, because he says they're too expensive!'

A chill crept into Miranda's heart. 'That's not what I asked, Lily. I said, have you missed *me*?'

Lily looked confused. 'I just said so, didn't I? I can't wait for you to come home, so that things'll go back to normal and . . .'

'Lily . . .'

'What?'

'I . . . I'm not coming home.'

Lily turned white. 'But it's Christmas! You've got to!'

'I haven't *got* to do anything. And I'm not coming home. I can't. Not yet, at any rate.'

'But . . . When, then?'

'I don't know. Maybe not ever. For the moment, I'm staying here.'

'Here? In this . . .' She looked around at the bare bulb dangling from the ceiling light, the cracked, mouldy walls and the threadbare carpet, '. . . this dump?'

'Yes. In this dump, if that's what you want to call it.'

'Mum?' Thomas called out from the kitchen.

Lily ignored him. 'You'd rather live in this dump, with *him*, than come home to us? You can't really mean that!'

'I'm afraid I do, darling. You see, I'm happier here. I feel fulfilled for the first time ever. I feel appreciated. And wanted. And before you say anything, I'm not talking about sex – although that's wonderful, too. I'm talking about having somebody who really cares about me, and likes me as I am, and – yes – loves me.'

'*Mum, are you coming?*'

'Just a minute, Thomas.'

'Dad loves you, too!'

'No, he doesn't, Lily. I'm afraid he hasn't loved me for a long time.'

'How do you know?'

She turned away from her daughter's accusing eyes. 'I don't want to go into it.'

'For God's sake! I'm your daughter! I've got a right to know!'

'No.'

'I don't suppose it matters that we love you?' Lily persisted in her angry voice.

'Of course it matters!'

'But not enough to make you come home?'

'Darling . . . It's just not that simple.'

'You mean that you don't want to.'

'No . . . It's complicated. I . . . I can't explain.'

Thwarted, Lily fumed in silence for a good thirty seconds – which was twenty seconds longer than Miranda had ever seen her silent before. Then she said bitterly. 'I don't know what's happened to you. You used to be so nice, but now you've become so . . . so *incredibly* selfish!'

Miranda smiled sadly. 'I suppose I have. It was about time, too, don't you think? I'd been a doormat for far too long.'

'A doormat?' Lily rolled her eyes. '*Puh-leease!* Don't tell me you've gone all women's libby as well! That would be the last straw.'

'Come on,' Miranda said, putting an arm around her. 'Let's go back into the kitchen. It isn't fair to leave Thomas all alone.'

'That hasn't seemed to worry you for the last six months!'

Thomas and Lily sat silently at the table while she bustled round them, making toast and tea, and talking nervously about trivialities. A few minutes later Justin slunk back in, his face washed out.

'How come Justin's here, Mum?' Thomas asked. 'Justin, how long have you known that Mum was still alive?'

Justin looked at Miranda. 'Just a few weeks,' she said quickly. 'We bumped into each other in the street.'

'Why didn't you tell us, Justin?' Lily demanded.

'I . . . er . . .'

'How could you keep quiet about it? I mean, Christ! You know what we've all been going through.'

'It's my fault,' Miranda said quickly. 'I swore him to secrecy.'

'Why did you have to keep *her* secret? You're supposed to be *our* friend.'

Justin shrugged.

'Why did you cut all your hair off, Mum?' Thomas said. 'And you've dyed it.'

'I . . . I fancied a change.'

'You mean, you didn't want to be recognised.' Lily was right, of course. 'If she'd have been recognised, Thomas, that would've meant she'd have had to come home to us. Christ, we must really be *terrible*!'

'Mum?'

'Yes, Thomas?'

'I wish you'd explain. I want to understand. Why did you go off like that without telling us? And why did you let everyone think you'd been killed? I mean *did* you get kidnapped or what?'

Torn between the need to explain and her desire to protect them from the awful truth, Miranda spread her hands helplessly. 'It's a long story, darling.'

'I bet!'

'Lily, please try not to be so sarcastic.'

'Why the hell should I?' Just then, Ed appeared in the doorway, fully dressed, with a fat duffle bag slung over his shoulder. Lily shot him a furious look. 'Does *he* have to come in here?'

261

Ed scowled at Lily, his face like a storm cloud. 'Don't worry. I'm clearing off. The game's over, isn't it, Miranda?'

'What game?' said Lily sharply. 'What game, Mummy?'

But Miranda never got as far as an explanation. Because, just then, the kitchen door swung open and Les walked in. The moment he saw Lily and Thomas, his tiny eyes lit up, and his lips spread in a wide grin.

'Ah-ha!' he said cheerfully, rubbing his hands together. 'And what have we here?'

Sixteen

Jack lay in bed, staring glumly at the thin grey light which filtered under the curtains while Sue Lawley and her Desert Island guest talked into his ear. Rolling over onto his side, he forced enough strength into his hand to switch off the radio. The conversation, like the music – a predictable selection including Mozart's 'Requiem', Imagine, and the three tenors singing 'O Sole Mio' – had drifted over his head, just as everything drifted over his head nowadays. At one time waining, his power of concentration had now completely vanished. Even Freud's *Standard Edition* and the *Guardian*'s Women's Pages failed to keep his attention for more than two sentences before the words began to dance before his eyes in Bridget Rileyesque confusion. Now that, for the first time in his life, he had all the time in the world to read, he seemed to have lost the ability to do it. Maybe he needed a new pair of glasses. At his age, bifocals. If only he could summon enough energy to walk the quarter mile or so down to the local opticians.

With all the agility of a frail octogenarian, he heaved his sluggish body out of bed and stumbled through the crop of abandoned shoes, socks and dirty underpants which had proliferated all over the carpet since Mary had moved back next door to her own house on Christmas Eve. 'No one wants me here – not even you any more,' she wailed as she crammed her clothes into a suitcase. 'Frankly, I've had more than I can swallow. I can just about stomach that theft inquiry, Jack, but this rape business has been the last straw.'

In vain had he tried to explain that it wasn't rape he'd been accused of, only sexual harrassment, and that, apart from the fact that it had been perpetrated from his computer terminal, using his password, there was not one single other shred of evidence to link him to the robbery of £300,000-worth of university funds. But his professions of innocence seemed to count for nothing. As far as Mary, and his children, and his employers, and the police were concerned, he was guilty on all counts until proven innocent. And, in all probability, still guilty after that.

Out on the landing, he stubbed his toe on a mud-encrusted football boot which had been abandoned on the carpet, then fell into the bathroom where he subsided onto the sticky lavatory seat and looked around in dismay. An army of oozing shampoo bottles – all without tops – were crammed onto the windowsill, the mouldy shower curtain had come unhooked from its rail, the bath was coated with thick black scum, and a line of stripy toothpaste had dried to a crust across the splashback above the grimy sink, upon which lay, in disarray, five toothbrushes with splayed bristles, half a bar of cracked Imperial Leather, and a grey, wet face flannel dripping water onto the cork floor. What, he wondered, had happened to his housework rota? None of the children did anything any more. He'd do it himself, if only he could be bothered . . .

He closed his eyes and strained. When he'd finished, he reached for the lavatory paper. A bare cardboard tube rattled on the wooden holder.

'Thomas! David!'

Through the thin skin of the ceiling he heard his sons stop talking for a moment, then carry on. He called again. This time nothing at all happened. In desperation, he tried the girls' names. After a short pause, angry footsteps thumped up the stairs.

'Yes?' said a curt voice outside the bathroom door.

'Diana?'

'What?'

'There isn't any paper.'

'What?'

'There's no lavatory paper.'

'Honestly! I'm in the middle of breakfast!'

He hesitated. 'Perhaps Lily could bring some up?'

'She went out early.'

'Oh. Oh, dear. Well, could you bring me up a roll? Please?'

There was a deep, impatient sigh. 'Can't you do anything for yourself any more?'

'Please.' Thoroughly humiliated, he sat tight while the footsteps trudged downstairs, then, reluctantly, up again.

'There *is* no more loo paper,' Diana barked. 'Because *you* haven't gone to the supermarket for weeks. You'll have to use kitchen roll.'

'Thanks, love!' he called out. There was no reply. Lurching to the door, he opened it a crack and pulled the roll in. 'Thanks!' he said again. Diana, on her way downstairs, didn't look round.

Jack climbed into the bath, rehooked the plastic curtain and, flicking the lever, stepped under the shower head. Lukewarm water drizzled onto his head and down his spine. After twenty seconds, the drips turned scorching hot, then ice cold. Jumping out, he groped blindly for one of the limp towels crammed onto the small towel rail. With a terrible crunch, the rail fell off the wall and came crashing down on his toe.

As he hopped around in agony, clutching his foot, he caught sight of his haunted, unshaven face in the over-the-sink mirror. What was happening to him? The house, like his life, was falling to pieces around him, and he felt powerless to do anything about it.

Back in the bedroom, he glanced with dread at the heap of crumpled clothes in his once-immaculate wardrobe, then pulled on the same socks, jeans and jumper he had worn every day for the past week. What did it matter what he wore? Downstairs, he grabbed his duffle coat from the hatstand, and headed for the Tube. He needed to get away from Tufnell Park. He needed intensive analysis, but he couldn't afford it. Maybe Prozac would help him? He'd ask his doctor for a prescription – if only he could be bothered to book an appointment . . .

For the first time since she'd disappeared, he missed Miranda. He thought of her not sadly, but reproachfully, almost angrily, as if the disasters that had befallen him were all her fault.

As the white Rolls Royce drew up on the corner of Regent Street and Sackville Street, the manager of Morpeth's came rushing through the mahogany doors and skipped across the pavement. 'Sheik Aziz!' he said, opening the passenger door before either the Rolls' chauffeur or his own uniformed doorman had had a chance to. 'How very good to see you again!'

Small and squat in a dark blue suit, and with a camel coat flapping loose from his shoulders, the 'sheik' slid out onto the pavement and, holding out a plump, dark brown hand encrusted with gold and diamonds, heartily shook the man's hand. 'My pleasure, Mr Carew. But you look so surprised to see me! Did I not tell you when I bought the diamond ring yesterday that I would return? Did you doubt that I am a man of my word?' Aziz's eyes twinkled as he watched the slow stain of embarrassment spread across Carew's face. 'Ah, trust, Mr Carew, trust! Back home in Bahrain, a man's word is still his bond – just like it used to be in your famous City.'

As Carew clicked his fingers, the shop's doorman rushed over with an open umbrella. 'I assure you, I was only, um, thinking that our terrible weather might be keeping you in your hotel.'

Aziz gestured towards the Rolls, in the back of which was sitting a single figure shrouded in black. From the eyeslits of her golden visor, two dark kohl-rimmed eyes blinked at Carew modestly. 'It would take more than a little drizzle to keep my wife in our suite at the Dorchester on the first day of Harrods' winter sale!' Laughing heartily, he clapped Carew hard on the back. 'But, as I said to her while we were breakfasting this morning, "Before you go bargain hunting, Yasmin, I have a little shopping errand of my own I want you to accompany me on." In short, Mr Carew, I have brought her here this morning to have a look at that little set of diamonds you so kindly showed me yesterday.'

'Of course! If you'd like to bring Madam in . . .'

Les turned towards the car. 'Yasmin, my dear, come, come inside, before we both catch our death of cold in this British climate. Sutton!' He signalled to the tall, uniformed chauffeur, 'Help her out!'

Lifting her black, floor-length *abbaya* a few inches to reveal a slender, black-stockinged ankle in a Gucci shoe, Miranda inched over to the door and, giving Pete her hand, stepped out into Regent Street, her movements hampered by the thick padding underneath her clothes. Having acknowledged Carew with a silent nod, she followed the two men towards the shop with a slow, stately waddle.

Round the corner, on the pavement in Sackville Street, Justin, dressed in bright blue overalls, looked out from a small tent emblazoned with the words London Electricity and gave Miranda a wink.

Les stopped by the doorway, smiling, and held his hand out to her. Miranda gritted her teeth. Just this one more job, she told herself, and then the whole sordid business would be over. She might not have her children with her, but she'd have Ed, and her freedom. First, she had to get through today.

'Keep that bloody thing still!' she hissed at Pete as his umbrella dipped slightly, allowing raindrops to fall on the few visible patches of her otherwise covered face. With the £3,500,000 diamonds within tantalising reach, the last thing she needed right now was for her fake tan to run.

*   *   *

Pa-pa-pa-pah. Pa-pa-pa-pah. The Northern line rattled on through the soot-blackened tunnels, stopping, now and then, at bleak dimly-lit stations. At Kentish Town, a red-faced drunk stumbled on, beer can in hand, and, though the carriage was half-empty, sat down next to Jack. His beige trousers were stained brown on the fly and his matted hair was crawling with vermin. Too polite to actually move seats, Jack surreptitiously edged away from him and tried hard not to breathe. When the train stopped at Camden Town, he pretended he was getting off and moved to the next carriage where a black youth and a pallid skinhead with the word WAR tattooed on his forehead were hunched over a packet of crack, clinching a deal.

Pa-pa-pa-pah. Pa-pa-pa-pah. Euston Station. Warren Street. Tottenham Court Road. Just as the train was about to leave the platform, Jack jumped up, squeezed through the closing doors, and rode the escalators up through the colourful Paolozzi mosaics. A small crowd was clogging the station's entrance, for outside rain was falling in a steady drizzle. Pulling his hood up, he trudged purposelessly down Oxford Street past shoe shops and clothes shops and fast-food outlets sporting glass-fronted counters filled with garish slices of hot pizza which oozed grease under bright hot lights. A mulch of squashed burger cartons, broken plastic cups and soggy newspapers littered the pavement. Lakes of black rain overflowed from the clogged gutters. Every few steps, a cracked paving stone attempted to trip him up. Jack took it all in with blank resignation: the infrastructure of London was slowly but surely collapsing, just like the infrastructure of his life.

While he dodged deep puddles in which cigarette butts floated like small turds, he thought about the disasters that had befallen him over the past six months. In the past he'd always believed that, if things happened to you, they happened because, consciously or unconsciously, you'd brought them upon yourself. But where did this leave him now? Was he really to blame for Miranda's murder, and for the false accusations made against him, and for Mary dumping him in order to go back to Brian, and for his children treating him like shit?

He bit his cold, cracked lips. What did it matter, when there were practical things he ought to be thinking about, like how he was going to pay the mortgage and feed the children if, or rather when, the university gave him the sack. Academe was tough enough nowadays even for those with an unblemished record – not so much a matter of how good a teacher you were, as how much money you brought into the department in research grants. With blots like sexual harrassment and suspected theft on his CV, what chance did he have of attracting grants in the future, or ever convincing a new employer to take him on?

'Spare some . . .' A youth, squatting under a sodden sleeping bag in a doorway next to Marks & Spencers, took one look at him and stopped halfway through his plea. 'Sorry, mate!' he said with a wink. Jack turned away. What hope was there for him, when even a beggar took pity on him? It was obvious, even to this homeless bloke, that he had fallen as low as could be. Though still suspended on full pay, he already felt and looked like a member of the underclass – penniless, alienated, dispossessed. He saw himself in a year's time, sitting outside the same shop, holding the same pathetic, misspelled cardboard sign as this young man was now clutching: *No job, No home, No freinds*.

He shivered. A thin line stood between him and penury. If only he *had* stolen that missing £300,000!

Outside Oxford Circus tube, he contemplated buying a bag of hot chestnuts from a street vendor, but at £1, dismissed them as too dear. As he crossed Great Marlborough Street, he plunged off the kerb and into a deep puddle, turning his ankle. Icy water sloshed over his socks and into his shoe.

Bitterly resigned to his fate, Jack limped slowly on down Regent Street. Tourists and shoppers bustled around him, looking smart, purposeful and busy. Unlike him, they seemed to belong there. He was the only outsider, a lone, lonely traveller in a foreign land.

Morpeth's *salle privé* was a spacious room in the firm's basement, sumptuously furnished with huge chintz sofas and distressed-leather armchairs. Limed oak panelling clad the walls, and a huge gas-log fire blazed in a white marble Adamesque fireplace, the top of which was adorned with a large pair of Staffordshire china dogs and a silver-framed photograph of the Prince of Wales. Only the lack of any windows, the battery of video surveillance cameras positioned discreetly, but strategically, overhead, and the solid steel security door reminded one that this was not the sitting room of an expensive English country hotel, but in fact a vast, electronically-controlled safe.

With a small click, the steel door slid open and Carew came in carrying a silver tray, upon which was a large, flat leather box.

'Sorry to have kept you waiting.'

Les put down his gold-edged Wedgewood coffee cup. When he spoke his well-rehearsed accent was a melange of Oxbridge vowels and gutteral Middle-European consonants, overlaid with the occasional tones of an East End wide boy. It amazed Miranda that the manager of Morpeth's was taken in by it. 'Not at all, Carew. My wife and I have been making the most of the silence – enjoying the calm before the Harrods storm.'

Carew gave a short laugh, and placed the tray on the walnut coffee table in front of the sofa. 'Sooner you than me, I must say. Buying at sales has never been my strong point.'

'Yasmin, on the other hand, is a well-practised shopper, aren't you my dear?' Miranda's eyes smiled through the slits in her *batula*. 'By the way, Carew, you must forgive us if I speak for her. Her spoken English is a little ropy. But don't go saying things about her, because she understands everything. Moreover, she understands a good bargain. And she understands diamonds. Oh yes, Yasmin is something of an expert when it comes to diamonds. The jewellers back home quake in their boots when they see her coming. They know only the best will do.'

'Well, I can assure her that these are amongst the best she will ever see.'

As Carew clicked open the case, Miranda sat forward in expectation. When Carew lifted out the necklace, she gave an involuntary gasp.

'Exquisite, isn't it?' Carew said, holding it up under the recessed spotlights. 'I have to say, in all my years in this business, I've never seen anything quite like it. To find forty stones of this quality, all so perfectly matched . . . But, here, please, have a close look at them yourself. Ah, I see you're already wearing the ring which *sir* bought for you yesterday,' he remarked as Miranda held out a darkly tanned, bejewelled hand. 'A delightful emerald-cut stone!'

Miranda's fingers closed on the heavy necklace. Carew talked on, but she could think of nothing other than that she was holding several million pounds' worth of diamonds in her hand.

'A diamond river of this length, and this quality – well, as you must know, it's unheard of. Each stone is, quite simply, perfection – five carats in weight – except the clasp, of course, which is six carats – the colour E, E-F, internally flawless. But more than that, to find so many stones of this grade, in an oval brilliant cut! And what a cut! Done by one man – the best cutter in New York. The symmetry is absolutely perfect. One could gaze into them for ever. Seldom in my career have I seen such marvellous refraction and fire! As for the bracelet . . .' Here he turned away, plucked the bracelet from its velvet shell and held it out to her. 'See for yourself. Fifteen stones, of exactly the same grade, but of course three carats . . .'

Surreptitiously, Les glanced at his gold Rolex. 'All this talk of carats and suchlike is most interesting, Carew,' he interrupted. 'But unless we, as you British say, get a move on, Yasmin is going to miss all the best bargains in Harrods' cashmere department.' Turning to Miranda, he patted her hand. 'Is that not right, my dear?'

Carew flushed a flustered pink. 'Yes. Oh, yes, of course! Perhaps Madam would like to try them on now? Shall I leave you for a few minutes, so that you might have some privacy? If you need anything, I shall be right outside.'

As if he were dealing with eighteenth century royalty, he backed out of the room. The electronic door slid shut behind him and the lock engaged with a click. Les took the necklace from Miranda, and examined it.

'Come on, come on, damn you!' he muttered under his breath. 'Pull the plugs!'

A moment later, right on cue, the lamps and spotlights flickered, then went out. Overhead, the tiny red lights on the video surveillance cameras faded to black. Only the fire carried on burning.

'Good lads!'

As rehearsed, Miranda let out a small scream. Outside, someone thumped on the door. 'Sheik Aziz? Are you both all right?'

'What is happening, Mr Carew?'

'I'm most dreadfully sorry. We appear to be having a power failure. I can't understand why our emergency generator hasn't come on.'

'Most unfortunate. Will you kindly let us out of here?'

'I'm so sorry – I can't.'

With the speed of an expert, Les pulled on some leather gloves, took the silk handkerchief from his breast pocket and began to polish his fingerprints from the coffee cup. 'Why not, Carew?'

'Unfortunately, the lock is electronically operated. If I can find my way upstairs, I'll go and get someone immediately to try to sort it out.'

His slow, lurching footsteps grew fainter.

'How long have we got?' Miranda whispered.

'Fifteen or twenty minutes. Better get a move on, gorgeous.'

Miranda pulled apart the abbaya, reached up her long black skirt for the small soft package taped to her inner thigh and ripped it off. The square of velvet unrolled onto the desk, spilling its bright crystal contents next to the real diamonds.

'Fucking brilliant!' Les murmured. As he got out his torch and shone it on the two necklaces, a thousand rainbows danced around the room. 'OK, fucking brilliant in the dark. It's not going to fool them long when the lights come on, is it?'

'We'll have to make a quick getaway.'

'We bloody will,' he whispered back. Suddenly, he turned the torch beam full onto Miranda's face, forcing her to shield her eyes. 'It's funny, I never thought you'd go through with this, gorgeous.'

She squinted into the light. 'Why not?'

'I thought you'd gone cold on me. That that CCV job before Christmas had put you off.'

Miranda hesitated, sensing a trap. 'Business is business.'

'True enough. A villain's got to do what a villain's got to do, eh? Which is why I brought this along.' The beam moved away from her face as he reached into his inside pocket and pulled out a small Smith and Wesson. 'If Carew cottons on, we'll shoot our way out of here. Maybe I'll do it anyway.'

'Oh?' Her heart skipped a beat. She got the feeling he was saying this to test her. 'Why bother?' she said as calmly as she could. 'When we know we can get away the way we've planned it?'

'It'd be neater. No witnesses.'

'But . . . But if we get caught, we could be done for murder.'

'Armed robbery, murder – who cares? There's not much difference in the sentences nowadays.'

If this was a bluff designed to scare her, it was succeeding. Still, determined not to show him she was frightened, she stared unflinchingly into the light. 'Please, Les. You know I don't want any violence. Put the gun away.'

'I might, gorgeous.' There was a long pause. 'On one condition – that you hand over the other necklace.'

Her blood seemed to stop flowing inside her. 'What other necklace?'

'Don't fuck me around, gorgeous. The second fake necklace. The one you've been planning to switch for the diamonds when we get outside.'

Her heart crashed against her ribs. 'What on earth are you talking about? You must be crazy!'

He pointed the gun at her. 'No, you're fucking crazy, gorgeous, to even think of screwing me. Now, you'd better hand it over, or I'll come and get it myself.'

The next moment, Les slid the torch back into his pocket and, pushing her down on the sofa, threw himself on top of her.

'For Christ's sake!' she hissed as his hand shot up under her skirt. 'What the hell do you think you're doing? We're in the middle of a job!'

'Where've you put them? In that tight little pussy Ed loves so much?'

Sharp as a knife, his fingernails clawed up her thighs, pulled down her pants, and groped inside them. 'Ah!' With a deep sigh, he withdrew, holding a lumpy roll of velvet. He jumped up, unfolded it, and spilled its contents onto the desk. Now there were two crystal necklaces side by side with the real diamonds, glittering in the dim light of the gas log fire.

Les turned towards her with a look of contempt. 'Get up!'

Feeling sick, she struggled to her feet. As soon as she was upright, he grabbed her by the throat. 'Stupid cunt! Did you really think you could get away with it?' He shook her fiercely, but Miranda was too frightened to answer.

After a moment, she whispered, 'How did you know?'

He laughed coldly. 'It's my business to know everything. Remember that day when we had lunch in San Lorenzo's?

Well, while we was there, I got a mate to change all your plugs. I'm telling you, these new transmitters are fucking brilliant. They look just like adaptors. Only I could pick up every fucking word you said.'

'You bugged our house?'

'Only the kitchen and the front room. And the bedroom. *Very* interesting, that was. Oh, yeah, and I bugged the phone. Want a bit of advice for the future, gorgeous? Next time you're planning to double-cross someone, don't ever do business over the blower.'

Miranda cursed herself for her stupidity. She'd thought she'd got the criminal world sussed, but it turned out she was as much a victim of it now as she'd ever been before. As her dreams of escaping abroad crashed around her, she asked herself how she could ever have been so foolish to think she'd get away with double-crossing someone as hardened as Les. Frightened as she was, she did her best to control her voice. 'If you know everything, you'll know that Ed and Justin had nothing to do with this. I suggested it, but they wouldn't buy it.'

'Save your breath, gorgeous. You can't tell me anything that I don't already know.' A sad sigh escaped from his blubbery lips. 'I could fucking kill you. Want to know something? I really liked you. I must be losing my instinct, because I trusted you for a while back there. Now, listen to me. In ten minutes, lover boy outside and Justin will switch the juice back on, and you and I are out of here. You know the plan, and we stick to it. Except, at the last minute, I'm going to plug that little shit Carew. And you, if I feel like it. And there's fuck-all you can do about it.'

Wasn't there? In a gamble to gain power over him, she lunged for his gun, and knocked it to the floor. Before she could grab it, he kicked it across the room. Throwing herself down, she groped for it underneath the table. A moment later, she felt the warm metal in her hand.

'I'd rather go to prison than let you kill Carew for nothing,' she panted as she scrabbled to her feet. 'I'd rather shoot you myself now.' Her hands shook as she pointed the gun at him.

'Sheik Aziz?' said a voice out in the corridor.

'Carew?'

'Many apologies. It appears that the power down the whole side of Regent Street has cut out. As for our generator – well, I don't understand what's gone wrong. I've telephoned the security company responsible for this door and they assure me an engineer's on his way.'

'Good.' Les didn't move, just grinned at her in the semi-darkness. 'You'll never pull that trigger, gorgeous,' he whispered. 'Like to know why?' She said nothing. Slowly, his left hand reached inside his jacket. Miranda pulled back the catch. 'I wouldn't do that if I were you.' He pulled a small white square from inside his lapels. 'Not till you've had a butcher's at this.'

Was he bluffing? Something in his manner told her to take him seriously. Miranda jerked her head towards the coffee table. 'Put it there.' She picked it up, and held it towards the firelight. It was a small Polaroid photograph of a bound and gagged young woman, crouching in the open boot of a car. Above her taped-up mouth, two red terrified eyes stared up at the cameraman.

'What is thi . . .'

Miranda's voice faded as she realised that the woman was Lily.

For a moment, she felt like she'd been shot. Strength gushed out of her like blood, leaving her arms limp, her whole body stone cold. When she looked up, Les's eyes were gleaming at her. A hard smile was scored into the plump creases of his face.

'Where is she?' she whispered.

'Outside. In the boot of the Rolls.'

When he put out his hand, Miranda handed the gun to him. For the first time in her life, she wanted to kill another person. She wanted to crack his skull open, and smash his brains to the floor.

'*You bastard!*'

Les slipped the gun back into his inside pocket. 'Now, you can't blame a man for taking out an insurance policy. You're not the only one around here capable of making plans.' The next moment, he bunched his fingers into a fist and sent her reeling towards the desk. 'To tell the truth, I'm disappointed in you, gorgeous. I expected more loyalty.' He came up to her and, cupping her bruised chin roughly, yanked her face towards his. 'That's where the difference is, see? Between a fucking piss-artist like you and a real pro like me.' Abruptly, he let go of her. 'But I'll deal with you later. First, let's get out of here.' Bending over the table, he scooped the diamonds into one of the velvet squares and slipped them into his pocket. Then he wrapped up one of the fake sets, and handed them to her. 'Stick those back up your pants.' She did as she was told, her cheeks burning as he watched her. When she'd finished, Les arranged the other fakes in the jewellery case.'Beautiful,' he murmured. 'No one will ever know till we're out of here. Right, nice and calm then. Don't try anything on when they come back, or you'll pay for it later. And so will Lily. To tell you the truth, I'm half-hoping you will try it on, so I can give her one myself. Before Pete and his mates do. Understand?'

She understood all too well. What she could not understand was how she could ever have trusted him and thought she liked him, and even looked on him as a friend. 'You disgust me, Les.'

He laughed. 'That's really something. Coming from you. The only woman I ever met who could shower in shit and come out convinced she still smelled of Chanel No 5. Now, do we understand the score, gorgeous?'

'How do I know you'll let Lily go if I do what you say?'

'Good point. To tell the truth, you don't. You'll just have to trust me, won't you? Just like I trusted you.' He glanced at his watch, then at her dishevelled clothes. 'Pull that shmutter straight, will you? And when the mugs come in, keep schtum and move your stupid arse down that corridor. Ah, and don't look so serious. Remember, it's all a big fucking joke!'

A few moments later, the chandelier overhead came on, and the red lights on the security cameras blinked back into action. The door of the strong room swung open and Carew rushed in, closely followed by a security guard.

'What a thing to happen! My most sincere apologies about this power cut. Quite beyond my control.'

'That, Carew, is the trouble with this country!' Les exploded, his face dark with pent-up fury. 'No one is willing to accept responsibility. There's always the same answer: *It is beyond my control!* Frankly, I cannot express my fury. For me, it is nothing. Only my Yasmin, as you see, is very upset. Too upset to make up her mind about whether she wants your diamonds! We must return to the hotel straight away!'

He stormed out into the corridor, closely followed by the now grovelling Carew. Miranda followed behind him, into the lift. She could think of nothing except Lily, and how her own stupidity had put her in mortal danger. She remembered suddenly the day, long ago, when she had accidentally shut Lily's finger in Horace's door. She could hear her screams still, echoing across the years. The dreadful guilt she had felt afterwards hadn't gone until the blackened blood had grown out of Lily's nail. Try as she might, she had not been able to escape from the knowledge that it had been her fault.

What was that, compared to this? If anything happened to Lily now, Miranda knew she couldn't live with herself.

The lift gates slid open, and Les walked briskly towards the shop door. The uniformed doorman opened it, and he strode out into the street. Miranda followed two paces behind. Pete was waiting by the open Rolls door, his face impassive under the chauffeur's hat.

On the corner, Ed and Justin were standing side by side looking into Morpeth's window, surreptitiously watching her pass by. She glanced at them in desperation through her visor, but it was useless.

'Come, my dear!' Les snapped.

She swung round, panicking. She didn't care what happened to her, she deserved whatever was coming. But she had to do something about Lily. She had to stop them driving off with her in the car.

Hesitating, Miranda took a step back, and bumped into someone behind her. Before she could stop herself, she turned round and, in her own voice, instinctively said 'Sorry!' at the very same time as the other person did.

He was a stooped figure in a shabby duffle coat and un-laced trainers. Under his hood was a pair of rain-spattered glasses, through which two watery eyes looked back at her from sallow, freckled skin.

His hood fell back, but even so, he had changed so much that for a moment she didn't recognise him. Only the thin, pinched line of his mouth was exactly as she remembered it. The halo of his hair barely stood out above his receding hairline, and what there was of it had turned a dull, lifeless sandy grey. Above his concave cheeks, which seemed to have fallen in on themselves, his eyes nestled in two hollows, deep and dark as caves. She had always thought of him as stronger and more powerful than she herself was. What she saw was a defeated-looking, unkempt, middle-aged man. This, then, was what she had done to him.

Perplexed at the sound of her voice, Jack peered short-sightedly at the visible portion of her face. Turning away, Miranda headed for the car, but suddenly found herself caught by the wrist. Jack swung her round, and squinted at her incredulously.

'*Miranda?*'

Just then a siren blasted out from Morpeth's back door. Miranda looked round in alarm for Ed, but he seemed to have disappeared. Les was standing by the Rolls, beckoning to her wildly while Pete ran round to the driver's door.

'Yasmin!' Les shouted.

Miranda wrenched free of Jack, and flung herself at the car, but Jack got hold of her again. 'Miranda!'

Les stepped forward and grabbed her other hand. 'Let go of my wife, you bastard!'

'But she's my wife! Mine!'

A police siren sounded in the distance. Les swung his arm back and punched Jack in the chest, and Jack sprawled across the pavement, taking Miranda with him. As the siren grew louder, Les ran towards the Rolls, leaving Miranda behind.

'Let go of me, Jack!' Miranda screamed. 'They've got Lily in that car!' When he still didn't release her, she appealed to the passersby. 'Somebody stop that car! My daughter's in it!'

Just then, Carew came flying through the shop door. 'Stop that car! They're thieves!'

'I've got her! I've got her!' Jack yelled. 'She's over here!'

Tyres screeched as Pete pulled away from the kerb, with Les's door still hanging open. Miranda tried to fight Jack off. But it was too late – they were driving off with Lily. Desperate to get free, Miranda pulled back her arm and punched Jack hard on the chin. As he fell back, yowling, she again caught sight of Ed and Justin among the crowd of spectators who'd gathered. 'Ed! Stop them! They've got Lily!'

Ed looked at her without recognition. With cold incredulity, she watched him turn away and melt away into the crowd.

Then, heedless of the moving traffic, Miranda lifted up her long skirt and ran into the road behind the Rolls-Royce, her black abbaya flying behind her. When one of her shoes came off, she kicked off the other, and ran on, oblivious of the cold, wet tarmac underneath her stockinged feet.

The Rolls lurched through the heavy traffic. Headlamps flashing, a squad car was racing down on the opposite side of the road.

Miranda ran on, panting, breathless. A stitch, sharp as a knife-wound, cut through her side. When she could run no more, she slowed to a fast walk, screaming out, 'Lily! Lily!' But it was hopeless, hopeless. Despite the traffic jam, the car was gaining ground, spiriting Lily away.

A moment later, a moving shape caught up with her. '*I'll get her, Mrs G!*' Arms and legs pumping like pistons, Justin shot up the centre of the road. A second squad car, heading down towards Morpeth's, screeched to a halt when he passed it. Someone jumped out of the back and crouched down, a gun in his hand.

'No!' Miranda yelled.

Sweat pouring down his face, Justin was closing the distance between himself and the Rolls. Ten yards, five . . . Now, he was neck and neck with it. Reaching out, he grabbed the handle of the back door, and clung on as the car accelerated forward, pulling him off his feet. As he regained his balance, he yanked the door open and tried to climb inside, but the Rolls shot back onto the pavement, hitting a lamp post and throwing Justin out. Justin scrambled to his feet, threw himself on top of the bonnet and lunged at the windscreen.

'Justin! No!'

Behind the wheel of the Rolls, Pete put his foot down, and the car shot back down Regent Street, swerving from left to right in an effort to throw Justin off. As it neared the parked squad car, the side window opened and the barrel of a gun appeared.

The police marksman lifted his automatic, and took aim at the car.

Miranda's yell was lost in the noise of the traffic. She had to stop them – had to stop them before Lily and Justin got hit.

Running across the road, she placed herself in the path of the Rolls. Faster and faster, Pete accelerated towards her. Someone on the pavement screamed, 'Get out of the way!' Between Justin's spreadeagled arms, she could see Pete's grimly set face, and the whites of Les's eyes and the barrel of the gun, pointing at her.

She closed her eyes. This then was it, the moment of her death. It wasn't a gun in the back, or a mad intruder in the night, or a mugger on the corner, or cancer, or old age. She wondered how quick it would be, and whether she would feel any pain, and whether, after the car hit her, Lily would be saved.

Just when she thought it must hit her, there was the deafening crack of bullets. Opening her eyes, she saw the Rolls spinning out of control towards an island in the middle of the road. As it hit it side on, Justin was catapulted off the bonnet. A moment later, the driver's door was flung open and a crouched figure jumped out and scuttled towards the nearest side street.

Miranda started to run towards it. But before she got there, Ed ran out from between two taxis and grabbed her by the arm.

'Come on!'

She shook her head, sure that he would stay with her once he knew what had happened. 'Lily's in that car! And Justin's hurt!'

'Don't be an idiot!' He pulled her again. 'You can still get away! Come on!'

'I can't!' Didn't he understand that there were more important things than her freedom? Ed stared at her angrily for a second, then turned and fled. Somehow Miranda knew it would be the last time she'd ever see him.

'Keep back!'

Ignoring the police instructions, Miranda ran over to the car and wrenched the boot open. Lily stared up at her, looking shocked but unhurt. Miranda swung round as she heard a loud moan behind her. Justin was lying in the road between two cars. His eyes were closed, and his leg was at a funny angle. Blood was seeping through a hole in his shirt, and bubbling through a tear in his jeans.

'Oh God!' Miranda fell to her knees beside him. 'Oh, Justin!' He opened his eyes suddenly, and gazed at her, his eyes large as a terrified dog's.

There was a loud click. Glancing up, Miranda found herself staring down the barrel of a gun.

'Don't just stand there!' she yelled furiously at the policeman aiming it at her. 'For Christ's sake call an ambulance! Can't you see he's been shot?'

Seventeen

'Miranda! Well, well, well!'

Jack walked across the visiting room towards her, his arms outstretched.

'Hello, Jack.' Without getting up from her chair, Miranda smiled at him coldly. 'Welcome to Holloway Prison. Thanks for standing bail for me.'

Now his arms fell to his sides, and a muscle in his jaw started to twitch. There was a loud squeak as he pulled out the red plastic visitor's chair and sat down on the opposite side of the table.

'What did you expect?' he said in a defensive voice. 'Besides, where was I supposed to find £100,000?'

'I don't know. Somewhere. You could have re-mortgaged the house.'

'And risked losing it when you ran off again?' He raised his eyebrows. 'If you examine your conscience, Miranda, I think you'll agree that we're all better off if you stay here.' This short lecture over, he readjusted his disapproving expression into a cool but helpful smile. 'Now, I've brought you the clean clothes you asked for. And the underwear. They made me leave them outside with one of the warders. I'll suppose you'll get them eventually.'

'Thanks.'

'Diana packed everything, so don't blame me if anything's missing. She even got you the make-up you asked for. Though quite why you need make-up in here, I've no idea, particularly since you never wear it. What is it, some kind of affectation? Oh, yes, and I put in the book you asked for. Very appropriate, if I might say.'

'Oh?'

He smirked. '*Crime and Punishment.*'

'It so happens I was reading it before I . . .' She hesitated for a moment. '. . . disappeared.'

'Well, I can't see why you insisted on me bringing that old, leather-bound copy of yours. It's quite valuable, you know – a first edition translation. It's sure to get stolen in a place like this.'

'Did you get the cigarettes?'

'No, I didn't! You can smoke yourself to death if you want to – you always had a self-destructive urge, didn't you? – but I'm certainly not going to collude with you!' Leaning back, he crossed his arms tightly over the hollow of his chest and licked the thin, pinched line of his lips. 'Now, you and I have got some serious talking to do.'

'Funny, I thought you were going to say that.'

He paused, peering at her over the top of his glasses like a biologist examining a frog he was about to dissect. Then, in an aggrieved tone, he said, 'How could you do it, Miranda?' He waited for an answer, but she remained silent. 'You've got a hell of a lot to answer for, you know.'

'Oh, please, Jack! You sound just like my old headmistress.'

'Is it any surprise if I do, after what you've put me through?' The thin halo of his hair trembled as he shook his head. 'I've thought about it and thought about it, but I just can't understand you.'

'Can't you?'

'Letting the children and me believe you were dead? Stealing money from the university and framing me? Robbing that jewellery shop! And as for that business with Gwyneth Barton . . . Don't look at me with those innocent eyes, I bet you were behind that, too! I could still lose my job over it, you know. If you were pleading insanity, well, it

286

would all just about be forgivable. As it is . . .' Leaning forward, he took off his spectacles and squinted at her. 'What exactly were you trying to prove?'

She considered this for a moment. 'I really don't know, Jack. Maybe I was just trying to prove that I was still alive. Maybe I wasn't trying to prove anything.'

His eyebrows shot up again. 'Oh, come on! Swapping motherhood for a life of armed robbery? For the gun? Why, it's as classic an example of penis envy as I've ever seen! My God, if only I were an analyst! What I'd give to get you on the couch!'

'That would make a change,' she snapped. 'Given that you couldn't wait to get me off it before.'

'Come on, Miranda!'

'I wish you wouldn't keep saying that.' Before he came, she'd sworn to herself that she'd stay calm and detached. Now, only five minutes into his visit, her determination cracked like a glass cafetière, and all the boiling hot, bitter-tasting detritus she had held back for nineteen years gushed forth. 'Let me make something clear, Jack – if I was suffering from penis envy, it certainly wasn't envy of yours!'

His nostrils flared like an angry horse's. He glanced over at the prison officer in the corner, then leaned across the table and muttered, 'That remark is below the belt. And, if I might say so, rather pathetic. Do you know, I almost feel sorry for you? It makes me wonder what happened to you in your youth that you should hate men so much.'

Miranda wondered suddenly how she could have stayed married to him for so long. 'I don't hate *men*, Jack, I just hate *you*. You're such a hypocrite. You cheated on me. You lied to me. You . . . you bullied me for years.'

'I did nothing of the sort!'

'Oh yes, you did! You systematically destroyed all my self-confidence. You never encouraged me in anything I did. In fact, you criticised me all the time. Do you know, I couldn't even do the shopping without incurring your disapproval? My God, you even stopped me wearing make-up, and then fell into bed with that . . . that painted tart from next door!'

He flushed red. 'I don't know what you're talking about. If I did try and . . . well, try and guide you now and then, it was only because you wanted me to. It wasn't my fault that I happened to have a clearer idea of your identity than you did. But there's no getting away from the fact that you allowed it to happen, Miranda. You didn't have to listen to me or do what I said. You could have told me I was wrong. It so happens that it suited you to . . .'

'Oh, don't give me that crap about the victim wanting to be oppressed! I don't have time for it any more.'

The black beads of his eyes glared at her furiously. 'Look, I didn't come here to quarrel but to make peace with you – though I'm beginning to wonder why. You're very lucky that I'm so understanding. Plenty of husbands would have nothing to do with their wives in a case like this.'

'A case like what? Honestly, Jack, aren't you pre-judging the outcome of the trial rather and . . . ?'

But he interrupted her before she could finish speaking. 'Most men in my position would leave their wives without a thought!'

Miranda gave a short laugh. 'How can you leave me, when I've already left you?'

Without seeming to hear her, he went on, 'Still, when you've served your sentence, I insist that we all go into family therapy together. After what you've put the children through, they're certainly going to need it. And the moment we can afford it I want you to go into proper psychoanalysis yourself. Five times a week if necessary. There are definitely a lot of critical things in your past which you need to sort out.'

She bit her lip, but after a moment the words burst out of her mouth. 'Yes. Like why I wasted so much of my life with a creep like you. Face it, Jack – you're not an analyst, you're just an anal retentive. You want to keep control of everyone and everything. Well, let me tell you something – you're no longer in control of me. When I come out, what I do or don't do will be my business, and my business only.'

'Don't be stupid, Miranda. Look where a few months of being without me's got you. Besides, how would you live?'

She hesitated. 'I'll manage somehow. I'll get a job.'

'That won't be easy. What, a woman in her – how old will you be by the time you get out? Mid or late forties, maybe even in your fifties – with no work experience, no qualifications and a criminal record? Do you think employers will be queuing up for you? Isn't it time you let go of this ridiculous fantasy life and came to your senses? Face up to the truth, Miranda – you depend on me and you need me. More now than you ever did.'

'Do I?' Seething with fury, she pushed back her chair and walked over to the door. Turning round, she took a long, last look at her husband. 'We'll see, Jack. We'll see.'

'Darling, will you ever forgive me?'

The glossy burgundy gash quivered dangerously. Underneath it, the crisp, pinstriped jacket rustled as, padded shoulders heaving, its wearer rested her elbows on the table and clutched her trembling chin.

'What on earth are you talking about?' Miranda asked.

The crop of geometric hair flopped over the immaculately made-up face until five immaculate maroon fingernails pushed it behind her ears. Shaking with emotion, Suzanne Jones looked up, her close-set eyes overflowing with crystal tears.

'I just feel so, well, so *responsible* for everything! I mean, if I hadn't stopped and talked to you by that pasta counter, the gunman might have picked on someone else, and this whole ghastly mess would never have happened.'

Miranda squeezed her friend's hand. Contrasted with Suzanne's soft white skin, her own hand looked at least a decade older. Veins stood out on the back like thick ropes, her cuticles needed cutting, and her skin was red and sore from having been washed too often in harsh prison soap.

Strangely, none of this seemed to matter as much as it would have done in the past.

'Don't be crazy, Suzanne. You had nothing to do with it. The robber was stalking me. Of course it'd have happened. Anyway,' she added with a smile, 'All in all, I'm not sorry that it did.'

'Really?'

'The experience had a few plus points.'

'Oh?' From her black patent bag, Suzanne took out a tissue and blotted her eyes dry. Not a single smudge of black stained the white paper. Ever efficient, she must have planned for the emotional visit by wearing waterproof mascara. 'Such as?' Miranda jerked her chin at the watching warden, then raised her eyebrows. Suzanne's small, dark-rimmed eyes widened. 'You don't mean you . . .' She mouthed the words *had an affair*. When Miranda nodded, she added a silent, *With the gunman*?

'Strictly off the record.'

There was a small gasp, then Suzanne leaned closer and whispered, very quietly, 'What was he like?'

Miranda shook her head. 'I'd rather not talk about it at the moment, if you don't mind. It's all too painful. Anyway, that's enough about me. I need news of the real world, to reassure myself that there's still life outside these prison walls. Tell me how you are, and what you've been doing. Apart from making programmes about me.'

'Darling, you don't really want to hear about me?'

'Of course I do. You're my one famous friend.'

'Not as famous as you are now! Well, I'm still exactly where I was the last time I met you. On that bloody TV treadmill and running fast. Except now I'm divorced, and Nick and the bitch are married and expecting a baby.'

'Oh, no! That was quick!' Looking at Suzanne's pinched, unhappy face, Miranda wondered why she had ever been jealous of her. 'I'm so sorry.'

'Yes, well, what can you do? They were featured in *Hello*! last month. Slobbering all over each other in front of Designer's Guild wallpaper samples. *"TV personality Nick Shaver and his new wife Justine decorate their house in Primrose Hill."* '

Miranda grimaced. 'And have you been seeing anyone?'

'Not really.' The padded shoulders shrugged. 'A few scrapings from the bottom of the barrel. You know – the kind of man who spends the whole of the first date telling you that he's no intention of ever being tied down, and then expects you to sleep with him. If you don't, you never hear from the bastard again.'

'And if you do . . . ?'

'You still don't hear from him!' Suzanne giggled. Then she looked down at her ringless hands. 'Miranda . . .' she began slowly.

'Yes?'

'There's something I need to get off my chest.'

'Yes?'

'After I'd made the documentary, I invited Jack to a couple of dinner parties. I thought he might be lonely.'

'That was kind of you.'

'I didn't know at the time that he was seeing someone else. Anyway, he never came in the end, and I didn't think anything else of it.' She paused. 'Then, last night . . .'

Her voice trailed away. Already, Miranda knew what was coming. 'Yes?'

Distinctly miserable, Suzanne looked her straight in the eyes. 'Last night, he phoned me up and asked me out.'

A dull pain began to throb in Miranda's head. 'Ah.'

'I'm sorry, darling. I know this isn't the time and place to talk about it, but . . . You see, he told me that you and he are, you know, completely finished. Well . . .' She bit her lips. When she next spoke, there were burgundy stains on her front teeth. 'Oh, this is so difficult! What I was wondering is, if that's really, really true, would you mind if I went? It's just that . . .' Bowing her head, she started to cry again. 'Oh, Miranda! Since Nick left, I've been so incredibly lonely! I can't stand living by myself, in fact I simply hate it! I'm forty-one years old. In a few years time I'll be menopausal. I'm afraid it'll be more like meno*stop*al. If I can, I want to get married again. At least, to go out with someone. Or live with them. Maybe even have a baby, before it's too late. And Jack, well . . . Frankly, he's the only half-decent, single-ish straight man around.' She covered her face. 'Oh, God, I'm so ashamed of myself! And so horribly embarrassed!'

Reaching across the table, Miranda stroked her cheek and smiled sadly. 'It's OK, Suzanne. Really, I understand.'

'Hello, Mummy.'

'Diana! Thomas! Come here, both of you! Let me give you a hug.'

The two of them ran forward. As she clasped them in her arms and breathed them in, she made believe for a moment that everything that had happened to her was part of a dream. She was still at home, in her house in Huddlestone Avenue, ironing, cooking and cleaning for her four children, just being there and doing all the ordinary things that ordinary mothers did.

Opening her eyes, she saw David hanging back on the other side of the bare visiting room and the dream died. She held out her arms, but he simply stood where he was, his full lips, so like hers, pressed together in the sullen pout she'd all but forgotten, his chin-length, flaxen hair masking evasive eyes. He'd grown taller and more gangly during the seven months since Miranda had last seen him. He looked as if someone had grabbed his head and his feet and simply stretched them apart. 'Gosh, you've quite grown up!'

'Yeah. Well, I had to, didn't I?'

He hadn't been in the room for thirty seconds, and he'd already put her in her place. 'How are you?'

'OK.' Looking down, he kicked at the floor with the toe of his trainer.

'Come and sit down. Please.' He refused of course, leaving her in confusion, unsure quite what to say next. She'd so been looking forward to seeing him, but now he was here she felt a loss akin to bereavement. He was a stranger to her. Had it been like this before, and had she simply forgotten? Or was this terrible emotional distance between them something new, caused by what she had done?

Determined not to waste a minute of the precious visit, she turned her attention on the others. 'I like the perm!' she said, patting Diana's long curly mane. 'It looks gorgeous! And so different. I'd hardly have recognised you.' As she stroked her shoulder, she was surprised to feel actual flesh under her fingertips. Perusing the half-hidden face, she saw that Diana's once sunken cheeks had filled out a little. Before she could censure herself, she blurted out. 'Why, Diana, you've put on . . . '

She stopped. Diana drew back, her eyes narrowing. 'Go on, say it! I've put on weight.'

'Only a tiny bit. It suits you,' she added tentatively.

'Well, it hasn't taken you long to start nagging me again!'

'I'm not nagging, darling, I just . . .'

'I mean, what do you expect me to look like after six months of Mary's greasy cooking?'

'You didn't have to eat it, Di!' Thomas said suddenly. 'I didn't notice anyone forcing you!'

'Well, there wasn't anything else to eat, was there? Besides, I was . . .' She stopped.

'Go on, say it!' said Thomas, his voice breaking in the middle of the sentence. 'It won't kill you to admit it. You were *hungry*. And, what's more, you liked Mary's cooking. Sausages and chips and beans and things. Honestly, Di, eating's nothing to be ashamed of. You're only human after all.'

Miranda stared at Thomas in surprise. Never before had he sounded so sensible. Pride and sadness mingled in her heart as she realised that her 'baby' had grown up in her absence. As if sensing what she was thinking, he smiled at her, seeking support.

'Thomas is right, Diana. And you look stunning. Just like Kate Moss. Only much prettier.'

'Don't lie to me. Anyway, what business is it of yours? You haven't exactly taken much interest in any of us lately.'

Thomas shot Miranda a pregnant look, then turned on his sister. 'How do you know she could? For all you know she was kept a prisoner and . . .'

'Daddy told me that Mum's been behind everything bad that's happened!'

'You don't have to believe everything he says!'

'Oh, shut up, Thomas. You're just a little mummy's boy!'

'I'm not!'

'Just look at you, wearing that stupid make-up!'

'Just because I . . .'

'Shut up, both of you, or I'm leaving!' David spat out suddenly.

Miranda looked up, horrified. 'No, darling!'

'I just can't stand to listen to any more of their bloody bickering! Besides . . .' He turned away from her. 'There's no point in staying. I don't know why I came.'

'Please don't go! I . . . I haven't seen you for so long!'

'Whose fault is that?' put in Diana.

'I . . . I haven't had a chance to talk to you yet.'

David kicked at the floor again, and mumbled something.

'Sorry?'

'I said, what is there to say?'

'Loads of things!' she said quickly, anxious to keep him there. 'Goodness, I haven't even congratulated you on passing your GCSEs!'

'It's a bit late for that.'

'Yes. Yes of course it is. I'm sorry but I . . .' She tried in vain to swallow down her guilt but it was rising fast inside her, burning her throat like acid. 'Wh-what are you going to do now? I mean, which A-levels are you taking?'

'I don't know. I'm probably . . .'

'Yes?'

'I might leave school.'

'But you're only just seventeen! Why?'

He shrugged. 'What's the point in staying on?'

'But, David . . .' She wanted to argue with him, to present all the sensible reasons, but she knew she didn't have a leg to stand on. 'What will you do if you leave?'

'I don't know. I don't care. Probably go on the dole like Justin. Don't look at me like that. What do you expect me to do, with a criminal for a mother?'

When she saw the look of shame in his eyes, the pretence of normality she'd been nurturing broke down. Her head dropped into her hands, and her shoulders hunched with sobs.

Thomas rushed towards her. 'What is it, Mum?' Then he turned angrily on David. 'How could you say that to her?'

Miranda clutched his hand. 'No, Thomas, David's right! He's absolutely right! I've failed you all completely!'

'No, you haven't, Mum!'

'Yes, I have, darling! I've ruined everything! Oh God, I'm so ashamed of myself!'

'Oh, Mum!' Now Diana started to cry, too. David looked on, stony-faced.

'I so badly wanted to set you all a good example, and instead, I've completely messed up all your lives!'

There was a long silence, broken only by her sobs, and the sound of someone shouting in the corridor outside.

Then, at long last David spoke. 'I . . . I don't care what you've done, Mum.' The catch in his voice made her look up in astonishment. 'I . . . I'm just glad you're alive.'

She stood up and faced him. His green eyes, so like her own, were overflowing with tears. Throwing his arms round her neck, he clung onto her like a small child, his shoulders heaving with sobs.

'Oh, Mum! Mum! I've missed you so much!' She tried to say something, but her tongue seemed to be paralysed. 'I don't want you to stay in this horrible place. I . . . I don't want the jury to convict you! I couldn't bear for you to be taken away from us again. I . . . I need you, Mum.'

'I need you, too, darling!' she said with difficulty.

'I . . . I love you!'

He hadn't said those words to her for eight years or more. It was almost worth being in prison, just to hear him say them again. She hugged him even tighter. Tears cascaded down her cheeks.

'I love you too!' chimed in Diana, anxious not to be left out.

'And me!'

'And I love you all.'

Arms intertwined, the four of them hugged for a long while. Embraced in her children's warmth, Miranda felt herself thawing for the first time in months. This was where she belonged – not on the emotional heights and depths of life, but here, on solid ground, with her children. Her heart swelled with pride at their generosity of spirit. She may not have brought them up to be perfect, but they were as near as dammit, and far better than she, or Jack, deserved.

'Oh, we mustn't cry like this,' she said at last, extricating herself from the tangle of arms. 'Maybe I'll get off. You never know. Maybe the jury will find me not guilty.'

'Maybe they won't!' sobbed Diana. 'Maybe you'll be sent to prison for years and years and years! Maybe we'll all be fostered out and never see each other again!'

'Nonsense.' She wiped her daughter's flushed, damp face, and put an arm around her shoulder. 'You're old enough to take care of yourselves, aren't you? Besides, Daddy will look after you. Just like he's been doing.' The children glanced at each other and snorted through their tears. 'What is it? Why are you laughing? What have I said?'

'Dad didn't look after us at all!'

'Didn't he?'

'No! He was completely mega-useless. We had to look after him!'

'He once tried to grill our Linda McCartney veggie-burgers in the toaster!'

'He didn't!'

'Yes, he did! And he made us do all the shopping, and the housework.'

'It's been bloody awful, Mum. At first he tried to run the place like it was some ghastly army barracks and . . .'

'I wish I'd thought of that.' Miranda smiled at them. 'It's a jolly good idea.'

'Mu-um!'

'Please!'

'And what we didn't do, he handed over to Mary.'

'And what she didn't do didn't get done. You should see the place now!'

'Under the circumstances, I'm rather glad I can't. You see, there are some advantages to being in prison.'

The laughter quickly died down, and the four of them lapsed into silence.

'Is it ghastly being in here, Mummy?' Thomas said eventually.

She hesitated, anxious not to burden them more than she had to. 'It's a bit grim, and very squalid, I suppose, but . . . Some of the screws – I mean, the prison officers – are really OK. And one or two of the inmates are something else. Believe me, you see all the world in here. People with such terrible, tragic lives, lives like you can't imagine. The worst bit's the boredom – being banged up so much in my cell.

'You sound like a real criminal, Mum.'

'I guess I am one, Thomas.'

'No, you're not. You're only on remand, aren't you?'

'Anyway, they ought to let you off. It wasn't your fault you got kidnapped by an armed robber.'

'Unfortunately, David, it's not quite as simple as that.'

She glanced at Thomas, and he winked at her complicitly. From what the police had said to her, she knew without asking that he hadn't breathed a word about his visit to Ed's.

As for Lily . . .

A shiver passed down Miranda's spine.

Lily was in no position to grass on her. Of that she was sure.

She came in the door, chin defiantly raised, flicking her waist-length hair over her shoulder. Striding over to the table, she shrugged off the black leather biker's jacket she was wearing, and, sitting down opposite Miranda, crossed the long black Lycra-clad legs that led down to her black patent Doc Marten's boots. Then, with a useless but demure gesture, she yanked down the micro-skirt which had ridden up her thighs.

'Hello, Lily. How are you feeling?'

'Fine. No thanks to you, I only got a couple of bruises when the Rolls crashed. The police said it was a miracle I hadn't been badly injured, being tied up in that boot.'

'Actually, I wasn't talking about the car crash.'

'Then what were you talking about? Oh, that!' A hostile look flashed in Lily's large blue eyes. 'I'm fine.'

'Really?'

'Don't sound so surprised. Would you rather I wasn't?'

'You're not feeling sick, or anything?'

'Of course not!' Her pale, pinched pasty face belied these words. 'Morning sickness is just a figment of the feminist imagination. A psychosomatic symptom of the victim mentality.'

'Goodness, Lily, you sound just like your father!'

'I do not! Anyway, don't insult Dad!'

'What makes you think it was an insult? I'm sure your views will be of great interest to millions of pregnant women all over the world.'

Lily narrowed her eyes suspiciously. Miranda stared her out, guilty for feeling so angry, but unable to control her raging pride. 'So, are you going to tell me about it?'

She yawned. 'What is there to tell?'

'How far gone are you?'

Her lips curled. 'God, what an old-fashioned expression! I'm eight weeks pregnant, if you must know.'

Under the table, Miranda did a short calculation on her fingers. 'You didn't waste much time.'

'It wasn't exactly planned,' Lily snapped. 'It just sort of happened.'

'And you're sure you want to go through with it?' Try as she might, Miranda couldn't keep the tone of disbelief out of her voice.

Only if Miranda had suggested she get her long hair cropped, or give up using the telephone, could Lily have looked more scandalised. 'What are you saying – that I should have an abortion?'

'There are worse things. You're only seventeen. That's incredibly young to saddle yourself with a child.'

'Unlike you, I don't happen to regard motherhood as being *saddled.*'

'That's not what I meant, and you know it. I don't think you've got a clue what having a baby entails.'

'Of course I have.' She gazed down her retroussé nose with a superior expression. 'You just open your legs and the thing comes out, doesn't it? Then all you've got to do is feed it and change its pooey nappies.'

'Lily! Really!'

'For heaven's sake, it can't be that difficult! Everyone does it! Christ, even you did it!'

'But you're so young! Don't you want to go to university, or have a career, or travel? Don't you at least want to have fun before you settle down?'

'I am not *settling down.* And I *am* having fun.'

Frowning, Miranda searched her daughter's face for some sign of this.

'And I *am* going to travel. We're going to Spain.'

'When? Where to? How long for?' Lily didn't answer. Miranda felt a chill creep up her spine. 'To live?'

Lily nodded, then cleared her throat uneasily. 'Ed said . . .' Just hearing his name made Miranda feel cold. 'Ed said to tell you that he'll take good care of me.'

She contemplated this with a sinking feeling. 'Don't rely on him Lily. Watch out for yourself.'

'Honestly, Mum, you're so cynical!'

'If I am, it's because I've good reason to be.' The burning desire to find out the truth overcame her pride. Leaning forward, she took Lily's hand urgently. 'What are you *doing* with him, Lily?' she whispered. 'How did such a thing happen?'

'How do you think? We fell in love.'

'But . . . When?'

'Must you know?' She sighed. 'I suppose, right at the beginning. I mean, I knew I fancied him the moment he opened the door.'

Miranda thought back to the antagonism between Ed and Lily that day in his house, and everything suddenly fell into place.

'But nothing happened till after the robbery,' Lily added quickly. 'I just knew I had to see him again, so I discharged myself from the hospital that afternoon, and rushed straight round to the house. I knew that if I didn't go then, he'd have disappeared for ever. And I was right. He was just clearing out.' A wistful, faraway look came into her eyes. 'And then – well, it just kind of happened. We kind of fell into each other's arms.'

The image rattled through Miranda's head like a scene from a cheap made-for-TV movie. 'Isn't he a bit old for you? Besides, what were you thinking of? He was my lover.'

A red flush stained Lily's cheeks. She drew back, a snake about to go on the attack 'And you were my mother. You found it easy enough to forget that when it suited you.'

Miranda's fingernails bit into her palms. Lily was right: she'd given up any right she might once have had to criticise or influence her daughter's behaviour. But something more than jealousy concerned her here.

'Listen to me,' she said urgently. 'Don't stay with him. He's trouble. Bad news. Underneath the charm, he's ruthless and weak and selfish. Darling, I beg you to think seriously about what you're doing before you muck up your whole life! You don't want to end up like me, do you?'

Lily drew herself up. 'You can rely on one thing, Mum – I'll never do that.'

'Thanks, Lola.'

Miranda closed her book and put it down on the table as a petite, raven-haired Philipino beauty pushed Justin's wheelchair into the room.

'I stay with you. Yes?' The young woman looked down at him adoringly.

'Er, no, thank you. Will you wait outside? Please? I'll call you if I need you.'

Lola shifted her eyes to Miranda, and gave a loud, disapproving sniff. 'You sure you be all right alone here with *her*?'

Justin grinned at Miranda across the table. 'Don't worry, she's not Hannibal Lecter.'

'OK. But I be just outside. OK? Anything wrong, I hear you shout, and I come running. OK?'

'OK, Lola. Thanks.'

The moment the door closed, Miranda burst out laughing. 'You've made quite a conquest!'

Justin looked embarrassed. 'Yeah, well, she got to kind of like me when I was in hospital. She was my nurse, see? She had to look after me, and now she can't stop. I don't have to be in this chair any more, you know – she just likes pushing me around. I'm like a baby in a buggy to her.' He grabbed Miranda's hand across the table and smiled broadly. 'Hey, it's brilliant to see you!'

'Justin! Oh, Justin!' Suddenly choked with emotion, she lowered her head and broke into sobs.

'Here, what're you crying about? I thought you'd be pleased to see me.'

'Of course I am! I thought . . . I thought . . .' The words caught in her throat. 'I thought I might never see you again.'

'Why not? Going somewhere in a hurry, were you?'

She laughed through her tears. 'I thought you were, dummy! I thought you were dying right there on Regent Street. Thank God you're all right!'

'Funny, that's what my Mum said. I don't think God had a lot to do with it. More that the officer who shot me couldn't hit a bullseye twice off. Once he'd shot the Rolls's tyre out, his aim went kaput. Lucky for me. Here, how do you stand this place? There's so many rules, I'd go berserk. And that's just for the visitors. They wouldn't even let me bring in the flowers I brought you. Said they got to check them for drugs! And they said I've got to take away the magnum of Bollinger!'

'That's prison life for you!' Her smile fading, she added meaningfully, 'If you don't like it, make sure they never have a reason to put you away.'

He nodded, his eyes suddenly round and fearful. 'Thanks for keeping me out of it,' he whispered, leaning across the table.

She took his hand and squeezed it. 'I'm only sorry I got you into it in the first place.' Raising her voice for the benefit of the warden, she added. 'It was an amazing coincidence you happened to be passing by.'

'Yeah, well I was following Jack, wasn't I?'

He winked. Miranda lowered her voice again. 'I really can't forgive myself. I keep going over and over what happened, and realising that, but for a few centimetres of flesh, you might have been killed.'

'Yeah, but I wasn't, was I? And do you know – being shot's turned out to be the best thing that's ever happened to me? Because when I was lying there in the hospital, this cool solicitor come round to see me, see? She says a chest wound and a leg wound like these have got to be good for a hell of a lot of police compensation. The

Old Bill are going to have to pay *me*! Besides that, I'm a hero, aren't I? You should have seen the headlines. "Youth Shot by Police in West End Diamond Chase". "Hero Shot In Bid To Rescue Friend". I was on the front pages, and the inside pages, my scar was even on Page Three. I've been on ITV, and BBC and Capital Radio. And because of all the publicity, I've met all kinds of important people. I got offered six jobs, Mrs G!'

'Oh, Justin, I'm so pleased for you!'

He straightened up in the wheelchair. 'Thanks to you, I'm a merchant banker now. Well, I will be when I'm old enough. Till then, I'm a trainee. I'm on my way up, Mrs G! I'm going to make it! What's more, I'm going to make it legit. I'm going to be *rich*.' With great relish, he rolled the word on his tongue. 'My Mum's going to have that house in Antigua. I'm going to have a new BMW, and a flat, and a wardrobe stuffed with real Armani suits!'

Reduced to tears again by his enthusiasm and excitement, Miranda covered her face. Justin put his hand on her shoulder. 'And I'm going to be there for you when you get out. So don't you worry about nothing. I'm going to take care of you.' Delving into a trouser pocket, he extracted a crumpled, torn tissue and pressed it into her hand. 'Look, Mrs G, there's something I never told you before.'

'What?' Looking up, she blew her nose.

'I think you're one cool lady.'

'Thanks, Justin.'

'Don't smile, I'm serious. You've done more for me than anyone else ever has – except Mum, of course. You've been a real friend.' He hesitated, biting his lip, then, grabbing her hand, he blurted out, 'I . . . I love you.'

She sniffed back more tears. 'I love you too, Justin.'

'Do you?'

'Of course I do. You're like a son to me.'

He looked disappointed. 'I'm not talking about that kind of love. I mean, the other kind. *Real* love. *In love* love. Know what I mean?'

'Justin!' Genuinely shocked, she pulled her hand away. 'I'm older than your mother!'

'I knew you was going to say that. But it doesn't make no difference.'

'Of course it does! I've known you since you were at primary school!'

He lowered his voice again. 'And even then I thought you was the sexiest lady I ever seen. And I still do. And before you say anything else, I know what I want, and I'm going to wait for it. And that's that!'

Before she could move away, he lunged across the table and pressed his lips against hers. As her own parted with surprise, his warm, smooth tongue slipped deep into her mouth.

So, here it was at long last, the fulfilment of Miranda's old erotic fantasy: Justin was kissing her. For a moment she felt nothing at all. Then, slowly, a melting sensation seeped through her, bringing her half-dead senses alive. But just as she was starting to enjoy herself, he pulled abruptly away.

'And if there's anything I can do for you while you're stuck in here, just ask,' he went on breathlessly. 'OK?'

'OK.'

They kissed again.

'As a matter of fact there is something you could do for me now.' Taking a small carrier bag of clothes from the back of her chair, she put it on the table. 'Drop these clothes home for me, will you? There's a dear. Oh, and this,' she added, picking up her book. 'I've finished it now.'

Justin took it from her, and examined it. '*Crime and Punishment*? Never heard of it. Worth reading, is it?'

Miranda nodded. 'It's a priceless work of art. Put it back in the living room bookcase, will you? If you give it to Jack, he's bound to lose it.'

'Sure. Talking of books, Mrs G . . . There's this funny American I met when the PM invited me to Downing Street. And I don't know why, but he seemed real interested in meeting you.'

* * *

'Miranda Green? Brad Brownhammer.'

Tall, broad and extremely handsome, the man in the unstructured grey suit clasped her hand in his outsize palms.

'Why,' he drawled in his lilting Texan accent, gazing at her with sky-blue eyes. 'The newspaper photographs don't do you justice. You're far more attractive in real life!'

He was lying, of course. If anyone in the visiting room was attractive, it was Brad Brownhammer. In his mid-to-late fifties, he was ageing in the way that only a wealthy American male could. His upright stance and pancake-flat stomach bore testimony to daily work-outs. His perfect, whiter-than-white teeth were monuments to good dentistry. His swept-back, abundant hair shone like highly-burnished platinum. His lightly-tanned skin bore the deeply etched patina of a full, intellectually stimulating and prosperous life. Next to him, Miranda felt like a member of some small, undeveloped sub-species might in the presence of Superman.

'Come off it, I look terrible. My hair needs cutting, my dark roots are growing out, and the food here is bringing me out in spots. So, please, let's have no more bullshit, Mr Brownhammer.'

Unperturbed, he carried on smiling, while he continued to hold onto her hand. 'Call me Brad.'

When they had sat down, Miranda regarded him curiously. 'Justin told me you wanted to see me, but I can't imagine why you do.'

Instead of replying, he put his fingers in his jacket pocket and fished out a pack of Sobranies. 'Am I allowed to offer you one of these?'

'Thanks,' She took one. 'I didn't know any Americans still smoked.'

He reached across the table and lit it for her. 'Only in secret, Miranda – I may call you Miranda, mayn't I? Smoking's a federal crime in the States nowadays. Become a serial killer, and you're a national hero. But puff on one

305

of these within two miles of a human being, and you're an instant moral and social outcast.'

'Well, you can relax now – we're all social outcasts in here.' She smiled back at him, beginning to enjoy his company. 'I understand that you're a literary agent.'

His face expressed mock-horror. 'Please! Not *a* literary agent. *The* literary agent. I am to other literary agents what Leboyer was to obstetrics. I re-invented the whole God-damn profession. You see before you the man who presided over the waterbirth of the blockbuster novel, the midwife of the first million-dollar deal!'

She laughed. 'In that case, I don't understand what you want from me.'

'Isn't it obvious? I want to sign you up, Miranda.'

'Why?'

'I want you to write your story – the story of what happened to you. I've got a hunch it'll be a major international hit. And, let me tell you, I'm never wrong about these things.'

'Aren't you?' Her calm voice hid her excitement. She felt like a large plum was suddenly dangling over her head; one false move and she might stop it dropping in her lap. 'How can you be so sure it'd be a hit when you don't even know if I'm guilty or innocent?'

Thick, dark and perfectly shaped, his eyebrows rose slightly, forcing his forehead into evenly-ploughed furrows. '*Frankly, my dear, I don't give a damn.* Either way, whatever happened must have been a hell of an experience. People will want to read about it. About you. The crime scene, seen from a woman's perspective. The women's market is very big nowadays.'

She sighed wistfully. 'I did want to be a writer once, but I came to the conclusion long ago that I haven't got any talent.'

'Talent?' He sounded shocked. 'Who needs talent? No, Miranda, you've got something much more important than that!' As he leaned towards her, his eyes glittered like

306

sapphires. 'You're *famous*, Miranda. Better than that – you're *infamous*.' He nodded, slowly and confidentially. 'That alone has got to be good for a six-figure advance! And let's not forget the feature rights, and the mini-series rights, and the serialisation rights, on both sides of the Atlantic. And the Australasian market. And the Far East. Oh yeah, and the CD Rom and the musical.'

'The *what*?'

He grinned. 'Why not?'

She shook her head. It was all too ridiculous. 'You're having me on!'

'Excuse me?'

'You're teasing me.'

Crossing his hands behind his head, he tipped his chair back. 'Want to know the secret of success, Miranda? The only secret? *Think big*. It's as simple as that.'

'But . . .' She faltered. 'What if I can't write?'

'Dictate the story into a tape recorder, and we'll clean it up for you. In a literary sense, I mean. If you can't spit it out that way, we'll get it ghosted.'

'You mean, you'd hire someone else to write it? But it wouldn't be my book then!'

'Sure it would! It'd be *your* story. It'd have *your* name on the cover. And *you'd* rake in the royalties.'

'But that wouldn't be honest!'

Amused, he winked at her. 'In that case, it should be right up your street!'

Torn by conflicting emotions, she thought deeply about what he said. 'There's something I'd better explain, Brad,' she said at last. 'This whole experience I've been through has left me feeling, well, sickened by the idea of anything dishonest.'

He pushed back his chair and stood up, dwarfing her. Somehow, he didn't look convinced. 'All I'm asking you to do is think about it, Miranda,' he said, handing her a business card. 'When you've made up your mind, give me a call collect. I'll be there. Just promise me one thing,' he added, taking her hand and gazing deeply into her eyes.

'What?'

He paused for a moment, then muttered in a husky voice, 'That you won't sign up with anyone else.'

Fizzing with excitement, Miranda walked back down the corridor, contemplating her future literary success.

And why not? If the past seven months had taught her anything, it was that anything was possible in today's world. If the old maxims she'd been brought up with had ever been true, they'd now been turned on their head. The meek didn't inherit the earth, they went to hell and back, whilst criminals prospered and inherited, if not the kingdom of Heaven, then the meek's just desserts.

All good things need not come to an end.

Because – and this was the big one – crime paid.

Yes, crime paid.

In her case, it looked like it might pay very well indeed.

For with Les having been killed in the car crash, and Ed in Spain with Lily, who was going to grass on her now? Pete? Lily? Justin? They all had a vested interest in keeping their mouths shut.

As far as the police were concerned, no one but she herself knew what had happened to her between the day she'd disappeared in Sainsbury's and her arrest.

In those missing seven months since Les, yes, Les, had taken her hostage, she'd been through hell on earth, as she'd told her solicitor. She'd been bound, gagged, blindfolded. She'd been abused, brainwashed and beaten, and, even worse, forced at gunpoint to carry weapons and commit dastardly crimes that went against the very essence of her moral fibre.

Her lawyer had assured her that the jury were bound to be sympathetic. So was the judge.

As for the psychologists and their batteries of tests – well, years of living with Jack had prepared her for those.

Given all these points in her favour, she might well get away with it. Today, one could get away with anything.

Brad Brownhammer was right. One day, her book might well be up there on the shelves with the greats of twentieth century literature. She had to face it, she'd never rate as a Nabakov, but she might at least rake in some cash.

Not that she'd need it.

Oh, no!

As she walked into her cell and flung herself down on the narrow bed, Miranda smiled a sly, secretive smile. One thing was certain: she'd never be short of money again. Dostoyevsky had seen to that.

With a glow of excitement, she thought of her copy of *Crime and Punishment* – thanks to Justin, now safely back in her living room bookshelf. She didn't think of the story, but of the book itself – in particular, its thick leather binding, within which forty five-carat diamonds were safely embedded.

In the semi-darkness of the strong room, Les hadn't noticed that he'd given her the real necklace to take out of Morpeth's. Then, when the police at Vine Street had discovered that their so-called robber was none other than the missing Sainsbury's housewife, well, instead of being searched immediately, she'd been treated as something of a heroine: given cups of tea and chocolate biscuits, offered tissues and shoulders to cry on; and she was even allowed to go to the lavatory by herself. Which was where she'd discovered Les's mistake, and where she'd hidden the diamonds until after the intimate body search had been completed.

Then she'd retrieved them from the cistern, and hidden them deep inside her, and so brought them with her into Holloway.

Who was ever going to disprove her statement that Les had handed the real diamond necklace to the driver of the Rolls Royce – the man who'd got away?

She smiled. It pleased her to think that Jack was unwittingly keeping her nest egg safe until her release.

Once the furore had died down, she'd sell the stones off

one by one, and buy herself a large house in Hampstead, with a swimming pool, and a Jacuzzi, and a burglar alarm, and security lights, and a live-in cook. David, Thomas and Diana would live there with her.

And, just maybe, Justin, too.

Miranda shivered in anticipation. Till then, she'd sleep the deep sleep of the truly wicked in her cell in Holloway, dreaming lustful dreams about him, secure in the knowledge that no one, but no one, was trying to break in.